DIAMOND RUBY

A Novel

Joseph Wallace

A TOUCHSTONE BOOK
Published by Simon & Schuster

New York   London   Toronto   Sydney

Touchstone
A Division of Simon & Schuster, Inc.
1230 Avenue of the Americas
New York, NY 10020

First Touchstone paperback edition May 2010

TOUCHSTONE and colophon are registered trademarks of Simon & Schuster, Inc.

For information about special discounts for bulk purchases, please contact Simon & Schuster Special Sales at 1-866-506-1949 or business@simonandschuster.com.

The Simon & Schuster Speakers Bureau can bring authors to your live event. For more information or to book an event contact the Simon & Schuster Speakers Bureau at 1-866-248-3049 or visit our website at www.simonspeakers.com.

Designed by Ruth Lee-Mui

Manufactured in the United States of America

1 3 5 7 9 10 8 6 4 2

Library of Congress Cataloging-in-Publication Data

Wallace, Joseph E.
Diamond Ruby: a novel / Joseph Wallace.
p. cm.
Summary: In early twentieth-century Brooklyn, Ruby endures many hardships including the flu epidemic, the death of family members, and even starvation, until her pitching talents open new opportunities in the changing world of sports for women.
[1. Survival—Fiction. 2. Baseball—Fiction. 3. Sex role—Fiction. 4. Influenza Epidemic, 1918–1919—Fiction. 5. Brooklyn (New York, N.Y.)—History—20th century—Fiction.] I. Title.
PZ7.W15675Di 2010
[Fic]—dc22
2009021565

ISBN 978-1-4391-6005-3
ISBN 978-1-4391-6631-4 (ebook)

For Sharon, Shana, and Jacob

And for Jackie Mitchell,
who didn't get the chance to show what she could do

I

*r*uby Thomas had never seen anything as beautiful as Ebbets Field, with its brick exterior and half-moon windows that reminded her of slices of jelly candy. Nor had she ever been inside such a huge building, so new that it smelled of sawn wood, fresh cement, and sticky paint. Familiar odors, *comfortable* ones, the same as those that filled the air on East Twenty-first Street, Ruby's street, as the new houses went up all around.

Nor had she ever before been in the midst of such an enormous crowd. Thousands of women wearing long white dresses and plumes and men clad in dark sacque suits with blue or peach shirts, striped ties, and black bowler hats. All of them had chosen to put their responsibilities aside to gather for an afternoon in the spring sunshine.

Down below, the Brooklyn Superbas moved around the field. In their brand-new uniforms, bright as flags against the shining grass and rich dark earth, they looked nearly as elegant as the spectators.

Today's game was merely an exhibition between the Superbas and the New York Yankees. Its real purpose was to celebrate the new ballpark, so everyone could just relax and enjoy the balloons, the speeches, and the military band playing "Killarney" and "Here Comes My Daddie Now."

For Ruby, the best part was that they were all here. All the Thomases. They never went *anywhere* together, but somehow all of them had managed to show up for this game. Mama was missing one of her meetings, Papa had taken the afternoon off from the ironworks, and Ted, with their permission, was skipping school. Nick *was* working, but his job, writing for the *Brooklyn Examiner*, required him to attend the game anyway. Evie, Nick's wife, was on leave from her position as a nurse at the Norwegian Hospital, and the baby, Ruby's niece Amanda—well, she went wherever Evie did.

They sat flanking Ruby, Evie and Amanda on one side, Papa on the other. She felt covered, protected, safe.

And invisible. Of all the people in that enormous crowd, not a single one paid the slightest attention to Ruby. No one stared at her and then looked away. No one flinched or frowned.

Sitting there, listening to the music and to Mama and Nick squabbling about something, watching the players down on the field, inhaling the odors of the new ballpark, Ruby had a thought that made her stomach swerve inside her and brought sudden, unexpected tears to her eyes.

I'm happy.

The date was April 5, 1913. Ruby was seven.

It was the first time she could remember having that thought, and the last.

Their seats were along the third-base line, just behind what Papa called "Clerical Row." And it *was* filled with priests and ministers, young and old, looking flushed and excited in the sunlight. Many carried pads and notebooks and stubby pencils, bending over to scrawl notes before the game even began.

One young priest grinned at them. "We're writing our sermons," he said. "Tomorrow, every congregation in Brooklyn will be treated to many metaphors comparing religion to baseball."

Nick was gazing at the field and ballpark with a critical eye. "They forgot the scoreboard," he said. Then, pointing at two rows of out-of-sorts men sitting up in the second deck, definitely not clergymen though they, too, were writing in pads, he added, "Not to mention a press box on the field level."

Nick himself would be writing a short article about the game for the *Examiner*. He was just getting started as a sportswriter, so even a short piece would be exciting for him.

Not that Nick ever allowed himself to seem pleased about anything. In Ruby's memory, he was always forbiddingly tall and loud, quick with a joke, a sharp comment, a sarcastic aside. Only Evie could bring out his gentler side.

A procession of dignitaries walked out to the white flagpole in center field, chased almost immediately by a second, more ragged deputation carrying the enormous American flag the first group had forgotten. Nick stood. "I've got work to do," he said, then looked down at Ruby. "You can come with me."

When Nick invited her, she went. Ruby stood, and together they worked their way through the preachers and the rest of the crowd toward the stands directly behind home plate.

"I have to get some quotations from Miss Ebbets," Nick told Ruby.

"Who?" she asked. But he just took her hand—a strong grip, good for a rescue from a crowd but not nearly as soft or warm as Evie's—and led her on. As they went they were joined by another man, the senior reporter from the *Examiner*, Nick's boss. He was a big, bull-like man with a sour face and a rumpled suit. Nick introduced him to Ruby—he barely glanced at her—but all she caught was his first name: George.

Grumpy George. That was how she thought of him.

The two reporters cornered Miss Ebbets in the front row of the grandstands. She was a pretty young woman wearing a long dress, a fur stole, and an enormous flat-brimmed hat. She smiled as Nick and Grumpy George asked her a few questions. Then a man on the field, dwarfed by a huge microphone, boomed something Ruby couldn't understand, and an assemblage of dignitaries joined Miss Ebbets at the railing.

Ruby asked Nick what was happening.

"She's going to throw out the first ball," he said. He pointed at an umpire standing on the field. "To him."

Everyone around Ruby was remarking on Miss Ebbets's wonderful dignity and sense of fashion, but Ruby didn't care about any of that. She was more interested in the way the young woman threw: with a weak, stiff-armed flip of the wrist. The umpire was standing no more than twenty feet away, but the ball barely reached him. The crowd cheered anyway.

Ruby found herself looking down at her arms and thinking, I bet I could throw harder than that.

And: Maybe these will be good for *something*.

Back in her seat before the game started, Ruby decided on her favorite player. He had a long jaw, a big brash nose, and amazing ears that put Ruby in mind of the rib lamb chops they sometimes had for dinner. He always seemed to be wisecracking, laughing at something a teammate said, pulling a prank or two. During warm-ups, he threw the ball like his body was going in three different directions, and ran like his legs were all cramped up.

Ruby couldn't take her eyes off him. "Who is *that*?" she asked Nick.

Her brother frowned. "Casey Stengel," he said. "And he

could be a useful ballplayer, if he'd just stop with the shenanigans."

As they watched, Casey snuck up on one of the other players
and stole his cap.

That's who I'd want to be if I played baseball, Ruby thought.

In the fifth inning Casey Stengel rapped a hard one to center
field. Everyone, the priests and ministers included, leaped to
their feet, yelling, and Papa hoisted Ruby up so she could see.

Running in, the Yankees' center fielder somehow kicked the
ball. As it rolled toward the fence, Casey went steaming around
the bases on his bandy legs, his face red, his cheeks all puffed out
as he rounded third and headed for home plate. He got there
ahead of the ball, scoring the first run ever at Ebbets Field.

Ruby was giddy with pleasure.

Other than that, though, she had trouble following what was
going on. She did notice that the Superbas' pitcher, Nap Rucker,
threw strange floating pitches, and that Papa turned quite red in
the face when Brooklyn's Jake Daubert, his favorite player, hit a
home run of his own, a tremendous clout that cleared the fence
in center field. Ruby watched her father cheering, Ted, who
was always drawing, sketching the afternoon shadows cast by the
grandstands across the green outfield grass, Nick taking notes,
blue-eyed, blond-haired Evie crocheting something for Amanda,
who was sleeping in her lap.

Ruby, content, took in a deep breath and leaned her head on
Evie's shoulder.

In the seventh inning, Casey Stengel came up to bat again. On
the second pitch, he took a mighty swing and hit a high, looping
foul ball toward the third-base stands. All the fans leaped up, and
Ruby, standing on her seat, watched the ball appear to grow larger
as it approached.

At the last moment, it looked like the minister in front of her was going to catch it. But he pulled his hands away, Ruby stretched out her long right arm, and somehow the ball evaded the reaching, grasping hands all around and smacked into her palm.

It hurt worse than a bee sting, but Ruby wrapped her fingers around the ball and thought that she would never let it go.

All around her, clergymen and other fans were clapping her on the back and patting her on the head, which she usually hated. But right now she didn't care. She was staring down at the ball, stained, brown, scuffed . . . and perfect. Direct from Casey Stengel to her.

It felt comfortable in her hand, solid and substantial. Again and again she looked down at it and once or twice, when no one was looking, she pulled her left arm back and imagined she was a baseball pitcher.

That night she slept with the grimy ball beside her pillow. And the next morning, right after breakfast, she waited till everyone was out and took the ball and herself down the street.

She hoped no one would see her, no one would follow.

She headed toward the big vacant lot on East Twenty-third Street. Unlike some of the other lots in the area, though, it wasn't overgrown and filled with snakes, or so muddy she'd risk ruining her clothes if she ventured into it.

And, best of all, it wasn't often visited by bullies. In fact, it was deserted this morning, since most other families in the neighborhood were at church. (When Papa, a Catholic, and Mama, who was Jewish, got married, they'd stopped attending religious services, and Ruby had never set foot in either a church or a synagogue.)

Standing in the middle of the field, Ruby swung her left arm and threw the ball upward. It flew quite high, seeming to pause for a moment against the blue sky before plummeting down again. Ruby had no trouble catching it in her right hand.

After a few such tosses, though, she got bored. At the game she'd asked Papa how far it was from the pitcher's mound to home plate, and now she picked a spot she guessed was about the same distance from one of the apple trees that shaded the lot. When she turned and looked at the tree, it seemed very far away.

She took a minute to scrape some dirt into a bump, a miniature version of the mound the pitchers at Ebbets Field had used. Then she mimicked the stiff-armed throwing style of Miss Ebbets (maybe that was how girls were *supposed* to throw?), but the ball popped high in the air and bounced in the grass no more than halfway toward the tree.

As she went to retrieve it, she remembered something Papa had told her as they watched the Superbas' Nap Rucker throw his odd, floating pitches. "Ol' Nap gets hitters out with tricks, but many other pitchers rely on speed," he'd said. "They just rear back and let fly."

Ruby took the ball in her left hand, her fingers finding a natural position across the raised seams. She stepped onto the little bump of dirt and peered at the distant tree. Standing there in her black dress with its tight sailor waist and her black patent-leather shoes, she shook her shoulders and let her muscles relax.

As she did, she felt her vision sharpen. Everything else—the movement of the grass in the wind, a flock of pigeons flying on whistling wings overhead, the sound of a distant trolley rattling along its tracks on Ocean Avenue—fell away, and all she saw was her target, a tiny knothole about three feet off the ground in the apple tree's gnarled trunk.

She took a deep breath, reared back, and let fly.

An instant later, the ball smashed into the tree with a sound like a small thunderclap. Bark exploded from the trunk, and the ball rebounded as if the tree had thrown it back, coming to rest no more than twenty feet from where Ruby stood.

After a moment, she walked over and picked it up. There

was a fresh brown gouge in the horsehide, and a corresponding yellow-white gouge, she saw, in the tree trunk. Already sap was leaking from the new wound, perfuming the air with a sharp, sweet odor.

"Do it again," a voice called out.

Ruby looked around. Without realizing, she'd attracted a small crowd of children. They stood on the edge of the lot, staring at her, staring at the damaged tree. It was a boy, perhaps her age but bigger, stronger, who'd spoken.

Ruby thought about it. The throw had felt good. Her arm wanted to try again. But looking at the ball, she knew that one more throw like that and it might come apart. Her Casey ball was too valuable to risk destroying.

She shook her head.

Most of the children looked disappointed. But the boy crossed his arms over his chest and stuck out his chin.

"Do it again," he said, *"Monkey Girl."*

At least he didn't try to stop her, to strike her, as others sometimes did, as she ran past him for home.

That night, just before she fell asleep, Ruby told Mama what she had done, what she hoped to do.

But before she had even finished, Mama had stopped listening. She was frowning and shaking her head.

"No," she said, and again, "Ruby, no. Girls don't play baseball."

Ruby felt a mix of confusion and disappointment and anger. Even though no one but Nick ever questioned Mama's pronouncements, she found herself saying, "But you always tell me girls can do anything."

Mama blinked. Then her face hardened. She peered down at her daughter, her eyes as cold and unforgiving as black stones.

"Girls *can* do anything," she said.

Ruby said, "But—"

"Anything *meaningful*," Mama said.

Ruby had never questioned Mama or disobeyed her orders. Not until now.

When the house was empty, she took the pillow from her bed, retrieved a coil of rope she'd taken from Papa's workroom in the basement and hidden in the closet, and carried them and her Casey ball back to the empty lot. This time she knew she would be left alone, because it was a weekday and all the other neighborhood children were packed away in that new public school they'd built over on Avenue L.

Mama didn't approve of organized schooling, at least not as it was practiced now. She thought that it "put shackles on young girls' minds," so she and occasionally one of her suffragist friends taught Ruby themselves.

Ruby had learned how to read and do basic arithmetic from these lessons, working slowly through the textbooks that Mama had brought home from somewhere. But Mama and her friends had so many meetings to attend that sometimes days went by between sessions. Ruby was frequently lonely, but she also knew that if she was forced to sit in a classroom with twenty other kids, the shouts of "Monkey Girl!" would ring in her head from dawn till dusk.

She carefully took the cotton case off the pillow and tucked it into the small cloth bag she'd brought along, then tied the pillow to the apple tree with the rope. Retreating to the little mound of earth, she peered in, then reared back and threw.

The ball still made a loud thump when it hit, but careful inspection revealed that it had survived the impact with no damage. The pillow, however, had acquired a deep dent and a small brown smudge.

For the next half hour, Ruby threw the ball, went and

retrieved it, and then threw it again. Every time but one, the ball went exactly where she aimed it, as if it were traveling down a tunnel to its destination. She seemed to know instinctively how to send it exactly where she wanted to.

By the end of a half hour, she was dripping under the warm spring sun. She was tired, especially her left arm, but it was a kind of weariness she'd never experienced before. A *satisfied* weariness.

She untied the misshapen, thoroughly stained pillow, covered it again with the clean case, and carried it, the rope, and the ball home. No one saw her—or if they did, no one said anything—not that day, or any of the ones that followed.

Ruby was smart enough never to breathe a word to anyone about what she was doing.

If she did, she knew that someone would eventually tell Mama. And that would be the end of it.

2

On July 2, 1913, two months after Ruby caught her Casey ball, she and Mama sat on the flagstone steps in front of the house on East Twenty-first Street. Under the hot summer sun, they paged through newspapers saved from the day of Ruby's birth, exactly eight years earlier.

Even in the heat, Mama was wearing a double-skirted black dress with long sleeves and a broad collar, as she often did. By pulling her dark, wiry hair back and holding it in place with a band gleaming with white and green flakes of glass, she seemed to be saying, "Look at me," to be challenging everyone to notice her high white forehead, flashing dark eyes, sharp chin, and thin-lipped mouth.

Ruby couldn't imagine ever saying, "Look at me!"

Together they leafed through the yellowing, crackly pages. It was a hot, steamy day, August weather, with brownish skies, a smeared sun, and heat waves rising like wiggling dancers from the melting tar of the new street.

And the smell.

Mama had told Ruby that before all these new streets had been laid and houses built, the neighborhood had been part of a poultry farm. But Ruby would have known *that* without being told, because an odor so thick it was like a fog rose from the dark earth on days like this, making Ruby's eyes water as she tried to breathe only through her mouth.

Funny enough, they'd moved here from Brownsville two years ago in search of what Mama called "healthy air." The air in the tenements, she said frequently, carried sickness with it, and she would be damned if she would let the past repeat itself again and again, not if she could help it, not if her life depended on it.

"Or my children's lives!" she'd said, Papa standing there, quiet, just nodding and nodding. When Mama talked like that, saying words like "damned," standing stiff and straight, her pointy chin like a knife and her dark eyes flashing, your only choice was to listen and nod and do what she told you. Whether you were Ruby or Nick or Ted or Papa himself, you listened and obeyed.

So they'd left the brick tenement with its bad air and bad memories and moved into the house at 1394 East Twenty-first Street, a real house made of wood. And Mama seemed happy, or *happier* at least, even if the healthy air smelled worse than what they were all used to.

When they'd first arrived, there'd been more fields than houses in the neighborhood. And there were still a few, like the one where Ruby went to throw her Casey ball against the tree. Not for long, though. Every day brought the sound of hammers and saws, the clatter of horses' hooves and cart wheels against the cobbles as building materials arrived. Irish families like Papa's were moving into the new houses, and German ones, and Jewish ones like Mama's, who came from Russia and other parts of Europe.

There were lots of kids, too, though most of them didn't have anything to do with Monkey Girl.

As they did every year, she and Mama inspected the *New York Times* "Pictorial Section" from Ruby's birth day. On the top of the page was a photogravure of a beautiful woman, tall, with a mass of curly black hair and thick dark eyebrows, standing straight-backed in a white dress, staring out of the page in a way that reminded Ruby of Mama.

"That's Alice Roosevelt," Mama said proudly. "Daughter of Teddy, of course."

Ruby had heard of Teddy Roosevelt, but not of Alice.

"You're named after her."

Ruby looked up in confusion, and her mother laughed. "Alice Lee Roosevelt," she said. "Ruby Lee Thomas."

"Oh," Ruby said. She was a little disappointed to have just the same middle name as someone famous. Ted was luckier—*he'd* been named after Alice's father.

"When you grow up, I want you to be like her," Mama went on. "Do what you want to do and don't care what anyone thinks about you. Show the world that women matter as much as men, just like Alice does."

Ruby didn't say anything. How did you show the world something like that?

They looked back at the newspaper, at the actresses and baronesses and opera singers who filled out the rest of the pictorial section. If they didn't resemble the languid, passive "ideal girl" described in one of her birth-day newspapers, none of them looked much like Ruby either, or anyone Ruby was likely to grow into.

Ruby was slender, with a narrow, serious olive-toned face, high cheekbones, wiry black hair that resisted brushing, and eyes that since birth had been an odd deep blue shading to violet. Her face was nothing like the little buttercup faces of the movie stars and society women, with their rosebud lips and helmets of curls and sparkling dark eyes.

"Just look!" Mama said, turning a page. "Look what women can do!"

None of them had arms like Ruby's, either.

Usually their journey through the newspapers would be a leisurely one, with plenty of time for articles about whales and pygmies and other oddities that the tabloids used to fill their pages. But this year they hurried through the ritual. At first Ruby thought Mama was merely bored, but it turned out she was planning to march in a parade up in Manhattan later that day.

"You'll come, too," she told Ruby.

When Ruby asked if she had to, Mama gave a sharp nod. "Oh, you're going," she said. Then, with an effort, she made her voice gentler. "You'll enjoy it, Ruby. There'll be other children there."

As if *that* was a convincing reason!

Ruby looked at her arms, hidden within the sleeves of a white cotton sweater. Mama noticed the direction of her gaze. "Ruby, no one will care," she said sharply. "You're not going to hide out here for the rest of your life. Let's go."

And so they went.

As they sat on the elevated heading toward Manhattan, the brick tenement buildings passing by almost within arm's reach, windows open like gaping mouths, Ruby asked what the parade was about.

"The vote, of course," Mama said.

Ruby knew *that*. Mama had brought her to a few suffragist meetings. There were usually pastries and little cakes to eat, and someone always brought her a glass of Coca-Cola or milk. Sometimes the speeches were like the humming of bees in Ruby's ears, while other times the speakers shouted and pounded tables and turned red in the face, their hair escaping from ribbons and pins, damp patches appearing under their arms.

"But why a parade?"

Mama's eyes gleamed. "Because we're finally getting close," she said. "Because by the time you're of age, you'll be able to vote. You and all other women."

Ruby knew she was supposed to be excited. But she merely looked out the stained window. The train was rattling across the Manhattan Bridge, and she caught a glimpse of the blue water and ships below and the city skyline ahead.

Mama was already on to something else, dipping into the big black bag she always carried over her shoulder on excursions and pulling out some newspaper clippings. Wherever she went, Mama brought old newspapers with her.

"Why a parade?" she said. "Because we're winning against minds like these."

Ruby looked. The paper on top showed a cartoon of two severe-looking matrons in plain dresses and ugly shoes and funny hats carrying signs that said VOTES FOR WOMEN. They were looking at a beautiful girl strolling past, wearing slender high-heeled shoes, a dress that hugged her slim body, a flowing fur stole, and a fashionable hat adorned with egret feathers.

One of the matrons was saying, in apparent admiration of the pretty young thing, "Isn't she feminine?"

Mama said, pointing, "According to the man who drew this cartoon, this one is me."

Her forefinger indicated the uglier, more witchlike of the two suffragists, the skinny one with a big nose and dead black hair and ruffles on her coat that looked like leaves of cabbage.

"No!" Ruby said, shocked. She stared at her mother. Yes, Mama was tall, yes, she was thin, yes, she had a somewhat prominent nose, but she was beautiful, not like the woman in the drawing. "You don't look anything like her."

"Doesn't matter. Just by being a suffragist, I look like that to him."

She showed Ruby another cartoon. It depicted a pretty young woman in a modest floor-length dress, eyes downcast; a professional man dressed in a suit and tie, rubbing his chin as if he was befuddled by something; and another skinny, unfashionable, witchy suffragist. The caption: "The Three Sexes."

"This one won a prize of fifty dollars," Mama said.

The three sexes. Men, women, and people like her mother.

"We're having a parade," Mama said, "because, damn it, we deserve one."

Several people in the train car stared at her disapprovingly, pursing their mouths or frowning, but Mama either didn't notice or didn't care.

The day Ruby turned thirteen, July 2, 1918, she sat beside Mama on the stoop as always, the old newspapers open on their laps. Ruby was still skinny and bony, unfinished, but she'd grown four inches in the past year. She was now taller than Mama and almost as tall as Ted. Nick and Papa, who'd reached six feet in height, still towered over her, and she didn't think she'd ever catch up to them.

For the first time they were being joined in the birth-day ritual by Evie and her and Nick's two daughters, Amanda and Allie. Amanda was halfway between five and six, tall for her age and slender like her father, with a long, severe face and a reserved manner that made people sometimes mistake her for Ruby's sister. Only their eyes were different: while Ruby's were that odd shade of blue violet, Amanda's were such a dark brown that they appeared almost black.

Allie, on the other hand, was the image of Evie, round and pink, with broad cheeks and blue eyes and blond ringlets. Little more than a year old, she was already into everything, but somehow escaped censure—even from Mama—because it was impossible to resist her endless good cheer and ready smile. She never cried and rarely complained about anything.

Amanda sat properly, looking down at the pages and asking the same questions that Ruby had asked years before. Meanwhile, Allie was crawling into and out of Evie's lap, climbing the metal railing alongside the stoop, picking the little red berries off a bush in the garden and putting them in her mouth, then thoroughly enjoying her mother's prying them back out again.

But Evie never got angry at her irrepressible younger daughter, no matter how tired she was. She still worked at the hospital part-time, and Ruby didn't know how she could manage to be so calm and cheerful at the end of a long day.

Amanda looked up from the photograph of Alice Lee Roosevelt and said, "Did you keep the newspapers for me, too?"

Mama smiled. It seemed she'd been expecting the question. "Of course," she said. "You and Allie both, just like I did with all my children. All kinds of interesting things happened on the day you were born."

Ruby knew that Ted still sat patiently as Mama paged through the newspapers every year on his birthday in December. Nick, on the other hand, had given up the practice even before he and Evie got married, moved around the corner onto Ocean Avenue, and produced Amanda and Allie.

"And will you show them to me?"

"Of course. Your next birthday, if your mother says it's all right."

Evie laughed. "I think it's a wonderful idea. I wish my own mother had thought of it."

Mama folded the newspapers carefully for return to the drawer in her study, where they would remain untouched till the next year. "And then, when your sister is just a little older—"

"And can sit still for more than six seconds," Evie said.

"We'll include her, too."

"And we'll still have cake?" Amanda liked to be certain of things.

"Of course." Mama reached out and patted her on the shoulder, as much physical affection as she was disposed to give. "Newspapers and cake."

"A birthday celebration unlike anyone else's," Evie agreed.

"Newspapers and cake, for each of us," Amanda said. "Promise?"

"Promise," Mama said.

3

*i*t was a hot, sticky August day, the kind where you'd break into a sweat merely by thinking about moving. The neighborhood dogs lay flat in patches of shade like dead things, and even the crows searching for scraps on the lawn seemed listless and out of sorts. Ruby thought the blank blue-gray sky itself must be perishing of thirst.

Mama called it sickness weather, when diphtheria and typhoid and infantile paralysis and other illnesses spread with special speed and ferocity. Those diseases seemed to thrive in the wet heat, as if they used it for fuel as they swept through the neighborhoods of New York City.

Sickness weather.

Ever since the United States had entered the war in Europe, Ruby's parents seemed to spend every night poring over a pile of newspapers, following the latest news with all the focus and intensity Papa had once reserved for baseball scores. They'd sit there, heads close together, murmuring to each other in voices so somber that Ruby wanted nothing more than to stick her fingers in her ears.

That was when Papa was home. The ironworks were in operation many a night and all weekend, producing depth-bomb casings (whatever *those* were) for the war effort, and he was working such long hours that his face seemed somehow always both flushed from the heat of the foundry floor and drained of all color by weariness. His gentle smile was the same, even if it came much less frequently than before.

Nick still worked for Grumpy George, still wrote about sports for the *Examiner,* but that was just a job. He spent most nights out with his journalist friends, arguing politics and social change and who knew what else, sometimes coming home for dinner with Evie and the girls, sometimes not. When he stopped by at 1394, he always had two or three of his friends with him, and from what Ruby could see, they took great pleasure in shouting and waving their fingers in each other's faces.

With America entering the war, Evie had gone back to work full-time at the Norwegian Hospital. Sometimes Mama took care of the girls, but more often that responsibility fell on Ruby's shoulders. It was easy work—not work at all, really—though chasing after Allie sometimes tired her out.

Ted's bad lungs had disqualified him from service, so he spent his days either at the Chase School in Manhattan, studying art, or drawing broadsides in support of President Wilson's entry into the war. Ruby would see his thrilling, dynamic illustrations of shouting men, women in peril, and children in rags, nailed to telephone poles and fixed to storefront windows.

When he was home, his classmate Jim McKay was usually there, too. Jim was planning to become a political cartoonist after graduation. He and Ted made much less of a fuss around the house than Nick and his gang, preferring to sit and draw instead of shouting.

The news was frightening. When German U-boats sank steamers and lightships all up and down the East Coast, two and sometimes three a day, Ruby imagined them lurking off the beach at Coney Island. When a German ship released mustard gas, sickening lighthouse keepers and others onshore, she could almost feel it prickling her lungs.

But by that hot August day it seemed like the war would be over soon. Papa said that the Germans were fighting and dying for pride alone. Soon an armistice would be declared and things, he said almost every night, would be "back to normal, or as close to normal they ever get in a madhouse like this."

To which someone would always say, "A madhouse like the world, like America, like New York, like Brooklyn, like Midwood, or like 1394 East Twenty-first Street?"

And Papa, smiling, would always reply, "All of the above."

Evie's face was still streaked with perspiration when she brought the girls over for dinner. Her white-and-blue nurse's uniform hung limply over her compact, rounded body, and there was a dark purplish stain spattered across the front of her blouse. Her blond hair had come loose from its pins, strands clinging to her cheeks like tiny feathers from a down pillow.

Ruby was sitting on the front steps, hoping for a little late-afternoon breeze and lifting her thick hair off the back of her neck. She'd been splashing water on her face all day, but it hadn't done much good.

Evie looked weary, and so did Allie, her fair cheeks and chubby legs speckled with heat rash. Propped restlessly in her mother's right arm, she barely mustered the slightest grin for

Ruby, though normally she had a smile for everyone. Amanda was a few steps behind, her thin face anxious.

"Don't say a word," Evie told Ruby. "I know I'm an absolute mess. There's no water in the whole apartment building. Nick and some other men are trying to figure out what's wrong."

"When I turned the faucet, brown stuff came out," Amanda said.

"Browner than usual, she means." Evie leaned over and handed Allie to Ruby. The toddler reached out and wrapped her arms around Ruby's neck. She smelled like sweat and powder and wet zwieback. Her arms felt like sticky little rubber hoses against Ruby's skin.

Amanda plunked down on the steps beside her. "Will you go hunting caterpillars with me?" she asked.

Amanda was fascinated by the fat green caterpillars that showed up occasionally on the trunks of the sycamore trees. They hatched out into big, dusty-green moths that had spots like eyes on their wings and looked like goggling angels when they flew against the gas lamps at night.

Ruby nodded. "After dinner."

"Are your parents home?" Evie's voice was casual, but Ruby heard something in it that made her skin prickle. Allie must have heard it, too, somehow, because her arms tightened around Ruby's neck, and she made a low, complaining sound that Ruby felt as a vibration in her breastbone.

"Mama's inside, but Papa's not back yet," she said.

"Okay, then, I'll go in and have a bath."

Ruby looked up into Evie's eyes. They were the palest blue, and guarded only by the faintest of blond lashes, which made it nearly impossible for her to hide how she truly felt about anything. And there was an expression in her eyes that Ruby had never seen before.

"Evie?" she said.

But Evie cut a glance toward the girls and said, "Later."

"The *Bergensfjord*," Evie was saying as Ruby returned to the dining room from saying good night to Amanda. With Allie long asleep in the crib that Evie and Nick kept there, Ruby had put Amanda in her own bed, as she often did, but only after they'd watched the caterpillar they'd found for what felt like hours. Ruby had remained patient, although she could hear the murmur of voices from the living room, and was curious to find out what everyone was talking about.

"From where?" That was Papa asking.

"Norway," Evie said. "A place called Christiania—though apparently the first case came aboard at Bergen."

"First case of what?"

All eyes swiveled toward Ruby, as if they'd momentarily forgotten who she was or that she lived there. Mama and Papa exchanged glances, but after a moment Mama nodded. Ruby understood that they'd decided to let her remain in the room. Being thirteen made her old enough, barely, to hear what they had to say.

"Just listen, honey," Mama said to her.

Even in the sodden heat, Ruby felt cold. There was a mood in the room—in Nick's unusually somber expression, in Evie's odd posture, very upright in her chair beside him—that was new to her.

"It was a Finnish woman," Evie went on. "She and the ones that followed—they were almost all in steerage."

"Of course they were," Nick said.

Evie grimaced. "They think she was sick when she came aboard, but no one checked, there was no way to keep anybody ill off the ship. Who knows if she even had any symptoms."

Nick said, "Between the war and the epidemic, it's not likely that there are enough healthy men left in Europe to enforce any sort of quarantine."

Evie sighed. Her face was scrubbed and clean now, but there were dark smudges under her eyes, and for the first time Ruby could see lines etched on either side of her mouth.

Ruby thought she looked . . . afraid.

"The next was a cook for third class, and the two after that were passengers."

"Were there doctors on board?" Ted asked. He'd been sitting quietly at the end of the table, his pad lying forgotten on his lap.

"Yes. But do you want to guess how much time they spent in steerage?" Evie's expression was scornful. "Anyway, those first four died, and—"

"What did they do with them?" Ruby asked.

Her mother shot her a warning look, but Evie chose to answer. "When people die aboard ship," she said, "at least people without much money or family connections, well, they're buried at sea. Especially when they're carrying an epidemic disease."

Ruby's face felt numb. She imagined the scene: the cold ocean, tumbling waves, the body wrapped in—did they wrap the bodies in shrouds?—the still form sliding off the deck and disappearing into the black water.

Unlike her parents, unlike Evie, Ruby had never seen a dead body. Not even in the moving pictures.

"What epidemic?" she said.

"The Spanish influenza, honey," Evie said.

Even Ruby had heard of this. Thousands of people had died of it in Europe, especially soldiers in the trenches, in just the past few months. Entire factories, schools, even shipyards had had to shut down because there was no one healthy enough to occupy them.

Ruby didn't know what the Spanish influenza looked like, or what it did to you. Nor did she want to.

"*Maybe* it's the influenza." Mama spoke sharply. "You told us that the health office says it was just the ordinary grippe and pneumonia."

Ruby didn't think that an illness that had killed four people should be called *just* anything, but she didn't get to speak before Evie flared up. "That's because they're cowards, all of them," she said. "If they quarantined the ship, word would get around that New York was hysterical over people with head colds, and soon enough all the freighters and merchantmen would be heading to other ports, down to the Amboys or up to Boston. Better to cover it up and risk a million lives than to lose port fees."

Nick put a hand on her arm, but she shook it off. "Listen," she said, "by the time the fourth patient had died, more than half of those in steerage were affected. Two hundred or more at one time. In just a few days!"

"Have you ever seen a case of Spanish influenza?" Mama asked.

Red spots rose in Evie's cheeks. "Of course not," she said. "No one around here has—not even Dr. Cofer, who's the health officer for the ports, who passed the ship. How can you already have seen an illness that's never been here?"

She sat back in her seat and looked at the faces around her. "But now it *is* here. I'm sure of it, as sure as I am that Mrs. Olsen, who they brought to the hospital this morning, will die within the next few hours, despite all we've tried to do for her. I doubt she'll ever wake up, poor woman, and maybe she's luckier that way."

They sat in silence for a long time, it seemed to Ruby, before Nick said, "What will happen next?"

"It will spread." Evie raised her eyes. "It's already spreading. You don't need to be a doctor or a nurse to know that, because it's what the influenza does. It spreads. How far it will go, no one can tell. Maybe not so far, if we're very lucky."

But her expression was bleak.

"How?" Papa asked. "How does it spread?"

"I don't know," Evie said. "We know diseases are caused by germs, and we know that germs pass from person to person, but we're not sure how. Some even say you get sick from eating old bread."

She shook her head. "I don't know," she said again. "Maybe the disease spreads when people breathe on each other."

Ruby saw the realization in everyone's eyes. You could get sick from *breathing*?

Papa slapped his palms together as if to interrupt their thoughts. "Okay, now we know what happened on board. What are we going to do about it?"

"Well, the first thing," Evie said, "is that you should stay away from me." Her mouth turned down. "I shouldn't have even come here tonight. I should have quarantined myself."

She looked over at her husband. "But I wanted to see my family."

Nick put an arm around her shoulders. "We have nothing to worry about," he said. "After all, we're strong . . . and we only eat good bread."

After a moment, Evie smiled. "You're right," she said. "But there are a few other things we can try, which might help protect us."

She reached down and picked up her white leather nurse's bag. "Here," she said, pulling something out of it.

If Ruby had expected to see some powerful medicine, she was disappointed. Evie was holding a pile of clean, white handkerchiefs. "Everyone take some of these," she said. "And use one whenever you have to sneeze. If you're with someone who has the grippe, give one to him as well, and tell him to use it. And keep them clean!"

She passed around the handkerchiefs, and everyone took a few, Ted reaching back to hand Ruby her supply. They were stiff and starched, and Ruby thought they might leave scratches on her nose.

"And wash your hands!" Evie went on. "That's very important. The germs might spread through touch. So keep your hands clean."

Ruby blinked. That was all?

How could it possibly be enough?

4

*r*uby and her family ate good bread, and sneezed only into
their handkerchiefs, and washed their hands with resolute
dedication.

But did anyone else? It seemed as if the whole of New York
was ignorant, unknowing, unconcerned, while the Thomases
alone were trapped with knowledge they would have given anything not to have.

Another patient at the Norwegian Hospital died, a seventeen-
year-old boy who'd come off the *Bergensfjord.* "The doctors said the
cause was pneumonia," Evie said. "They're wrong."

She was unshakable in her beliefs, but after a few days Ruby
began to wonder, because no one else seemed to notice the epidemic at all. There was never a headline in any newspaper. The
front pages were always devoted to the war, to the local boys who
had given their lives for the cause, to the vast sweep of soldiers
across places Ruby had never heard of and knew she would never

visit. All eyes were pointed toward Europe. None looked close to home.

A few days after the arrival of the *Bergensfjord,* eleven more patients with the disease ("Spanish influenza, or whatever it is," one of the newspapers called it) arrived on another ship. But because none of them seemed to be in any danger of dying, this ship, too, was passed, its passengers sent from the dock to disappear into the city.

Dr. Cofer, the health officer, explained why he hadn't quarantined the passengers. "We quarantine against smallpox, leprosy, yellow fever, plague, typhus, and cholera," he said. "You may notice that influenza is not on that list."

"Because it's not on the list it's not dangerous?" Evie said as Mama read the announcement in the paper. "That's the most foolish thing I've ever heard."

"This country is at war, and besides having on our hands the winning of the war, we also have the job of supplying our allies," Dr. Cofer added. "This port cannot be clogged for a minute longer than necessity requires."

"Oh, stupid man!" Evie burst out. "How will we be able to supply the Allies when half of our workers are lying sick to death in bed?"

"There is not the slightest danger of an influenza epidemic breaking out in New York," the health officer proclaimed.

"Stupid, murderous man," Evie said.

Without fanfare, the city announced that it was sending 250 nurses and doctors house to house to find the people who had disembarked from the two afflicted ships, to investigate their health and isolate those who showed signs of the illness. According to officials, there was nothing to worry about. The follow-up was strictly routine.

But Evie merely shook her head. "Too late, too late," she said. "The disease has already escaped."

"Have you seen new cases at the hospital?" Papa asked.

Evie nodded.

"Many?"

"No," Evie admitted. "Not many . . . yet."

Mama said, "Perhaps it will all just blow over—"

"Perhaps," Evie said. "We'll wait and see."

They waited. Every day Evie was at the hospital from dawn till dinner, and often enough she went back for another shift after dark, leaving the girls with Ruby. She and Nick had kept their apartment on Ocean Avenue, but had as good as moved back into 1394 while she was working so hard, taking over Nick's old room while Amanda and Allie shared Ruby's.

And every day she came home and went immediately to the bathroom to scrub herself. Her daughters waited patiently, knowing the routine, until she'd emerge in clean clothes, her hands chapped from the soap and hard water, her mouth smelling of Cascara Quinine, reputed to head off influenza.

Only then would she bend over for hugs, her face, hidden from the girls, showing a mix of love and fear.

They waited.

More disease-ravaged ships arrived in the busy harbor and were passed without quarantine. More passengers died at the Norwegian Hospital, and at other hospitals as well—but these patients, being mostly East Indians and Negroes, did not seem to matter as much.

Could you catch the influenza from a Negro? Ruby couldn't see why not.

The city's department of health, headed by a man with the absurd name of Royal Copeland, announced that any spread of the illness would be curtailed by his antispitting campaign, his warnings not to share the punch bowl at social functions, and his cautions to avoid kissing one another on the mouth.

"The influenza epidemic, if such it may be called," was how the newspapers now described it.

And still, oblivious, as if the reports were from somewhere far away, people went on with their lives.

And Ruby watched.

Behind the counter at his candy store, Lenny's normally ruddy face was pale as he fixed their egg creams, one for Ruby and one for Amanda. Allie didn't like the bubbles, but loved watching the seltzer hiss from the shiny nozzle into the tall glasses. So Ruby stood close as she always did, holding Allie on her hip to see, while Amanda inspected the rows of penny candy and fingered the coins in her pocket.

As Lenny worked, blinking his watery eyes, Mrs. Cohen from down the street came into the store, trailed by two of her four young sons. She picked up a pack of cigarettes from the rack and said, "You still feeling poorly, Len?"

"Like a bell my head is." His voice was raspy. "And my throat, it's like—"

But he didn't finish the sentence before a cough took him. It seemed to Ruby that it came from deep in his lungs, and he was barely able to put the glasses down on the counter before it shook his thin frame. He turned away, both hands in front of his face, and Ruby saw the muscles on his neck tighten like strings.

Inside the small store, the sound was awful, like a hundred pieces of stiff paper being ripped apart at the same time. Ruby took a quick step away from the counter, turning Allie's head toward her shoulder with the palm of her hand. Amanda, eyes wide, raised her hands to her ears, and Mrs. Cohen gave Lenny a sympathetic grimace. Even her usually noisy children fell silent for a moment.

When the spasm had passed, Lenny pulled a grimy cloth from his pocket and wiped first his mouth and then his hands on it. Then he looked down at the cloth, frowned, folded it up, and put it back in his pocket. Taking a long spoon from under the counter, he began to stir the chocolate syrup into the first of the egg creams.

"You should take a day off," Mrs. Cohen told him. "Get your strength back."

"I take a day, who opens the store?" Lenny said. "My wife, she's already in bed."

Ruby watched his fingers on the glass, the wrinkled fingers that had just clutched the dirty cloth, that had just covered his mouth when he coughed. As she watched, a bit of liquid splashed up onto his forefinger, then dripped back down into the glass.

Without hesitating, she spun away from the counter, so fast that Allie laughed out loud. Amanda, curious, turned her serious face toward them and said, "What's wrong, Aunt Ruby?"

"Let's go," Ruby said. "Now."

Amanda shot her a look, but followed without question. As they reached the door of the little store, she heard Lenny say, "What? You don't want your drinks?"

Too polite just to walk out, Ruby looked back at him and said, "I just remembered we have to go. I'll pay—I'll pay you later."

Her heart was pounding. She was desperate to be out of there.

The old man began to protest, but before he could say anything Mrs. Cohen said, "Don't fret, Lenny—we'll take them."

Ruby stiffened. "Don't," she said to Mrs. Cohen. "You and your boys, just leave. Please."

Lenny stifled another cough. Ruby could see that he was laboring for breath. He looked much worse now than he had when they'd entered the store a few minutes before.

"And you go home, too," she said. "Close the store and go home and . . . rest."

He shook his head and looked over at Mrs. Cohen, who was smiling. "Young people!" she said.

"They don't understand the value of work," he agreed in a hoarse voice.

At Ruby's side, Amanda had caught some of Ruby's near panic. She tugged at her free hand and said, "Let's *go.*"

A moment later they were out the door and back in the open. But a gray haze seemed to obscure the sun, and the air seemed tainted, harsh and smoky on Ruby's tongue.

When they reached home, Ruby marched the girls upstairs and ran a bath. "Now?" Amanda asked. A creature of habit, she was accustomed to having a bath just before dinner.

"Now," Ruby said.

"Why?"

Ruby didn't answer.

"Because Lenny was coughing?"

Smart girl. A watcher, like Ruby.

"We won't cough like that if we take a bath?"

"That's right," Ruby said, pulling Allie's blouse over her head.

I hope not.

She started feeling better when they were sitting in the big old tub, all three together, the water so hot they could barely tolerate it, the steam rising in billows to the ceiling. Amanda, her dark curly hair sticking to her neck and shoulders, played with the metal cups that had long been her favorite bath toy, pouring water endlessly from one into another. Allie sat on Ruby's lap, as slick and energetic as a golden seal.

Ruby kept them all there for almost an hour, until they were as wrinkled up as old plums, until Allie, hungry, began to whine and struggle, and even Amanda complained of boredom. "Okay," Ruby said, pulling the plug and gaining a few more minutes because both girls loved to watch the water swirl down the drain.

But speaking for herself, she could have stayed in there forever. All she'd been able to think about since they'd left Lenny's was the old man's knotted hands, and the way those hands had touched the glasses right after he'd coughed into them.

How many hands were there in this city?

And how could you ever tell what they'd touched?

Evie closed her eyes. "This is how it happens," she said.

It was late, past midnight. Even Mama and Papa had gone to bed, and Ted, too. Nick was out at the newspaper, and the two girls had been asleep for hours. Exhausted by their unusual bath, they'd barely made it through dinner.

Only the two of them sat in the living room, Ruby and Evie, one lamp in the corner casting dim yellow light across the darkened room. Ruby had chosen to wait until they were alone to tell Evie of the visit to Lenny's that afternoon.

"I'm sorry!" she said suddenly, the words loud in the quiet room.

Evie opened her eyes wide, the whites gleaming in the lamp's glow. "What?"

"I shouldn't have brought them to the store." Suddenly there were tears on Ruby's cheeks. "I should just have kept them home. If they get sick—"

But before she could go on, Evie stifled her words with a hug that stole Ruby's breath.

"Oh, baby," she said, pulling back a little and cupping Ruby's face in her hands, "if they get sick, it won't be your fault. It won't be *anyone's* fault. It'll just be the disease. And you were so smart to take them out of there, to not drink those egg creams. Most people wouldn't even have noticed."

Ruby shook her head against the soft palms, but Evie didn't

let her go. "Listen, Ruby," she said, keeping her face close. "People we know are going to get sick. Some of them might die. Do you understand that? I mean, truly understand it?"

Ruby didn't reply.

"It's the way epidemics work," Evie went on, releasing her. "I've been talking to people who saw the influenza in Europe, who saw how it went, and that's what they've all been telling me. It's like a tornado, touching down here, and there, and then over there. You can't tell where it will hit—you just know it will be somewhere."

Ruby rubbed at her eyes. Suddenly she was exhausted.

"Will he die?" she asked. "Lenny?"

Evie shrugged. "I don't know," she said. "There's no medicine. Many people get better eventually, but some die. Lenny would be doing himself a favor if he'd listen to your advice and just go home and rest as much as possible."

"So what will happen?"

The silence went on for so long that Ruby decided that Evie had chosen not to answer. But finally she heaved a sigh and said, "To epidemics like the influenza," she said, "people are like coal. Like wood or oil. They're simply fuel. The disease burns through them, and then eventually it burns out. That's the way it always works.

"As to how many it will consume—well, that's something none of us can guess."

5

*t*he flames spread across Brooklyn and on into the rest of the city, seeming to gain in strength and size with each passing day.

Remarkably, Lenny survived, and so did his wife, even though the candy store sat locked and empty for many weeks. But two of the Cohen boys died within a day of each other. Ruby never learned whether they were the ones who'd drunk the egg creams meant for her and Amanda.

It didn't seem to matter. You didn't need to drink an egg cream to become ill, to die. Strong young men went off to work in the morning, fell down in the street in the afternoon, and were dead by nightfall. Four women played bridge one evening, and three didn't survive until dawn the next day. The Royal Italian Grenadiers Band played a concert at the Lexington Avenue Opera House, after which six band members could not rise to acknowledge the audience's applause and were taken to the hospital.

Through a window, Ruby and Amanda watched a small group

of girls skipping rope on the street one bright autumn morning. They were singing, "I had a little bird, its name was Enza. I opened the window, and in-flu-enza."

"Can I go out and play?" Amanda asked.

"No."

The newspapers finally took notice, listing the number of new cases in each borough, a number that grew each day through September and on into October. Two hundred new cases, three hundred, nine hundred, twelve hundred in each twenty-four hours. Twenty deaths, fifty, a hundred.

And almost always, the most new cases and new deaths occurred in Brooklyn, just as a fire always burns hottest at its core.

Mrs. Cohen died a week after her two sons. Mr. Cohen and the surviving children packed up and fled, leaving so hurriedly that there were still toys scattered across their front lawn—toys that no one dared to touch. "Wherever they've gone," Evie said at the dinner table that night, when she thought Ruby wasn't listening, "they've brought the plague with them."

Ruby was always listening.

Old Mr. Higgins at 1416 was next, and then the Giles baby, a little girl so recently arrived that no one even knew her name. When Mama heard about that death, she went pale and barely spoke the entire next day.

It was so strange. The weather was warm and placid, the sun shone bright, the news from Europe was good—it looked as if the war would be over within weeks. Movies opened, stores held sales, people went to work or on vacation. But always new names were added to the list. Jonathan Silver, who worked at Essex's down on Seventeenth Street. Rebecca Samuel, a teacher at PS 193 on Bedford Avenue. Miss Ellen Ziegler, a nurse. Billy O'Reilly, a bully who had terrorized the children of East Twenty-first Street for years, who had happily called out "Monkey Girl!" whenever he had the chance.

The health department, while denying that it had mishandled any aspect of the epidemic, tried this and that to halt its spread. Placards appeared in shop windows, literature was handed out on street corners, health experts visited the schools, theaters projected slides up on the screen. All recommended keeping homes and businesses well ventilated, avoiding sweeping where you might raise a cloud of dust, and staying at home if you felt the onset of headache, fever, or congestion of the lungs.

Written above Health Commissioner Copeland's name on every placard was the following inscription: "To prevent the spread of Spanish influenza, sneeze, cough, or expectorate—if you must—in your handkerchief. You are in no danger if everyone heeds this warning."

"Look!" Amanda said to her mother. "Just like you told us to do."

"Yes," Evie replied. "Weeks ago, when it might have made a difference."

How did you stay healthy, how did you stay alive, in a city so crowded with people who didn't expectorate into their handkerchiefs? Mama still went to her meetings, Nick to the *Examiner*, Ted to his art classes, and Evie to the Norwegian Hospital or the district nurses' office up on Schermerhorn Street in Brooklyn Heights, which sent her to care for patients too sick to make it to the hospital.

And every day Papa went off to the foundry. Though he'd been a manager for years, with his own office, he'd recently returned to working on the floor, along with every other healthy man they could find. Some days fifty men would be out sick, sometimes a hundred, and even those who returned to work were pale shadows of their former selves and not good for very much.

When they could, Nick and Ted went to the foundry to help. At least they could carry boxes or hunks of scrap metal, even if they couldn't do much else. Ruby almost never saw any of them, and when she did they were gray-faced with exhaustion and covered with fresh burns and blisters.

Rest, and good food, and fresh air, and separation from sick people. Those were the tickets to surviving influenza, to surviving the inferno.

But who had the time?

When the epidemic finally came to their door, though, it wasn't exhausted Papa who was struck first, or Evie, or either of the two little girls.

It was Ted. Ted with his gentle disposition and his lungs scarred by some unnamed disease that had swept through the tenements when he was just two years old.

Ted, *of course.*

He walked in the front door early one afternoon when only Ruby and the girls were at home. "I'm going straight to bed," he said. "My head hurts."

Ruby felt herself grow cold and still, as if something within her, some gear or spring, had stopped working. She walked over and put the back of her hand against his temple, and felt the heat radiating through her skin and all the way into her bones.

Somehow, this only made her feel colder.

But she kept her voice businesslike. "All right," she said. "Off to bed with you. I'll get you a drink and a compress."

"Okay," he said vaguely, in a way that made her wonder if he'd understood anything she'd said. So she took his arm and ushered him up to his bedroom. Though she was prepared to help change him into his nightclothes, he merely tumbled onto the bed and lay there, eyes closed.

"I'll be right back," she said, and nearly ran down the stairs to the kitchen. Wetting a cloth in cold water at the sink, she hurried back upstairs. He hadn't moved. She brushed his lank, damp hair away and placed the cloth across his forehead. He sighed and half opened his eyes, and the corners of his mouth twitched upward. "Feels good," he said. "Thanks, sweetie."

He was blazing.

Ruby said again, "I'll be right back." Then, even though it was nonsensical, "Wait for me."

She headed toward the stairs, but hesitated and went instead to the bathroom, where she scrubbed her hands under hot water. Then, taking the steps two at a time, she headed toward the front door.

Amanda followed her into the hallway, Allie holding on unsteadily to one of her legs.

"Ted's sick," Ruby said.

Amanda's face was solemn. "Is it influenza?"

"I don't know." Though she did. "Listen, Amanda, I have to go around the corner to buy something for him. You two stay here, and I'll be back as quick as I can. I'll bring you a Coke. Okay?"

Eyes wide, Amanda nodded. Ruby never left them alone.

"Don't let your sister get into trouble." Ruby turned toward the door, then looked back at them. "And don't go near your uncle Ted's room!" Seeing Allie's chin begin to quiver at the tone of her voice, she added, "I mean, he's very tired, so leave him be so he can rest."

Then, almost running, she headed down the block and onto Avenue M, past the Cohens' empty house and Lenny's shuttered store, down to the Empire City Food Mart. Here she bought two bottles of Coke and, her actual goal, four bottles of Phez, a loganberry juice.

There'd been an advertisement in the *Examiner* recently, featuring a drawing of a smiling nurse and claiming that Phez was a tonic against fever caused by influenza. ("It soothes, refreshes, and nourishes!") Seeing these boasts, Evie had given a great snort of disbelief. "At least Bacardi Ron, which claims the same thing, has alcohol, so you feel less pain," she'd said. "But loganberry juice? Sorry, but no."

Still, maybe Evie was wrong. Maybe the makers of Phez knew something even she didn't. Carrying the bottles carefully, Ruby walked home as fast as she could, past people who—perhaps because her face was flushed, her eyes wild—gave her a wide berth.

The girls were waiting for her just inside the front door. Amanda looked very solemn.

"Uncle Ted coughed," she said.

Ruby felt something click and spin inside her head. "How many times?"

"Just once." Suddenly the six-year-old seemed to understand how upset the information had made Ruby. "But he didn't sound as bad as that man in the candy store."

Ruby put her free hand on the top of her niece's head for a moment. It was cool to the touch. "Thank you, Amanda," she said. "Come with me."

In the kitchen she popped the metal top off a Coca-Cola, poured some into a glass, and handed it to Amanda. "Share with your sister," she said. "Don't spill it."

Then Ruby levered the top off the Phez bottle, poured some of the fragrant purple-red juice into a glass, and added the coldest water she could get out of the tap. With a long spoon—which reminded her of egg creams, of hands—she mixed the concoction.

The two girls never took their eyes off her.

Carrying a newly soaked compress in one hand, the glass of diluted Phez in the other, Ruby walked carefully up the stairs. As soon as she stepped into Ted's room, though, she realized that he was in no shape to drink loganberry juice or anything else.

The entire room was as hot as if someone had brought a wood-burning stove inside. It was suffused with the cloying smell of sickness, and Ruby wondered if the odor came from her brother's lungs. Ted lay on his back, and though his eyes were open, he didn't appear to see anything. Nor did he turn his face in her direction when, panicked, she called out to him. His cheeks were bright red, as if he'd been slapped, and sweat streaked his forehead. It had already drenched his shirt and soaked the bedclothes.

Ruby placed the useless glass of Phez carefully on the little night table, went over and opened the room's only window, then returned to the bed and sat down beside her brother.

As she took his wet, burning hand in hers, he coughed, a weak, wretched sound. Ruby fought off a wave of terror stronger than any she'd ever felt. Was he about to die, before anyone else even came home? Should she try to take him to a hospital? How could she even get him downstairs?

And Ruby herself. Was she sick already? Had the germs spread into her body, her lungs? Would she, too, die?

She wanted nothing more than to run from the room. But she stayed where she was, holding his hand, saying words to him that he couldn't hear and that she never was able to recall. Perhaps they weren't words at all, only sounds.

Shaking her head to clear it, she reached out and picked up the cool washcloth. She placed it gently on his forehead, and for a moment his rigid muscles seemed to relax a little.

While he lay there, not helping, not even seeming aware of what she did, she struggled to unbutton his limp shirt, then to wriggle it out from under him. How white his chest was! How thin! The skin, stretched tight, seemed barely to cover the ribs.

As she bent over him, readjusting the cloth, he drew in a sharp, spasmodic breath—his frail chest expanding so that Ruby thought for an instant that it might burst—and coughed again. This cough made a deep, harsh sound, and it brought Ted back closer to awareness, though still his red-tinged eyes were unfocused.

"It *hurts*," he said.

"I know," she said to him. "I know. Just rest, Ted. Rest, and you'll feel better."

Already the cloth was as steamy as if she'd been running it under the hot tap. She went to the bathroom and rinsed it in cold water, then returned and mopped his brow, and his chest, once more. Again and again she did this, replenishing the cloth, mopping away the sweat, speaking even if he could not hear her. For hours and hours, until she thought that this was the way she'd live out the rest of her life. Standing, running to the sink, wetting the cloth, returning, sitting, applying the compress, speaking into his unhearing ear.

When someone, Evie, Mama, finally came into the room that evening, Ruby was nearly blind, staggering, and only when someone else, Papa, Nick, took the cloth away from her and steered her downstairs, to the kitchen, to the table, did she allow herself to stop, to loosen her muscles, to let go.

She sat there, exhausted, head resting on her arms, drenched in sweat—her own or Ted's, she didn't know—a glass of water in front of her, moisture beading up on its rim and sliding down like raindrops. Her family moved around her, a blur, a commotion. Ruby listened to their conversation as if it were coming from miles away. Sometimes their words just sounded like babble, but other times she could follow the thread.

They talked, they argued, two or three at a time, while one of them tended to the patient upstairs. At first Nick marched around the room, insisting that they take Ted to the hospital. But Evie, quiet and calm, was equally firm that they leave him where he was.

"There's no point," she said. "Worse than no point. All the hospitals are overfull already, and there aren't enough doctors or nurses." Ruby saw her give a strange smile. "Many of us are sick, too, you know. We're not immune."

Nick stopped his stamping around and stared at her.

"No, not me," Evie said. "I'm fine. But many others are ill. Of course they are. What would you expect?"

No one said anything to that.

"During an epidemic," Evie said, "the hospital is the worst place for a sick person."

But what was the best place?

No one slept for more than a few hours at a time during the next three days, and afterward, Ruby honestly couldn't remember sleeping at all. She recalled drinking tall glasses of cold water and juice and even the Phez, which had a sharp tang and left her mouth feeling dry. She supposed she ate every now and again, though she could never say what.

For all of them, attending to Ted became a mechanical enterprise, an endless round of cold compresses, doses of aspirin and salicin and salt of quinine to bring the fever down, and, when that didn't work, cinnamon mixed with warm milk. (Though Ruby could tell by Evie's expression that she put little stock in *that*.)

On the third night Ted's cough became worse, a thicker, more frequent, agonized sound. A doctor came at some unearthly hour, a gruff, haggard man doing a favor for Evie, and injected oxygen under Ted's skin. "An oxygen mask would be better," he told the family, "but I have none to spare."

"We understand," Papa said, but his face was washed free of humor, of life. He looked like he didn't understand anything.

By now, Ruby was no longer allowed in Ted's bedroom. She stayed with Amanda and Allie, reading to them from books and magazines, her eyes seeing and her mouth moving but her mind somewhere far away.

She made sure they were fed and bathed, since no one else seemed to remember they might need such care. That was something Ruby could do.

Evie and Mama and Nick and Papa took turns upstairs, always making sure to scrub themselves in the bathroom sink before coming back down.

Even so, Ruby could see the bright red drying droplets scattered across the areas they'd missed, on their arms, their cheeks, soaked into their shirts. Still the coughing went on, echoing through the house.

Ted died at eight-thirty on the fourth morning after taking to his bed.

But Ruby had given up hope long before.

They buried him at the Evergreens out by the Queens border, the cemetery Mama and Papa chose because it was nondenominational. His grave was set on a small rise amid pine trees and stretches of grass, with a view of Manhattan in one direction and the expanse of Jamaica Bay in the other. As the gravediggers dug, Mama leaned on Nick, Papa stood off by himself, and Evie, with Allie on her hip and Amanda holding on to the hem of her skirt, made sure that everything that was supposed to happen happened. Ruby watched a big white bird flap its way across the glimmering marsh on long, unhurried wings.

Afterward, the hearse drove them back to the house. They sat in silence the whole way.

Ted had been with them in the car on the trip to the cemetery, and now he wasn't with them, and that was that.

The house still smelled of sickness when they walked through the front door. Evie went around opening windows.

It seemed very quiet without the sound of Ted's coughing.

Ruby sat at the kitchen table, thinking, I should feel like something has ended.

So why do I feel like it's just begun?

6

*O*nce the newspapers finally discovered the epidemic, they couldn't get enough of it. Alongside the advertisements for Cascada Quinine and Phez and the lists of newly dead were announcements that all classes in a local college would be held outdoors, regardless of the weather; that the New York City Police Department was vigorously enforcing the new antispitting regulations; that health experts were set to lecture in public schools throughout the city, emphasizing hygiene as the first line of defense against the ravages of what people had begun to call "the flue."

It was all too late. At one elementary school in Williamsburg, nearly a thousand students were absent, and teachers were dying at the rate of one every three days. Shops, offices, factories, and theaters were ordered to stagger their opening and closing times to ease congestion on the subways, elevated lines, and trolleys, which the newspapers called "death traps." In a single day, one Queens cemetery buried more than a hundred victims.

Nurses were among the hardest hit, of course. Evie reported that nearly half of those working for the Brooklyn Bureau of Charities were out sick, and two of her friends at the district nurses' office died within a day of each other.

"Are you scared?" Ruby asked her.

"Of course I am," Evie said, though she seemed just as strong and unflappable as ever.

Until Nick started coughing.

"I'm fine," he kept saying. "I'm fine."

But his voice was different when he spoke, less robust, and at the end of sentences his eyes looked a little wild as he drew in a breath that sounded a lot like a gasp.

"To bed with you," Evie said, and, protesting, Nick went. They could hear him coughing, and the entire family felt a renewed sense of horror at the sound. But his coughs never progressed to the chest-wrenching sound that had characterized Ted's last two days, and he never drifted in and out of consciousness, or suffered from as high a fever. He was a terrible patient, getting out of bed at the slightest provocation, neglecting to take the medicines they brought to him, and insisting that he was fine.

His weakness only made him even noisier and more resentful than usual. In the mornings he sneered at the convalescent menu of oatmeal gruel and hot lemonade. At lunch he insisted that he was ready to go back to work. In the evenings he complained that he wasn't feeling like himself.

"He's going to live," Evie told Ruby after herding him back to bed one more time. "The flue won't get him, though he may be the end of me."

When, after an eighteen-hour shift at the foundry, Papa came home with a fever, no one was entirely surprised.

Ruby awoke the next morning to the sound of her father's

deep, harsh cough. Outside, a dog barked and a child laughed, and then her father coughed again.

She hurried into their room to find him and Mama both in bed. She couldn't remember the last time she'd seen them together like this. Even before the epidemic began, Papa had always been up before dawn to head to work, and Mama, who rose nearly as early, usually went to bed after everyone else in the family.

But there they were, lying side by side. Like Ted had been, Papa was sweaty and restless. His eyes were glazed, coughs shook his broad chest, and air whistled down his throat as if someone had poured asphalt into his lungs. Beside him, Mama was quieter, but her eyes were wild, too, and when Ruby touched her burning forehead she did not react at all.

Ruby must have called out, because a moment later Evie was standing beside her. Evie's jaw clenched, her mouth becoming a thin line the same color as her sallow face. Then she took a deep breath, looked at Ruby, and said, "I'll rouse Nick. You go get the compresses."

Ruby nodded, and they got back to work.

They did what they could, the three of them, with silent Amanda bringing the wet cloths to the foot of the stairs. By now there were no doctors available to deliver oxygen injections, no ambulances, no room in the hospitals, nothing but this insignificant trickle of activity in the face of the inferno.

Papa spent all his time and dwindling energy trying to breathe. By late afternoon his cough had acquired a liquid sound, and perhaps once every three times, he brought up a fine spray of red droplets that spattered the bedsheets, his drenched nightclothes, Mama's face, and Ruby's as well.

Lying beside him, Mama came in and out of awareness. Sometimes she managed a smile for Ruby, even a few words, an apology for causing trouble, but at other times she stared with terrified eyes, as if she didn't know her daughter, as if she were seeing a monster instead.

When Evie would come to take her place, Ruby would go into the bathroom and wash her hands and face, then stand there, head down, and watch the reddish water swirl into the drain.

I'm thirteen years old, she thought, and the mere idea of it was incredible. She felt like an old woman. She felt like she was a hundred.

I'm thirteen years old.

What will I do when my parents are gone?

The first explosion came at seven-thirty in the evening, loud enough to rattle the windows and send Ruby's heart thudding up against her rib cage. It was quickly followed by another and then, soon after, by a third, even louder. Every dog in the neighborhood began to bark.

She was sitting at the kitchen table when the barrage began, and immediately Amanda came in, carrying Allie. Both of them looked at her with wide eyes, and Amanda said, "Is it the war? Has the war come to us at last?"

Ruby said, "No, I'm sure it hasn't." But even as she spoke there was another blast, the loudest yet. She could hear cries of confusion and fear outside.

Nick and Evie came bursting into the room. "What the hell is that?" Nick asked. Then he said, "I'll find out." And a moment later he was gone, the front door slamming behind him.

There was a lull, followed by a long series of explosions, the last of which shook a coffee cup off its hook and sent it shattering onto the floor. At that sound, so much less ominous than the others, Allie's face crumpled and she began to cry.

Her mother scooped her into her arms and looked at Ruby. With a nod, Ruby stood, walked over to the sink, rinsed out a cloth, and headed upstairs.

During the next hour, there was an almost continuous barrage. Looking down at her parents, both of whom had sunk into fitful unconsciousness, Ruby was glad that they were unaware of it.

When Nick finally returned, he was sweaty and distraught. "It's not the Germans," he said. "The Gillespie Shell Loading Company, over in New Jersey, in Morgan, caught fire, and we're hearing its shells exploding."

Another blast rattled the windows. "Well, that's a relief," Evie said. "At least the Huns aren't invading."

"No, you don't understand." Nick's voice was too loud. "The fire is completely out of control. South Amboy, Sayreville, Tompkinsville—they're all in ruins. People are fleeing. Who knows how many have died? And as if all that's not bad enough, the wind is blowing the flames toward a stockpile of TNT."

Evie said, "What fool thought it was a good idea to keep munitions so close to the city?"

No one had an answer to that.

"What will happen if the stockpile ignites?" Ruby asked.

Nick looked at her. "The explosion will be powerful enough to bring down half the skyscrapers in Manhattan."

Ruby said, "And our house, too?"

Nick and Evie said nothing.

Through the night and on into the morning, the explosions continued. No one slept, and every so often Nick reported back with a further update. The wind was freshening, the fire line still moving steadily toward the TNT dump. Troops had been dispatched to keep order and help with evacuations, and firefighters from every nearby town had gone to battle the flames.

Through the open windows, Ruby thought she could smell smoke on the chill autumn air.

At ten o'clock in the morning they heard the largest blast yet, one so loud and sustained that Ruby heard glass fall from windows all around. The house shook to its foundation, and Ruby was shocked to see tears come to Evie's eyes.

"This is so unfair," Evie said.

Thousands of refugees were streaming through the tunnels and crowding onto ferries to reach New York, Nick told them. Parents were separated from their children, and the weak and sick and old were being abandoned, sometimes even trampled by the panicked crowds. In Manhattan, buildings as far north as Chambers Street were being evacuated.

Ruby sat beside her parents. Papa was no longer coughing. His breath came shallowly now, quickly, as if his lungs had given up the battle. And though his blood no longer sprayed, it had crusted brown around his mouth, and Ruby thought she could hear it gurgling in his throat.

He died just a few minutes before the biggest explosion of the day, which came at noon and which sounded to Ruby like the end of the world. The neighborhood dogs set up a hoarse, desperate howling, and Ruby heard confused shouts once again from the street outside. The house seemed to shift sideways a few inches beneath her before settling back, but she didn't move, just stared into her father's gray, still face. Already she could barely recognize it.

Beside him, her mother stirred. Ruby shifted her gaze to see the fierce, dark eyes fixed on hers.

"Mama," she said.

"Ruby."

"Papa is—"

"I know." Her voice was barely above a whisper.

"I'm sorry," Ruby said.

But Mama shook her head, as if not wanting to be distracted from what she had to say. "Ruby," she said, with a trace of her old spirit, "listen."

"Yes, Mama?"

"Just listen. I want you to do one more thing for me."

Ruby took her mother's hot, wet hand in hers. "What?"

"Don't waste your life."

Ruby sat still for a moment as her mother stared up at her. Finally she moved her mouth and said, "Yes, Mama."

Her mother nodded, as if satisfied, then closed her eyes and rolled over, resting her head on Papa's still chest.

And that's what Nick and Evie found when they came into the room a few minutes later to announce that the threatened catastrophe had been averted.

One catastrophe.

Jim McKay, Ted's old school friend, offered to drive them and the bodies to Evergreens in a Model T truck he'd borrowed from someone.

Most people, Evie said, had to pay a taxi driver fifteen dollars to transport the deceased, and then had to follow in a trolley or on the subway. If you didn't have the fifteen dollars, or if you couldn't find a willing driver, you were out of luck.

They left the girls alone at home. What choice did they have? There wasn't room in the truck for all of them.

When they arrived at the cemetery under a drizzling gray sky, there were no workers to be seen, no one to help them carry the coffins to the grave site, no one to dig the graves. Caskets were piled in every available space, sometimes five or ten high, just left there to rot in the rain. There must have been hundreds of them, yet only a few dozen mourners milled around.

"What are we going to do?" Evie asked.

"We'll dig," Nick said.

"I'll help," said Jim. He reached into the back of the truck and retrieved two long-handled spades. He must have known what they would find here.

They dug for hours, taking turns, until they were all covered in mud, until their hands blistered, the blisters broke, and their blood soaked into the dirt. Finally they had gone deep enough, and then still they had to take the coffins from the auto and lower them into the holes, and replace the dirt they had removed.

The sky was darkening when they were finally done. Before they left, Nick, barely able to stay on his feet, said a few words over the fresh graves, but Ruby was unable to make them out.

By the time they got back to the house, Nick was consumed with fever. Together, Ruby, Evie, and Jim half carried him up to bed, while Amanda and Allie, pale, thin, ghostly, watched from the bottom of the stairs. When Nick was settled, Jim left—refusing any payment—and Ruby got some food into the girls while Evie tended to her husband.

It was only after everyone else was asleep, and Evie and Ruby were alone in the kitchen, that Evie allowed herself to cry. She wept silently, her mouth stretched open, her tears falling unblotted to the tabletop.

But Ruby didn't cry. Tears were impossible.

Nick recovered again, but his relapse seemed to have broken something inside his head. No longer the self-confident, decisive man they'd known, he was now jumpy and easily distracted, quick to show anger and remorse. They learned to be careful to measure their words around him.

"Will he get better?" Ruby asked Evie.

Evie said, "I'm sure." Then she sighed. "No, I'm not sure. I'm not sure of anything."

She gave Ruby a direct look. "It's just us now, you know," she said. "Just the two of us to take care of everyone."

I'm thirteen years old, Ruby thought again.

·　　·　　·

By the end of October the epidemic was waning. The newspapers still reported hundreds of new cases, but every day seemed to bring fewer than before, and fewer deaths as well.

"It's what happens," Evie said. "Eventually it just goes away. The fire burns out."

Ruby didn't say anything, but she thought she knew why: because it had already consumed all the dry wood. Because most of the people it had intended to kill had already died.

Now that there was no one at home to tend to, Evie was working full-time for the district nurses, taking the Brooklyn Rapid Transit train to their office up in Brooklyn Heights. She spent all day visiting housebound influenza victims, but always tried to get home in time for dinner, or at least before the girls' bedtime.

On the morning of November 1, they awoke to discover that the Brotherhood of Locomotive Engineers had gone on strike. No one knew if the trains would be running. Evie considered hiring a taxi but decided that was too expensive, especially with Nick on leave from his job at the *Examiner.*

It turned out, though, that most of the subway lines were unaffected, so Evie went off to work as usual.

As Ruby found out later, the BRT ran that day, despite the strike, because the company had called in inexperienced motormen to drive the trains. One of them was a man named Edward something who was assigned a five-car train running from Park Row terminal in Manhattan to Brighton Beach in Brooklyn.

Edward was normally a crew dispatcher. He had only a couple of hours' experience as a motorman, had never operated an elevated train at all, and was unfamiliar with both the Brighton Beach line and its wooden cars, the oldest still in regular operation.

In addition, Edward himself was just recovering from the flue, and had buried his three-year-old daughter just a week earlier. Still, like so many others, he could not afford to miss work, so on November 1 he showed up at the Culver Depot in Coney Island and did his best to get through the day.

Late that afternoon, he accepted an assignment to take one of the company's trains on its regular run through Brooklyn. He climbed into the motorman's cab at the front of the train at the Kings Highway yards, drove it uneventfully through the borough and across the bridge into Manhattan, turned it around at Park Row, and began its return journey.

No one was ever sure at what station Evie boarded the train. She'd had three patients to visit in downtown Brooklyn, and each lived near a different stop. Nor was it certain which car she was in—only that it was one of two, the second or the third, two non-powered trailer cars that, despite strict rules to the contrary, were coupled together.

Nor did anyone ever determine why Edward was operating the train at a speed of thirty or forty miles per hour as it encountered the sharp curve in the newly opened Malbone Street tunnel, where the posted speed limit was just six miles per hour.

All they would ever know was that the train derailed within the tunnel at 6:22 in the evening. Though the motorman and most of those in the powered first car survived, the top-heavy, vulnerable, unpowered second and third cars came flying off the tracks in the curve and shattered against the tunnel walls, leaving behind unrecognizable wreckage and dozens of bodies.

Only when the dazed, bloodied survivors began emerging from the tunnel on foot did those in the area begin to realize that a disaster—another disaster—had occurred.

Nick and Ruby learned of the accident at the same time they realized that Evie was late. Without a word, Nick went out the door, leaving Ruby alone with Amanda and Allie, alone with her terror.

He came back hours later, long after the girls had gone to bed. He was distraught, railing in a high, anguished voice, carrying something in his hands that he dumped on the table. "This is all," he kept saying. "This is all they could find."

A nurse's shoe, its white canvas stained with soot and blood, Evie's name still discernible on the tongue.

"This is all," he said once more, then turned and went back out.

As the front door slammed, Ruby sat very still for a few moments. And then, at last, she began to cry.

She cried so long and so hard that she did some sort of damage to her voice box. Ever after, her voice was hoarse and an octave lower than it had been before.

I'm dreaming, she kept saying to herself. This is a bad dream.

But still the tears went on, and on, and still she didn't wake up.

At dawn she heard the girls stirring in their room upstairs. And then, because she had no choice, she stopped her tears, stood, and went to get them dressed for the day.

7

*t*he squirrel perched on the top of the wooden telephone pole above a rats' nest of wires sprouting in all directions. A moment later it was humping confidently along in the cold winter sunlight, its bushy gray tail waving in the air for balance.

The stone hit it in the side of the head, crushing its skull and killing it instantly. Without a sound it fell straight down, through the tangle of wires and twenty feet to the frozen snow, where it landed with a thump. There it lay, blank eyes wide, a few drops of blood running from its mouth, its feet twitching, claws spreading as if it were reaching for something. Then it went limp.

Ruby walked over and picked it up by the tail. It was a big one, close to a pound and a half, which meant the meat would be tougher but would go further.

Anyway, Ruby thought, beggars couldn't be choosers. And squirrels were harder to find and kill than pigeons, and also less tiresome to eat, though not much.

She'd been hunting this way since that first winter, four years ago, after everyone had died. Only her strong left arm and un-erring accuracy had kept them from starving. Since then, they'd eaten pigeon or squirrel most every day, when they had any meat at all.

Once Ruby had brained a fox that was sniffing around a gar-bage pail—as if there was likely to be anything good to eat there! As if Ruby hadn't searched it herself earlier, and found nothing.

There'd been no recipe for fox in the Marion Harland cookbook that had been Mama's favorite. Ruby and the girls had improvised, but the fox had been hard to clean, and even after rinsing and soaking it for hours and hours, it had main-tained a gamy, off-putting flavor that spread to the potatoes that shared space with it in the pot. If they all hadn't been so hungry, it would have gone into the garbage pail for some other fox to sniff around at.

One time, in the stunned, nightmarish first weeks, Ruby had come upon a bedraggled, half-dead chicken huddling in the cold in an alleyway off Elm Street. Though it had likely escaped from the nearby poultry market, Ruby hadn't even considered return-ing it. She'd snatched it up, wrung its neck, and carried it home as carefully as if it had been made of the finest crystal.

They ate soup from that skinny bird for days, and even now she could remember how warm it made her feel, when the nights were frigid and there wasn't money for enough coal.

Fortunately, it had never been *that* cold that first winter. As if nature was finally relenting after the influenza epidemic had burned itself out, the winter of 1918–19 was the mildest anyone could remember. Hardly an inch of snow had fallen.

If it had been a brutal winter, or even a typical one, they might have starved, all four of them. Allie, who hadn't turned two until March, certainly wouldn't have survived.

With the cooling body of the squirrel tucked under her jacket, Ruby stepped through the front door of the apartment building on Ocean Avenue. She still thought of the building and the apartment as Evie and Nick's, even though it had been her home since soon after the epidemic.

It turned out that Papa had no savings. The family had been living from paycheck to paycheck, and when the checks stopped coming, there was almost nothing to live off.

They'd sold the house on East Twenty-first Street as soon they could, her and Nick. But people were fleeing New York City in the wake of the plague, thinking that anyplace else would be less dangerous. (Ruby could almost hear Evie's voice in her head: "If they think there's safety anywhere on this earth, they've got another think coming!")

Because many families had lost children or parents, or seen their breadwinners return from illness weakened, good for almost nothing, there were many houses on the market, and few potential buyers. Plus, 1394 had acquired a reputation as a death house, a place that, even months later, seemed to have tragedy infused in its beams.

And, as if all this wasn't enough, who wanted to buy a house whose nearest elevated station was on the ill-fated Brooklyn Rapid Transit line to Brighton Beach? The BRT had gone bankrupt, the line was now called the BMT, and the city had stricken the name Malbone Street from the records in exchange for the forward-looking Empire Boulevard, but it didn't matter. No one even wanted to ride the train to visit Midwood, much less live there.

The upshot was that the house Ruby had grown up in, the one that was supposed to save them from the dangers of tenement life, had sold for a tiny fraction of what it would have been worth just a few months before. The return was not nearly adequate to keep them warm or full or well clothed, and barely enough to keep them alive.

And Nick had taken most of it. He'd promised to make them all rich, but they'd never seen any of that money again.

Ruby walked down the dark hallway to Apartment 4G to find her older niece waiting for her at the door. At ten, Amanda still shared Ruby's slender, willowy build, long jaw, and high cheekbones, as well as her serious, almost solemn demeanor. Neither of them talked much or smiled freely.

Sometimes Amanda came along on the hunting expeditions. She couldn't throw nearly as well as Ruby, no one could, but she was quick to spot possible prey and did not hesitate to go after an animal that had been injured but not killed by one of Ruby's throws. Carrying a jagged-edged stone, she'd scramble over fences and up trees if it meant meat for dinner, and she never flinched at finishing the job.

Ruby had made her stay home on this hunting expedition so she and Allie could work on their reading. Neither of them went to school, but Ruby insisted that they know how to read and spell and do sums. Every day had to include at least an hour of study.

They couldn't afford schoolbooks, but Amanda was so quick at mathematics that she could be the teacher, effortlessly creating work sheets and quizzes for her reluctant younger sister. They had sold almost all of their books, so for reading and spelling they used Nick's old collection of *Baseball Magazines*, a copy of Emily Post's new book *Etiquette* that Nick had brought home with no explanation, and Mama's old Marion Harland cookbook—though on days when food was in short supply it was painful to read about "beef with sauce piquante" or the proper ingredients for afternoon tea.

But schoolwork was forgotten when Ruby brought home a fresh kill. With a nod, Amanda took the squirrel from her and went into the kitchen to clean it. She'd learned to use the cleaver and the butcher's knife when she was six, and had long since become expert at the task.

Hanging her coat on the wooden peg near the door, Ruby went into the bathroom to wash her hands. By the time she got to the small, crowded kitchen, its walls covered with grease spatters, Amanda had already quartered the squirrel and set the big cast-iron pot to boil on the stove. Sitting beside her on a high stool, Allie was peeling potatoes and dumping them into the pot.

Allie never came on the hunt because she thought squirrels were cute. But she put her natural sympathies on hold because she knew they had no choice. Grinning, she looked up at Ruby and said, "Yum! Squirrel stew *again!*"

Despite herself, Ruby smiled. No one could lighten her mood like blond, plump Allie, at six still the image of her mother, and with the same upbeat, we'll-get-through-it temperament to boot. The blond ringlets, blue eyes peering out of her round face, rosebud lips always ready to smile—well, Ruby would have done almost anything, and had, to keep her happy.

Allie had grown so thin that first winter, though even then she'd rarely complained. Still, every day Ruby had waited for some illness, a return of influenza, or typhus, or infantile paralysis, to strike her down. There were so many plagues—how did any young child survive?

Somehow Allie had been luckier than many. It took just a little food, a little milk, to put the weight back on her bones. As Ruby learned how to cope, learned the rules of their new lives, she stopped fearing that a new disaster would strike their shrunken family.

Or at least stopped fearing it every waking moment.

Thinking on your feet, learning how to fend for yourself, and judging everyone around you by what they could do for your family. That was life.

Those first weeks, Ruby had told no one what had happened to them. Strangely, she'd felt ashamed, as if losing one's parents and brother and beloved sister-in-law was a sign of weakness.

But she'd gotten over it. Sitting down at the table with a pile of bills and receipts one January night that first winter, she'd finally made a cold calculation and realized that they weren't going to be able to make it without help, at least not right away.

First she'd contacted various service organizations she'd found listed in the newspaper, but they hadn't been much help. What could they do for her and the girls? In New York alone, she heard again and again, twenty-one thousand children had been left either half or full orphans by the influenza epidemic, and at least two thousand were in dire need of aid.

"And really," one harried-looking woman at the Hebrew Orphan House in Manhattan had said to her, "after all, you and your nieces aren't orphans, are you?"

Ruby had come to the Hebrew House because it had a reputation for caring, and because she was more than willing to embrace her mother's Jewishness, even if her mother never had, if it meant more food on the table.

But apparently it didn't. "I mean, their father, your brother, is living," the harried woman had explained. "And of age."

Ruby had heard this before. She'd sighed, gathered her papers, and stood. Thanked the woman politely, received her wishes of good luck with a nod, and headed out onto the rain-slicked street.

No one understood about Nick. She wasn't sure she did.

Nick entered, slamming the door behind him. Dropping a big wooden box onto the floor, he swept Allie up in his arms to cries of laughter and whirled her around, then stopped and took a deep sniff. "Smells great," he said. "What are we eating?"

His face was ruddy, his lips chapped, his voice as always a little too loud.

"Stew," Ruby said. Her eyes strayed to the wooden box. "What's that, Nick?"

His gaze followed hers, and for a moment he stared blankly

at it. Then he grinned. "Oh," he said. "Look! I bought us all a present."

Ruby felt as if a hole had opened in her stomach. She saw Amanda frown, but Allie, as always, was joyful. "What is it?" she asked. "Papa, what is it?"

"Well, let's see," he said, putting her down. Ruby wondered if he was just being playful, or if he'd actually forgotten. "Go open it."

Allie crouched beside the box. A moment later she'd swung the top open, revealing wires and a strange wand with a head like a little mushroom.

"What on earth is that?" Ruby asked.

"It's a violet-ray generator," Nick said. "To keep us healthy."

He sounded so proud of himself that Ruby bit back on her words. She'd seen the advertisements for such devices, which supposedly prevented illness by sending out electrical rays, and she knew they cost upward of ten dollars.

Ten dollars they couldn't afford to waste.

"Where did you get it?" she asked.

"Up at the United Electric store, on Eighty-ninth Street and Broadway."

"In *Manhattan*?" Ruby felt the hole in her stomach open wider. "What about your job?"

Nick made a dismissive gesture with his hand. "I didn't feel like going in today."

"Nick—" His latest position had been as a handyman at a building over on Coney Island Avenue—though Ruby thought "handyman" was a kind term for someone who mostly wielded a broom. But even a menial job brought in a few dollars a week, and every penny helped them eat another meal.

When you were hungry that was all you were allowed to think about.

Allie was playing with the wand, while Amanda squatted

beside her, reading the instructions on the inside of the box's top. "Be careful," Ruby said, her voice coming out harsher than she'd intended.

They all stared up at her. "Why?" Amanda said.

"Don't touch," Ruby said. "Tomorrow I'm going to have to return it, and we need to be sure nothing's broken."

Hours spent on the subway, lugging that big box, when she could have been working.

"But I thought you'd like it," Nick said.

How many times had they had this conversation?

"I do like it," Ruby said, walking over to him and looking up into his stricken face. "Nick, it was very thoughtful of you to buy this, but we just don't have the money for—such things. I'll just have to bring it back. But I promise, when we can afford it, we'll go right back and buy it again. Okay?"

He stared down at her. Ruby's heart thumped inside her chest, because she knew that this was the pivotal moment. How would he react? He might rage, scaring his children. He might even lash out at her with his fists—he'd done it before.

But instead his face crumpled, which she almost hated the most. It meant that she'd have to listen to his fumbling apologies, his self-hatred, his understanding that he wasn't the person he'd once been.

She listened, or pretended to, until he went off into his room, his shrine to his dead wife, leaving Ruby with the work of comforting Allie while Amanda, pale, eyes shadowed, silently set the table for dinner.

Ruby had held almost as many jobs as her brother had since the fall of 1918. It hadn't cost much to get a set of fake identification papers that said she was fourteen and therefore eligible for a variety of factory jobs. In just the first year, she'd packed dates in South Brooklyn, wrapped chocolates in Bushwick, stocked shelves at a cloak-and-suit company in Brownsville, and boxed cigarettes in lower Manhattan.

Unlike Nick, however, who could lose a job the first day he had it through inattention, distraction, or thoughtless words, Ruby was an efficient, competent worker. She only moved on when she found a new position that paid a little more.

Or when she thought a job might kill her. Surrounded by girls with stories at least as unfortunate as hers, she'd find herself working for twelve straight hours in conditions that were obviously dangerous: pipes spouting scalding steam, floors with jagged holes through which you could see the jagged holes in the floor twenty feet below, air filled with cleaning fumes that made your head spin in rooms whose windows had been painted shut and would never open again.

She remembered one fifth-floor room where she and thirty other girls were beading crochets. As soon as they were all settled on the splintery wooden benches lining the worktable, she heard the slide of a bolt across the only door and knew that at the end of the day she was going to walk away without looking back.

Perhaps working conditions had improved since the great Triangle Factory fire—which she remembered hearing about as a child—but it was hard to see how. And she had no intention of dying and leaving her two nieces in the care of their father.

She couldn't even leave them with him for a day, to be honest. He was too mercurial, too unpredictable. There were times when she came home to find that he'd abandoned them for hours while he went out on some never-explained mission.

Ruby knew that the only way to guarantee their safety was to stay with them at all times. But that wasn't possible.

For a while, when the girls were three and eight, she'd brought them down the hall to Apartment 4B, where Mrs. Baker lived. Thin, sallow, with dull button eyes, Mrs. Baker had been widowed in 1918, and while she didn't seem poor, word got around that she was looking to make some extra money by minding other people's children. Ruby had jumped at the chance, even though it meant giving Mrs. Baker nearly half of what she made at work.

But the result had been a sad disappointment. Ruby had thought that Mrs. Baker's own tragedy might make her more sympathetic to theirs, but all it did was make her mean. Allie and Amanda didn't complain—they never complained—but to her everlasting shame, Ruby, desperate to keep working, had ignored signs that the girls were being mistreated. Allie grew uncharacteristically silent and went back to her habit of sucking on the second and third fingers of her left hand, and Ruby once spied Amanda weeping silently in the bed the two girls shared.

But on the day Amanda came home with a blackened eye, saying that she'd taken a fall, Ruby marched down to 4B, unearthed the truth, and spoke quietly until Mrs. Baker's sallow face went quite white. After that, the old woman never came out of her apartment when any of them were in the hallway.

It was still only January, but already the winter had been brutal. Nature had long since ceased giving the people of New York a helping hand. Sleet had quickly turned the streets to ice, the temperature had stayed below freezing for days at a time, and a big storm had just covered everything in nearly two feet of heavy snow. They'd been hungry through it all, and then the snow made it impossible for Ruby to find any fresh meat.

For four days after the storm, they huddled in the apartment, unable to go anywhere. The streets were deserted and all the stores were closed, as men with shovels slowly dug pathways through the snow.

During those four days, Allie again became a thin, pale ghost of herself. And Amanda's ribs began to show through her translucent skin, since she insisted that her little sister take extra portions of the beans and rice and potatoes that was all they had left to eat.

Ruby knew, even if the girls didn't, even if Nick was too scatterbrained to see, that there was no help coming. No one would promise them their next meal, or the one after that. Hundreds of people, maybe thousands, starved to death in New York City every winter. People died all the time, and they didn't need an epidemic to send them on their way to the next world.

When she was little, Ruby had thought of New York City as a gigantic circus. You never knew what you were going to see next. But now she knew the truth: it was an ocean, a vast sea. And you had a simple choice: you swam, keeping your head above the surface, or you sank and quickly drowned. Then it would be as if you'd never existed.

The weather finally broke, and Ruby was able to go out and replenish their food supplies. She walked down to the Food Mart on Avenue M and used a little of their scant savings to buy condensed milk (fourteen cents a can), bread (twelve cents a loaf), and, because she'd read something about scurvy once, three grapefruits (on sale at twenty cents). She also bought a can of coffee for thirty-five cents, even though they couldn't really afford it, because it killed your appetite and one can lasted for a while.

Finally she added a Baby Ruth candy bar for Amanda, because she liked how chewy it was, and a package of Chuckles for Allie, because the different colors made her smile.

It was the least Ruby could do, especially now that Amanda had started working, too, from home. She was cutting out patterns for cloth flowers and then attaching them to the flexible metal stems, work that left her red-eyed and squinting, her hands cramped and clawlike. All for just a few cents a day.

Then, on the way back from the market, Ruby had spotted the

squirrel venturing out across the telephone wires after the snow-fall, so they had meat for dinner that night as well.

But it wasn't enough.

After Nick and the girls were asleep, Ruby got up from the sagging sofa where she slept and went to the bathroom.

She stood there, barefoot on the cold tile floor, and looked at herself in the mirror. Her violet-blue eyes seemed enormous in her gaunt face. She'd grown some in the past year, and her thick black hair had as well. She tied it back in a ponytail, though any girl with money these days had her hair cut into a bob.

Ruby took a deep breath and brought her hands up to cover her eyes. She missed Mama and Papa and Ted fiercely. And Evie, too. Evie would instinctively have known how to face every challenge, how to keep them fed, alive.

But Evie wasn't here. Ruby was alone.

After a few moments she let her long arms drop to her sides and stared into her determined face, seeing her chin lift and her mouth set. She was seventeen years old now. It was time to start looking for a different kind of job.

8

"Don't move."

Ruby sat on the slick red-velvet love seat, her back rod-straight, her arms folded over each other on her lap. When she snuck a look down at her body, she didn't even recognize it.

"That's better," said Mel Walters, proprietor and chief photographer of the Posatype Corporation on West Fifty-seventh Street, just a stone's throw from Fifth Avenue. Ruby had seen his name and address on the back of a photograph she'd found when cleaning Nick's room several weeks earlier. A grainy image of a blond woman who looked like a nightmarishly haggard and aged version of Evie, dressed in a white feather boa and little else.

The photograph had given Ruby an idea that she'd quickly banished from her mind. Until last night.

Mel Walters fiddled with a big camera that looked like some weapon brought back from the Great War. Even though his eyes were no longer on Ruby's body, she felt as uncomfortable as she had when she'd walked through the studio door to find him staring at her with unabashed curiosity.

And something more than curiosity.

She wouldn't let herself show her discomfort. Not to this little man with a mustache like a bottle brush and dandruff that flaked down onto the sloping shoulders of his shiny black suit jacket.

Even when he told her to undress in front of him. "I need to see what I'm going to be working with," he said, his eyes scanning her body. Then, even though she'd kept her face as still and expressionless as a stone, he'd shaken his head and added, "Or you can get a wiggle on and walk out the door, and we'll call it even."

Get a wiggle on. Ruby had never heard that phrase before. But in her various jobs, she'd learned that while she'd been struggling to keep her family alive, others had been inventing a whole new language to accompany the young decade. People these days had silly ways to refer to everything from borrowing a cigarette ("butt me") to a woman's legs ("gams"). Ruby had no patience for it, but no one had asked for her opinion.

"Show me your chassis," Mel Walters said, "or get out. That's your choice."

After another moment's silence, Ruby pulled her blue cotton blouse up over her head, folded it, put it on a small wooden table beside the love seat, and then lifted her head to look up at him again.

He was regarding her with renewed interest. "I didn't expect that," he said, then pointed at her chest. "Take it off."

She looked down at the gauze bandage she'd been wrapping across her breasts ever since they'd grown. It had happened soon after she'd turned fourteen. That was when she'd missed Evie, and even Mama, the most, when all those changes happened, when her breasts appeared, when she bled. It had been awful facing that with no one to confide in.

"Unwrap," Walters said. "Or you having second thoughts?"

She looked into his eyes until he glanced away, then slowly unwrapped the bandage. She hadn't started wearing it because her breasts were too big; she had a boyish figure, which even a cursory look at the newspaper revealed as every girl's dream. It was the full-figured women who usually sought to squeeze themselves into current fashion.

But to Ruby, fashion was the least of her concerns. She wrapped herself every morning because otherwise, as she'd also discovered when she was fourteen, men would want to touch her. It didn't seem to matter that her arms were still freakishly long, that she wore patched and mended clothes dating from a decade before, that her hair was far from stylish, that her mouth rarely smiled, or that her expression was usually cold and unwelcoming. Only by squashing her breasts down under layers of gauze could she hope to avoid men's wandering hands. And even this hope was often dashed.

She'd worked so hard to be invisible. But now she was sitting here, on a stranger's love seat, naked from the waist up, enduring Mel Walters's penetrating gaze.

"Huh." Walters scratched at his chin. "Nice enough bubs. But that bandage doesn't do you any favors."

She didn't say anything, just kept her eyes on his face.

"You should be wearing a brassiere, a side-lacer."

"Buy me one and I'll wear it," she said.

He looked startled, then grinned, and she realized she'd made a mistake. "Ah, a gold digger," he said. "And such a voice! You should be onstage."

Her deep, husky voice that reminded her of the night Evie died.

She said nothing. After a moment, he pointed. "That, too. You can keep your frillies on."

She slipped off her simple ankle-length checked skirt, folded it, and placed it on top of the blouse, leaving on only her white slip. She made to sit down again, but he waggled a finger at her and said, "No, stay standing."

So she stood, half naked, arms at her sides because she didn't want him to think her vulnerable, as he took his sweet time going across the room and rummaging in a big steamer trunk. Then, eyes never leaving her, he returned, carrying a small pile of flimsy black cloth. Only when he handed it to her did she realize what it was.

A set of sheer, nearly see-through black cami-knickers. The camisole, with its plunging neckline, would show off her arms and breasts and back, while the knickers, made of the same material, would come down only to the middle of her thighs.

And a pair of black stockings, too.

"Are these silk?" she asked.

Walters grinned. He was a man who enjoyed his job. "Put it all on," he said, "while I get ready."

"How much will people pay for these photographs?" Ruby asked.

He scowled. "That's not your business. I'm paying you twenty smackers for each outfit you wear, not to ask questions. So shut up and get dressed."

While Walters went around turning on glaring, hot lights, Ruby did as he'd instructed. She'd never felt anything softer against her skin than these sheer undergarments, and for a moment she let herself dream of what life would be like if such things, such possessions, were routine. Oddly, the idea made her think of food, not fashion, and she imagined wearing silk and eating . . . what? Fresh cherries? Lamb? The asparagus-and-shrimp salad she'd seen in Marion Harland's cookbook?

She had to swallow to keep her saliva from leaking out. She hadn't eaten anything at all that day.

When she was done donning the lingerie, she looked up to

see Walters standing there. His lips were wet, as if he was hungry, too, and in his right hand he carried a short glass filled with an amber-colored liquid. Even from where she stood, Ruby could smell the bitter odor rising from it.

Ruby knew what the glass contained, of course. Prohibition had been in effect for more than two years, but anyone who wanted to could still get their hands on gin or vodka or whatever else suited their thirst. And "anyone" frequently included Nick, who came home plastered at least twice every week, and sometimes more often than that. If he even came home at all.

Ruby herself had never tasted alcohol. When you worked as hard, and worried as much, as she did, the last thing you needed was something that clouded your mind and laid your emotions bare.

"It's giggle water," Walters told her. "Bourbon. It'll give you an edge."

She shook her head. "No, thank you."

After a moment, he shrugged, took a gulp of it himself, and went back to his camera. He fiddled with it awhile longer—on the wooden legs of its tripod, it reminded Ruby of a head, a golem's head, with two staring black glass eyes—then said, "All right, I'm ready. Let's pose you."

He pointed at the love seat. Ruby sat down, then leaned back against the scratchy cushion. He laughed. "You really are new at this, aren't you?"

"I told you that."

He raised a placatory hand. "I know, I know, no problem. Anyway, I like working with—newcomers." He reached out and arranged her body the way he wanted it.

Walters's hands were damp, and lingered on her longer than they should have. He talked all the while, a low, steady mutter that seemed to flow into her ears and dull her brain. "This is good, very good," he said, bending one knee while leaving the other extended along the love seat. "Now you're on the trolley! Look at that length of muscle and bone, though I have to say you could stand to gain some weight. Ten years ago, they would have called you a boy, said you had no flesh on your bones, but lucky for you, styles have changed. Everyone wants your figure today—you should see the girls I meet, little round dumplings with curves in every place you could imagine. But they're starving themselves to look like the girls they see in moving pictures. To look like you. Just starving themselves! A leaf of lettuce is lunch to them."

Ruby tried to imagine what it would be like to starve oneself by choice.

"But these—" Walters held up her left arm, looking at it like it was some strange snake. "I've never seen anything quite like them."

Ruby stayed quiet.

"First I thought we should keep them out of view, behind you or to the side, or under a stole or silk scarf." His gaze went to the trunk where he kept his models' costumes. "But then I decided that I was being hasty. There are some men who find this sort of—disfigurement—appealing, even exciting, you know."

Yes, Ruby knew.

He ran his hand along her upper arm. Ruby felt goose bumps rise all along the trail left by his moist fingers. "So we'll take some photographs that, er, *emphasize* your special attributes," he went on. "And others that hide them."

He pondered for a moment, then dropped her arm along the back of the love seat. Took her chin in his hand and tilted her face to look up at him. "That way," he said, "we can appeal to all sectors of New York City society."

He brushed his lips against hers.

"Stop it," she said.

He grinned, then went back behind the camera. "Now, let's see a nice pout," he said.

· · ·

When he was done with this pose, he came back over and rear-
ranged her, his hands always staying in contact with her body a
moment or two longer than necessary. Once, then again, Ruby
felt herself begin to blush, but each time she grasped hold of
something cold and hard in her chest—the same knot of ice that
anchored her when she was facing one of Nick's bouts of anger
or self-hatred—and felt the color, the embarrassment, drain out
of her.

Mel Walters kept talking all the while, his face close to hers,
sweat gleaming on his temples, the flood of his words washing
over her, his voice and his hands growing ever more insinuating.
"Loosen up," he said repeatedly. "Relax. The camera magnifies
emotions, you know. It's like a microscope. If the customer sees
fear, then that's all he'll see, not your remarkable eyes, not your
beautiful figure, not your—"

"Stop that," Ruby said.

He let go of her, stepped back, and let his eyes roam over her
body once more. "Though, of course, there are some people who
like to see a little fear. Quite a few people, in fact."

Ruby said nothing. But she made sure there was no fear in
her face, even if her heart was thumping.

He was back behind the camera now. The sound of the shut-
ter opening and closing reminded her of some scratchy late-night
insect, a big crawly thing with sharp, hooked legs and a wet chewing mouth. And the lens just seemed like an extension of the
photographer's eyes, staring unashamedly at her body.

Katy-did, Katy-didn't.

Why did she care? The camera and Walters were far from the
only eyes that would be seeing her in this lingerie. Dozens, hundreds, thousands of others would soon share the view.

"Okay," Walters said. "Now stand up. Look at that! I love the
shape of your legs, so slim and muscular, and your neck is like a

swan's. Face me. Drop your arms, fold them behind you, good, very good. Now one leg up on the chair. Good! Just bend it a little more, so the calf muscle flexes. No, not that much. Let me show you."

He came up behind her. She could hear his breathing, hoarser and louder than it had been. Then feel his moist, soft hands on her.

"Don't touch me," she said.

But he was no longer listening. One hand strayed upward, the other down.

Enough.

More than enough.

Ruby pulled away from him and turned. The expression on her face made him hesitate for a moment, but then his grin widened and he stepped toward her again. "What are you, a Mrs. Grundy?" he said. "This is part of the deal. Take it or leave it."

His hands shoved aside the camisole. Now they were rougher, more aggressive, more demanding.

"I'll leave it," she said, and knocked his hands away with a swipe of her arm.

He reached for her again, and this time she didn't back away. She didn't slap his face or pull his hair, the way girls in moving pictures always seemed to do when they fought. She didn't push at him, or simper, or scream, or fall into a swoon.

Jerking her strong left leg upward, she felt it connect solidly with something hard and something soft. An instant later, Mel Walters was lying on the floor, clutching himself, his back heaving as he desperately attempted to draw air into his paralyzed lungs.

Standing over him, Ruby shook her shoulders. The sweat was cooling on the back of her neck.

That had felt good.

Walters struggled to his knees before her. Ruby noticed with interest that his face had turned purple. She stepped past him to the table that held her clothes and slowly took off the silk undergarments. As she wrapped the bandage carefully around her breasts, she heard him take a deep breath, then another.

When she was back in her blouse and skirt and flat-heeled shoes, she stood with the lingerie puddled in her hands, wondering what to do.

"You—" Walters gasped out. "You bluenose *bitch*."

Ruby nodded. Now she knew.

She picked up her beaded swag purse, one of the few things of Mama's she'd kept, and pushed the lingerie inside. Then she walked back to where Walters was slowly getting back to his feet, still breathing heavily, mopping at his face with a handkerchief.

"Stay away," he said. She saw that his hands were shaking. "Beat it."

"First you pay me," she said.

"What?" The injustice of that seemed to clear his head. "You—you hit me!"

"I also posed in a costume. You said you pay twenty dollars for each one. So pay up."

"No," he said.

Ruby made a fist. Her whole arm wanted to hit him so badly it itched. But he didn't require it. Cringing, he scrabbled in his pocket and pulled out a faded leather wallet. Taking two tens out of it, he held them out in the tips of his fingers. She put them in the purse with the underthings.

"You're making a big mistake," Walters said. "No one's ever going to take your picture again. Not for love or money."

"That's not my problem," she told him.

·   ·   ·

But it *was* her problem. A big one.

Ruby knew it from the moment her excitement wore off, somewhere on the long, clanky elevated ride across Brooklyn. What had she done? Turned her back on a sure-thing paycheck, and for what? Pride?

Pride wasn't something she could afford.

She got off at the Avenue M stop and walked the five blocks to the apartment through a fine, blowing mist. There were still scraps and heaps of old gray snow in the shady spots.

She hesitated, then stopped outside the candy store, which had been taken over by a silent, scowling old man after Lenny and his wife had fled the epidemic. The twenty dollars Ruby had earned from Walters wouldn't last long, even if she succeeded in keeping it from Nick. She might as well spend some of it right away.

From the toy shelf she selected for Allie a small, hammered-tin bus, painted a shiny red and white, with seats that came out. Amanda was getting old for toys and had never been much for such things anyway, so Ruby found an issue of *Photoplay* magazine, with a painting of dashing Douglas Fairbanks as Robin Hood on the cover.

Amanda still had vivid memories of her mother and father taking her to the pictures when she was little. Ruby occasionally took them to the Kingsway Theatre over on Kings Highway, a grandly opulent palace a world away from the old nickelodeons, to see whatever was playing, to escape from the world they were trapped in.

While Allie loved the comedies best, Amanda tended to sit through them stone-faced, even if they starred Charlie Chaplin or Harold Lloyd. She much preferred adventure stories, and Douglas Fairbanks was her favorite. Whether he was playing Zorro or d'Artagnan or Robin Hood, she'd smile, looking for once like the child she was as he swung and jumped and flew through the air. When the movie was over, she'd heave a deep sigh of satisfaction, and her good mood would last the rest of the day.

The girls met her at the door. Amanda looked haggard, her eyes red from rubbing, her hair oily and hanging down out of its braid. Allie's left hand was swaddled in gauze, through which spots of red showed. She looked pale.

"I've been cutting patterns," Amanda said, "and Allie hurt herself on the scissors."

"I was trying to help," Allie said, chin quivering.

Ruby took a breath. How many times, she wondered, can the same worn-out heart break?

"Come here," she said, wrapping both girls in a hug. Then she picked up Allie in her arms, the little girl clinging to her neck. "Let's look at that cut. We don't want you getting lockjaw so you can't talk."

As they headed for the bathroom, a loud snort came from Nick's room. Ruby stopped and looked at Amanda.

"He came home and went to bed," Amanda said, expressionless.

"He said he was fried to the hat." Allie pulled her head back to look at Ruby. "He was funny."

Tending to the cut, Ruby didn't feel like laughing. She was thinking of Mel Walters, and of the mistake she'd made.

Late that night, after the girls were in bed, Nick unconscious till morning at least, she dressed once again in the lingerie she'd taken from Posatype Studios and looked at herself in the flaking bathroom mirror.

She tried to picture what it would be like to wear such things as a rule. To lie on luxurious pillows on a Sunday morning, with nothing to do but pick at breakfast off fine plates while music played and the sun streamed in through unstreaked windows.

Your family arrayed around you, your husband smiling, your children on the carpeted floor playing with their toys—

She couldn't even imagine it.

On the other hand, she knew exactly what could happen if you were poor in New York. You could sink beneath the surface, and no one would ever, *ever* be there to rescue you. You could starve to death, and your nieces, too, and you'd all end up buried in Potter's Field, with no headstone and no one to remember you.

If you were lucky enough to make it to Potter's Field. Funerals, coffins, and grave sites cost money. Sometimes, she knew, you just got hidden in a basement, or in the foundation of a new building going up.

Today, because of her pride and her stupid temper, Ruby's family had taken a step closer to that fate. So what was she going to do about it?

There were places she knew of where she could earn more money. Maybe. If she were lucky and skilled, and if enough men came by who considered her—what was the word Mel Walters had used?—her *disfigurement* to be something they wanted to see more of.

To touch.

It would be funny, and not funny at all, if this was what her pride led her to.

But what choice did she have? Ruby had heard of children permanently ruining their eyes doing what Amanda did; going blind, even. And one bad winter, one unavoidable accident that laid Ruby up for any length of time, and Allie *might* starve.

Ruby stretched her arms out before her. The lingerie felt like a second skin, but skin she could shuck off, discard. Leaving what beneath? Merely bare flesh.

She looked into her own depthless eyes, the steady, unblinking gaze, and went over all the possibilities again. And again, for hours, as behind her Nick snored and Amanda, stoical Amanda, whimpered in her sleep.

And finally, just before dawn, Ruby reached a decision.

There was one other place you could still go when you'd fallen as far as she had.

And it was just a subway ride away.

9

the man wore a white jacket with mother-of-pearl buttons on the pockets and down the front, a white shirt with blue stars woven into the fabric, and a red, white, and blue bow tie.

Oh, and a spectacularly large white cowboy hat.

"Let me take a gander at you," he said.

And that's what he did, took a gander, while Ruby looked back at him, absorbing not only the garish clothes but also the down-sweeping mustache, the weather-beaten cheeks, the black eyes that looked as if they might, under different circumstances, twinkle.

Cooper, his name was. Samuel Cooper, and he was staring at her because she'd asked him to. Because she'd walked past a crowd of people waiting to see him and into his office without an appointment, risking being tossed out on her ear if her bold gamble didn't work.

And she'd done it in front of the girls, no less. She'd brought them with her, had no choice, not with Nick awake, half hungover, half still drunk, occupying the apartment. She couldn't leave them alone with him.

But she had to admit she'd also thought that Samuel Cooper might treat her more politely in front of Amanda and Allie. She wasn't sure about that yet. Silent and pale, the girls looked poorer, closer to drowning, outside the apartment than they did within it. Under orders not to speak unless spoken to, Amanda clutched the cloth bag that she carried whenever she went out, and Allie sucked on her fingers.

At least they'd gotten past the first hurdle. When Cooper's secretary had come racing in after them, he'd waved her away and said, "No, I reckon I'll listen to what they have to say."

Now he said to Ruby, "Turn around, young lady." He had a funny, creaky voice, and he drew his words out longer than most of the fast-talking New Yorkers Ruby saw every day.

She'd never met Cooper before, but she'd certainly heard of him. Everyone had. He'd started out riding horses in Buffalo Bill's Wild West Show, back in the last century. Maybe his accent was held over from those olden days, or maybe it was just an act, a costume, like his cowboy clothes. Like Mel Walters's modern-day slang, or the kohl some girls painted around their eyes to make them look like movie stars.

If Ruby remembered right, Cooper had moved from bucking broncos to P. T. Barnum's circus and then to the famous Dreamland Park, which had burned when Ruby was five. But the only thing that mattered was that he now ran the Fantasyland Circus Sideshow, which showed off midgets and giants, alligator men and bearded ladies, Dr. Green and the Man Who Cried, Bert the Lion Boy, and Tig the "Who Am I?"

Mama had loathed the sideshows. If she hadn't been so busy with suffrage, she often said, she would have gone after Cooper and the rest of the impresarios. "Those poor unfortunates," she'd fumed. "Did they have a choice to be who they are? Did they dream of this when they were children, sitting there to be laughed at, to be jeered at, to be objects of derision?"

Papa, in his mild way, had disagreed. "Where else would they go?" he'd asked. "What else would they do? No, they didn't ask to be—different—but that's the way they are."

Just as I am the way I am, Ruby would think and shiver.

"At least here in Coney Island," Papa had said, "they're in company with others who have shared the same kinds of experiences . . . and here, they can earn enough money to survive. The alternatives are worse."

"Are they?" Mama would ask, unconvinced.

And Ruby would take Mama's part. The last place on the entire earth that she had ever wanted to be was anywhere near the sideshows. She'd always been sure that if she ever went, someone would look at her arms and say, "Why aren't you up there with the rest of the freaks?"

But that was then. That was *before*.

Samuel Cooper's expression was thoughtful, and, Ruby decided, not unkind, as he shook his head and said, "No. I'm real sorry, Miz Thomas, but I just don't see it."

Ruby felt her heart thump in her chest. She spread her arms out and said, "People call me Monkey Girl."

She heard Amanda give a little gasp of protest.

Underneath his opulent mustache, Cooper's frown was sympathetic. "Do they now," he said.

She nodded.

"But you're not, are you?" he went on. "You're not, in fact, Monkey Girl."

Ruby looked at her arms. "I could—"

He was already shaking his head. "No, ma'am," he said. "Not for me you couldn't. I only use real living curiosities. No stunts, no fakes, no make-believe. My Bantoc headhunters truly came from the Philippines, my Wild Men from Borneo. I do not paint the tattooed ladies, glue beards to my bearded women, or use tricks of the light on my midgets. My performers are all who they truly are, and even if we pasted hair all over you, you, my dear, would be no Monkey Girl."

At another time, Ruby thought, this would be one of the kindest things anyone had ever said to her. Just not now.

"I sure am sorry, though," Samuel Cooper said. He stood, polite but unyielding. "Now, if you could see your way out—I got some people out there waiting who actually thought to call ahead."

Ruby didn't have anything else to say. She turned to go.

"Wait," Amanda said.

They all looked at her.

"Aunt Ruby has another—" Amanda faltered for a moment. Then her chin lifted. "There's something else that—that Aunt Ruby can do."

Ruby opened her mouth to say, "There is?" Then she closed it again.

"Oh, is there?" Cooper asked. He looked amused by the set of Amanda's mouth as she faced him. "And what would that be?"

Amanda shook her head. "No," she said. "She needs to show you. Outside."

"Outside?"

"Yes, on the beach." Amanda stood very stiff and still, a small figure dressed in battered clothes and unassailable dignity. "But I can promise you, Mr. Cooper, that you won't regret it."

Cooper smiled, a twitch of the lips under his mustache. "I have a good imagination, you know, little girl," he said. "You tell me about it, and I'll picture it just fine."

"Do you *tell* people about your Wild Men," Amanda asked, "or *show* them?"

For a long moment Cooper stared at her. Then he laughed.

"Well! You certainly outdrew me on that one. What is your name, young lady?"

Amanda kept her eyes on his. "Amanda Florence Thomas," she said. Then, "My mother was a nurse. She died in 1918."

"I'm sorry," Cooper said.

"Thank you." Amanda took in a breath. "Now Aunt Ruby takes care of us. Will you let her show you what she can do?"

Cooper stood still for ten seconds, fifteen. Then he nodded and reached for a fringed leather jacket, like something a frontiersman would wear, that hung on a peg on the wall beside his desk. "Well, Amanda Florence, you've convinced me," he said. "I certainly hope your aunt lives up to your faith in her."

"Of course she will."

Cooper smiled and shook his head. Amanda took Allie by the arm, ushered her toward the door, and said, "Let's go show him, Aunt Ruby."

Following, Ruby thought, Show him what?

For fifty years, and especially since they'd improved the subway service in 1920, enormous crowds had come here to Coney Island in the summertime. Sometimes a quarter of a million or more on a single Sunday, the newspapers said, to ride the dip-the-dips and the carousels, blush in the Blow-Hole Theater, admire the strolling elephants and camels at Steeplechase and Luna Park or visit the sideshows and speakeasies and other, less savory attractions along the Bowery and Surf Avenue.

More than anything else, it was the beach that drew those untold millions each summer. The miles-long stretch of sand by the blue-green water, filled beyond imagining with partially clad men and women who rarely otherwise found ways to get so intimate with each other. All that bare flesh, all those sunburned faces, the smells of sweat and oil and salt and cooking food, the screams and laughter—no one who had been here would ever forget it.

And Ruby had been here. She'd visited the beach when her mother and the other suffragists had set up a tent. She'd even gone with her family a few times just to lie in the sun and splash in the water and eat the cold roast chicken, coleslaw, and apples they'd lugged from East Twenty-first Street. The food always got sandy, but no one seemed to care.

Oddly, Ruby had been less self-conscious in Coney Island, even in a bathing costume, than almost anywhere else. There were simply too many people on every small patch of sand for anyone to focus on her for more than a few seconds. Mostly they didn't notice her at all.

But now, on this late-winter afternoon, there were few people in evidence. The great amusement parks were closed for the season, and the huge new Boardwalk, set to open in the spring, looked more like a moldering ruin than a massive achievement near to completion. The windswept beach was nearly deserted.

They walked in silence down West Eighth Street and Amanda led the way onto the beach, stirring the gulls into fitful, complaining flight. Pieces of newspaper flew around in the gusty breeze, and the sky and sea were almost the same shade of silvery gray. A small fishing boat was heading out into the choppy winter waters.

"Now, young lady, what did you want your aunt to show me?" Cooper asked.

Amanda's cheeks were already chapped by the cold breeze, but her eyes were clear as she met his gaze. "Just watch."

She reached into her bag and pulled out a baseball.

Ruby looked at it. It was new, shining white against all the day's gray shades. "Where'd you get that?" she asked.

Amanda looked at her full on. "I took some of our money when you were out."

As if anticipating an angry response, Allie stepped up beside her sister. "I helped," she said.

But Ruby wasn't angry. She was staring at the baseball in her niece's hand, and beginning to understand what she was supposed to do.

Cooper's mustache, however, was pointing downward. He looked cold. "Appears to be a baseball," he said. "So?"

Ruby ignored him. "Where?" she asked Amanda.

Amanda gazed down the beach, where a couple of other people were walking, huddled deep in their coats. Then back toward the Boardwalk, before finally pointing toward the ocean. "There."

Ruby looked out and spotted a cylindrical red-and-white buoy, perhaps three feet around at its widest and about as tall, riding the waves a hundred feet off the beach.

"You can do it," Amanda said, "can't you?"

Ruby said, "Sure."

"'Course you can," Allie agreed.

Ruby shrugged out of her coat and laid it on the sand. She looked at the sea, at the whitecaps running in confused directions over a sandbar, at the gray line of the horizon. The breeze was coming from onshore, pushing against her back, supporting her, on her side.

Not that it mattered much. She wouldn't have cared if there was a gale blowing into her face.

"I'm sorry, young ladies," Cooper said, turning away. "Have to hit the trail."

"No," Ruby said, and something in her voice stopped him. "Just look."

She took the baseball from Amanda. She hadn't thrown one in five years, but she'd thrown plenty of stones. The ball sat comfortably in her left palm.

"Watching?" she asked Cooper.

He nodded.

Ruby stared out at the buoy. Then she went into a windup,

feeling her muscles move in concert, her joints mesh like the gears of the old clock Mama and Papa had kept on the living-room mantel. Everything felt . . . smooth . . . as she reared back and let fly.

A white dot against the silver sea, the ball flew straight and true, and *fast,* eating up distance at a remarkable rate before slamming into the buoy with a loud bang. Woodchips flew as the float rolled over, revealing a scummy, greenish bottom before righting itself.

Allie gave a low whistle. Beside her, Amanda looked positively smug.

"Hope they don't make me pay for repairs," Ruby said.

She turned to Cooper. He was still staring at the wobbling buoy, and his mouth was open. Finally, slowly, he swung his head to look at her. His eyes were wide beneath his broad-brimmed hat.

"Diamond Ruby," he said.

Ruby blinked. "What?"

He reached out and grasped her shoulder. "Can you do that again?"

Ruby nodded. "Sure."

"How often?" His face was close to hers. "How many times a day?"

She shrugged, then took the time to pick up her coat, shake the sand off it, and put it back on. "I don't know," she said at last. "A hundred?"

He stared at her.

"A thousand?" she said. "How many do you want?"

He laughed, a sharp bark of disbelief. "You could hit a target that often? You can be that accurate?"

Ruby thought about squirrels. But she merely said, "Of course."

Cooper walked a few steps down the beach in his bowlegged way, then came back and faced Amanda. "Sweetie, you asked me to watch this. Why?"

Amanda looked nervous. "I think—" she said. "I mean, I was thinking—wouldn't boys, men, want to see if they can throw as hard as Aunt Ruby does? Couldn't you make them pay to try?"

"Yes." He paused. "Wait. There's someone I want to see this. Then we can all talk about it together." He began to turn away, but stopped and looked back. "You all will still be here when I get back?"

Ruby nodded. As if there was a chance they'd be going anywhere else.

He strode away up the beach, his leather jacket gleaming with mist, his hair a little in disarray under his cowboy hat.

They walked on the sand, Allie searching for shells, Amanda looking out at the water, for about ten minutes before they saw Cooper returning. He was accompanied by a heavyset man with a broad, ruddy face and a bluff and tolerant expression. Unlike Cooper, he wasn't wearing a cowboy costume, merely a long coat over a dark suit.

"This is David Wilcox," Cooper said as Ruby went to meet them. "He runs our arcades—the shooting galleries, penny-arts, and our other games of chance. David, this is—"

"Ruby Thomas," Ruby said.

David Wilcox nodded to her, then turned toward Cooper and chuckled. "Samuel, you got me out here in the cold and the wet, just for a girl?" His voice was gravelly, as if he'd smoked too many cigars. He was holding the smoldering stub of one between the fingers of his right hand.

Cooper smiled. "She's more than 'just a girl,' I assure you."

Then his face fell. "Tarnation!" he said. "I forgot to bring another ball!"

Ruby was already scanning the beach for a stone when Amanda pulled a second baseball out of her bag. It was brown with dried mud and age, its seams worn with use. Ruby could still make out the gouge from where it had struck the apple tree all those years ago.

Her Casey Stengel ball.

Amanda saw the expression on her face and flinched. "I thought you might need two," she said apologetically, "but we only had money for one."

After a moment, Ruby shrugged. "It doesn't matter."

She took the ball, then turned to make sure Wilcox was watching. He was, his expression showing only mild interest. The cigar was dangling from the corner of his mouth.

She wound up and threw. For a second time a ball streaked across the water, a meteor traveling parallel with the earth. This time, though, the impact made a hollow cracking sound, and the buoy split in half. Both halves floated away from the mooring like tiny red life rafts fleeing a sinking ship.

"Uh-oh," Ruby said.

No one else spoke for what seemed like a very long time. Then David Wilcox broke the silence.

"Samuel," he said, "wherever did you find her?"

"We found *him*," Amanda said with immense satisfaction.

Ruby was still staring out at the water. The Casey ball, her most prized possession, her one memento of a vanished life, was gone. But she showed nothing on her face as she turned to look at the two men.

Cooper was beaming. "Imagine the possibilities!"

"I am," Wilcox said. He was smiling around his cigar, though the expression in his eyes was more calculating. Ruby thought he was already counting the money she might make for him.

"How old are you, dear girl?" Cooper asked.

"Seventeen," Ruby said. "Eighteen in July."

"Good! That's just about perfect. The younger you appear, the better."

Ruby thought about the bandage wrapped around her torso.

"Until word gets around, we'll be raking it in on that arm of yours," Cooper went on. "And even after that, every young swain with a girl on his arm will want to prove he can throw harder than you. Just like he wants to become the champion of the High-Striker or knock down all the Red Indians in the shooting gallery."

Wilcox took the cigar out of his mouth. "Have to lose sometimes, you know, won't you?" he said, pointing it at her. "On purpose, if no one shows up who's faster than you."

Ruby felt her face get hot. "No."

Wilcox merely looked thoughtful, but Cooper said, "He's right, Ruby. People have to have some hope of winning, or they'll stop coming."

He smiled at the expression on her face, then turned to Wilcox. "Between those eyes and that voice and that four-alarm temper—oh, and her left arm—well, I think we have ourselves a new attraction."

Wilcox was nodding. "Right you are, Samuel. Glad you got me out here in the cold."

He paused. "What did you call her again?"

"Diamond Ruby. We'll get someone working on her costume right away."

Wilcox thought about that. "We can put her in that space beside Karissa on Fifth Street."

"Good."

Ruby was about to point out that no one had discussed how much she might earn as "Diamond Ruby," when she saw Wilcox's eyes widen.

"Wait just one second," he said, frowning. "How do we prove that she throws faster than the paying customers?"

Ruby saw the problem. Her heart sank.

Cooper was staring out at the foam-flecked water, as if seeing the hurtling baseball again. "Know what you're getting at. If we don't have a way of *proving* it, every single palooka will argue for fifteen minutes, and we'll have to get the strongman in to kick 'em out. It'll be a real mess."

The two men regarded each other, and Ruby could see what they were thinking: Another promising idea bites the dust.

Then Amanda said, "I know how we prove it."

The two men stared at her, this thin little girl with the pinched face and dark eyes. She was rummaging in her bag again. This time she pulled out not a ball, but a small pile of glossy, crumpled pages. When she unfolded them, Ruby saw they'd been torn from a copy of a magazine.

An old issue of *Baseball Magazine*, from Nick's collection.

Allie recognized it, too. "We just read that one!" she said. Then she looked up at the two men. "Amanda taught me how to read."

"An old magazine?" Cooper's mustache indicated disapproval. "I don't get what you're gunning at."

"It was what gave me the idea," Amanda said. "Look."

They all looked down at the creased pages. ONE HUNDRED AND TWENTY-TWO FEET A SECOND! blared the headline. Beneath it was an odd photograph that appeared to show the inside of a long, narrow room, with something that looked like a wire-mesh window screen on a stand in the middle and a massive steel plate against the far wall.

HOW THE VELOCITY OF A PITCHED BALL WAS ACCURATELY MEASURED FOR THE FIRST TIME IN HISTORY, said the next headline. Cooper read it, then raised his eyes to look at Amanda.

She gulped a little, but went on. "They use this thing, this machine, made by the Remington Arms Company up in Bridgeport," she explained. "That's in Connecticut, where they make their guns. They needed to measure the speed that bullets fly—"

"Why?" Allie asked.

Amanda gave an irritated shrug. "I don't know, Allie," she said. "Anyway, the magazine thought that it could also measure the speed of a fastball, so they brought in Nap Rucker and Walter Johnson to test it."

Nap Rucker, whom Ruby had watched pitch all those years ago on the Superbas.

And Walter Johnson, the greatest pitcher of all time.

A gust of wind sent stinging sand whirling up into their faces. Amanda held on to the pages like they were a lifeline. "The pitchers threw the ball through the screen," she said, "and the speed machine, it measured when the baseball brushed or broke one of the wires and then again when it hit the steel plate."

They stood in silence for a moment, thinking about it. Then Samuel Cooper gave a nod. "Yeah, sure, I can see just how that would work," he said. "They'd know how far the screen and the plate were from each other, so by calculating the time the ball took to pass between those two points, they could tell how fast it was moving. That's—" He smiled. "That's just fine. Very smart."

He looked at Wilcox. "Shouldn't be hard to unearth one of those machines, should it? Or build one of our own with a little help from Remington, if we have to."

Wilcox shook his head. "Naw. Bet we'll be able to buy one, cheap."

He looked back down at the headline. "Hundred and twenty-two feet a second," he said. "How fast is that?"

Amanda said, "About eighty-three miles an hour." Then, seeing their startled expressions, she said, "I used a pencil and paper."

"Eighty-three!" Wilcox whistled. "Faster than a racehorse, or an automobile."

He turned his eyes back on Ruby. "Think you can throw anywhere near that fast?"

Ruby said, "What do you think?"

It wasn't really an answer, but the two men looked at each other. Then Cooper laughed.

"Think you should come back to my office," he said. "Let's have ourselves a parley."

10

"Wow," Allie said, her face alight. "This is the *berries*."

Even Amanda seemed impressed for once, her eyes shifting back and forth as if each time she looked away from something, it flew from her mind.

The front of the building was painted to mimic the gate of a ballpark. The flat stone of the exterior walls now resembled bricks, the painted-on windows above seemed to reflect an unseen sun, and a painted boy was leaning out of one of the windows, scorecard in one hand, the other gesturing excitedly to passersby. "Come on in!" he appeared to be shouting. "It's a great game!"

DIAMOND RUBY, SPEED PITCHER EXTRAORDINAIRE! shouted a banner above the door. RUBY, THE BELLE OF THE BALL! screamed another. CAN YOU THROW FASTER THAN THIS TEENAGE GIRL? taunted a third. COME IN AND GIVE IT A TRY!

And there was a painting of her, too. An idealized version of her, with normal arms. She was wearing a white baseball uniform with ruby-red pinstripes and a red cap with the letters *DR* in white above the brim, and she was holding a baseball in her left hand. Peering out at the street like she was waiting for the sign from the catcher, glossy hair spilling out from underneath the cap, face stern and challenging with its high cheekbones and large, dark eyes.

Samuel Cooper came up beside her as she stood there staring at her portrait. "I take it," he said, "that you're impressed."

Actually, Ruby had been imagining the expression on Mama's face at such foolishness. "Don't waste your life," she'd said, and to her this would have been nothing but a waste.

Ruby kept such thoughts private, merely nodding. "Hope the customers aren't disappointed, though. The painting's ten times as pretty as I am in real life."

Cooper's mustache bristled at the very idea. "My dear," he asked, "are you *spifflicated*?"

Ruby smiled and shook her head. "Seriously," she said, "what will people think when they go inside and find that it's only me in there? Won't they be disappointed?"

He laughed at her question. "Disappointed? Not when they think they can win money or other prizes just by throwing a ball faster than you can."

Distracted as quickly as they'd been enthralled, the girls had wandered down the street, past the restaurants and arcades, all still closed for the winter, and toward the new Boardwalk. And they weren't the only ones. Even with the official opening still weeks away, crowds of men in suits and homburgs and women in fashionable dresses and furs came every day just to stroll along the pine planks.

They came as well to stare at the enormous refurbished bath-houses, the freshly painted restaurants, and the newly festooned sideshows, all of which anticipated booming attendance this summer.

And, of course, Luna Park and Steeplechase themselves, the crowning glories with their roller coasters and equestrian races and smash-'em-up cars.

Who would pay attention to a girl in a baseball uniform when there were so many other distractions nearby?

But Cooper, today dressed in a long black coat and a big black cowboy hat, like a villain in a Douglas Fairbanks movie, seemed unconcerned. As Ruby called the girls back, he bent, turned a brass key in the heavy steel lock on the front door, swung the door open, and stepped inside. Before he allowed them to follow, Ruby saw him reach to push up a row of heavy switches. The windowless room was suddenly illuminated by a row of electric globes up near the ceiling—globes encircled, Ruby noticed, by heavy links of chain.

"For protection," Cooper said, "against errant tosses."

"Not by me." Ruby stepped into the room. As the girls ran ahead, she got her first real look at what she guessed would become her true home in the months to come.

It was, as she'd known it would be, a long, narrow chamber much like the gun shed *Baseball Magazine* had used, paralleling the front of the building and the street outside. Unlike the magazine's spartan testing area, the floor here had been painted grass green and the walls to resemble grandstands, with blurred figures in the seats and a blue sky dotted with white clouds and quickly sketched birds above. A bright yellow sun placidly observed the entire scene.

Ruby could see how welcoming it seemed, how you might want to step inside and stand under that blue sky and glowing sun.

A counter ran along the shorter wall to the right of the door, and behind it rows of shelves held cigarettes, candy, little stuffed animals, dolls, and other small knickknacks of one sort or another. A large banner hung over the counter, proclaiming TRY YOUR LUCK! *One Throw: 10 cents. Three Throws: 25 cents.* CAN YOU THROW HARDER THAN DIAMOND RUBY?

Below was a second banner: *Watch Your Score Appear on Our Me-chanical Scoreboard—Brought to You Straight from the New Yankee Stadium, the Greatest Ballpark on Earth!*

Ruby looked at the scoreboard, big and green with white zeros marching across it, and then at Cooper.

"Yankee Stadium?" she said.

With a sweep of his hat, he gave her a rakish bow. "My dear girl," he said, "can you prove it *wasn't*?"

Throw 50 miles per hour or more, and YOU WIN! a third banner blared. *The faster you throw, the BIGGER THE PRIZE!*

Ruby said, "A lot of people can throw fifty."

"Not as many as you'd think," Cooper said. "Anyway, so? Let them win a Baby Ruth, or a doll for their girl. It'll keep them coming back."

OUT-TOSS DIAMOND RUBY AND WIN $2!!!

For a moment, Ruby felt a twinge of nervousness in her stomach. It was a lot of money. What if every second man who came in could outthrow her?

But then she dismissed the thought. "How often do you want me to lose?" she asked.

Cooper smiled at her tone. "We'll see how that goes," he said. "Depends on the traffic, on how much we're pulling in."

THROW 100 MILES PER HOUR, WIN $100!

Ruby shook her head. She'd read the article Amanda had found, and knew that even Walter Johnson didn't approach that speed. "Poor saps here will be breaking their arms," she said.

"Always promise," Cooper said, "what you'll never have to deliver."

In front of the prize counter, in plain view of anyone who peeked in the front door, was a concrete platform painted brown to resemble dirt. "Is that the pitcher's mound?" Ruby asked.

Cooper nodded.

Ruby stepped up onto it, finding it a little higher than she'd expected. That was okay. The higher the mound, *Baseball Magazine* said, the easier it was to throw hard and accurately at a target. Her challengers would feel like they were throwing better than they ever had before, which was just fine with her.

Because, unfortunately for them, she'd be throwing off the same platform.

She sighted down the length of the room toward the large framework of copper-wire mesh that stood on a solid wooden stand about thirty feet away. It had been her idea to make it substantially larger than the one *Baseball Magazine* had used—six feet on each side. The article had revealed that even Walter Johnson had frequently missed the entire screen of the smaller original, and Cooper didn't want to frustrate the paying customers. Someone whose throws never went through the wires wouldn't come back.

"We've got three of them," Cooper told her. "Three screens. Too many of the wires break, we'll bring out a new one until we fix the first."

Ruby nodded. "Tell you what. I won't throw slower than anybody, but sometimes I'll miss the screen."

No matter how hard you threw, if the ball didn't touch the wires and register on the speed machine, you lost.

Cooper smiled. "That's fine."

Bolted to the far wall and heavily braced stood a large sheet of steel shaped like home plate—the target. Like the wire screen, it was attached to the speed machine by snaking wires that ran along the floor toward the sturdy wooden shack on the side. Following Ruby's gaze, Cooper said, "Those wires will be placed in grooves in the floor and covered with green rubber mats before we open."

Ruby went over to inspect the steel plate. For now, shiny and untouched, it looked more like a fun-house mirror than the future recipient of a fusillade of hardballs. Ruby looked at her distorted reflection, the rippled surface of the steel making her arms look, if anything, even longer, and then turned away.

"That thing is going to take quite a beating," she said.

Cooper shrugged. "It'll hold up for quite a while. And when it wears out, we'll replace it."

Ruby didn't say anything, but standing there, she felt a little dizzy. For the past five years, she had never thought that way about *anything*. There had never been a moment, not one, where she could allow herself to think, Oh, I'll just replace that. Everything had to be saved, repaired, mended, its natural life span extended as far as possible, and then even further.

Cooper had offered her thirty-five dollars a week to start, far more than she'd ever earned. But no matter how much money she saved—a hundred dollars even—she wondered if she'd ever think of objects as *replaceable*.

"Aunt Ruby! Come look at this."

It was Amanda, standing beside the little wooden shack that housed the speed machine. It had taken David Wilcox only about a week to get hold of an old one ("It might even be the same one that *Baseball Magazine* used," Cooper had said), and now it sat inside the shack's protective walls beneath the big mechanical scoreboard that hung on the wall.

Ruby walked over to take a look. To be honest, she couldn't make head or tail of it, the sprouting wires or the glass gauge or the rows of white buttons and red switches, some flipped one way, some the other.

Lucky for her all she had to do was throw the ball.

"We could most likely charge a nickel just for people to watch that machine at work," Cooper said. Then he smiled. "Well, not yet. Maybe someday."

It had taken Amanda about a minute to learn how to operate it. This was going to be her job, along with operating the pulleys and levers on the mechanical scoreboard that would reveal, in big white numbers, the speed of each pitch.

Meanwhile, Allie would gather up the used balls and return

them to the metal bucket that would stand beside the pitcher's mound. And both girls would repair or replace the wires broken in the mesh framework after closing each day.

Ruby's heart had been in her mouth when she'd suggested this setup to Cooper, but the impresario had taken the request in stride. "That'll be fine," he'd said. "A family of girls working together—people will just eat it up."

Her relief at his response had been so strong Ruby felt she could almost touch it. She'd had no idea what else she'd have done with Amanda and Allie during the hours she was here. She certainly couldn't have left them in the apartment every day.

She looked back at the mound, at the bin of baseballs sitting beside it. "Do you want me to try it out?" she asked.

Cooper nodded. "Sure. Throw a few—let's see how she works."

He looked at Ruby, standing there in the faded blue Peggy-cloth slip-on dress she wore when she wanted to be comfortable, the one whose length she'd outgrown when she was fifteen, and said, "Can you throw in those clothes?"

She nodded and headed back to the mound. As she did, her heart took a funny little jump in her chest.

Amanda called out from the shed, "Ready in here."

Allie, safely off to the side, said, "Ready over here, too!"

Cooper, standing beside her, nodded and said, "At your convenience, my dear."

Ruby reached down and retrieved a ball from the bucket. It was new, they all were, shiny and slick, with the printed "Spalding" on it still clear. Ruby rubbed it between her callused palms. After a few impacts with the steel plate, it—and all the rest of the balls—would lose some of its shine.

She didn't even bother to sight in, just went into a windup and threw the ball through the screen. It was far easier than throwing at a tree trunk, much less a squirrel or pigeon. The ball hit the plate with a clang loud enough to send Allie's hands up to her ears and to make Cooper give a little jump.

He smiled. "Perfect."

"Not too loud?" Ruby asked.

"Oh, no," he said. "The reverse. People feel like they're getting their money's worth if something makes a racket. It's one of the secrets behind shooting galleries and lion acts and those men Barnum shoots out of cannons."

"Hundred and twenty-two feet per second!" Amanda called out from the speed shack. A moment later, the scoreboard rattled, and two of the three blank, staring zeros were replaced with an eight and a three.

Amanda popped out from behind the scoreboard. "Eighty-three miles per hour," she said. "That's as fast as Walter Johnson in the magazine."

Ruby shook her head. "Maybe that's all he could do when he was aiming at that little screen, but I bet he was faster in a real game."

"Fast enough for me," Cooper said. "Now do it again."

So she did, maybe twenty throws. She'd intended to throw as hard as she could, but Cooper seemed impressed enough by her speed—eighty-four miles per hour, eighty-six—that she kept herself under wraps.

When she was done, Cooper let Amanda and Allie throw a few. Allie's tosses tended to go higher than they did far, but Amanda, with a few words of advice from Ruby, put one through the wires and against the metal plate with something on it.

"When I'm tired," Ruby told her, "you can take over."

Earning a rare smile from her serious niece.

Afterward, they stood outside in the weak early spring sunshine, Ruby and Cooper with cups of coffee, the girls with Cokes that he'd found somewhere. Most of the crowds were gone from the

Boardwalk, taking the neighborhood's life and energy with them, and the street again had a ramshackle, spiritless feel to it.

"It'll be different on opening day," Cooper said. "I can promise you that much."

Ruby looked at him. "Is this going to work?"

"Diamond Ruby?" He smiled behind his mustache. "Well, I guess we're going to find out."

Seeing the unconvinced expression on her face, he raised a hand. "But to help make sure," he went on, "I'll place a barker out here, at least at first, and some ballyhoo also."

"I don't know what that is," she said.

"Well, it's anything colorful and noisy that attracts attention." He pondered for a moment. "I was considering bagpipes—you can hear those for blocks—but I think I'll have someone dressed as Babe Ruth march around out here with a giant bat and a big voice. He'll describe you and challenge the crowd to try their luck, and I promise you'll have plenty of people coming to take a look."

He tilted his head at her. "After that, of course, it'll be up to you."

Ruby waited while he locked the door. Then, as he straightened, she asked, "And you? Will you be here, too?"

"I'll come when I can," he said after a moment. "But it won't be often. I have a lot of other places I need to be every day—and anyway, this is really Wilcox's bailiwick. He's in charge day to day."

Cooper smiled at her.

"You two will get along just fine," he said.

II

"*T*he what?" Ruby said.

The seamstress—her name was Tania—grinned. Her teeth were stained, and one on the top was missing, but there was life and humor in her dark eyes, and Ruby could tell from the lines that bracketed her mouth that she smiled a lot.

"The Birdcage," Tania said. "That's what we called this place before."

She laughed at Ruby's confusion. "Believe me when I tell you it was silly," she went on. "Some poor girl with a face like—like an eagle, can you imagine? Sad story, sadder because I had to dress her in feathers. They called her the 'Bird with the Golden Wings,' and she'd dance around for people. Not very many people, though. No surprise this place was empty when you came along."

Tania shrugged. "Nice enough girl, she was, just—it was sad. But anyway, yes, the Birdcage, that's what we called it."

"We should change its name to the Ballpark or something."

"Call it what you like."

It was opening day for the Boardwalk. Ruby and Tania stood in the dressing room that opened onto one wall of the—well, Ruby was already thinking of it as the Birdcage. The dressing room was square, with white walls, a couple of splintery wooden chairs, an equally worn table, a clothes rack, two metal-framed cots with saggy mattresses, and a bare globe casting harsh light from overhead.

There was a second, solid wooden door on the dressing room's back wall. The first time Ruby had visited, this door had been open, and she'd seen an empty, dusty storage room occupied only by spiders and cockroaches, and finally another door that opened onto a trash-strewn alley that ran between Fifth and Sixth streets. Since that day, the door to the storage room had been locked from within, which was fine with her.

Tania was holding out her Diamond Ruby costume. "You like it?" she asked.

An immigrant from some city in Europe that Ruby had never heard of, short, dark-haired Tania was just one of a battalion of seamstresses and costume designers employed by the Fantasyland Sideshow to clothe the midgets, giants, bearded ladies, and others who couldn't shop at Abraham & Straus or that new place, Loehmann's, up on Bedford Avenue.

"I love it," Ruby said, "almost as much as my girls love theirs."

Each of them had been given a baseball uniform made of white flannel with ruby pinstripes, matching the one worn by the painted girl out front. Amanda's and Allie's had their first names sewn on the back in red, while Ruby's said "Diamond Ruby." Amanda's and Ruby's had long trousers, but Allie's had shorts, designed to show off her chubby legs and dimpled knees. Each uniform was accompanied by red baseball shoes and a red cap with the letters *DR* embroidered in white above the brim.

Allie had shrieked when she first saw her costume, and Ruby had seen how pleased Amanda was as well.

As Ruby changed, she said to Tania, "Everything looks beautiful. But that's not what matters, is it?"

Tania thought about it as she watched Ruby with a critical eye, noting where she'd have to take in the costume, where she'd have to let it out. Then she said, "No, it matters. 'Course it matters—you don't look good, you got no chance here." She raised her eyes to look into Ruby's. "But what you're asking is, does it make *all* the difference? And no, it doesn't, of course it doesn't. *You* got to do it, whatever it is you do."

When she was finished dressing, Ruby walked back into the Birdcage. Allie and Amanda, already in their uniforms, were waiting for her, and so was David Wilcox, cigar dangling.

He looked her up and down with his pebbly gray eyes and nodded his approval. "That's okay," he said. "That's good."

Then he gestured toward the front door. "Let's go. Show's about to start."

Ruby and the girls followed him outside into a wet, dreary morning. The weather didn't seem to have affected the crowd's enthusiasm, though. People were streaming toward the Boardwalk, hundreds of them, thousands, men in suits and bowler hats, women in fine dresses, girls wearing white gloves and knitted jerseys and serge skirts against the unusual chill, boys in the knee-length black trousers they wore summer and winter alike.

"Aunt Ruby!" Allie sounded thrilled. "Look at this!"

Standing beside David Wilcox outside the door of the Birdcage was a young man, maybe twenty, with knotty muscles and a nose that looked like it had been broken at least once.

He was wearing a sandwich sign. On one side it had a painting of Diamond Ruby, a smaller version of the one that adorned the front of the Birdcage. On the other was a baseball with linked dollar signs instead of stitches, and the word WIN! in big letters.

"What you do," Wilcox said to Ruby, "is walk, slowly, to the big party over on the Boardwalk. Don't say a word, don't look at anybody, don't do anything except be mysterious, like you live in a different world and are just visiting this one. No giggling, no beating your gums, no acting like a bearcat, no trying to meet some prince who'll take you away from all this. Got that?"

Ruby nodded. "Got it."

"Jimmy here will follow you, and if people have any questions, *he'll* answer them."

"Easy," Jimmy said, grinning. "I know all about you."

"And then, when you've gotten yourself noticed, come back here and we'll see if anybody stops by and pays their dime. Got that?"

Ruby nodded again.

"So go."

As she maneuvered her way through the crowd, Ruby saw heads start to turn in her direction. Pretty soon people were pointing, coming up to read the sign, asking Jimmy for details. With the easygoing self-confidence of the born showman, he answered every question just vaguely enough to leave onlookers wanting more.

"Does she throw like a girl?" Ruby heard him say. "I don't know—maybe. What does a girl throw like? Real question is, does she throw faster than *you*?"

Ruby didn't meet anyone's eye, didn't say a word, just stood there, occasionally stretching out her arms in a gesture that brought gasps when people saw their length.

Gradually the reviewing stand overlooking the Boardwalk filled. Amanda and Allie ducked and darted their way to the front of the crowd where the military bands sat. As the first speech began, something long and dull by the mayor about the future and progress and other subjects that didn't concern Ruby, someone bumped into her, hard. She turned to see a skinny man whose grin revealed three missing teeth, and whose breath in her face smelled like alcohol.

"Hey, pretty girl," he said, reaching for her, "come play on my team."

But the words were barely out of his mouth before Jimmy had gotten between them. Ruby thought there'd be a fight, but what Jimmy did instead was give the man—and all the onlookers nearby—a spiel. He went on and on about how yes, she was beautiful, yes, she was mysterious, yes, look at her long arms . . . but they'd have to come to her ballpark, just a few blocks away on Fifth Street, a mere baseball's throw from the Boardwalk, to see what she was really capable of. Not here, not now, but there, and soon. Very soon.

Even Ruby found herself mesmerized by his patter.

And wondering how she could ever match the buildup he was giving her.

"Did you see that soldier's furry hat?" Allie, wide-eyed and breathless, asked as they headed back to the Birdcage. "And he let me play his drum!"

"There's a dance tonight," Amanda said. "There'll be a band next to the Giant Racer—and, Ruby, it's free. Can we go?"

Her normally pale face was flushed, and there was a light in her eyes Ruby had rarely seen.

She felt her heart twist. It was worth it, all of it, wearing this costume, people staring at her, at her arms. All worth it, if she could see her girls happy, at least for a moment.

"Of course we can," she said.

The arcades that flanked the Birdcage were already open for business, and attracting a steady stream of visitors, when their little procession returned. Below the painting of Diamond Ruby stood a big, burly man dressed in a pin-striped uniform and navy-blue cap much like that worn by the Yankees. Though he was old, about forty, it was obvious that he was supposed to remind passersby of Babe Ruth. He was swinging a giant baseball bat made out of some lightweight wood, and as they approached he took a big swing and bopped a large metal plate hanging beside the door. It rang like a gong.

"Ballyhoo," Ruby said.

Jimmy nodded. "He'll make noise, and when they come over, I'll try to get them to go in and hand over their dough."

"Will it work?"

He shrugged. "How would I know? Haven't even seen what it is you do yet."

"Come in and I'll show you."

He thought about it, then nodded. "Fast, though," he said. "Mr. Wilcox wants me out here."

Inside, the place looked spiffed up, clean and shiny under the electric globes. A middle-aged man with broad, stubbly cheeks leaned against the wall behind the counter, his arms crossed over his thick chest.

"Art," he said.

"Ruby."

"You gonna keep me busy, Diamond Ruby?" he asked her.

"I hope so."

Jimmy was looking around with an experienced eye. "Huh," he said. "Pretty cute."

He turned his gaze to Ruby. "So show me your trick."

"It's no trick." She walked with a measured pace to the mound. When she bent to pick up a ball, she saw that all of them had been painted red. They looked less like hardballs than big round jewels.

She picked one up and hefted it, then reared back and threw with an easy motion. The ball powered through the screen and clanged off the steel plate—a louder, duller echo of the fake Babe's gong outside. Allie went scampering after it, picked it up, and inspected it. "Some of the paint came off," she announced. Then her face brightened. "I could repaint them every night!"

Amanda's head emerged through the door of the speed shack. "One hundred eleven feet per second," she called out. She bent down to work the levers and pulleys, and a moment later the number clacked up onto the scoreboard: 75.7 miles per hour.

"Huh," Jimmy said again. "Let me try."

"Sure."

Ducking out from under his sandwich board, he folded it and leaned it against the wall, then reached into his pocket. He withdrew a dime, showed it to Ruby, then handed it over to Art. With a flourish, the cashier banged open the cashbox and dropped the coin in.

"Our first customer," Amanda said.

Jimmy stepped past her and up onto the mound, peering in at the target before reaching down and getting himself a ball.

Then he went into a windup, looking more comfortable than Ruby had expected, and let go a pretty fair fastball. It hit off the steel plate with a satisfying sound and rolled away, Allie in pursuit.

"Seventy-eight feet per second," Amanda reported. A moment later the scoreboard clattered to read 53.1 miles per hour.

"Hey," Ruby said, pointing up at the sign. "You win!"

Jimmy grinned, reaching up to catch the candy bar that Art tossed to him.

But when he looked back at Ruby, there was a new expression on his face, as if he was working something out. "I pitch for a neighborhood team on my days off, over in East New York," he said.

Ruby nodded. "You've got a good arm."

"But not as good as yours."

She shrugged.

"I could throw harder, you know," he said.

Ruby said, "I know."

"But then," he said slowly, figuring it out, "so could you."
She just looked at him.
"Huh," he said.

Three hours later, it was time to close up. There'd been a steady stream of men willing to try their luck against her, a steady patter of dimes and quarters into Art's cashbox. Some of the contestants clearly knew they were going to lose, but liked having the chance to throw the ball against the steel plate and enjoyed seeing Ruby hurl fastballs that were (in the words of one older man) "something you'd expect to see from Smoky Joe Wood back in the day, not a girl."

Others got furious when they couldn't throw harder than she could. One man was so determined to outdo her that he spent something like four dollars trying, then stomped away (under Art's no-nonsense guidance) with an arm so sore and weak he could barely lift it.

As she'd promised she would, Ruby let two customers win. And as she'd promised herself, she never let anyone throw faster than she did, but just missed the screen. The winners were thrilled anyway.

Somewhere during the busiest part of the evening, David Wilcox and Samuel Cooper came in. They stood near the door, watching, and neither said anything to her. When she looked over, Cooper smiled. A few minutes later she looked again, and the two men were gone.

When Tania returned from wherever she'd been all afternoon, Ruby knew they were finally reaching the end of the day. One more customer, and she was able to step from the mound.

Jimmy poked his head in the door and said, "Good start."
"Thank you, Jimmy," she said.
He grinned. "Back at it tomorrow, doll."

. . .

When the door was shut for the day, Tania helped her remove her costume. A quick inspection revealed no tears or pulls, and the uniform was carefully hung on the metal rack in the corner of the dressing room.

The girls, long since changed into their own clothes, were waiting expectantly near the front door.

"What?" Ruby asked.

Amanda said, "Well, can we?"

Ruby wanted nothing more than to get on the elevated and go home. She'd almost fallen asleep on her feet as Tania stripped off her costume. "Can we what?"

"Can we go to the parade? The dance?"

They both looked so eager, and they'd both worked so hard, that Ruby didn't have the heart to say no. So off they went, back to Surf Avenue, arriving in the midst of a sturdy crowd defying the drizzle just in time to see the Street Cleaning Department Band march by. Other bands followed, and camels, and horses, and even an elephant. The girls were in raptures.

After the parade the bands stationed themselves all along the Boardwalk, beside Feltman's, and near gaudy Steeplechase Park, and the parade turned into a party under glaring white arc lights that hissed and snapped in the blowing mist. First one or two, then dozens, then hundreds of people began to dance, their wet hair and clothes gleaming in the sparking streetlights, laughing and shouting at the sheer happy improbability of it all. Could this really be happening here? Now?

Of course it could. This was 1923, after all, when anything was possible.

Or so Ruby was beginning to learn.

She let the girls join the dancers, and soon they were twirling like everyone else, slipping and sliding across the Boardwalk's slick new planks as if they were skating, or flying. There was pure joy on their faces, Amanda's as well as Allie's. They looked lighter than air, as graceful as birds.

And if Ruby was unable to join in, to set herself free the way they could, well, she was content anyway.

Nick was waiting when they walked in the door after midnight.

Allie had fallen asleep on the train, and Amanda's eyes had grown heavy. Ruby's native wariness had kept her awake, but she was bone-tired. The last thing she needed to see was her unpredictable brother sitting at the table, a cup of coffee in front of him and an accusatory look on his face.

At least it's only coffee, Ruby thought, and not some bootleg liquor with kerosene or something in it.

And then she thought: He's probably dosed the coffee with the liquor.

"Where have you been?" Nick asked her.

Ruby didn't reply. She looked at the girls, awake now, worried, waiting for the explosion, and said, "Say good night to your dad, and get to bed. There's another day coming tomorrow, whether we're ready for it or not."

A moment's hesitation, and then Amanda walked over and gave her father a stiff hug, followed by Allie's slightly warmer one. Nick looked at them, Ruby thought, like he wasn't sure who they were. Or maybe he'd just forgotten what you did when someone hugged you.

"Good night, Daddy," Allie whispered.

"Good night," he said.

Then they came over to Ruby. These hugs were heartfelt, the two warm children smelling of wet hair and cigarette smoke and the candy she'd gotten for them from the Birdcage prize booth.

"Thank you, Aunt Ruby," Amanda said into her neck.

Ruby put her arms around them for a moment, then let go.

Before the girls had even left the room, Ruby's gaze was back on Nick's face. He looked, she thought, *old*. He had lines around his eyes and mouth she'd never noticed before, and there was a papery quality to the skin of his badly shaven cheeks. The whites of his eyes were yellow.

How old was he? It took Ruby a minute to remember. He was thirty, just thirty.

"Where were you today?" he asked.

"Coney Island."

"Why didn't you tell me?"

There were many ways Ruby could have answered this. But all she did was say, in a mild tone, "Sorry, Nick. I didn't think. I was at my new job."

He blinked at this information, then said, "How much do they pay you?"

She didn't answer, just looked at him. After a moment, his gaze shifted away. "I have a new job, too," he said.

This was the first she'd heard of it, but that wasn't unusual. Nick had had plenty of jobs. How long he kept them was a different question.

"You do?"

"Yeah. Fact, it's down your way."

Ruby felt a chill creep along her skin. "What kind of job?"

But Nick, grinning, proud of his secret, wouldn't answer.

12

"*i* f it's okay with you," the man standing near the door said, "I'd just like to watch you pitch."

He was an older guy, a little thick around the middle, dressed in a gray sacque suit that was shiny in the elbows and knees. The lenses of his eyeglasses were smeared, and in his knobby hands he held a scuffed bowler. He had a long jaw and a beaky nose, and brown eyes that were sharp for a man of his general shabbiness.

"Can't throw since I had my accident," he said, lifting his right arm a little but explaining no further. "Always admire a pitcher's form, though, so I had to come see you."

Hmm. *A pitcher's form.*

He didn't *seem* like a masher.

Ruby looked over his head at Art. Wide-eyed, the cashier lifted his hand, and Ruby saw a five-dollar bill dangling from it. He shrugged his shoulders, but his look said, "Hey, the man's money is good. Go ahead."

It wasn't like she had a whole lot else to do. It had been a slow morning. They'd *all* been slow mornings. Slow days. A few people here and there, some kids, every once in a while someone who wanted just to test his arm against the speed machine, not against Ruby. But more times than not, no one there but her, the girls, and Art, who Ruby thought was getting ready to look for his next job.

That first hopeful night had only been a week ago, but already it seemed like the distant past. If Ruby had thought that the excitement and enthusiasm of those brief hours would carry over, she'd been wrong.

On these beautiful spring days, with all the parks open and all the other sideshows and shooting galleries and restaurants ready to grab their share of the customers' cash, there just didn't seem to be enough left over for Diamond Ruby.

"Love watching someone throw a baseball," the man said to her.

Ruby knew she was supposed to stay silent. But she found herself saying, "Most people head over to that new stadium in the Bronx. I hear they throw baseballs up there, too."

The man blinked, either at her deep voice or because he hadn't realized she could talk at all. Then he grinned. "Yes, and most of those balls go flying off the bat of Babe Ruth," he said. "No, I think I'll see what you can do. Name's Gordon, by the way."

He stuck out his hand. After a moment, she shook it. She could feel the bones and tendons under the skin, but his grip was surprisingly strong.

"Where do you want to stand," she asked, "just to watch?"

He looked around, then shrugged and leaned against the wall. "Might think about bringing in some chairs for folks like me," he said. "Maybe even bleacher seats."

Ruby couldn't let this pass. "Bleacher seats?" she said. "Folks like you? You think anybody else's going to pay just to sit and watch me?"

The man looked into her eyes. "You throw as hard as I've heard, 'course they will."

There was no point in arguing. With a shrug, she stepped onto the platform, took a deep breath, and put all the pent-up frustration of the past empty days into her first throw.

She knew as it left her hand that it was the hardest pitch she'd ever thrown. The ball sliced through the wires and hit the steel plate with an impact like a small explosion. Paint dust flew off the wall around the bolts. The ball rebounded through the air like a line drive struck by a bat, and as it went past her Ruby could see that it had lost a big patch of red paint from one side.

Allie, staring, forgot for a moment to chase after it, Amanda popped out of her shack like a jack-in-the-box, and Art dropped his cigarette.

Gordon gave a low whistle. "Who needs the Bronx?" he said.

Ruby didn't reply, but inside she was smiling. That had felt *good.*

Amanda disappeared into the shack again, and stayed there for longer than usual. When she stood up, her mouth was open, her eyes wide. She looked like one of the big dolls you'd win if you threw the ball seventy miles per hour.

"One hundred and thirty-six feet per second," she reported, her voice breathless. She ducked back down, and a moment later the scoreboard read, "92.7 miles per hour."

"My God," Gordon said, peering at the numbers.

"Look!"

Everyone turned toward Allie. She was holding the ball up in one hand like it was a trophy, and pointed at a part where the paint had been stripped away. "This side is . . . *flat.*"

Gordon laughed. "Young lady," he said to Ruby, "would you please do that again?"

She reached down from her concrete platform, took another ruby baseball from the bucket, and went into her windup.

. . .

She threw pitch after pitch with Gordon as her only audience. None were as hard as the first, not quite, but he applauded every one.

Or she thought he did. She soon lost track of him and his reactions and found herself slipping into a strange kind of dream state. Everything else seemed to disappear, the room, her audience, the worry that always seemed to gnaw at the linings of her gut, leaving only the ball and the target.

After every pitch, she'd see, as if from a great distance, the numbers on the scoreboard change: 87 . . . 89 . . . 85 . . . 90. But that didn't matter to her, either. Usually she didn't even wait for the calculation before throwing her next pitch, and eventually Amanda simply gave up trying to keep track.

The point, Ruby thought, wasn't throwing as hard as she could. The point was shutting down her thoughts, her worries, her memories, and concentrating only on the pleasure of the pitching motion and its repetition.

By the time she'd finished, sweat was running down her face and her chest was heaving. She came out of her trance and looked around the room. But no one moved or said a word until Gordon let out a laugh and pushed himself away from the wall.

At the door, he turned and looked back at her. "Ruby," he said, "the world's *got* to find out about you."

"Yeah."

He frowned. "But how?"

And at that moment, Ruby figured it out.

"Yeah, I remember you." The sour-faced man sitting across the cluttered desk didn't look happy about it. "You're Nick Thomas's kid sister all grown up—I met you at that Superbas game when you were, what, seven?"

"Nearly eight," she said, surprised.

"Uh-huh," he said. "You were hanging around Nick, looking like a kid at a candy shop."

"I caught a foul ball that Casey Stengel hit."

"Yeah? Well, I'm sure ol' Case would be happy to hear that."

George Littell, his nameplate said, though Ruby still remembered him as Grumpy George. He was the sportswriter who'd been Nick's boss at the *Brooklyn Examiner* all those years ago. A lifetime ago. But here he still was, in the newspaper's bustling offices downtown, a long subway ride from Midwood, the place smelling of ink and cologne and odors Ruby couldn't identify.

And he was just as grumpy. Already, looking down at the piles of papers on his desk, then back up at Ruby with quick, almost silvery eyes set incongruously in a pouchy, sallow face, he seemed ready to ask her to leave his office. "We went through this when you wrote to me," he said, "and we did what we could."

Years earlier, that had been. When Ruby and the girls had been starving, that first awful winter.

"We tried," he said. "We set your brother up with one job after another . . . but he couldn't hold any of them."

"This isn't about Nick," Ruby said.

"No?" George put his hands down flat on two piles of paper on his desk, as if he was about to push himself to his feet and usher her out of there. But then he sighed and settled back a little. "Then what is it about?"

"Me."

He looked at her. She knew she was an unprepossessing sight in her old clothes. Her only distinguishing feature was her arms.

"Yes? What about you?"

Ruby took a breath. There was only one way to approach this.

"I can throw a baseball as hard as Walter Johnson," she said.

George stared at her. Then he laughed, a sharp sound that echoed in the dusty office. "Sure you can."

"And I can prove it."

He opened his mouth to reply, then closed it again. But his face was closed, too, unforgiving, willfully uninterested.

"Mr. Littell," Ruby said, "please listen to me."

After a moment, he said, "All right, I'm listening."

She took a deep breath and plunged in. "It seems like I see an article in the newspaper every week about woman athletes," she said. "Some girl swimming the English Channel or diving off the high board or, I don't know, running the mile faster than anyone ever did it before. Or going off to Africa on safari, or flying her own airplane across the Atlantic Ocean or—"

But George was holding up a hand to stop her. "Yeah, I read the newspapers, too," he said. "But what does it all have to do with you?"

Before she could answer, he went on. "I mean, you're not doing any of those things, are you? You're not swimming across the ocean or piloting your own hot-air balloon or diving into a teacup." He widened his eyes, and she could see exactly how much he wanted to be done with her. "You're dressing up in a costume," he said, "and throwing a baseball in a sideshow on Coney Island."

Ruby's stomach twisted. She hadn't realized he knew.

Grumpy George's face was expressionless. "Yeah, 'Diamond Ruby,' I've heard of you. Made me feel sorry for Nick all over again."

There were a hundred responses to that. But all Ruby said was, "Come see me."

"Not worth my time. Didn't that old cowboy tell you? I don't write about sideshows."

"Even ones who throw as hard as Walter Johnson?"

This time he didn't laugh. "You keep saying that. It didn't slay me the first time, and now I'm getting tired of it. You sound like that guy who thought he was the Human Fly last week and climbed the outside of the Studebaker Building. You hear about that? He was no fly, and he didn't bounce when he hit the pavement."

He stood. "And you're no Walter Johnson."

Ruby got to her feet, too. "Guess I won't convince you," she said.

Grumpy George grinned and shook his head.

"But I bet I'll be able to convince someone else."

He didn't like that as much.

"Like maybe someone at the *Brooklyn Eagle*." Ruby paused, thinking. "You know, I bet I could even call Grantland Rice at the *Herald* and get him to come down from Manhattan. He likes 'human interest' stories. Maybe he'd even write a poem about me."

Grantland Rice was probably the most famous sportswriter in the whole country, known not only for his descriptions of the games, but also for the poems he put in his columns. Amanda loved sharing them with Allie as part of their reading lessons, and Ruby listened in when she could.

Grumpy George was looking grumpier with every word she spoke. When she took a breath he said, "The *Trib*."

"What?"

"Rice writes for the *Tribune,* not the *Herald*."

Ruby shrugged. "Oh, right. Well, wherever he is, I think I'll be able to find him."

Then she leaned over the desk. "Listen, Mr. Littell, it's your choice," she said. "You either leave this office and come see me throw, or somebody else will. Grantland Rice or John Kieran or Jack Lawrence—I don't know. But somebody. That much I can guarantee. And I can also guarantee that afterward you'll feel pretty stupid for missing a scoop that I brought right to your desk. But that won't matter to me." She paused. "I'll give you a week for an exclusive. That's all."

It was the longest speech she'd ever made. Long enough? Too long? She had no idea.

She could feel his eyes on her as she walked away.

·   ·   ·

"One more week, and Jimmy and the ballyhoo are out of here," David Wilcox told her that evening. "There's better places for us to use them."

Ruby would rather have heard the bad news from Mr. Cooper himself, but she hadn't seen him in days. It was, she thought, another sign that her sideshow was failing.

"I need more time," she said.

She could see that Wilcox didn't care. The unfortunate bird-faced dancing girl or the one with the freakish arms, it didn't matter. They were all the same to him. If they didn't make money, they were out the door.

"We're not running an orphanage here," he said. "Or a monkey house."

Two days later, just before closing time, Grumpy George showed up.

Ruby was on the mound, showing a teenage boy how to grip the ball, when she saw him walk in the door accompanied by a photographer. Following her advice, the boy threw the ball through the wires much harder than he had before. A moment later Amanda stood and called out, "Seventy-seven feet per second," and the number came up on the scoreboard: 52.5 miles per hour.

A bell clanged, and Art's voice, magnified by a bullhorn, echoed around the room. "And we have a winner!" he called. "Please come to the counter and collect your prize!"

"Your turn now," the boy said.

"You sure?" Ruby asked. "You've already won a prize."

He was tall and skinny, with long arms, and his pretty sweetheart was gazing at him with adoration after his fast throw. Ruby didn't want to make him feel bad, but she'd already missed the screen a couple of times that day, and wasn't ready to do it again quite yet.

Especially not in front of Grumpy George.

The boy grinned at her. "Know you're faster than me," he said. "Stop jawing and show us what you got."

So she did, making sure before she went into her windup that George was watching. He was leaning against the wall, his face betraying nothing, but Ruby could see that he was paying attention.

She went all out. The ball hit the steel plate with a tremendous bang and went rolling back, by luck, right toward Grumpy George.

Or maybe not entirely by luck.

He picked up the ball, inspected its flattened side, then tossed it back to Ruby, his face expressionless.

The numbers clacked on the scoreboard.

Ninety-one miles per hour.

The article came out on Sunday, on the front page of the *Examiner*'s sport section. BROOKLYN GIRL IS WONDER "HURLER" read the headline, and in letters scarcely smaller, *Miss Ruby Thomas Is New "Queen of Diamonds" at Coney Island Attraction.*

Amanda had run down to the candy store at the crack of dawn to get the newspaper, and now she and Allie bent over the smeary black type and read every word of the article out loud, commenting over the parts they liked best.

Sore, weary from her long Saturday, Ruby lay on the sofa and listened.

"Look at this!" Amanda marveled. "'Though only a stone's (or a baseball's) throw from such attractions as Jolly Irene the Round, Lady Olga and her beard, and Captain Fred Walters (the "Blue Man"), Ruby Thomas is no sideshow. Instead, she is a talented pitcher with a gasoline-packed left wing, and some onlookers think there isn't a player in the major leagues—not even the great Babe Ruth—who could stand at home plate and return her speedy offerings with any consistent degree of success.'"

"Huh," Ruby said.

"I'm in here!" Allie said proudly. "Oh, and Amanda, too."

The photographer had taken pictures of Ruby on the mound, of the girls in their uniforms, of the speed machine and the painted backdrop and the fake Babe Ruth.

"And listen to *this*," Amanda went on. "'Walter Johnson is widely acknowledged as the fastest pitcher ever; even the great Ty Cobb has said that the Big Train's fast one intimidated him. The question that this reporter now must face: Does Diamond Ruby Thomas's fastball match the Big Train's in his prime? Well, we can't say it does—but we can't say it doesn't, either.'"

Ruby glanced at the clock. It was time to get up and go to work.

"Aunt Ruby?" Amanda said.

"What, sweetie?"

"Will this make a difference?"

"Let's hope so," Ruby said.

13

*t*heir elevated train got delayed at Kings Highway, which meant they reached Surf Avenue a few minutes late. Then, when they turned the corner onto Fifth Street, there was such a crowd milling about that Ruby thought there must be a fire somewhere.

But as usual, Amanda and Allie figured things out before she did. They were looking around, Allie's golden hair flying, her white teeth shining like Chiclets. Amanda's sparkling dark eyes and closed-mouth smile were filled with no less realization and pleasure.

"Aunt Ruby, don't you understand?" Allie said. "They're here for *you*."

And she was right. The crowd was lined up at the door of the Birdcage. They were here for Ruby.

"Guess they read the *Examiner,* too," Amanda said. Her face was calm, but her eyes were filled with something that looked a lot like joy.

Ruby said, "Guess so."

Jimmy was waiting for them at the front door. He stepped forward, shaking his head, and said, "You better not come up with a lame wing today—" He looked around and puckered his lips into a whistle. "Or any other time, either."

Ruby went in, the crowd murmuring as they recognized her. Art was standing behind the counter, the line snaking back toward the door as people handed him their money. "Glad you bothered to show up," he said to her. "Thought we might have a riot here if you stayed in bed today."

She just stood there, looking around.

He gave her a sudden, unexpected grin. "Wake up," he said, "get dressed, and throw the damn ball."

That day, and those that followed, were a blur. Ruby could barely distinguish one from another, and by the end of the week she felt like a clockwork girl made of gears and pulleys and levers, just like the scoreboard that Amanda could now operate without even looking.

Take the ball, throw the ball, watch the numbers click over.

Stand aside to let others throw.

Smile and wave.

Take the ball. Throw the ball.

Within two days of the surge in business, Samuel Cooper had installed three rows of bleacher seats near the front door, just as Gordon had suggested. BLEACHER SECTION: 50 cents, the sign hanging on the wall read, and during quieter moments Ruby began to recognize some of the regulars who chose merely to watch. There was a massively heavy man who sat for hours for his fifty cents, smiling all the while, a young man with only one arm, and a thin older woman with wiry hair. Ruby wondered what brought them here nearly every day.

But she was most curious about the lanky man of about

thirty-five who showed up several times, always dressed more colorfully than most visitors in a perfectly tailored but loudly checked suit, a bright red or blue bow tie, and a white straw hat with a colorful patterned band. When his gaze met hers, she saw that he had a long, narrow face and odd eyes that were as slanted and watchful as a cat's.

He would always tip his hat, but he never approached her. Once, curious, she held out a ball, offering him the chance to throw. He just grinned, shook his head, and continued to watch.

One morning Ruby noticed that her audience contained more than the usual number of children, thirty or forty of them with just a few adults. Art said they were orphans, residents of the Hebrew Orphan House up in Manhattan, brought out for a day in Coney Island.

Ruby remembered going to the Hebrew Orphan House for help. Like many others, it had turned down Ruby's pleas that first awful winter.

"A lot of those poor kids were orphaned during the epidemic back in '18," Art said, as if reading her thoughts. He looked at them sitting in neat rows in the bleachers, well behaved, their faces scrubbed for their big day out. "Poor kids," he said. "A lot of them probably don't even have any memories of their folks."

Ruby didn't reply. She wasn't sure what he knew about her own history.

And anyway, maybe it was a blessing not to remember those who had died. She often thought that Allie had an easier time of it than Amanda, for instance. To Allie, her father had always been the way he was now, and Evie had never existed. But Amanda knew what she'd lost.

This was all too much for Ruby to think about when she had to work. But that morning she paid almost no attention to the young men showing off for their girls, the older guys who used to play for neighborhood teams, the ones who swore they'd once hurled a ball past Honus Wagner.

Instead, she focused almost entirely on the orphans, teaching them how to throw, helping them get the ball through the wires, shooting a look at Amanda that her whip-smart niece understood, which resulted in the scoreboard telling the smallest children they were throwing the ball thirty, forty, even fifty miles an hour, making sure that everyone got a Baby Ruth bar, so that their scrubbed faces became chocolate smeared, as they should be.

"Is there a field near the House?" she asked Deborah, the harried young woman who was in charge.

"We use one in Central Park—it's not so far away," the woman replied.

"Good," Ruby said, and promised to come by someday soon to continue the lesson.

On another day a young man assaulted her.

She'd noticed him earlier, hanging around near the bleachers. He was in his early twenties, maybe, and showed all the familiar signs of a hard, brutal life: pale skin, bony wrists and skinny hands protruding from his patched, poorly fitting shirt, a long, barely healed scar alongside his jaw, close-cropped blond hair.

His staring dark eyes never seemed to leave her. He glared at Ruby like she'd done something terrible to him, like they had a history together. But she had absolutely no idea who he was. She knew they'd never met.

Even when she was throwing, even when her back was to him, she could feel his ferocious gaze on her, a cold sensation along her spine, the fine hairs rising on the back of her neck.

He went for her just as she finished throwing the ball, when she was off balance. She heard a shout from the crowd, and then the sound of footsteps, but only got half turned before he was on her.

They went down in a tangle of limbs, the back of Ruby's head hitting the edge of the concrete mound, dazing her, slowing down her reactions. For an instant she thought he'd be reaching for her breasts, like Mel Walters had, but this man, this lunatic, had a different goal.

She felt his hands going for her throat, saw his eyes staring down at her, spittle at the corners of his wide-stretched mouth. He was yelling something, but she had no idea what it was.

Then she woke up. Struck at his wrists until his grip loosened, then got both arms between them and hurled him off her.

She rolled over to get to her feet, saw him scrambling onto all fours, then gathering himself to spring on her again. But before he could do so, about ten people piled onto him. Ruby saw Art in the middle of it, and Gordon, too, red-faced with outrage.

With a last paroxysm of strength, her attacker broke away from the crowd, plowed his way to the door, and escaped. A few people chased after him, but most stayed close to Ruby, helping her up, asking if she needed a doctor. She felt like she was drowning in a tide of concern.

"I'm fine," she said again and again. "Really, I'm fine."

Finally she held up a hand to stop them. "He kept saying one word over and over," she said. "What was it?"

People exchanged glances.

"Tell me," Ruby insisted.

Someone said, "Jew."

"Who was he?" Ruby asked Art. "And why did he want to kill me?"

She was behind the counter with him and the girls, sipping a Coca-Cola someone had gotten for her while the uneasy crowd milled around.

Art shrugged, frowning. "Well, he was making about as much sense as a Chinaman, but my guess? The guy was with the Klan."

"The what?"

Amanda, sitting close by, said, "Aunt Ruby, the Ku Klux Klan. You know, the ones that don't like Negroes."

"Or women doing what women shouldn't do." Art gave Ruby a quick look. "Or Jews neither."

"I know what they are," Ruby said. "But don't they just live down south somewhere?"

"Not no more." Art frowned. "They're everywhere these days. Couple of times last year, they tried to close down our Wild Men of Borneo. You know, because they're darkies."

He shrugged. "But Mr. Cooper didn't put up with it, and after a while, they went away."

They sat in silence for a few moments. Then Ruby got to her feet to go back to work.

Art gave her another look. "*Is* you a Jew?" he asked.

Ruby started to say no. She'd never practiced the religion, never been to a synagogue or cracked open a Bible, didn't honestly know the first thing about it.

Then her chin lifted.

"My mama was," she said.

Art said, "Never would have guessed."

That evening, her brother Nick came to the Birdcage for the first time.

He showed up during what had become a regular evening break—a fifteen-minute pause when everyone was shooed out and the speed machine and Ruby herself given a rest. She was sitting on a wooden chair tilted back against the wall, her feet up on a bucket of balls, her eyes closed, when she heard Allie make a funny little sound and then say, "Daddy!"

Ruby opened her eyes. Nick was standing in the doorway, looking around. Even from across the room she could see the pale, taut skin of his face, the gleam of sweat on his forehead.

He had a black eye, a shiner that couldn't have been more than a day or two old.

Allie was hugging him, and he rested one hand on the top of her head. But Amanda still stood near the speed shack, as if unsure whether to go to him or run away.

Ruby brought the chair and her feet down to the floor with a bang, making everyone look her way. She stood and walked slowly across to her brother.

Before she could say anything to him, he said, "Ruby, I'm sorry."

"Sorry for what?" she asked. But he didn't answer, just turned his head to look at the man crowding through the door behind him.

Ruby took a look at the new arrival. Actually, she smelled him first, the strong whiff of some fancy cologne laid on thick. The next thing she noticed was his suit, easily the fanciest she'd ever seen, black with white pinstripes and a perfect fit. The tailoring must have been a challenge because the man was big, more than six feet tall with powerful shoulders and arms. The pants fit equally well over legs that were like tree stumps, and his polished shoes and brilliantined, combed-back hair both reflected the light from the hanging globes above.

He stepped inside and looked around, his big face settling into an expression of amusement. Then he focused his eyes, half hidden behind the rise of his thick cheeks, on Ruby.

"The star," he said, his voice a deep grumble.

She nodded. "Ruby Thomas. And you are?"

In the periphery of her vision she saw Art flinch.

The big man gave her a considering look from his deep-set eyes. But before he had the chance to answer—if he'd even meant to—a third man entered the room.

This one Ruby knew. It was David Wilcox, turning to close and bolt the door behind him.

Ruby, and Amanda with her, took an involuntary step back. Allie let go of her father's hand and hurried to their side.

No one spoke for a moment. Nick looked miserable. The big stranger strode past on a waft of cologne, looking up at the painted backdrops, examining the wire mesh with interest, paying no attention to anyone else in the room.

Wilcox was giving Ruby a hard look she hadn't seen from him before. "Doesn't matter who he is," he said. "Just keep your nose out of it."

Ruby looked at him. "Where's Mr. Cooper?"

His face darkened. She had the feeling that he wanted to hit her.

Instead he merely said, "We'll be here for a while, and then we'll be gone, and whether we're here or not is no bother of yours, either. Understand that?"

After a moment, Ruby gave a nod.

She heard a knock on the door, and then a voice calling out, "Hey, are you guys open?"

Wilcox glanced at Art, who without a word headed toward the door. Then he looked at Ruby again. "What are you waiting for?" he said. "We pay you to work, not to stand around."

"*You* don't pay me," she said.

He laughed at her.

While she threw for the evening crowd, Ruby saw the three men moving around the room. They checked out the speed machine and its shack—Amanda standing very still, white-faced, as they closed in on her—and then moved over to the prize counter, where Art looked barely less terrified than Amanda had. Ruby couldn't tell what they were looking at, or for, but their inspection was careful, and involved a lot of low talk between Wilcox and the big man.

As far as Ruby could tell, Nick never spoke.

After that, they headed into the dressing room. It felt like an invasion to Ruby, but there was nothing she could do about it.

They were in there a long time, and a couple of thumps and a slammed door indicated when they'd moved into the storage room beyond. After that it got quiet, and a few minutes later Ruby realized that they must have gone out the back door.

When the last customer was gone, and it was time to close up, Ruby went over to Art. "Who was *that*?" she asked.

But Art shook his head.

"Ain't saying a word," he said.

14

*a*t lunchtime a few days later, Samuel Cooper told her that the Birdcage would close early that evening. "There's a special guest coming, the daughter of a friend of mine, a fellow who has passed on, and she has a particular interest in seeing—in meeting Diamond Ruby. I won't be able to be here, but I'd like you to give her a private tour."

Ruby, halfway through her turkey on rye, nodded.

Cooper looked at her, as if waiting for questions. When she didn't say anything, he gave an uncomfortable shrug and went on. "Please treat her well."

"Sure," Ruby said.

After another moment, he said, "Thank you, dear," and turned away.

Ruby wondered what part of the story he wasn't telling her. She almost called out to ask, but decided not to bother. Whatever it was, she'd learn soon enough.

.　　.　　.

Samuel Cooper's special guest was a slender young woman of about Ruby's height, with full black hair cut into a bob, a sharp chin, lips that curved upward at the corners, and deep-set dark eyes beneath sculpted eyebrows. She was dressed in a dramatic wine-red dress and matching satin damask shoes.

Ruby had seen plenty of women with that haircut and dressed in similar clothes, but something about the visitor piqued her interest. It took a moment to figure it out: even half-obscured by the dress, the woman had powerful shoulders, muscular arms, and strong calves. She looked like an athlete, like someone better suited to a track-and-field uniform or swimming costume than to the elegant clothes she was wearing.

And there was something else interesting, too. The woman was blind.

It wasn't easy to tell, not at first. The woman's eyes weren't hidden behind dark glasses, and she seemed to be gazing around with great interest. Yet it became clear that she was depending on the descriptions being provided by her two companions, a roundish young man in a tan suit and a gray-haired woman wearing a flowing black dress.

Ruby went to meet them, with Allie and Amanda, suddenly shy, trailing a bit behind her.

"Thank you for inviting us," the young woman was saying to Art. She had a warm, musical voice. "And for letting us visit after hours." Her hands went to her ears. "I know how popular this show has become, and when there's so much noise indoors—well, it's a challenge for me."

"No problem," Art said. "Anytime."

"Let's see what I can learn without help," the woman went on. "Well, I smell fresh paint. And—the sharp smell of electricity, and several different kinds of cologne—and—"

"And perspiration?" Allie asked. "That's Aunt Ruby."

"Allie!" Amanda said.

The woman tilted her head. "Does that mean that Diamond Ruby is nearby?"

Ruby thought the woman knew very well that she had approached. After a moment's hesitation, she took the proffered hand. It, too, was strong, and what the woman did with it was half a handshake, half an exploration.

"You have long fingers," she said. "Do they help you grip the baseball?"

"Sure," Ruby said.

"I never thought of that," the woman said. "It must be a great aid to a pitcher to be able to wrap his—" She smiled. "*Her* fingers around the ball."

She let go of Ruby's hand. "I've heard these are quite extraordinary as well," she said, reaching for Ruby's left arm.

Ruby stepped away and said, "Please don't."

The woman's face colored, and her hand went to her mouth. The young man standing beside her grinned and said, "Our dear Helen takes liberties she never would have dared before she had her accident."

Helen's hands hung at her sides. Her face was still red. "It's true," she said. "Sometimes I can be quite thoughtless."

She shook her head. "Worse yet, we haven't even introduced ourselves. I'm Helen Connell, and this is my mother, Margaret, and our friend Paul Fitzsimmons."

With her dark eyes and wiry hair streaked with gray, Mrs. Connell had a fierceness about her that reminded Ruby of Mama. Paul seemed soft and unobtrusive beside her, with his round cheeks, thinning blond hair, and kind eyes. Yet, as Ruby shook his hand, he looked her over carefully. She felt as if she were being judged.

Both of the girls were much more interested in Helen than in her mother and friend. "Was it your accident that made you blind?" Amanda asked.

Ruby sighed. Clearly, discretion was one of the things she'd neglected to teach her nieces.

Helen recognized her discomfort and smiled. "Don't worry," she said. "I've heard that question many times—and I much prefer when people ask rather than merely wonder silently." She tilted her head, seeming to fix Ruby with her gaze. It was disconcerting. "Didn't dear Samuel tell you my story?"

"No," Ruby said. She hesitated. "He didn't have time."

"Oh, yes. No time." For a moment Helen's expression darkened. Then she smiled again and said, "Well, I *certainly* have time."

They walked over to the bleachers, Helen feeling her way through the unfamiliar territory, Paul helping her with gentle touches and quiet words. Perching on the edge of one of the benches, she said, "You don't even know me. Are you certain you want to hear this?"

"Of course we do," said Amanda. She and Allie were clearly consumed with curiosity.

"If you like," Ruby said.

"Okay." Helen took a breath. "I was a butterfly, a high diver in a show called *Pure Joy* up at the Majestic Theatre back in '19. I would dive one hundred and twenty-two feet from a platform into a water tank."

Don't waste your life, Mama had said. She would have considered Helen's chosen career unforgivably inconsequential.

The thought made an odd spark ignite somewhere inside Ruby. "I could tell when you came in," she said.

Helen tilted her head. "Tell what?"

"That you're . . . very strong."

"Oh!" Again Helen's face colored. "I'll take that as a compliment, so . . . thank you."

She turned back toward the girls. "Well, that year I dove every day for nearly six months. But then, on my one-hundred-and-seventy-fifth dive, I made a mistake. I got distracted by a firework someone set off in the crowd and neglected to tuck my chin. You have to do that, bend your neck, to take the impact of the water on your forehead. But I didn't, and the water hit me right across the eyes."

Her expression darkened. "Two days later, I was blind in my right eye. My left followed a few days later."

"Was there nothing—" Amanda looked stricken. "Nothing that could be done?"

Helen's smile was wistful. "We tried everything we could."

"Fourteen surgical operations in Europe," Paul said.

Mrs. Connell brushed the back of her hand across her eyes. "Too many!"

"Yes, too many." Helen took a breath. "And they didn't succeed. So now I can see only shadows."

She shook her shoulders. "But I'm not complaining. I'm learning to read Braille—I'm back to reading children's books! I've made many new friends, I can still sing and dance, I can even get to the subway by myself, as long as I don't trip over a baby buggy on my way." She smiled. "And, since I could see once, I know what everything looks like. I feel so sorry for those who have been blind all their lives—how terrible not to know what the blue sky looks like, or the green of a good friend's eyes."

Paul grinned.

"Our uniforms are white, with ruby-red stripes," Ruby said.

"Are they?" Helen nodded. "Yes, I can *see* them."

They sat in silence for a moment. Again, Ruby felt Paul's gaze on her. She took a breath and said, "Helen, would you like me to show you what I do?"

Helen smiled. "Yes," she said, "if you would do me that kindness."

But before they could stand, there was a sharp rap on the door. A moment later a loud voice came through. "Know you're in there, Connell!" it said. "Let me in or I'll knock it down!"

Helen gave a smile of unabashed pleasure. "He's here!" she said, getting to her feet.

"Who?" Amanda looked immediately suspicious, even alarmed, as if the mad Klansman was about to make a return appearance.

But Art was already swinging the door open, and his eager look put Ruby's mind at ease.

Two men walked in. The first was a middle-aged gent wearing a fine suit and swinging a polished wooden cane. The second, also dressed elegantly, was carrying three Nathan's hot dogs in each hand. He was big, with a broad chest and thin legs and a moon-shaped face that crinkled up into a grin when he saw Helen standing there, and again when he took in Ruby in her pin-striped uniform.

"You know, kid," he said to her, through a mouthful of hot dog, "that guy you have swinging that big bat out front? You should tell him he doesn't look a bit like me."

Allie and Amanda were, quite simply, unable to move. Even Ruby was thunderstruck.

And how could she not be? She was, after all, standing before the most famous man on earth. Rudolph Valentino or President Harding would have been lucky to get their pictures in the newspaper half as many times as Babe Ruth did.

Helen, smiling, had her hands out. The Babe strode over to her, then looked down at his own hands, burdened with hot dogs. With a shrug, he handed them over to his well-dressed friend, wiped his fingers on his trousers, then took Helen in his arms and spun her around until her laughter rang through the Bird-cage like a pealing bell.

When he put her down again, she was breathing hard and red in the face. The Babe shook hands with Paul and kissed Mrs. Connell, looking for all the world like he wanted to spin her, too. Then he looked around till his gaze fell on Ruby again.

This time he really seemed to see her, and at once his eyes were filled with interest and speculation. He came over, put his hands on his hips, looked her up and down. "Huh," he said. "People have been talking you up to me, but here you are, just a little thing."

She looked up into his face, those odd, broad cheeks, flat nose, and eyes as pale and clear as a hawk's. "Don't have to be big to throw hard."

He stared at her for a moment, wide-eyed, then guffawed. "Think you could throw one past me?"

"I don't know," Ruby said. "I've never seen you play, Mr. Ruth."

He frowned. "First of all, kid, my friends call me Jidge," he said. "Second, you never seen me play? We'll have to do something about that. You need to visit that big stadium they built for me. I'll make sure you all get some tickets."

Helen linked her arm in his and said, "And Jidge will, you know, as long as someone reminds him. Otherwise, he'll forget before he walks out this door."

The Babe grinned at that, unoffended. "Didn't forget you, did I?"

"No, you didn't." Helen turned her head toward Ruby. "Jidge and I met when we made a moving picture together back in, oh, 1917 or so."

"I jumped into a pool from about twenty feet up," the Babe said. "That was high enough for me."

"Then, while I was recovering from all those surgeries, he visited me often." She gave an odd half-smile. "Everyone knows how much Babe Ruth likes to visit unfortunates."

"Hey!" The Babe looked very discomfited.

"But it's the truth. I was one."

The Babe covered up his embarrassment by going back to his dignified friend and retrieving his hot dogs. A minute later

Amanda and Allie were sharing his feast and laughing at something he'd said to them.

Helen, listening, smiled. "Once you're his pal, you're his pal forever," she said fondly. "It's just that he has so much going on, you know."

"I can only imagine," Ruby said.

"Hey, kid!"

Ruby looked over. The Babe was finishing up the last hot dog. "Didn't I hear you could throw a little?"

Ruby nodded. "You might have heard that."

He turned his palms up. "So am I gonna see it, or are you too busy yakking with Helen to show me?"

"I guess I could throw a couple," Ruby said.

The Babe rolled his eyes and exchanged glances with his dapper associate, who had been standing quietly in the background with Helen's mother, leaning on his cane. The man, who hadn't said a word that Ruby'd heard since he'd come in, looked amused at her manner.

Allie scurried over to her chosen spot for chasing rebounding pitches while Amanda walked more sedately to the speed shack. Ruby, not feeling like a clockwork girl now, got up to her position on the mound, her head down, studying the trail of scuff marks and worn-out patches she'd made, then bent and picked up a baseball.

She didn't do anything fancy, didn't even try to throw the hardest she could. For the first time, she wanted only to get the ball through the wire mesh and against the wall.

If she was wild, she knew that Ruth would lose interest in a hurry. He'd think it had all been tall tales, or that the people who'd been touting her didn't know what they were talking about, or that she was impressive not because she could throw hard, but merely because, as a girl, she could throw at all.

"Helen?" she said.

Helen, who'd been standing beside her mother, tilted her head. "Yes, Ruby?"

"This is going to be loud, so I want you to be ready."

That brought a smile. "Do I put my hands over my ears?"

"Not that loud."

Still, Helen squeezed her eyes closed like a little child. Ruby took a deep breath, wound up, sighted, and threw.

It wasn't the best pitch she'd ever thrown, but it traveled straight and true, brushing through the wires and hammering against the steel plate with a satisfying clang. The ball bounced toward the prize counter, Allie in pursuit.

"My goodness," Paul said.

Helen opened her eyes. "That was surprising even though I was waiting for it. How do you *do* that?"

Ruby didn't reply, but looked past toward the Babe, though she could barely bring herself to. She was afraid he'd appear disappointed, or even worse, bored.

But what she glimpsed was the Babe and the other man looking at each other. Ruth inclined his head a little, as if asking a question, and the older man waggled his back and forth, his lips pressed together in a thoughtful way.

Then the Babe turned to look at Ruby, a huge grin spreading across his face. "Okay, kid, maybe you *could* have outthrown me in my pitching days," he said.

The number clicked over on the scoreboard: 82.5 miles per hour.

"Can you get it over even faster than that?"

"A little," Ruby said.

"A *lot*," Allie interjected. Ruby shot her a quelling glance, but both Helen and the Babe laughed.

"Throw another," the Babe said.

This one was eighty-six miles per hour.

He whistled. "You got a curve, too?"

Ruby frowned. "I used to work on one, but it doesn't amount to much. They don't pay me for curveballs."

"Huh." The Babe walked unhurriedly over to her, then reached down and took a ball from the bin. "Look," he said, holding it in his callused left hand. "I gripped mine this way, with my middle finger on the top seam and my thumb on the bottom. See?"

Ruby said yes.

"Good." Talking baseball, he was all business, showing none of the jollity and recklessness and extravagance he was famous for. "Now, I lay my first finger here, beside the middle one, but I don't use it to hold the ball. It's just comfortable that way. Wait, let me show you."

He took off his suit jacket and dropped it on the floor. Then stood on the mound, peering in at the steel plate, a large man with an expanding waistline beneath his expensive white shirt and gray trousers. "You have to keep the same speed in your arm as when you're throwing a fast one, but the motion of your wrist is different," he said. "Watch."

Ruby watched as he went into a seemingly effortless windup and let go of a pitch that swooped and dipped through the mesh before striking the plate.

"Wow," Amanda said.

The Babe grinned. "You try," he said to Ruby.

It took her about ten pitches, seven of which didn't even touch the screen, and several more suggestions from the Babe, before she threw one that dipped the way she wanted it to.

"Quick learner," he said.

"Doesn't feel like it."

"Well, work on it when you can." The Babe paused. "How about another pitch? A fadeaway? A changeup?" He gave her a grin. "Any freak pitches? Shine ball? Spitter?"

Any pitch I throw, Ruby thought, is a freak pitch. But she shook her head.

"Well, you could get by with just the two, if you had to, with the speed you have." He looked at her. "But I'll teach you some other tricks next time."

"I'd like that," Ruby said. Her mouth felt dry.

She turned and, seeing that Helen was sitting on the bleachers beside her mother, walked over. "Sorry we got distracted. Would you like to see how this setup works?"

Helen smiled. "If it's not too much trouble."

Ruby led her to the screen, explaining its use as Helen ran the tips of her fingers over the fragile mesh. Then they moved over to the steel plate and the shed, where Amanda told her how the speed machine and the scoreboard operated.

Helen pulled the levers, listened to the clicking of the number tiles, and said, "I see."

Ruby took a breath, began to speak, then hesitated. She looked over at Paul, who was, as ever, watching her.

"Helen," she said, "I could show you what I do, if you'd like. I mean . . . how I do it."

After a moment, Helen nodded. "Yes," she said, "I *would* like that."

As the Babe stayed with the girls to play with the scoreboard, Ruby led her back to the mound and helped her step up onto it. When the two of them were standing there, Helen behind her, Ruby said, "Put one hand here, on my hip, and one here, on my left shoulder. Just the tips of your fingers—don't hold on."

Still, delicate as it was, she was uncomfortable with the contact. No one ever touched Ruby except for the girls.

"Like this?" Helen's face was flushed, and it seemed to Ruby that she was trying to make up with all her other senses what sight no longer provided. Everything about her seemed on edge, almost quivering—her fingers twitched, her nostrils flared, and she leaned forward to make sure she didn't miss a thing.

"Just like that," Ruby said. "Okay, I'm going to throw one now. Are you ready?"

Helen nodded. Ruby went into a careful windup—the last thing she wanted to do was knock Helen off the mound—and lobbed the ball through the wires and off the steel plate with a comparatively gentle thump.

"I felt it!" Helen said. Her face was aglow. "The way the muscles of your shoulder bunched and then released, the way you shifted your weight. Now I know why you can throw so hard."

No, Ruby thought. You don't know the most important part, because I haven't let you.

"Your turn," she said.

Helen's hand went to her mouth.

"You're an athlete," Ruby went on. "I told you, I saw it the moment you came in. So I'll bet you can throw."

"Well, I used to be able to . . ." Helen said.

"Then you still can." Ruby took her hand again and showed her the dimensions of the concrete mound and where to stand on it. Helen seemed to know instinctively in which direction the screen and steel plate lay. Maybe it was a matter of sound, Ruby thought, of echoes, of judging the movements of the air.

"Do you remember how far away the wires are, and how high off the ground?" she asked.

Helen nodded.

"And how far from the wires to the wall?"

"Yes."

Ruby handed her a ball. "Then you're ready."

For a moment, Helen stood very still, her expression apprehensive, her hands rubbing the ball, exploring the slickness of the horsehide and the ridges of the stitching. Then she leaned back, swung her right arm in a tight circuit, and let go.

It was a creditable pitch, reasonably straight though not hard.

It brushed through the wires (Ruby saw the corners of Helen's mouth turn up at the slight scratching sound) and thumped off the steel plate.

"I did it!" Helen said. There were spots of perspiration along her hairline.

"Knew you could," Ruby said.

But Helen raised a hand, waiting. A moment later, the clacking of the scoreboard came to them: 33.5 miles per hour.

Ruby relayed the total and Helen laughed. "I guess my career as a major-league pitcher was just nipped in the bud."

"You throw harder than plenty of the men who come in here," Ruby said.

"And look a whole lot better than the palookas who pitch against me," said Babe Ruth, an absolutely delighted Allie perched on his strong shoulders.

At the door, Helen said, "Thank you, Ruby. This was more fun than I've had in—well, in ages."

"True," Paul said, grinning. "Then again, she's usually just stuck with us."

But Ruby barely heard the words. She was struggling with herself, and wasn't sure whether she had won or lost when she found herself saying, "Helen, give me your right hand."

Helen blinked, then complied. Ruby placed the hand against her arm near the shoulder. "Now you'll be able to see where I get the speed on my pitches," she said, not yet letting go. "But be ready. My arms are—not like other people's. They're very long."

She released Helen's hand and stood rigid as the delicate fingers worked their way along her biceps and down the length of her forearm.

"Oh!" Helen's voice was barely more than a breath. "I do see."

Then, finishing the exploration, she said, "You know, they're not *that* long."

Ruby said, "What?"

"Well, of course they're long—and you're right, I'm sure that's a big reason why you can throw so fast. But I'll bet if you took a look at some baseball pitchers—men—you'd see that their arms are long, too. I mean, my shoulders are big and my legs are strong, always have been, which is why I was a good diver and swimmer. We all have something."

She paused and smiled. "I wonder if your arms seem longer in your eyes than in anyone else's."

"Well—" Ruby said. Her cheeks were hot.

"Yes," Helen said. "Well! Will you allow us to come back to visit sometime?"

"Of course."

"I'll come back, too, bring some pals," the Babe said, arriving at the door and dumping Allie back onto her feet. He turned to go, his quiet associate beside him.

"Wait a second," Ruby said.

The two men turned to look at her.

"I don't even know your name, or who you are," she said to the gray-haired man.

"Colonel Edward Fielding," he said, shaking her hand. "And I'm nobody important."

Babe Ruth grinned.

"Believe *that*," he said, "and I got a spanking new stadium to sell you."

15

*t*he press never got wind of Babe Ruth's visit to the Birdcage. Given the magnifying glass that he seemed to live under, Ruby had expected a battalion of reporters to invade the next morning, asking how many hot dogs the Babe had eaten, what he was wearing, and how hard he'd thrown.

But . . . nothing. When she asked Art about it, his face regained a trace of the awestruck expression it had had that night. "That's Jidge for you," he said. "He does it all the time, visiting orphans and poor children and the like."

Ruby kept her smile to herself as Art went on, oblivious to what he'd just said. "Think the writers and him have made this, you know, *deal*—he gets to make, like, 'secret' visits in peace, as long as he gives 'em what they need other times."

Ruby said, "I'm guessing the Babe lives up to his end of the bargain."

"You mean those pictures of him playing football and riding horses and boxing Jack Dempsey and all that other hoo-hah?" Art grinned. "Yeah, well, I think Jidge loves all that stuff. He'd do it anyway, just for fun, even if nobody was watching. Since it's what the sportswriters want, too, it works out for everybody."

Ruby said, "Think he'll come back?"

"You kidding? He might come back *tonight*. You're like his new toy, Diamond Ruby."

The Babe didn't return that night, but he did show up again, a week later, with some of his teammates. And it wasn't only Yankees who discovered the Birdcage as the days went on. Some Brooklyn Dodgers (Ebbets Field being only a short subway ride away) and some Giants from up in Manhattan, and a couple of players from a new minor-league team that played in Washington Park, would come by after the doors shut to get a look at the girl with the killer speedball.

Ruby guessed that the ballplayers, or their teams, were paying Cooper and Wilcox to have the Birdcage become their private after-hours club, a safe, quiet place to gather. If so, Ruby didn't see an extra penny. She didn't mind, though, not much. All in all, the ballplayers were good company.

They clearly liked coming by, especially since it meant they got to use the speed machine. In and around eating hot dogs and smoking cigars and sipping from flasks containing liquids that were never offered to Ruby, they'd engage in throwing contests that would last for hours, keeping Amanda and Allie busy well after their bedtimes.

The girls never complained. They loved what had turned into an almost nightly party. The men brought them sweets, especially candy bars from all the cities they visited with their teams. Soon Allie started collecting the wrappers, carefully pasting the Fat Emmas and Chicken Dinners and U-Nos into a scrapbook Ruby bought her. Every one represented a city she was determined to visit someday.

Most nights, the three of them used the sagging cots in the dressing room. It was easier to fall into bed here in a tangle of warm limbs and wrinkled sheets than to trek home on the elevated every night. It was also a relief to avoid the possibility of finding Nick there in one of his moods.

Ruby was introduced to countless ballplayers, but their names meant nothing to her. She'd lost track of the game and most of its players after 1918.

At first, looking at them, all she could think of was that these were men who made a living playing baseball. Real baseball, not some ridiculous sideshow version where the mound was made of concrete and "home plate" was steel and bolted to the wall. Ruby was embarrassed to be standing in front of them in her pretend uniform.

But they all took her costume in stride, making nothing but good-natured jokes about it. ("If Art Nehf looked half as good as you up there on the mound, I'd never get a hit off him!") And when Ruby threw the ball, all traces of humor fled from their faces.

"Wish we could sign you," one of the Yankees said. "Put you next to Shawkey, Bush, and Hoyt, we'd win hundred and forty games, easy."

"Might not lose a single one," another said.

"Guarantee we'd win the Series."

"Well, we're gonna do that anyway."

"Yeah, true."

"You want to go out sometime?"

That was actually part of a different conversation, a question posed to Ruby by one of the Giants, a lightweight, weedy guy with a sharp nose and little eyes. "I know a great juice joint just three blocks from here, open all night," he said. "Whatta ya say?"

Ruby said no.

She got asked that a lot of times, occasionally with a little more grace and charm, and she always said no.

. . .

The third time Babe Ruth visited, with a flock of other Yankees, one of them was an enormous young man Ruby knew she'd never seen before. He was barely more than a boy, maybe a couple of years older than she was, and so painfully shy that he blushed scarlet when Ruby even looked up into his face.

The whole time he was there, she never heard him speak a word.

"His name's Gehrig," the Babe told her. "He's just out of college, Columbia University, but I guess they didn't teach him much about the real world." He grinned. "Don't know if he's gonna make it—he stumbles around a lot in the field—but boy, can he hit the baseball."

Whenever the Babe stopped by, he spent most of his time eating, smoking, clowning around on the mound, and joking with his teammates. But he always made sure to give plenty of attention to Allie and Amanda, who idolized him. He seemed to get unending pleasure out of them—and out of the young children the other players sometimes brought along—arriving with little gifts, roughhousing with Allie, asking Amanda polite questions, and, most importantly, treating them both like equals, like he was still a kid, too.

"He's always like this," one of his teammates said, watching alongside Ruby. "Does what he pleases, and doesn't give a damn what anybody else thinks."

Something Ruby never forgot.

During working hours, a good number of girls and women came to the Birdcage, but almost always in the company of men. So when a small group of well-dressed older women came in alone and watched her carefully, Ruby took notice.

Though she was more subtle about it than Allie, who frankly stared.

During her next break, the ladies approached her. They were led by a particularly imposing woman in a suit, her face carefully made up and her ears and neck gleaming with diamonds.

Facing her, Ruby was reminded vividly of the imperious suffragists who'd filled the meeting rooms back when she was young. She'd rarely been able to speak a word in their presence, and now again she was tongue-tied.

Luckily, the woman felt perfectly comfortable doing most of the talking. "Miss Thomas," she said, "you are extraordinary."

Behind her, the rest of her cadre nodded.

"Thank you," Ruby said, feeling about six years old.

"My name is Josephine Collier, and I am the principal of the Collier School for Girls in Tarrytown," the woman went on. "I am also the chairwoman of the New York City Federation of Women's Organizations and head of the Committee for the Advancement of the Modern Girl."

Ruby didn't know how to respond to that, since she'd never heard of the school, the federation, the committee—or even, if she was forced to admit it, Tarrytown.

But Miss Collier appeared to be waiting for her to say something, so at last she said, "I don't think I have time to go to school right now."

Miss Collier blinked and then smiled, looking suddenly much more human. "That is not what I am asking—though I have no doubt that you would be a fine addition to our student body."

Again she waited for a response, and again Ruby was at a loss. Finally, thinking about current fashions and voting rights and movie stars, she said, "Honestly, I don't know very much about the modern girl."

Miss Collier blinked. "Oh no, my dear girl, you don't understand," she said after a moment. "We're here because you *are* one."

It was the silliest thing Ruby had heard in ages.

·　　·　　·

An hour later, all the lights in the Birdcage went out. Ruby was just going into her windup when she heard a loud buzzing sound. The hanging lamps flickered, grew very bright for an instant, and then, with a pop, plunged the windowless Birdcage into darkness.

It wasn't the first time this had happened, and alongside the squeals and laughter of the small crowd inside, Ruby could hear shouts and doors slamming that indicated that the Birdcage wasn't the only attraction being affected. She had heard talk about overloaded boxes, increased demand due to the streetlamps along the Boardwalk, and other gibberish, but hadn't paid any attention. All she knew was that with the speed machine not functioning, she and the girls would now have an unexpected break. That was fine with her.

Someone swung the door open, letting in a sudden flood of late-afternoon sunshine. The crowd dispersed, and Ruby headed out as well, the girls following.

Art was standing in the doorway, looking out at the street. "So much for setting any records with receipts today," he said. "Only shows doing business now are the ones don't need electricity."

He turned to look at Ruby. "Don't take too long. Sometimes they get the power running again in just fifteen minutes."

More like half an hour, Ruby thought. But she nodded and stepped out into the warm sunlight, blinking like some night creature until her eyes adjusted. All around them, the tidal crowds flowed past, and if anyone thought it was strange to see three girls in baseball uniforms, no one said anything.

Allie said, "Let's go ride on the Giant Racer!"

Amanda grimaced. "I hate that ride."

"No time." Ruby paused. "But I'll buy you shaved ice on Surf Avenue."

That seemed to be an acceptable alternative. They walked toward the wide avenue, with its custard stands and movie theaters and haberdashers, but after they'd gone only a few steps, Amanda said, "Something's burning."

Then Ruby saw it, too: dark billowing smoke rising against the blue sky a block or so past the avenue. A moment later the acrid odor reached them as well. Ahead they could see a scurry of activity, cars stopped in the middle of the street, people staring, some running toward the fire, others moving more slowly.

Drawn to the tumult, they made their way through the crowd. When they reached the burning house, a small thing built out of shoddy wood, penny nails, and tar paper, it was nearly consumed. Flames leaped from the broken windows and spread across the roof, and even the few paltry bushes that had stood near the front door were ablaze.

"Why aren't they helping?" Allie asked, pointing at the firemen who'd been at the scene when they arrived.

It was a good question. Three fire trucks were parked in the street in front of the burning building, two shiny new pumpers and an old one that looked like it had begun its life as a horse-drawn wagon. But the firemen were employing their hoses only to soak the houses on either side of the burning one.

"They probably got here too late," Ruby said.

"They made sure they got here too late," said a man standing beside them.

Ruby looked at him. He was elderly, with a sharp, bony face and thin white hair peeking out around the brim of his hat.

"It was *their* house," he said, jerking a thumb, "and now they'll go back where they came from."

Ruby followed the direction of his thumb. He was pointing at a family: a young father, a mother who barely looked older than Ruby, a little boy clinging to his father's leg, and a swaddled baby girl in her mother's arms.

A Negro family.

They were just standing there like all the other onlookers,

staring at their home burning down. There were tears on the woman's cheeks, but the man looked dazed, as if he couldn't comprehend what he was seeing.

Ruby wondered what she would do if it were *her* home. Certainly not just stand there.

She looked at the elderly man. He nodded and grinned a little at her expression. "They were warned," he said. "Didn't listen. Now they'll go."

"Warned by who?" she asked.

But the man just winked and made a gesture with his hands, sketching a hood in the air around his head.

Ruby thought about the newspaper headlines she'd seen about the spread of the Ku Klux Klan across New York City. The anger hot inside her, she grabbed Allie's hand and glanced at Amanda. "Come on."

"What will those people do?" Allie asked as they walked back to the Birdcage, carrying the smell of smoke on their uniforms and hair. "Where will they live?"

Ruby didn't reply. She was tamping down her anger and thinking about the man who had attacked her. Perhaps that, too, had been a warning.

If so, she hadn't listened, either.

She could tell something was wrong the moment they got back to the Birdcage. It took only one look at Art's pale face to see it.

"Mr. Cooper is dead," he said.

Ruby stood still in shock.

"Apoplexy, is what I heard," Art said, struggling with the difficult word. "He didn't show for lunch with some people. They found him in his office, stone cold."

Amanda straightened, expressionless, eyes glittering. Allie began to cry.

But Ruby didn't have time for any of that. Her mind was

working furiously. That was the only way to survive, by figuring out what was going to happen and then planning what to do about it.

"Is David Wilcox going to take over?" she asked.

"Sure," Art said. "He's been waiting a long time for this."

Wilcox stopped by that night at closing time. He was dressed in a black suit, his ruddy face suitably solemn as he came through the door.

He looked them over as soon as he locked the door behind him, surveying the Birdcage, the two girls standing very still with their eyes on the ground, and finally Ruby herself.

Then he smiled. For the first time revealing his real smile, teeth showing behind his ever-present cigar

"Everything's going to be different now," he said.

16

*n*ick stood there, holding in his arms a worn cardboard car-
ton, maybe a dozen others stacked four high on the concrete at his feet.

He'd jumped when Ruby entered the alley behind him, casting a heavy shadow across the trash-strewn pavement, and she'd
heard glass bottles clinking against each other. Now, his face half
hidden in the shadows, he looked at her as if deciding how to
react, which approach to take.

Finally he said, "You can't come back here."

"No one told me that rule."

"You're not supposed to know what we're doing."

Ruby put her hands on her hips. She could hear the sound
of laughter from the ballplayers gathered inside the Birdcage,
a happy shriek from Allie, and the thump of a ball off the steel
plate. Someone shouted down the street, and in the distance
she could hear blaring bagpipes, ballyhoo for some sideshow or
other.

"Come on, Nick," she said. "You think I was never going to find out?"

She'd guessed what was going on the first time Nick had shown up, when he'd trailed like a pet dog behind Wilcox and the man with the brilliantined hair. Since then, she'd heard thumps and bangs and, once, the sound of breaking glass from behind the locked door in her dressing room. You'd have to be an idiot not to know what it all meant.

Rumrunners from overseas and down south were flooding New York City with illegal alcohol—and their landing points were the beaches and inlets all along the stretch from Manhattan Beach up to Gravesend. The back of the Birdcage was one of countless way stations on the road that started with the manufacturers and ended in the stomachs of those thousands, millions, who didn't care that drinking booze was illegal.

"You're going to end up in jail," she said to Nick.

He met her gaze. "Only if you turn me in."

She stood in silence for so long that eventually he turned and walked into the dark storeroom. Ruby heard the bottles rattle as he put the box down, and then he was back, looking at her as if she was a stranger standing in his way.

"Clear out," he said. "I have work to do."

"Not this."

"Yes, this." For a moment, she recognized her brother. His hands went to his head. "Otherwise—I think so much. I can't stop. I have to stay busy."

"Not doing this," she said.

He stepped closer to her. His face emerged from the shadow, and she saw the nakedness of it, the anguish. She couldn't remember the last time she'd really looked at him.

"Ruby, I have to work," he said, "and no one else will hire me."

•   •   •

Before they parted, he promised not to tell Wilcox what she'd seen.

But maybe he forgot his promise, or maybe one of Wilcox's spies had spotted her in the alley. Whichever it was, that very evening the new boss of Fantasyland found out that she'd been poking around where she wasn't supposed to.

She could tell the moment Wilcox came through the Birdcage door after closing time that night. The stiffness in his back, the way his cheeks looked even more flushed than usual, a certain way he held his head, looking at her only out of the corners of his eyes like an angry dog or a bear.

He spoke a few words to Art, too low for Ruby to make out, and Art, stricken, went out the door without looking back. Wilcox bolted it behind him, turned, and came toward Ruby. No delay, no hesitation.

Allie, who'd run to the corner, stood frozen, mouth open, face drained of color. But Amanda, as brave as her mother used to be, and as quick to understand what was happening, stepped fearlessly in front of Ruby.

Wilcox barely flicked his wrist. Amanda cried out, her hands going to her mouth as she fell. She lay on her side, the first threads of blood welling up around her fingers.

Ruby went for Wilcox. But he was too quick for her, and too strong. She saw his fist coming, and then she was spinning around and falling onto her back, the overhead lights gleaming in her eyes, a strange whistling sound in her ears.

Before she could even take a breath, he had yanked her to her feet by one arm and shoved her into the dressing room. As he slammed the door behind them, Ruby heard Allie start to wail.

With a quick movement of his arm, he threw her back against the table. His fist went back up. She looked at him through swelling, blood-filled eyes and said, "You leave us alone, and I won't say anything."

He barely seemed to be listening, but at least his fist didn't move.

"But you hit me again," she went on, "and I'll bring in the feds."

He didn't say a word for a long time. Too long. But then some of the rigidity left him. He shook out his hand and drew in a breath. The angry gleam in his eyes faded a little.

But just a little. "Okay," he said. "Deal. But if you decide to sing, understand that I've got friends all over. *All over*. And you? Who do you got? Nobody. Sam Cooper is dead, and you're all alone."

He leaned in close and spoke into her ear. "You breathe a word of this, about what you saw, about what just happened, I'll know. I'll know right away," he said. "And then I'll come and kill your brother. I'll kill your little girls. And I'll make you watch when I do."

He went out the back door into the storeroom. When he was gone, Ruby, her right eye already almost swollen shut, her head spinning, made her way out of the dressing room. Allie was in her arms immediately, white-faced, crying. But Amanda, her mouth swollen, bloodstains all down the front of her uniform, stood apart.

"Is he coming back?" she asked, her words made indistinct by the swelling and pain.

"No," Ruby said.

Not right away.

Ten minutes later, though, Ruby heard the front door rattle, saw it creak open. She felt as dizzy, as sick as she could ever remember, but she stepped forward.

It was Tania, the seamstress, carrying a heavy cloth bag over her shoulder. She slammed the door behind her and looked at Ruby and Amanda.

"Well," she said, "ain't you two a sight."

Ruby said, "What are you doing here?"

"Giving some help to people who look like they need it."

"How—"

"Art knew where to find me. You think you're the first person who ever crossed Wilcox and paid for it?"

She dumped the contents of the bag onto the prize counter. Ruby saw jars of creams and liniments, a bottle of some thick green liquid, various tins whose labels she didn't recognize.

Tania grimaced. "You two, you're going to feel bad, next few days. These things, they'll make you feel better. At least a little."

Reaching for one of the small jars, she gestured toward Amanda. "Come here, sweetie," she said, prying off the top. "You first."

The man who followed Babe Ruth into the Birdcage the next night was so famous that even the other ballplayers seemed a little bashful around him. He was so famous that Ruby knew that the entire room would fill with photographers popping their smelly flashbulbs if they so much as guessed he might be here. He was so famous that even Ruby, who paid little attention to such things, recognized him right away.

It had been a long, tough day, her hardest by far. She'd never thrown worse. Despite all of Tania's best efforts, her head still had spun so badly whenever she went into her windup that she thought she might fall off the mound, and after her first few throws, she realized that she'd never make it through the day if she didn't conserve her strength.

So she did, aiming the ball at the wires and the wall instead of rearing back, as was her usual habit. Still, she missed her target half a dozen times, and even when the ball went where she wanted it to, it rarely traveled faster than sixty miles per hour. Sometimes she didn't break fifty.

Tania had come by with her makeup case before opening time and had worked hard to cover both Ruby and Amanda's visible bruises, but there was only so much she could do. Ruby had had to shrug off all sympathetic comments and questions about her black eye, while Amanda had brushed out her hair and let it hang down in front of her face.

She'd also spent the day crouched in the speed shack, showing herself as little as possible.

On top of everything else, it figured that this would be a day when the Birdcage was filled with ex-professional ballplayers, college athletes, and other fine specimens of modern-day masculinity, every one of whom had a better throwing arm than Ruby usually encountered in a week. In addition to those who won because she missed the wires, four young men (four!) outthrew her and walked away with their two-dollar rewards.

Art had spent the whole day behind the counter in a welter of embarrassment and guilt. Red-faced, tongue-tied, he'd tried to apologize, but Ruby had told him to forget it. She didn't blame him. He had a job to keep, a family to feed. He hadn't signed up to be her bodyguard.

By the time the endless day finally drew to a close, Ruby thought that her head might explode from the relentless pounding. If she moved too fast, lights and other objects still left trails across her vision. She hadn't been able to eat or drink anything all day except cups of some bitter elixir that Tania had brewed up.

Not recognizing the newcomer, Allie went running over to greet the Babe as she always did. Amanda followed more sedately, her hair over her face. Ruby went to join them, wishing she looked and felt closer to herself.

The Babe scooped Allie up onto his hip and reached out to brush Amanda's hair away. Then he froze.

"Someone hit you," he said.

He raised his gaze to look at Ruby, and there was an expression in his eyes she'd never seen before. She understood: He thought she might have done it. He thought she might have struck her niece.

She remembered that he'd spent years in a home for wayward boys. He must have known plenty of kids who were beaten by their parents or some other relative. Maybe it had even happened to him.

But then he got a look at her face. His went oddly still for a moment, and his eyes grew even darker. She could tell that his anger, just as fierce, was no longer directed at her.

"Who did this to you two?" he asked.

Ruby looked down at the ground, then back up. She'd been lying all day, but she found it much harder to lie to him.

Still, she had to try. "No one," she said, cursing herself that her voice didn't sound stronger and more convincing. "Amanda and me, we were in a car accident." She forced a smile. "A jitney we were on last night, a real broken-down old flivver."

He gave his head a tiny shake, back and forth, as if to say, That wasn't even a good try. Then, without taking his eyes off hers, he said, "Jack, come here. There's something I want you to see."

A moment later, the Babe's guest walked away from a knot of admirers and came up to them. He was a powerful-looking young man with a strong chin, curly black hair, eyebrows like stripes of war paint over dark, piercing eyes, the kind of beard you had to shave twice a day, and a nose that looked like it had been broken more than once.

"What happened to these two girls?" the Babe asked him.

His guest glanced at Amanda. "This one was hit with an open hand, I'd say backhand," he said in a surprisingly soft voice. "That cut on her lip came from a ring."

He raised his gaze to Ruby. "He wasn't fooling around with this one. It was a straight right, with a lot of force behind it." He brought his face in closer to hers. "You're lucky he didn't blind you in that eye, but I bet he still rung your bell pretty good, didn't he?"

She looked at him. What was the point of bluffing when no one believed you?

"Yeah, pretty good," she said. "Feels like my brain is still bouncing around in my head."

She took a breath, then added, "Mr. Dempsey."

Jack Dempsey nodded in sympathy. "Sure know how *that* feels. You know I worked as a saloon fighter back when I was a kid?"

Ruby shook her head and winced.

"Yeah. Not much bigger than you, I was, and sometimes I'd feel like that for weeks at a time."

He gave the Babe a sidelong look. "Still, the guys who fought me felt worse."

But Ruth wasn't listening. He was still staring at Amanda.

"Do you good to get some rest in a dark room, you know," Dempsey said to Ruby. His eyes strayed around the Birdcage. "But sometimes you got no choice but to work, right?"

"Right," Ruby said.

The Babe dragged his gaze back to her. "Who did this to you?" he asked again, almost spitting out the words. Ruby had never seen his usually jovial moon-shaped face look so dark. Her shoulders twitched in a shiver.

For a moment, she almost told him. But she couldn't imagine the consequences, couldn't be sure what would result from her confession.

She couldn't afford to say anything—*anything*—unless she knew for sure what would come of it.

"Jidge," she said finally. "I can't—"

He stared at her, and after a moment some of the anger went out of his face. "Okay." He nodded and took a deep breath. "Okay, I get it."

"Thank you," she said.

He smiled at her expression of relief. But it was not his normal crinkled-up, childlike grin, but something tougher, more predatory.

"When you're ready," he said, "make sure I hear about it. I want in on the action. Promise?"

"Promise," she said.

The Babe looked down at his own big hands. "Nobody gets away with hitting kids," he said.

"Looks like I've got a big fight this fall up in the Polo Grounds, the deal works out," Jack Dempsey said. "Against this ox from South America, Firpo."

They were clustered around the bleachers, maybe a dozen ballplayers and their hangers-on, the Babe, and Dempsey and a rumple-faced guy who'd come in with him, whom people called Doc.

Amanda and Allie were staying close to Ruby, but neither was saying a word. Both were in awe of the champion boxer, who people said was the richest man on earth, and might have been the most famous, too, along with the Babe.

"You going to be able to beat him?" the Babe asked.

Dempsey smiled. "Sure."

There was a commotion at the door. Art went to stop whoever was invading. But then he stepped aside, his mouth falling open in surprise.

It was David Wilcox, ushering in a newspaper reporter with a pad and a photographer with a camera. They were from the *American,* and they wouldn't have looked any more thrilled if they'd cornered Santa Claus.

Right away Ruby could hear a rising grumble of discontent among the ballplayers around her. Ruby had long assumed that Samuel Cooper had made a deal with the teams to keep their visits private. But David Wilcox wasn't Samuel Cooper. Ruby could only imagine how much Wilcox had gotten paid by the *American* for this exclusive.

She wondered if everyone would just walk out. But she'd underestimated Babe Ruth and Jack Dempsey's professionalism. The last thing they needed was an article about how they'd stormed away after being found by the newspaper's intrepid reporter.

So instead they smiled, submitted to interviews, pretended to box with each other for the camera, and posed throwing the ball from Ruby's mound. Then, with a quick look at each other, they hoisted her up onto their shoulders. The popping flashbulbs made her head swim.

Lastly, David Wilcox stood between them, an arm around each of their shoulders. All three of them grinned as the bulbs exploded. But then, as they drew apart, Ruby saw the Babe look down and notice something she had spotted the moment her boss walked in the door.

A small cloth bandage wrapped around the last three fingers of Wilcox's right hand.

The Babe glanced at it once and then a second time, his attention sharpening. Then, quicker than Ruby had anticipated, he turned his head and stared at her.

She hadn't prepared herself. She felt color rise to her cheeks, and saw understanding enter his eyes, quickly followed by a deep, intense anger. His face seemed to clench like a fist.

She saw what was about to happen, and knew she couldn't let it.

With a cry, she stumbled and went down to her knees. It wasn't even acting, not really—nothing but willpower had been keeping her upright for the last two hours.

She heard shouting, and a moment later the Babe was crouched beside her. Before he could move, before he could say anything, she sprang forward and grabbed hold of him, her cold cheek against his broad, warm one.

"Leave it—" she whispered urgently into his ear.

"What?" His voice was almost lost in the tumult around them. "But we have to—"

"Yes," Ruby said. "We do. But not yet. Leave it, Jidge. *Please*."

She was lying in his arms, so he couldn't move. She kept lying there, deadweight, until the urgency of her words filtered through his anger and she felt some of the tension drain from his body.

Then he hoisted her up, lifting her with no apparent effort. "Clear some space," he said, carrying her over to the bleachers.

By the time she'd assured everyone that she was fine, Wilcox was gone.

17

*i*n the days that followed, David Wilcox kept his hands off Ruby. But he was far from done with her.

He fired Tania as soon as he learned that she'd come to Ruby and the girls' aid that awful night. He also warned her to stay away, far away, but late one evening she came sneaking back into the Birdcage to say good-bye.

"Don't worry about me," she said, smiling away Ruby's distress. "You think I haven't been through worse? Remind me to tell you about the trip I took with my bubbie from Arkhangelsk when I was seven. This is nothing."

She shrugged. "Anyway, I already got a job at Steeplechase—people like me, we don't stay out of work long."

Her expression turned bleak. "But you, you'll still be here."

Ruby nodded.

"And so will he." Tania's face was somber now. "And he hates you."

Still Ruby didn't speak.

"Leave this place," Tania said suddenly. "Come with me."

Ruby said, "You know I can't."

"Yes, I know." Tania chewed on her lip, then sighed and said, "Just . . . be careful."

Ruby touched her temple. She was still getting headaches, three days after the blow. "I'll try," she said.

Although both of them knew that being careful might not be enough.

Wilcox's plan for Ruby soon became clear.

For a few days after he fired Tania, he was around the Birdcage a lot, much more than Samuel Cooper had ever been. Ruby could feel his gaze even when she was throwing the ball. While he was there, Amanda never emerged from the speed shack, and Allie would let others pick up the balls that bounced too close to him.

But he wasn't just trying to spook her. He was charting the ebb and flow of her day. After three days of this he came up to her and said, "You're not working hard enough."

Ruby looked at him. She'd long since learned not to speak until she knew exactly what she was going to say, and never to reveal exactly how she felt.

But the truth was, she'd never worked harder. The photos in the *American* of the night that Jack Dempsey and the Babe had visited had created another boom in popularity for Diamond Ruby.

The clincher had been the photo of the two men holding her on their shoulders, the Babe's moon face crinkled up, even Dempsey's usually dour expression lightening into a grin. To her own eyes, Ruby, perched precariously, looked dazed in the photograph, sick—even now, that whole evening felt like a bad dream—but she knew that no one else would notice, and the camera had been too far away to detect her fresh bruises.

These days, visitors flooded the Birdcage as if they might

catch a glimpse of the Manassas Mauler or the Big Bam mingling with the tourists. But Ruby knew that Dempsey was in Montana, a place out west she couldn't even picture, while Ruth was as likely to show up among the midday crowds as President Harding was.

Instead, other reporters came, from publications she'd barely heard of, like *The Saturday Evening Post* and *The Atlantic*. The articles, she was told, would concentrate on her being a woman in a man's game. As if she would ever read them. As if, in the blur of those days, she even cared.

Even *Baseball Magazine* sent someone to interview her. Normally this would have been at least a little thrill, but it was all she could do to answer the writer's questions, even to feign interest in the same topics she'd discussed endlessly with every reporter who'd come before.

The crowds kept coming. On Wilcox's orders, the Birdcage began opening at seven in the morning and didn't shut its doors until ten, then eleven, at night. Wilcox also cut lunchtime down to fifteen minutes and eliminated the other short breaks that Mr. Cooper had allowed even in the course of busy days.

They never got a day off. Not one.

How many pitches did she throw each day? Hundreds. For the first time, her pitching arm began to hurt. A knot formed behind her shoulder that felt hot to the touch at the end of the day.

Wilcox was wearing her out, using her up. The clockwork girl's gears were beginning to break down.

Mr. Cooper would never have let this happen. And Tania would have had something to put on her shoulder, something to cool the angry heat and soothe the constant ache.

But Mr. Cooper and Tania were gone.

They weren't the only ones.

Almost as soon as Wilcox betrayed them to the *American*, the ballplayers stopped coming by as well. If they couldn't rely on having freedom and privacy at the Birdcage, the place was of no use to them. Off they went to some speakeasy or club whose owner wouldn't sell them out.

The Babe, who always lifted her spirits, had never returned. Gordon, her faithful admirer, seemed to have been swept away by the tide of her popularity.

When Ruby closed her eyes, she could still see Evie's smile, the warm expression in her blue eyes. Evie would have remembered, if no one else did, that Ruby was still little more than a child herself.

So Ruby worked, and the girls worked, until their world became the Birdcage's four walls, and a concrete mound, and a bucket of balls. They rarely ventured outside, and when they did they walked in a daze through the crowds, hordes, *floods* of people, past autograph seekers and those who didn't recognize her. Blinking in the bright summer sunlight, overwhelmed by the rush, the bustle, the blue sky itself.

And when they'd return to the Birdcage, the crowds would be waiting there for them.

When they did finally close for the night, and fell onto their cots, they were hungry enough to wolf down sandwiches from a delicatessen around the corner but too tired to wash up. They could hear the thumps and muffled voices through the wall from the storage room as the cartons of bootleg liquor were brought in and carried out.

Ruby listened to the voices and tried to figure out if one was Nick's. She couldn't be sure. She and the girls hadn't seen him in days. He never walked through the front door of the Birdcage, and on those rare occasions when they made it back to the apartment, he was never in.

Lying awake one night, Ruby looked over at Amanda and Allie sleeping in their cot. Allie was sucking on her fingers and Amanda's brow was knotted even in sleep.

Come with me, Tania had said.

But where?

No matter how bad things are, they can always get worse. That was a lesson Ruby knew all too well.

Closing time had come early—before eleven—on this rainy Sunday night at the beginning of July. Art was on his way out when there was a knock on the door. With a frown and a shrug, he swung it open, then blinked when he saw who it was.

George Littell. Grumpy George.

"You here for an interview?" Art asked him.

"No business of yours what I'm here for," he said, walking past.

Ruby hadn't seen Grumpy George since his feature on her had come out, the one that had cemented Diamond Ruby's success. She saw that his face was grim, his eyes darting around before fixing on her. He was already beginning to speak as he walked up.

"Your brother's in trouble," he said, "and God only knows why, he decided to include me."

Ruby waited for the rest.

"He came to see me in my office—an hour or so ago. Begging me for a job, any job. When I said sorry, no, we'd already been through that, he started asking for you."

Ruby sighed and glanced at the door. "Did you bring him here?"

"No." George wriggled his shoulders. "I put him in a taxi, and sent him home."

Ruby looked at him.

"Listen, I gave the driver extra and asked him to see that Nick made it up to the apartment." He grimaced. "I know, mistake. Guy could have taken the money and dumped him in the street. That's why I'm here."

Ruby closed her eyes. She was so tired.

Then she opened them again and nodded. "Okay. Thanks. I'll go, make sure he's home sleeping it off."

"No." George was scowling. "I brought my car. I'll drive you."

Ruby blinked. She hadn't expected this. "Yeah?"

"Yeah. My mistake, my responsibility." He gave her a sideways look. "Anyway, I owe you something. You did come to me with that scoop."

Ruby glanced at the girls. Allie was asleep on her feet, and Amanda, too, was struggling to keep her eyes open.

"I'll take all of you," George said.

"Thank you."

From near the door Art, who'd been listening in, said, "Mr. Wilcox isn't going to be real happy you took off."

Grumpy George's expression showed that he was considering popping Art one. But Ruby merely shook her head, roused the girls, and headed out the door.

George pulled his white Studebaker into an empty space in front of the apartment building. Ocean Avenue was silent, nearly deserted, although Ruby could see headlights several blocks away. The trees that flanked the avenue hung over the road, heavy with their summer leaves, unmoving in the still air, leaving shadows like black paint against the tarmac and trolley tracks.

"Well, he isn't lying in the street," George said.

Ruby shrugged. "Small favors."

"I'll come up with you." He swung his door open, but before he could climb out, Ruby put a hand on his arm to stop him. He turned to look at her.

"No," she said. "Thanks for driving us." She glanced into the backseat, where the girls were sleeping. "But this is family stuff. I have to take care of it myself."

He looked reluctant. "Are you sure?"

Nodding, she leaned over and woke the girls. Even half asleep, they were compliant, obedient, struggling out of the car with only murmurs of complaint.

As she shepherded them toward the door, he said, "Call me if you need help—the newspaper can usually find me."

"Thank you," Ruby said, wondering what on earth he could do for her.

Nick was home. They could hear him in his room, his and Evie's old room, banging around like he was moving furniture—something he never did, since he'd left the room virtually untouched since the day she'd died.

The apartment stank of stale coffee and spoiled food. There were dirty dishes everywhere, on the tables, on the sofa where Ruby slept, in unsteady piles beside the sink. Pieces of stained clothing hung from the backs of chairs and lay on the floor where they'd been dropped. An ashtray bore a sodden mass of cigarette butts. Beside it stood a streaked tumbler that still held a half an inch of clear liquid.

Ruby heard the sound of glass breaking from Nick's room. She turned to the girls, who had made no attempt to enter the apartment, and said, "Go to your room, close the door, and don't come out till I tell you."

They looked up at her, a pair of pale blue eyes and a pair of brown ones, with identical expressions of worry, even fear.

"Do you understand me? I'll tell you when it's all right to come out, okay?"

There was a loud crash from Nick's room.

"Go—now."

They went, picking their way through the mess, Amanda shutting the door to their room behind them.

Ruby took a deep breath and walked across the cluttered floor, feeling something—food? glass?—crunch under her shoes.

She hesitated a moment outside Nick's room, then opened the door.

He turned, a wreck of a man, barely recognizable with his lank, greasy hair, hollow cheeks, and mad glittering eyes. He stood amid chaos. The room, carefully tended for all these years, looked as if someone had set a wild animal loose in it. Shredded books and papers lay everywhere, the bookshelf itself had been knocked apart, every picture had been pulled off the wall, and even the wallpaper was hanging in strips.

Nick was holding something in both hands, a glass globe that Ruby recognized as an award Evie had received at the Norwegian Hospital years and years ago. Before she could do anything, he drew his arm back and hurled it against the wall.

The globe didn't shatter—it must have been solid—but it left a hole in the plaster, and flecks of dust flew around the room like gnats.

Ruby took a few quick steps into the room and grabbed Nick's arm. Up close, he smelled like stale liquor, like putrefaction, like death.

"Stop that!" she said. "What are you doing?"

He stared at her as if he didn't know who she was. Then some of the madness left his eyes. "It's too much," he said, his voice low, hoarse.

Ruby said, "I know."

His shoulders slumped. "I can't—look at it anymore. Any of it. It's *too much*."

"Then don't." Ruby pulled at his arm. "Don't look. Let's go out for a walk. Get some air."

He shook his head, but when she pulled a little harder he came with her. She left him at the front door—head slumped, his wild energy gone, he now seemed unlikely to move without her—and went over to the girls' room. Peeking in, she was relieved to see that their room had been left untouched. They were sitting close to each other on the edge of their bed, Allie's head resting on Amanda's shoulder, reading Marion Harland's cookbook together.

"Looking for a new squirrel recipe?" Ruby asked, trying to keep her voice light.

They stared at her. "Is Daddy all right?" Allie asked.

Ruby nodded. "Yes, he's fine."

She knew that this wasn't even the beginning of a convincing lie. "Listen, he and I are going out for a while—so he can clear his head," she went on. "I want you to just stay here, try to get some sleep, and we'll be back as soon as we can."

Both of the girls nodded.

Neither made a move to see their father.

Two minutes after she and Nick were out the front door, Ruby regretted suggesting it. Nick never said a word to her, just walked ahead fast enough that she had to hurry to keep up. But he wasn't silent—in fact, he kept up a low monologue the entire time, a kind of back-and-forth argument, though she could not understand a single word of it. When she tried to make conversation, to calm him down, he ignored her.

At first he headed down Ocean Avenue, under the still trees and past a succession of four-story apartment buildings much like their own. An occasional car grumbled past, but very few people were out on the street so late.

They crossed the avenue at the corner of Avenue L. Then Nick doubled back, returning the way they'd come. Hurrying, Ruby stumbled over a bump in the sidewalk where the roots of a big old tree had upended some of the cement. She went down on her knees on the lawn beside the tree, catching a whiff of rich earth and chicken manure, reminded with a pang that went all the way to her heart of her long-vanished childhood. By the time she got back to her feet, Nick was half a block away.

She caught up with him at Avenue M. The stores that lined the avenue were closed, iron gates drawn across their fronts, but Nick, nodding to himself, strode along toward a destination only he knew.

He led them to Elm Street, hard by the elevated station. As they turned onto the street, Ruby heard the low rumble of voices and saw one half-hidden storefront among the ramshackle wood-frame houses that lined the street. It was a small brick building with a blacked-out window, light spilling around its edges, and a blank wooden door.

Nick knocked on the door, and a moment later it swung open. Ruby saw a muscular young man peer out, stare into Nick's face, then nod. He looked suspicious when he saw Ruby, but let her in as well when he realized they were together.

They walked into a small, low-ceilinged room so filled with cigarette and cigar smoke that Ruby felt nearly as cloudy-headed as she had after David Wilcox hit her. The room was packed, mostly men in suits but some women in dark dresses, too, sitting around tables or at a long wooden bar that ran along the back wall. Ruby saw rows of bottles and glasses of different shapes and sizes filled with brown liquid, and gold, and clear.

Nick walked right up to the bar. It was obvious that the blank-eyed man standing behind it knew him, because before he'd even sat on a stool, there was a tumbler on the bar. It was like the one Ruby had spied back in the apartment, filled halfway up with a clear liquid she assumed was gin.

Nick put a five-dollar bill on the counter. Ruby wondered how he'd earned it.

The bartender looked at her as she dragged up a stool. "One for you?" he asked.

Ruby shook her head. He glowered a bit at this, but ended up shrugging and letting her occupy the space.

Ruby had read about speakeasies, about how exciting they

could be, an all-night party fueled by alcohol and the thrill of breaking the law. But this was the most joyless place she'd ever been, with very little conversation and no laughter. It seemed to serve only one purpose: to allow people to numb themselves in company, to make the process of becoming spifflicated a group activity instead of a solitary one.

Nick drained his glass and pushed it across the bar for a refill. And then another, as his head hung lower and lower over the counter, as the alcohol missed his mouth and splattered on his clothes, as his steady monologue dwindled away to random mutterings.

Ruby sat there for hours, until finally his money was all gone and he was blind drunk, and then she took him home.

Somehow they made it back to the apartment, Nick's arm around her shoulders, his legs rubber, his weight heavy on her. Somehow Ruby managed to hold him up while she got the key into the lock, turned the knob, and swung the door open.

Trying to keep her brother from falling to the floor, she glanced into the girls' bedroom and saw them sleeping, arms around each other. Then, her muscles and joints aching from the strain, she pushed Nick into the bathroom, propped him on the chair that stood beside the tub, and went to work stripping his drenched, stinking clothes off him.

When he was down to his undershorts, she soaked a washcloth in hot water and sponged him off as best she could. He leaned back against the cool tile of the wall, head drooping, not helping but at least keeping his feet flat on the floor.

Eventually he was clean enough. She shook him partly awake, got him upright, and struggled with him the short distance to his bedroom. Maneuvering around the splintered wood of the bookshelves, over the torn-up newspapers and books, she let him fall backward onto his bed. With one last heave, she got his legs onto the mattress, then straightened to pull up the thin cotton blanket. When she looked up she saw that his eyes were open, though she couldn't tell how much he saw, and he didn't say a word as she left the room.

Then she went back to the bathroom and scrubbed herself for what felt like an hour, till her arms and face shone red in the mirror above the sink. But still she could smell the reek of the speakeasy on her skin.

Sighing, she walked back into the living room, then stopped in her tracks.

While she'd been out with Nick, the girls had cleaned up the living room and kitchen. They'd washed, dried, and put away the dishes, and the piles of trash had been collected and taken out to the chute. The papers that had been scattered across the floor had been gathered and placed in neat piles, and the dirty kitchen counters had been scrubbed.

Ruby took a deep breath and closed her eyes. When she opened them again, she saw something else.

There was a big piece of paper, creased but carefully unfolded, sitting on the dining table. When she came closer, Ruby saw that it was a poster for Coney Island, stolen off some wall or signboard, smuggled home, and flipped over so its clean, white side showed.

On this, in smeary red—it looked like they'd used one of Evie's old tubes of lipstick—the girls had drawn uneven rows of hearts, big and small, and written the words HAPPY BIRTHDAY, AUNT RUBY!!! *We love you!*

Ruby closed her eyes for a moment. They were right. It was her birthday. July 2, 1923. She was eighteen years old.

Beside the birthday message was a small round cake, untouched, with a candle in it. It was sunken on top and looked like someone might have stolen a bit from one edge.

They'd baked her a cake out of Marion Harland's cookbook.

Heaven knew how they'd scraped together the ingredients, or where they'd found the candle.

Ruby sat down at the table, all the strength leaving her body at once. She crossed her arms and laid her head down on them. She could smell the warm, sweet aroma of the cake wafting toward her, and her stomach gave a sudden jump of hunger, but she knew she would wait till morning to share the treat with her girls.

18

David Wilcox, stormy-faced, was waiting for them in the Bird-cage. "Where the hell have you been?" he said.

After one look at him, Amanda and Allie fled into the dressing room. Ruby stayed where she was and met his gaze.

He was right: they were late. She'd let the girls sleep as long as they wanted—though they'd still woken by seven-thirty—and then had taken the time to light the birthday candle and enjoy the sponge cake.

It was, Ruby had informed them, the most delicious cake she'd ever eaten, and they were the greatest nieces in the entire world.

Then she listened to their description of all the work they'd done, all the cleaning. How they'd managed to gather the ingredients without her knowing and struggled to use the oven. Allie did most of the talking, of course, telling each part of the story at least three times, while Amanda added an occasional detail, her eyes rarely leaving Ruby's face.

Only after they'd washed the dishes (making the birthday girl stay in her seat) and left a note and a piece of cake for Nick, who of course was still asleep, did they head downstairs and, sharing a growing sense of gloom, catch the elevated back to Coney Island.

"Sorry," Ruby told David Wilcox. "Family emergency."

She saw his gaze swing toward the room where the girls had gone, then sharpen and come back to Ruby. "Your brother," he said.

She acknowledged it with a small nod.

"He hasn't been around for a few days."

Ruby said nothing.

Wilcox's mouth was a hard line in his ruddy face. "Your brother's going to get himself into trouble, he doesn't show up when he's supposed to," he said. "We're going to wonder where he is. We're going to lose faith in him."

Ruby took a moment more, then said, "It's been years since anyone had faith in him. Something happened to—to his mind, after his wife died."

She hated herself for talking about her family's problems to this man, who didn't seem to care at all. "Well," he said, "since you seem to be the boss in your family, I recommend—" Drawing the word out. "I *recommend* that you make sure he comes to work on time."

Ruby stayed quiet.

"And you, don't ever show up late again," Wilcox said. "Or—"

"Or what?" Ruby took a step toward him, and saw him rock back a little at the expression on her face. "Or what? You'll beat me up?"

"You bet I will," Wilcox said. He seemed to be considering doing it at that moment.

But Ruby was too angry to be scared. "Well, the next time you do, you'd better kill me, because otherwise *I'm* going to kill *you*."

For a moment, Wilcox looked disconcerted. But then he smoothed his pouchy face into a small smile, and again his gaze strayed through the door to where Allie and Amanda were having a catch.

"Can you keep them with you every minute of every day?" he asked.

Ruby was silent.

"Can you keep your guard up forever?"

She kept her mouth shut.

"Poor little freak," David Wilcox said. "So much bravado, so little power."

Art handed her a cream-colored envelope. "Got here this morning," he said.

It was the most words he'd spoken to her in days, and he'd waited till Wilcox had gone to speak them.

"Who left it?" she asked.

He shrugged. "Some guy."

She didn't have time to read it until her fifteen-minute lunch, by which time she'd thrown at least a hundred pitches. Her shoulder hurt. Slumped back against a chair in the dressing room, the girls lying down on cots beside her with their eyes closed, she opened the envelope and pulled out the thick, embossed piece of stationery.

The letter was from Helen Connell, and was written in a flowing hand in blue ink. The lines were even, Ruby noticed, and never strayed to the edge of the paper.

Dearest Ruby:

I've thought of you often since our magical night in your lair. You were so kind to me, my mother, and Paul, and so generous with your time. I loved throwing the baseball, and you don't know how much I appreciate your generosity at allowing me such intimate contact with you. So much of my life depends on such generosity—if people didn't allow me to "invade" their privacy, I would never know what anyone looked like. (Though I would know who *you* were merely from your remarkable voice and your words, and those of your lovely nieces.)

I'm writing to discover whether Coney Island and "the Birdcage" can spare you for a few hours on July 4, when New York City will host its annual "Safe and Sane Fourth." I imagine you know of it. Perhaps you've even participated in previous years?

In any case, I have decided to join the festivities this year, for the first time since my accident, and I would consider it an honor if you would accompany me. Yes, there is baseball among the offerings, but perhaps you would find it more enjoyable to run in one of the many footraces that are also staged. I myself will join some of the swimming competitions.

I believe that Amanda and Allie would have a wonderful time as well. There are many races and other events designed for children of their ages.

I hope you are interested. If so, please join my mother and me outside the entrance to the Aquarium at Castle Clinton at nine o'clock in the A.M. on Wednesday, the Fourth. Then we will head across town to Seward Park, which as you may know is located at Canal and Jefferson streets, in close proximity to the subway for your return to Coney Island.

I look forward to seeing you there.

Yours fondly,

Helen C.

"Can you break that thing?"

Ruby was standing at the speed shack, Amanda squatting in her usual place beside the machine. It was late in the afternoon, and except for lunch all three of them had worked straight through to make up for their late arrival.

Amanda looked down at the apparatus, her face grim, and said, "I could break it with a hammer."

Ruby smiled. "Getting tired of your job?"

"Aunt Ruby, I dream about numbers."

Then she looked up, and for once her usually guarded expression was open, vulnerable. "Your arm hurts when you throw, doesn't it?"

Ruby nodded. No point in lying.

"What happens if you . . . can't?"

Ruby said, "We won't let it come to that." She paused, looked around. "Can you break the machine so no one knows you did it?"

"Um." Amanda pondered this surprising question. Then she nodded and bent over the machine. "Look—see this connection, with these wires? I've been fixing it all the time."

"It's been breaking?"

"With how hard we make it work? *'Course* it's been breaking."

"Can it break tomorrow night? I mean, really break, so it needs a replacement part?" Ruby leaned in close. "So we can do something fun instead?"

Amanda didn't need any convincing. "Ab-so-lute-ly," she said, and started figuring out how.

Art said, "I'll get Mr. Wilcox."

He'd stared at the broken speed machine and poked it with a thick finger, but that was the extent of his efforts. Looking worried, he headed out, closing the door to the Birdcage behind him.

Allie was lying on her back along one of the bleachers. She was staring up at the ceiling and singing a little nonsense song to accompany some mysterious counting game she was playing with her fingers.

Ruby walked over to her. "You all right?"

Allie tilted her head. "I'm *tired*," she said, though her voice was cheerful. "And *hungry*."

"We'll get some dinner soon, I promise."

Allie went back to the song, then interrupted herself again. "Aunt Ruby, can we have a vacation?"

"How about tomorrow?"

Allie sat up. "For true?"

"Maybe." Ruby looked at both of them. "We'll see. Just don't say anything when Mr. Wilcox comes, all right?"

"Like we would!" Amanda said.

Someone knocked on the door. Ruby went to answer it, readying herself to tell whoever had come by that they were closed for the day.

But it was Gordon, looking harried. Ruby hadn't seen him in the Birdcage in weeks.

"Can I come in?" he asked, glancing over his shoulder. "I need to talk to you."

"Sure." She stepped aside and he came in, bringing the smells of salt water and fried food with him. Without hesitating, he slid the bolt that locked the door from the inside.

Ruby stepped away from him, her arms hanging at her sides, waiting to see what happened next.

He looked at her and understood what she was thinking. "No, Ruby," he said. "Just talk."

She looked at the door. "Wilcox is coming back with Art."

"Not yet, though. Someone is keeping them busy."

He glanced up at the clock on the wall. "But let's not waste any time—we can talk in the dressing room."

After a moment, she nodded and followed him in, gesturing to the girls to stay where they were, that everything was fine.

Gordon entered, turned around one of the two wooden chairs, and sat in it. He looked different; though he was wearing the same shiny suit she'd seen many times before, now it seemed like a costume.

She began to suspect where the conversation might go.

"Is your name really Gordon?" she asked.

He blinked. Then he said, "Yes, it is."

He might well tell her so, she thought, even if it weren't true.

"And I *am* a big fan of yours," he went on, "but that's not all I am."

She looked at him, considering. "You're after my brother," she said finally.

His eyes showed amusement. "No," he said. Then, again, "No. But it is Nick I'm here to talk about, partly."

He leaned forward in his chair. "Ruby, I'm an agent in the Federal Prohibition Unit, and I'm tracking bootleggers here in Coney Island."

Close enough to what she'd guessed. Her gaze slid past him toward the locked door to the storage room, and he noticed. "Yes, Ruby," he said, "I know about the 'staging area' back there. We've been watching it for weeks."

"Then why—"

"Why is it still operating?" He raised his hands, palms toward her. "Because if we swept in now, who would I arrest? A couple of low-level box haulers, like your brother." He shook his head. "That's not what we're after. We're gunning for bigger game."

"Is that why you spent so much time here?"

That got a nod. "You gave me a good excuse to watch the comings and goings. And we've learned a lot—but not enough."

She thought about the first night Nick had showed up, with the stocky, well-dressed man with hair layered in brilliantine. Gordon hadn't been there that night.

She described the man, and Gordon looked thoughtful. "I don't know him. But he sounds like what we're looking for." He rummaged in his pocket, then reached out and handed her a white business card. It had only his first name and a phone number on it. "My office is here in Brooklyn," he said. "Call me if you see him again, will you?"

Then he leaned forward. "Look, Ruby, I'm telling you this because I want your help, but also because I like you. Your brother is of no interest to us, but that doesn't mean we won't sweep him up with the rest of the trash. You understand that?"

She nodded.

"Get him away from here and we'll keep him out of it. But better do it soon."

She took a deep breath and closed her eyes. People expected so much from her. How would she ever live up to everyone's expectations, much less her own?

When she opened her eyes again, Gordon was giving her a curious look. "How old are you, Ruby?" he asked.

"Eighteen," she said. "Today."

He blinked. "Well, then, happy birthday. There's my gift: a warning. We don't usually give people a heads-up."

"Thanks," Ruby said.

Thanks a lot.

"Any idea how to jury-rig this thing?"

David Wilcox's face was even redder than usual, and when he spoke his breath carried the bitter tang of bootleg liquor. Ruby knew he was counting all the money he'd lose if the Birdcage wasn't able to open on the Fourth. She also wondered how many drinks he'd had, thinking his working day was over.

"Know anyone who does?"

She shook her head. "Sorry."

Behind Wilcox's back, Amanda kept her mouth shut tight. She didn't have anything to worry about. Wilcox wasn't the sort to think that a ten-year-old girl could possibly help.

He was quick enough to blame her, however, turning his bloodshot eyes in her direction and saying, "This is your fault."

Amanda went pale.

"No, it's *not*," Ruby said. "This machine has to work as hard as I do every day. No wonder it's wearing out." She looked into Wilcox's face. "Mr. Cooper would have known better."

Wilcox scowled at her tone, and Ruby felt the hairs on the back of her neck prickle. But at least she had taken his mind off Amanda.

After a moment, his face loosened a fraction. He glanced up at the scoreboard with its row of zeros. "Then make it up," he said. "Who knows how fast a throw is?"

Ruby shook her head. "Every third guy in here or his sweetie comes over to watch the speed machine spit out its numbers. Word gets around that we're faking it, the public's not going to be happy."

She thought she could hear his teeth grinding, but he could figure out no way to argue with that.

"Okay," he said finally. "We'll close tomorrow—I'll get in touch with Remington first thing Thursday morning and get the new part."

He turned his gaze on Ruby. "But I want you to be here—all day. No more family emergencies." He looked at the door. "Starting tonight."

Ruby had known this was coming. "I have a better idea," she said.

He crossed his arms, his face dark, but he listened as she told him about her letter from Helen and the invitation to participate in the Safe and Sane Fourth.

He was shaking his head before she was done. "No chance," he said.

Because it sounds like too much fun for me, Ruby thought, and that can't be allowed.

"No, listen," she said. "That reporter and photographer from the *American* you brought the night Jack Dempsey came by—wouldn't they be interested in an exclusive about the famous Helen Connell participating for the first time after her terrible accident?"

Wilcox was no longer shaking his head. He could see the idea's potential.

"And I'll be there, just like I was with the Babe and Dempsey. I know Helen won't mind posing with me. Imagine the publicity we'll get." Ruby made her voice sound as cheerful and enthusiastic as she could. "We'll have to build a bigger Birdcage."

Wilcox looked thoughtful.

"Why waste me here with nothing to do when I can help drum up business?" Ruby asked.

He was still unsure, still suspicious, but at last he nodded. "I'll get on the phone. Where should they meet you?"

Ruby kept her face blank, as if she were struggling to remember the name of the location Helen had told her. What she was really doing, however, was standing on the precipice of a lie that would change her life—and her nieces'. There would be nothing ahead but uncertainty.

"Ruby," Wilcox said.

She looked at his thick hands. His fingers were twitching. His gold ring glinted in the light.

Ruby thought of Amanda lying on the floor, blood welling from her mouth.

"Isham Park," she said. "In upper Manhattan."

The lie.

"I know where it is," Wilcox said. "What entrance?"

"The one at Two Hundred and Fourteenth Street."

Mama had brought Ruby there once, for a speech by a suffragist who'd come all the way from England.

"And what time?"

"Nine o'clock."

Wilcox nodded. "Someone from the *American* will be there. You'd better be there, too."

"'Course I will," Ruby said.

No turning back now.

19

"Do they have whales inside?" Allie asked.

They stood in Castle Garden opposite the front entrance of the Aquarium, looking at its blocky white stone walls gleaming in the morning sun and the silvery-gray water of New York Harbor beyond. The aquarium hadn't opened yet for the day, but already there was a short line of children and their parents, waiting at the doors.

"I don't know about whales," Ruby told Allie. "I think they have seals, though. And lots of fish."

"Sharks?"

"Maybe sharks."

"Can we go someday?"

Ruby thought about it. Then she shrugged. "Sure," she said. "Maybe even tomorrow."

The girls exchanged glances. She'd told them repeatedly that they would never have to go back to the Birdcage, but they still didn't really believe her. They kept asking, phrasing their questions in different ways, as if expecting to trip her up and find out the truth. The actual truth.

"We're really—" Allie's hands grasped the air as she searched for the word. "We're really . . . *done*?"

"We're really done," Ruby said.

"What will we do instead?" Amanda asked.

Ruby thought of the photographer, Mel Walters, but said nothing.

Amanda's face was grim. "And what will Mr. Wilcox do?"

That was the question. Ruby had been looking over her shoulder all morning, and she did so again now, as if expecting to see Wilcox looming up behind her. It was ridiculous, this fear. He had no idea where she was. She'd told him to send the *American*'s reporter and photographer to the other end of Manhattan, and it would be hours before he learned that she had purposely led them astray. He wasn't going to find them, not today.

Even so. The bruises on her face and Amanda's had faded, but there were still times when Ruby stood up too quickly and her head spun, a reminder of Wilcox's blow.

"Will he come to get us?" Amanda asked.

Ruby didn't know that, but there was one thing she did know.

"He'll never touch you again," she said.

"There she is!"

It was Amanda who spotted Helen and Mrs. Connell first, of course. And Allie who ran and greeted them as if they were life-long friends, not new acquaintances.

"I believe you've grown since we last met," Mrs. Connell said.

"They never stop growing," Ruby said.

Allie was tugging on Helen's skirt. "We've quit being Diamond Ruby!"

"You have?"

"Yes, seems so," Ruby said.

"That means—" Helen bit back on her words, though an odd expression remained on her face.

"Means what?" Ruby asked.

Helen shook her head, as if irritated with herself. "Let's go over to the park," she said.

They were met at the entrance by Paul Fitzsimmons, as cheerful and easygoing as he'd been the night at the Birdcage. He was dressed in a beige suit and carried a canvas bag and a large paper sack. He gave Mrs. Connell and Helen each a kiss on the cheek, said hello to Ruby and the girls, and then asked, "So who wants breakfast?"

Smiling at Allie's unabashed enthusiasm, he opened the paper sack, revealing a pile of pastries and little cakes. "They're made by this Bavarian madman up in Yorkville," he said. "I wouldn't trust him with my car or my sister, but he sure can bake."

Ruby thought Paul looked like he sure could eat. His face was even rounder than she'd remembered under his lank hair, and as he wolfed down one of the pastries he said that he really needed to restrain himself. But when Helen, her lips curving in a grin, suggested he might work off some of his breakfast by joining them in the upcoming athletic contests, he laughed as if that were a ridiculous suggestion.

When they were done, he handed the canvas bag to Helen. She reached inside, and to gasps from the girls, began pulling out new, neatly folded athletic wear.

"Hope they are all right," Paul said doubtfully. "I'm no good with girls' clothes."

"Since you will need to dress for today's events, I took the liberty of asking him to buy these for you," Helen explained. "Mother helped me with the sizes."

Ruby began to protest. Then she saw the expression on her

nieces' faces as they held the dark blue V-neck blouses with white trim around the necks and sleeves and matching shorts. They looked so stricken at the possibility that these gifts might be taken away that she could only thank the Connells and Paul for their kindness.

Looking very much alike, mother and daughter shrugged away her gratitude. Paul grinned at Ruby. "Get used to it," he said.

"We also bought you swimsuits," Helen said.

"I'm sorry," Ruby said, feeling uncomfortable. "We're not much for swimming."

"But we love to run!" Allie said.

Helen laughed and gestured out at the park's lawns and fields. "So what's stopping you?"

After saying good-bye to Paul, they walked to the vast tent that served as the women's changing room. Ruby was struck by the easy camaraderie inside. Young and old, fat and slim, stranger and friend, the women laughed and talked as they stripped off their dresses and climbed into their athletic wear. No one paid the slightest attention to Ruby's arms—and why should they? Nearly everyone had something, some blemish or scar they could have been self-conscious about, yet no one was.

Almost as soon as they'd left the changing room, the girls were swept up in a mass of children of all ages. The officials on duty frantically blew their whistles and tried to keep things organized, but with only middling success.

Standing beside Mrs. Connell and Helen, Ruby watched her nieces begin to let their guard down. Pink and dimpled, Allie scampered this way and that through the horde. She finished next to last in her official race, a fifty-yard dash against other little girls, because she just had to wave at Ruby as she went by. But she didn't care in the slightest, and as soon as her race was over, she was swallowed up again in the mass of happy children.

Amanda, on the other hand, ran with the same quiet, unfussy efficiency with which she did everything, only her flushed cheeks and sparkling eyes betraying her joy. She finished fourth in the seventy-five-yard dash, mistiming her final sprint, but then figured out a better strategy in the one hundred and finished second. Panting, exultant, she showed her silver medal, strung on a red, white, and blue strand of fabric, to Ruby, then handed it to Helen.

"I want you to have this," she said. "For inviting us."

Helen smiled, ran her fingers over the medal's rough surface, and said, with a dignity equal to Amanda's, "Thank you. I'll hang it beside my own."

She insisted that Ruby sign up for some events as well, the one-hundred-yard dash for starters. Ruby resisted at first, but glowing looks on their faces when she finally agreed made it worthwhile.

When was the last time she'd run? She couldn't remember. And she was a little embarrassed by how she'd look, those wings of hers pumping. But again, no one seemed to notice, or to care if they did, and though she finished near the back of the group, it felt wonderful to just let go for once.

She did better in the running broad jump, hurtling through the air with her arms outstretched like she was suspended there, pinned for an instant beneath the blue sky, the summer breeze in her face, her hair flying back, free.

She landed in a flurry of sand to the cheers of the crowd and found that she'd finished third in the event. She took her bronze medal and hung it around Allie's neck, then turned and took Helen's hand in hers.

"Look at me," she said, and held her friend's hand to her face.

Helen's gentle fingers touched here, there. "You're smiling."

"That's what I wanted you to see," Ruby said.

·   ·   ·

As they walked over to the municipal swimming pool near the Hudson River, the girls running ahead through the crowded street, Helen said, "Have you really forsaken Diamond Ruby?"

"As of today." Ruby explained the subterfuge that had sent the newspaperman to the wrong park. "Now I can never go back."

"This Wilcox." Mrs. Connell looked as worried as her daughter. "Does he know where you live?"

"Yes."

"Then will he come to find you? Will he come to your home?"

Ruby didn't say anything.

"What will you do if he does?"

Ruby's chin lifted. "I'll throw him out."

But neither of the Connells looked reassured by her bravado. Helen reached for her mother's arm. "Now, Ma?" she said.

Mrs. Connell smiled. "Go ahead, dear," she replied. "You know you have my blessing."

Helen's face was red. "Ruby—"

Then she gulped and coughed, as if having difficulty getting words out. Ruby waited before finally saying, "What?"

"Come live with us," Helen said.

The pool was like a gigantic green fish tank with tile floors, and the hundreds of people who played in it looked like minnows or tadpoles. Helen seemed happy just to hear the sound of water, and went off to the changing room without her mother's help. "*This* place I know my way around," she said, smiling. "I'll meet you back here."

The girls, tired at last, found chairs by the pool and watched the swimming races. Ruby said to Mrs. Connell, "That Paul?"

"Yes?"

"Do you like him?"

"Yes, very much." She gave Ruby an amused look. "He and Helen have become—quite close. It doesn't bother him at all that she can't see."

"And why should it?" Ruby said.

Mrs. Connell laughed. "No half measures for you, are there, dear?"

When Helen returned, she was wearing a black tank suit, revealing the well-developed shoulders and strong leg muscles that were usually half hidden by the dresses she wore. As if understanding the effect she caused, she smiled and said, "I no longer dive, but I still swim here almost every day. I need to—to be in the water."

When it came time for her first event, the hundred-yard crawl, she walked up to the starting spot as if she could see as well as the other competitors. Ruby wondered if anyone else there even realized that Helen was blind.

"She knows every inch of this pool," Mrs. Connell said.

Helen clearly did. She swam with such strong strokes that she soon left the other competitors behind. When she reached the end of the pool, she flipped and pushed off as smoothly as if she'd seen the wall coming, then returned and won the race easily.

She bobbed in the water, her face alight under her white swimming cap, as Allie and Amanda knelt at the edge of the pool, their clothes getting wet. Ruby turned to Mrs. Connell.

"Was she serious?" she asked.

"About you living with us? Of course she was. She's talked of little else for days."

"But—" Ruby took a moment to gather her thoughts. "She barely knows us. We've met twice. How can she be so certain?"

Mrs. Connell smiled. "Helen is *always* certain."

"And you . . . how about you?"

Mrs. Connell tilted her head back and gave Ruby a long, cool

inspection. Then she said, "You heard me. I gave Helen my blessing."

Ruby said, "Why?"

Mrs. Connell held her gaze for a few moments more, then
sighed and looked down. "The house has felt empty ever since
Helen's father died five years ago—and even more so since she had
her accident. If this is what she wants, and it is, then I do, too."

"Well." Ruby took a breath. "Thank you."

Mrs. Connell smiled, then looked up as the others returned.
Helen, dripping, looked elated. Her medal was hung around
Amanda's neck.

"We've swapped," she said.

The next event was announced. As Helen headed back toward
the pool, her mother walked over to her. For a moment they
talked, heads close together, and then Helen turned and strode
unerringly back to where Ruby stood.

"Listen to me, Ruby," she said. "Don't think, don't question.
Just say yes."

But was it already too late?

They stood on the sidewalk, the late-afternoon sunlight il-
luminating the trees and housefronts along Ocean Avenue, and
looked at the car parked in front of their building.

It was the fanciest automobile any of them had ever seen, a
black Packard touring car with big wheels and shiny windows and
a removable leather top that looked like it was cleaned and oiled
every day.

Amanda and Allie looked at each other, then up at Ruby, the
joy of the long day draining out of their faces. "Is that Mr. Wilcox's car?" Amanda asked.

"I don't know," Ruby said.

Allie looked at the building's door. "Let's go," she said suddenly. "Let's just—go away."

It was an appealing prospect, to turn their backs and leave, but after a moment Ruby shook her head. "We don't even know it's his car," she said. "And we can't just go—this is still our home."

As they walked up the stairs, the girls, quiet and afraid, stayed close behind her. Ruby swung open the door leading to the fourth-floor hallway, and saw that there was no one lurking there.

She allowed herself to take a deep breath.

But when she opened the door to the apartment, someone was inside. Two people. Large forms, one of them looming up off the sofa, turning toward her, taking a step in her direction.

In that moment, Ruby felt real fear. Behind her, Allie let loose with a little shriek.

But then they saw that neither man was David Wilcox. One was a gray-haired gentleman dressed in a fine suit, holding a cane in his left hand. He was already speaking as he stood before her. The other, younger man, stood in the background. He wore a dark uniform.

As Ruby's heart pounded, she realized she'd met the older man before, weeks ago, at the Birdcage, in the company of Babe Ruth.

She couldn't remember his name.

Colonel—

Colonel Edward—

And what on earth was he talking about?

20

*C*olonel Edward *Fielding*. That was it.

And he certainly didn't *seem* like much of a threat.

"I'm so sorry to have startled you," he was saying for at least the fifth time, his lined, good-natured face filled with concern at the expressions he saw on all three of their faces. "I know how forward it seems, us waiting here unannounced."

"It's fine," Ruby said for about the fourth time. The girls, though still wide-eyed and sticking close to her, had begun to relax as well. Ruby could tell that all the Colonel's bowing and apologizing (what her mother had called *phumphering*), along with his expensive clothes, white hair, and polished wooden walking stick, were beginning to strike them—especially Allie—as reassuring, if not funny.

"As I said, your brother—Nicholas, is it?—was here when we arrived," the Colonel explained. "He was the one who let us in, of course, and told us to make ourselves comfortable."

Ruby looked at the dark living room, the tatty sofa, the full ashtray on the scarred table, and sighed. Well, it could have been worse. It *had* been worse, before the girls cleaned it up.

"But then—" Colonel Fielding looked intensely uncomfortable. "But then he just left without a word of warning, about an hour ago. We thought he might have stepped out for a short while, but he hasn't yet returned."

"He may not be back for hours," Ruby said. "I apologize for his behavior. It can be very—erratic these days."

"Oh." The Colonel paused, looking thoughtful. "Anyway," he went on, "here we were, Cesare and me—"

Cesare was the Colonel's driver, a slim young man with olive skin, a pointed chin and nose, and dark, amused eyes.

"We didn't know what to do," the Colonel said. "We considered leaving, but the door would have remained unlocked." He looked at the door as if it were the culprit, then turned his head to meet Ruby's eyes again. "Since I'm not very familiar with this neighborhood, I didn't feel entirely comfortable with that idea."

He had no idea how many times Ruby had come home to find the door not only unlocked, but swinging wide open. It was lucky that they owned nothing worth stealing.

"Thank you," she said. "That was very thoughtful."

He smiled at her, all the creases in his wrinkled face aligning and pointing upward. "You're quite welcome. Anyway, we kept expecting Nicholas to return, but instead you walked in, looking like you'd seen a ghost."

Worse than a ghost, Ruby thought.

"Can I see your stick?" Allie asked.

"Allie!" Amanda said.

But the Colonel seemed pleased enough to hand it over. He appeared to have no trouble remaining upright without it. Allie made a close inspection of its carved handle, which looked to Ruby like the head of a roaring lion.

"I imagine you're curious as to why I've come to see you," he went on.

Ruby merely nodded.

"I have a business proposition to make." The Colonel looked around at the sparse surroundings and said, "There's much to talk about. Are you hungry?"

It took only an instant for Allie to say, "Yes!"

Ruby rolled her eyes and said to the Colonel, "She's always hungry."

"Me, too," he said, smiling. "Is there a local restaurant you prefer? On my dime, of course."

Ruby hesitated. But Allie was delighted. "I know! Let's go to Steiner's!"

Steiner's. The restaurant Mama and Papa had brought the family to most often when Ruby was a child. But how on earth did Allie know of it?

Then Ruby remembered. Nick had taken them there once a couple years ago, after he brought home a small stash of money and insisted they go out. It had been a celebration, but a painful one, with Nick talking too loudly and Ruby aware at every moment of how shabby they all looked. Amanda had said very little, while Allie had been so overwhelmed by her first restaurant that she'd barely eaten a bite.

But clearly her memories of that night were better than Ruby's.

"Steiner's it is, then," said the Colonel. "Is it close by?"

Ruby shrugged. "Just a few blocks away."

"We'll drive."

Ruby thought he'd have come to the same decision if she'd said, "It's just two doors down." Why not drive everywhere when you had a car like the Packard?

Colonel Fielding sat up front beside Cesare, who drove easily, confidently, one hand on the big hoop of a steering wheel.

Ruby and the two girls sat on the deep, warm-smelling leather seats in the back. There was still plenty of room.

"Do you usually sit back here?" Allie asked.

The Colonel turned his head. "Yes," he said. "Yes, I do."

She slid around on the seat and stretched her legs. "I could *sleep* in here!"

"High praise indeed," he said, smiling.

Cesare parked just a few feet from the restaurant's front door. He stayed with the car while the rest of them entered the delicatessen. When the Colonel held the door for them, Allie giggled, prompting a glare from Ruby.

Though Steiner's looked exactly as Ruby remembered, she wondered if it seemed coarse, common, to the Colonel. She wished she'd insisted on someplace fancier, though of course she couldn't think of one.

But he appeared perfectly content in these surroundings. Anyway, Ruby decided, since he was acquainted with Babe Ruth, perhaps this was a step up from establishments where the hot dogs came twenty to the dollar.

They sat in a booth near the back. A harsh odor rose from the bowl of pickles their waiter clanged onto the table. The Colonel looked across at Ruby, then at Amanda, seeming to notice for the first time the gold medal still hanging around her neck.

"Safe and Sane Fourth, eh?" he said.

Amanda nodded, giving nothing away, dark eyes hooded in her long, severe face. She'd hardly spoken since they'd entered the apartment and found the two men waiting for them.

But now she asked, "Colonel Fielding, what do you do?"

"Do?" He looked surprised, but not put out. "I own ships that sail between New York and Europe, and Asia as well."

Allie perked up. "Pirate ships?"

"What?" He laughed. "Er . . . no. Nothing so exciting, honey. No pirates, as far as I know. We transport wheat, and automobiles, and farming machines, mostly, goods that each side of the world needs from the other."

The waiter came to take their orders. Allie ordered blintzes, Amanda roast chicken, and the Colonel, with evident enjoyment, brisket. Ruby had no appetite, but ordered potato pancakes with sour cream. Evie had always loved those.

The Colonel also ordered a pastrami sandwich to be brought out to Cesare. Ruby wondered whether the driver worried about dripping something on all that immaculate leather.

When the waiter had gone, the Colonel raised his eyes and caught her gaze. "And I also own a baseball team," he said.

Ah.

"The Brooklyn Typhoons."

Ruby looked at him, and for a moment he seemed a trifle embarrassed. "A typhoon is a big storm, like a hurricane," he explained. "I commanded a brigade in the Philippines when I was on active duty—and we had a lot of them. Typhoons."

"I like it," Allie decided. "Typhoon. It's a good word."

"I'm glad you agree." The Colonel smiled, but kept his eyes on Ruby. "We're part of the new East-Coast League that just began play this spring. Have you heard of us?"

The answer was yes, vaguely. Ruby knew that a few of the team's players had come to the Birdcage, though she couldn't remember any faces.

"You play at Washington Park," she said, in what was half a question. "Where the Robins used to play, back before they built Ebbets Field. Up on Fourth Avenue, near the Gowanus Canal."

Not far from Empire Boulevard, once Malbone Street, where Evie had died.

Colonel Fielding beamed. "Yes, that's us. The other teams we face are located in places like Bethlehem and Allentown, Pennsylvania, and Beacon, which is a couple hours north of us here in New York."

Ruby had never heard of any of those places.

"The teams spend a lot of time on buses and trains," the Colonel said.

"And you usually drive to see the games?" Allie asked. "I mean, you get driven?"

He laughed. "Why, yes," he said, "when I can."

"And you want Aunt Ruby to play on your team. You want her to pitch for the . . . Typhoons."

The Colonel looked down at her. Then he looked across the table at Ruby. His eyes were the palest shade of blue and a little watery.

"Why, yes," he said again. "Yes, I do."

A few years ago, when she was young, Ruby would have been thrilled. It sounded a lot better than what she had planned, which was . . . nothing. Still, she was suspicious. Who knew what Colonel Fielding was really offering?

"For an exhibition?" she asked. "A onetime appearance?"

The Colonel shook his head, looking a little surprised at her tone and expression. He'd probably been expecting joy.

"No," he said. "I want you to join my team and pitch for us every four days."

Ruby had the oddest feeling: that she was the sober adult in this conversation and Colonel Fielding, gray-haired and august as he was, the eager child.

"And your other players," she said. "Do they know about this? About your plans for me?"

"Not yet," he said.

"Well," Ruby said, "that puts an end to *that*."

The Colonel looked confused. "What?"

"Colonel Fielding," Ruby said, "do you really expect your players to accept me? Because if you do, you don't know from nothing. A jane out on the field? They'll put the kibosh on *that* idea fast enough."

"Oh, will they?" The Colonel sat up straighter, his back ramrod stiff, and something in his gaze hardened. For the first time, Ruby caught a glimpse of the strong will that soldiers under his command must have seen.

"I can tell you one thing without doubt," he said, his voice icy. "My boys will do what I tell them."

His tone brooked no argument, but still Ruby couldn't let it go. "And the players on the other teams?"

Colonel Fielding drew in a deep breath. "Ruby," he said more gently, "I understand your concern. But I can promise you that players throughout the league will go along with this. They'll have no choice. They are professionals hired by us, the owners, to do a job—just like the crews on my ships. If they don't want to do it, we'll find someone else who will."

Ruby thought about this. Colonel Fielding gave her time.

"Who runs the league? Is there a commissioner?" she asked after a while.

He nodded. "Herbert Landsman is president, and also the man who first organized the league. I've already discussed this with him, and he thinks it's a fine idea."

Amanda leaned forward. "I remember now," she said slowly. "You're the team that uses all these, these *stunts* to bring in the crowds, aren't you?"

The Colonel frowned at the term, but gave a little nod.

"Didn't you have a horse that could kick the ball over the plate?"

Allie, munching on a pickle, her face smeared with brine, perked up at this. But the Colonel just waited.

"And another time you had homing pigeons deliver new baseballs to the umpire. Right?"

The Colonel frowned. "I know what you're asking."

"Do you?"

"Yes. What you're asking," he said, "is do I see your aunt as merely another gimmick, another stunt, like the horse or the pigeons? And the answer is no."

The food came on big white chipped plates the waiter slammed down in front of them. Allie dug in right away, awkward with the knife as she always was, but refusing to let anyone cut her food for her anymore. Beside Ruby, though, Amanda stayed still.

The Colonel looked down at his brisket, then raised his eyes again. "Look, Ruby, I can't deny that I'd enjoy the publicity that signing you would bring. Look at the crowds that flooded Diamond Ruby's show every time someone wrote an article about it—"

Ruby raised her eyebrows.

Colonel Fielding smiled a little. "Yes, I went back after the night I came with the Babe," he said. "Several times, in fact, since this idea's been growing in my mind. You just never noticed me in the crowd."

"I saw you," Amanda said.

Of course.

"I brought some coaches and scouts along with me, too. And other than the fact that you were working so hard we thought your arm would fly off, we were just as impressed every time."

He leaned forward, making his own kind of pitch. "Yes, you could help us draw new fans. But I think you could also help us win." He grimaced. "Two things that we haven't been very good at so far."

"That's true," Amanda said, surprising them both again. "You've only won nine games, while losing sixteen."

The Colonel stared at her. "Remarkable girl," he said, as if to himself. Then he shook his shoulders. "Sometimes we only have a thousand or so fans at a game. It's very difficult—even more than

I imagined—to capture the attention of New Yorkers when they have the three major-league teams to distract them. Especially with everyone and his mother wanting to head up to the Bronx to see Jidge's 'Eighth Wonder of the World.'"

Ruby thought that anyone who believed the Colonel's new team could succeed against such competition was deluding himself, but she didn't voice her doubts.

"The other teams in the league are struggling, too," the Colonel went on. "Fans are enthusiastic . . . but sparse. We—all the owners—think that your appearances would boost attendance throughout the league. Especially if we promoted you properly."

Ruby stayed silent. The Colonel gave her a curious look and said, "To be honest, Ruby, I don't understand why you're hesitating. I happen to know that you're—" He gave a delicate cough. "In between jobs right now."

She sat back in her seat.

"I went to see David Wilcox this morning." The Colonel's voice was noncommittal, but Ruby thought she could see something change in his expression. He hadn't yet had a bite of his brisket, but he looked like he'd tasted something unappetizing.

"Wilcox was working today, even on the Fourth, and so was I," he went on. "I happened to be in his office, trying to find out where you'd gone, when he received a telephone call from some newspaperman who was also searching for you."

Now the Colonel definitely looked disgusted. "He grew extremely angry."

Amanda shuddered.

"He spoke so—intemperately—that I had to restrain myself from using my stick on him."

"Too bad you didn't," Amanda said at once.

"After he had calmed down somewhat, we had a civil conversation," the Colonel said, "during which he came to see that I was taking a problem off his hands."

"How much did you pay him," Ruby asked, "to set me free?"

The Colonel shook his head. "Just leave it that it was enough to satisfy him, while still being within the range of what I could afford."

He leaned forward. "But that's not important. What's important is that you're done with David Wilcox—and now you have a new opportunity. What do you say?"

The silence at the table was broken only by the clatter of Allie's knife and fork. Then Amanda put a hand on Ruby's arm.

"Say yes, Aunt Ruby," she said.

21

the Connells' brownstone on Henry Street in Brooklyn Heights was so clean, its white plaster walls so bright, its windows so clear and unstreaked, its mother-of-pearl inlays so shiny, that Ruby, carrying the cloth bag that contained all her clothes, felt poorer than she ever had before.

Including when she'd been killing squirrels for dinner.

Standing in the sunlit parlor, Amanda and Allie huddled close to her, one on each side, Ruby realized that the whole time she'd thought she was providing for them, protecting them, she'd been lying to herself.

What had ever gone right? Her nieces had been struck with fists. They'd gone hungry, been forced to work until they were gray-faced with exhaustion. They'd had no leisure, little education, no friends. They'd watched their father decline until he expressed more worry that Ruby might stop paying his rent than sadness that he would no longer be seeing his daughters.

She'd managed to keep them alive. That was about it.

The girls had no idea what Ruby was thinking. They felt only boundless, inexpressible relief to be out of the Birdcage and moving into this house that surpassed their most fervent imaginings.

Mrs. Connell stood beside Helen, her eyes widening as she scanned their meager possessions. "Is that all you've brought?"

Ruby met her gaze. "It's all we have."

"Hmm." Helen rubbed her chin. "We'll take a shopping expedition tomorrow to Abraham & Straus—"

"Helen!"

Four sets of eyes swiveled in Ruby's direction. She took a deep breath and tried again, this time more gently.

"Helen, thank you," she said. "And, yes, we need some new clothes. But before we go on any 'shopping expeditions,' you have to know that I'll pay you back."

Helen began to protest, but Ruby didn't let her. "We're a little short now, because I never got paid for my last two weeks. But after I sign my contract with the Typhoons, we'll be able to afford to pay rent, too."

Barely. Colonel Fielding had offered her forty dollars a week, less than she'd gotten at the Birdcage at the end, though with bonuses built in depending on how many additional fans her presence attracted. "You won't get rich," he'd said to her, an obvious truth if she'd ever heard one. "But . . ."

But you won't get hit.

Or worked until your body breaks.

"You can pay me rent when you're back on your feet," Helen said now, a mulish look on her face.

"No. Starting right away."

They stood opposite each other, neither willing to back down, until Mrs. Connell laughed, breaking the tense silence.

"Dearest Helen," she said, "at this late date, you've finally got the little sister you always wanted."

Helen laughed. "And quite the pill she's turning out to be!"

"Are you hungry?" Mrs. Connell asked the girls.

"Always!" Allie said.

"We have Eskimo Pies in the icebox."

Ruby heard Amanda swallow. Eskimo Pies were a treat they'd rarely been able to afford, though they'd certainly seen plenty of other people eating them in Coney Island.

"The girls would enjoy that," Ruby said to Mrs. Connell. "But we'd like to bathe first."

"No, we wouldn't!" Allie said.

Ruby gave her a look, and Allie put her hand over her mouth. "I'll go first," she said meekly.

Amanda shook her head. "We'll go together."

As the girls splashed and played in the bathtub upstairs, Ruby sat with Helen at the table and drank dark tea.

"Can I ask you something?" she said.

Helen smiled. "Of course. Anything."

"Why have you done this? Invited us to stay with you?"

The answer came without hesitation. "Because you let me touch your beautiful arms."

Ruby had nothing to say to that. Her cheeks were hot, and she was glad there was no one here to look at her.

But Helen's eyes sparkled, so perhaps she knew. Maybe she felt the heat.

"Listen, Ruby," she went on. "After my accident and all those surgeries, I had a difficult time, and not just for the reasons you might imagine. The worst of it—some of the worst, at least—came because my friends . . ." For the first time she paused. "Many of them didn't know how to treat me."

Ruby could see how that might happen.

"Some disappeared entirely. They couldn't bear it." Helen took a deep breath. "Even worse were the ones who treated me like I was a piece of china, something fragile, something different than what I'd been before." Her hands rose in the air before her. "But I was still me! It was they who had changed."

She put her hands back around the teacup. "The people I met afterward were worse yet. To them I was just the blind girl. And blind meant stupid, slow, retarded. A tragedy, a freak."

Ruby said, "You! Slow!"

Helen smiled. "Yes, well, that's what they thought. It's been awfully hard finding people who just treat me as . . . Helen. Jidge does. And you do, too."

They sat in silence for a few moments. Then Ruby said, "And Paul?"

"Oh, Paul." Now it was Helen's turn to blush. "I only knew him casually before my accident, but afterward . . . afterward he stayed with me through all the surgeries. He spent hours reading to me, talking, making me laugh. He's a true friend."

Then Helen's chin lifted and she looked directly at Ruby's face with her dark eyes. "Don't distract me, Ruby," she said. "What I wanted to say is that you've done me a great favor by agreeing to move in here, to this big empty house, you and the girls alike. And that's why I don't want you to pay me a penny of rent."

"Sorry," Ruby said. "No deal."

Later, lying in a claw-footed tub, luxuriously private and far bigger than the one in the apartment, Ruby let herself sink back among the warm bubbles. She stretched her legs out all the way, and her arms, too, and felt her burdens lift, just a little.

When she walked back into her sunlit new bedroom—for the first time in five years, she'd have a bed to sleep in, not a sofa, not a cot—there were clean clothes laid out for her. Clothes Helen had bought for her in the days since she'd agreed to come.

Clearly the battle had just begun.

But she didn't hesitate to put them on. A navy-blue skirt, a blouse of lighter blue, shiny T-strap shoes with a thankfully low heel.

And a side-lace brassiere.

Downstairs in the dining room, the girls had already finished their Eskimo Pies and were digging into bowls of chicken soup. Amanda was demurely dressed in a long dark skirt and a white blouse that buttoned up close to her chin, but Allie was wearing her athletic suit from the Safe and Sound Fourth.

"She insisted," Mrs. Connell said.

Ruby smiled. She saw that both girls were looking at her, and for a moment she felt almost shy in her new clothes.

"Does she look beautiful?" Helen asked.

"Of course she does," her mother said. "I'm sure you can see that as well as the rest of us can."

Ruby sat down at the table and accepted a cold, sweating ice-cream bar. She bit into it, feeling her teeth tingle, the delicious flavor filling her mouth. Knowing that the vanilla ice cream was smearing across her chin, but not caring. They could dress her in fine clothes, but she was still Ruby.

"Mother and I were talking before," Helen said, "about school. Where did you girls go last year?"

There was silence in the room. Ruby saw Amanda flush a deep red, saw Helen's eyebrows rise at the change in mood she detected.

"They haven't attended school," Ruby said.

There were so many other things she could have said, explanations she could have given. But, as so often happened, she couldn't find the words.

"There are laws now—" Mrs. Connell began, but Amanda jumped in before she could finish. Amanda never had trouble finding the words, once she chose to speak.

"We had to *work*," she said, ignoring Ruby's quelling look. She raised her hands. "Ruby had to take care of us, and Daddy, too, but it wasn't enough, so I had to work and Allie had to help."

Allie nodded, eyes wide. Amanda lost her reserve so rarely.

"I twisted the stems of silk flowers," Amanda went on. "I couldn't sleep at night sometimes, my hands hurt so much, but what else were we supposed to do?"

"Amanda," Ruby said.

Amanda paid no heed. "And then we worked in Coney Island," she said, her face still red. "We were part of Diamond Ruby. Aunt Ruby needed us. We were—necessary. When could we go to school?"

Mrs. Connell was trying to apologize, Ruby could see, but Amanda still wasn't done. "I can read, you know," Amanda said. "Really well. And do mathematics. Did you know I ran the speed machine at the Birdcage?"

Mrs. Connell gave a little nod. She seemed afraid to open her mouth, as if the slightest sound might set Amanda off again.

But it was too late for that. "And I've taught Allie, do you know that?" Amanda looked around, spotted a copy of the *Times* on the table, and dragged it over. "Read, Allie," she said.

Allie looked at her sister, then at Ruby. She *could* read, Ruby knew that, but it was unfair to expect her to perform in front of these near strangers.

"Allie, *read*," Amanda said.

"That's enough," Ruby said. "You've made your point."

Amanda turned her burning gaze on Ruby. She was breathing hard. "But—"

"That's enough," Ruby said again, with more emphasis.

The silence was tense. Then Helen interrupted it. "How about this?" she said in a mild voice. "They'll start school in the fall—"

Both girls looked horrified by the prospect.

"As all girls should," Helen said. "But before then we'll have someone come in and see where their studies have brought them. If necessary, we'll hire a tutor, so they'll be ready by the time the new school year begins."

Now the girls' eyes were on Ruby. "Do we have to?" Allie asked.

Ruby said, "Yes."

Helen smiled. "And in the meantime, they can brush up by reading to me."

The girls brightened.

"I'm still working on Braille," Helen said. "But it's tiring, and even now the most I can manage is *Peter Rabbit*."

"We'd be pleased to read to you," Amanda said in her most dignified tone.

"Good." Helen turned in Ruby's direction. "Now, girls, describe to me how your aunt looks. I want to know every detail."

Before they could begin, Ruby spoke.

"To be honest," she said, "I feel more comfortable in a baseball uniform."

Three days later, not long after first light, Ruby met Colonel Fielding at the entrance to Washington Park. It was the day of the public announcement of her signing with the Brooklyn Typhoons.

From the outside, the park looked like what it had been for years: an abandoned ball field waiting for demolition, much farther from Yankee Stadium than a mere subway journey from Brooklyn to the Bronx. The Colonel followed her gaze, and at least some of her thoughts, and looked grim. "I can see you're disappointed," he said.

Ruby stared at him. "Just promise me I won't have to throw at a wall."

He laughed. "You won't. And it does look a bit better on the inside."

It did. The clubhouse was clean and freshly painted, not that it would matter much to her: Ruby would be dressing in a small room, barely more than a closet, down the hall from a washroom that would be exclusively for her use.

Fine with her.

And the uniform was more than fine. It was dark blue with the team name spelled out in white script, navy socks, and a blue-and-white cap.

"There was some discussion about designing your uniform with a skirt instead of trousers," the Colonel said. "But I decided that you should wear a uniform just like the rest. You'll garner quite enough attention from the press and the public, I think, without dressing like a flapper on the mound."

He gave his head a little shake. "And anyway, Jake wouldn't hear of it."

Jake was Jake Conlon, the Typhoons' manager. He was a small, squirrelly man with a big nose, a sharp chin, and piercing dark eyes that repeatedly shifted to Ruby's face and away. His callused hands, with their big knuckles and old silver-white scars, were in constant motion as well.

He'd been a shortstop back with the Orioles early in the century, the Colonel had told her, the kind of rowdy little player who used his fists and spikes to get by. "You didn't want to cross him," the Colonel said, and Ruby wondered if that was a warning.

Jake Conlon's first words to her were, "Can you hit?"

Leading Ruby to assume that he'd already seen her throw.

"I can learn," she said.

He scowled. "Can't learn to hit," he said. "Got to know how to do it from the minute you're born."

Ruby stretched her arms out before her. "Heard the same thing's true for pitching."

Watching them, the Colonel gave a little smile.

Jake Conlon said, "Horsefeathers. You can learn a lot about pitching, you're willing to listen."

"All the listening in the world," Ruby said, "isn't going to help if you weren't born with the arm."

Jake stared at her. She met his gaze. By this point, she'd met a hundred men just like him. She knew how to handle them. You didn't win by deferring.

Finally he did what she expected: nodded, his face loosening a bit. "Okay," he said, "we'll start work on your hitting as soon as we get this circus over and done with. We got a lot to do, and a game tomorrow."

Dozens and dozens of people were gathered on the infield. The press and interested public alike were all waiting to get a look at her. This dog and pony show would be followed by her first practice with the team.

Ruby got a look at the field, grayish under lowering skies, and at the freshly painted stands, the tall light towers from when the outlaw Federal League had dreamed of holding baseball games at night, and the outfield walls plastered with billboards advertising Old Bushmills whiskey and Fatima cigarettes and BVDs. In center field a band played patriotic songs while jugglers tossed golden baseballs back and forth in looping arcs.

Ruby barely had time to take a breath before a surge of sportswriters, cameramen, and others flooded around her. She could see that Colonel Fielding was eating it all up, while Jake seemed to be in almost physical pain at having to endure the attention of the crowd.

Grumpy George was there, with his notepad and sour expression and a wink for her when no one else was looking. Amanda and Allie, dressed in blue and white, shepherded by Mrs. Connell, stood at the far edge of the crowd. (Helen, with apologies, was off to see the new Harold Lloyd movie with Paul.) Two or three familiar faces from the Birdcage had stopped by, though not Gordon. Ruby recognized a diamond-draped older woman as Josephine Collier of the Federation of Women's Organizations, champions of the "modern girl."

Oh . . . and David Wilcox was there, standing beside the burly, cold-eyed man with the expensive suit and brilliantined hair. Nick's boss.

Beside them stood three New York City cops, strong young men with beefy white necks jutting from their high collars, their brass uniform buttons shining in the misty light.

Wilcox saw her looking at him and gave a little nod. She knew he was sending her a message by being here, by bringing the man with the shiny hair, by surrounding himself with cops.

Ruby took a deep breath. She couldn't say she was much surprised.

You were never done with people like David Wilcox.

22

*t*he Colonel went first, leaning on his walking stick and speaking in strong, measured tones. He sketched in Ruby's history, touched on her family tragedies (which she hadn't even known he was familiar with), and described her Coney Island experiences in the Birdcage.

The sportswriters' pens scratched against paper, though most of them already knew her, and Ruby guessed they had a good idea what they were going to write. Many had seen her in action, and several had profiled her previously.

It was a story that almost could write itself: Long-Armed Girl Plays Man's Game.

Still, a quote was a quote, and the Colonel was an expert at turning a phrase that would look good in the newspapers the next day. For the first time Ruby began to understand how he could take a ramshackle old ballpark, build a team from castoffs, has-beens and never-weres, and hope to make a success of it.

"We're pleased to welcome Diamond Ruby, the Belle of the Ball, as the newest member of the Brooklyn Typhoons," he said.

Jake Conlon went next, and looked like he would rather have been anyplace else. Ruby saw all the tendons in his neck standing out, his hands knotting behind his back, as he said a few words about the team's prospects and her role in helping achieve them.

"When will Ruby pitch?" someone asked.

Jake shrugged. "Don't know," he said. "She just got here today. She's got a lot to prove."

Colonel Fielding stepped forward, smoothly taking control. "We plan for her debut to take place on Thursday, right here against the Allentown Silkworms, at one P.M.," he said. "At the very least, we'll bring her in for an inning so you can all get your first look." He grinned at them. "In plenty of time for the late editions."

Thursday. Three days away.

The Colonel turned toward her and made a courtly little half bow. "Assuming you feel that you'll be ready," he said.

She nodded. What was she going to do, say no?

But behind the Colonel, Jake scowled. Clearly this was the first he'd heard about the schedule for her debut, and just as clearly he didn't like it. Ruby began to see that Colonel Fielding might be a difficult man to work for.

The press noticed, too. "Jake," Grumpy George said, "any problem playing a girl on your team?"

"I'll play anyone who can throw the ball as hard as this girl does," he said right away.

Ruby thought he looked sour when he said it, and wondered how much he'd fought the Colonel's brainstorm. She understood that Jake could make her life difficult, if he chose to, especially once the work on the field began, and Colonel Fielding's focus turned elsewhere, as it inevitably would.

"I notice that none of the other Typhoons are here yet,"

someone said. "How will *they* feel about having a girl on the team?"

"They'll feel like we tell them to feel," Conlon said. "That's how they'll feel."

"And how about the other teams' players?" Grumpy George had moved to the front of the crowd. "Are they on board with this?"

The Colonel, eyes turning cold, answered. "As I assured Ruby herself," he said, "the ballplayers have no say in this matter. They are our employees, under contract. If they don't do the job they've been hired for, they'll pay the consequences."

Ruby saw some of the sportswriters exchange glances. But Colonel Fielding wasn't finished. "Remember," he said, "this isn't the major leagues we're talking about. It's not the Yankees and Babe Ruth threatening to walk off the field. We're a new league, we've only been playing for a month, and we can easily find as many young ballplayers as we need to fill our rosters . . . ballplayers more than willing to play behind Diamond Ruby."

That seemed to put the matter to rest. But Josephine Collier wasn't satisfied. Stepping out of the crowd, she fixed the Colonel with a steely look and said, "How do you intend to guarantee Ruby's safety and dignity?"

The Colonel looked startled. "Er, well," he said. "She will, of course, have her own private dressing area and washroom in every ballpark—"

"That's not good enough." Miss Collier took another step forward. "She is, I believe, the only woman playing in your league?"

It wasn't really a question. Colonel Fielding merely nodded.

"For this reason I—and all the women of the Federation of Women's Organizations—strongly urge that you provide her with a confidante."

The Colonel opened and closed his mouth. "A what?"

"A female companion who will join her here and accompany her on the team's travels."

Before she was done speaking, the Colonel was nodding and agreeing. Anything, it seemed, to get this officious woman off his back.

But Ruby was smiling to herself. They'd given her an idea.

Once Miss Collier was provisionally satisfied, the next question was back to the sportswriters and back to baseball. "How many pitches did you throw each day in Coney Island, Miss Thomas?"

Ruby felt the back of her neck prickle. But sometimes you just had to follow your instincts. She scanned the crowd till she found David Wilcox standing in the rear and off to the side. Beside him, the three cops stood like bodyguards.

"What would you say, Mr. Wilcox?" she called out. "Maybe about three hundred?"

She heard the reaction of the crowd, a sudden indrawing of breath. People turned to see where she was looking, and someone said, "That's crazy."

"I just did what Mr. Wilcox told me to," Ruby said.

Wilcox looked furious and uncomfortable under the weight of so many accusing eyes. "What were you thinking?" Josephine Collier asked him, her chin jutting. "Were you planning merely to use her up and throw her away?"

He didn't answer, just turned and walked off, a big rectangle of a man with a stiff, angry stride. After a moment, his police escort went with him.

The man with the shiny hair remained behind, his face impassive. As Ruby watched, a second man approached him, and a moment later she recognized this one as another former regular at the Birdcage. He was dressed now as he'd always been then, in a fine checked suit, a sharp bow tie—blue this time—and a white straw boater with a colorful pattern on its band.

As always, he looked like a swell, a darb, and Ruby noticed

that he moved with lanky, effortless grace. When he turned his head she saw his narrow face and those slanted, almond-shaped eyes as gray and canny as a cat's. Seeing her watching him, he grinned and tipped his hat.

Ruby moved her gaze back at the assembled writers. "Of course, I'll also do whatever Mr. Conlon asks," she said. "Pitch an inning, start, even throw three hundred pitches if I have to."

That got a laugh.

A freckled young reporter said, "Another question for you, Ruby. Where'd you get that voice?"

She looked at him but didn't reply.

Crying, she thought. I got it from crying.

He smiled, having no idea what she was thinking. None of them knew, or ever would. "You should be onstage," he said.

She looked around. "Aren't I?"

People laughed again. Then someone said, "So when are we going to see you throw?"

The Colonel paused, as if mulling the idea, as if he hadn't considered it until the question was asked. But Ruby knew better. She knew how showmen worked. She knew they always anticipated every question.

And Colonel Fielding was as much a showman as Samuel Cooper had been. For all she knew, he was planning some bally-hoo outside the ticket window, a guy with a sandwich sign, a big fat Babe Ruth look-alike.

Finally the Colonel nodded, as if he'd just reached a decision, and looked at Ruby. "What do you think, Ruby? You want to throw a couple?"

She shrugged. "Sure."

Magically a glove appeared, soft and old but suitable enough, along with a shiny major-league-quality baseball.

And then, for the first time ever, Diamond Ruby stepped up onto a real pitcher's mound.

After all those weeks on a concrete slab, standing on packed dirt felt strange. Still, she liked the view. The mound had a high, steep slope, which suited her just fine.

The writers and other onlookers cleared a space between the mound and home plate. Jake Conlon, wearing a black catcher's mitt, stood behind the plate, waiting for her to be ready.

"Want a couple warm-up tosses?" he called out.

She shook her head. Then she rubbed up the ball, kicked some pebbles off the mound, and stood looking in while Conlon squatted behind the plate. His hawklike face was intent, and for once his body was still. All around them, the crowd on the field fell silent, cameras focused, pens waiting.

Conlon stuck out one finger. Ruby knew enough about real baseball to recognize the signal for a fastball.

She felt her heart thump in her chest, the blood surge through her veins. It was hard to concentrate. Some ants or flies were hatching out of the grass halfway to home plate, swirling madly up into the air. Above the stands, a flock of gulls circled, feasting on them.

She peered in at Jake Conlon's glove, took a deep breath, and felt her muscles relax. It was the first time she'd ever been expected to hit a glove. But when she went into her windup, she knew that she wouldn't embarrass herself, knew she wouldn't throw the ball over the backstop and into the empty stands.

She let go and watched it streak away from her and smack into the glove. The crowd gasped, especially those onlookers who had never seen her throw before, and Conlon paused for a moment before pegging the ball back to her.

But Ruby caught the sharp look that Grumpy George sent her way, and the nearly identical glance, quickly covered up, that she got from Amanda, the person who knew her talents better than anyone.

Ruby didn't acknowledge their concern, but she knew what

had provoked it. At least on this pitch, there'd been no doubt that her fastball hadn't had its usual speed. Something felt numb in her left arm. Something was . . . missing.

Maybe she'd left some of her freakish ability back at the Birdcage.

Maybe David Wilcox was already getting his revenge.

She still had enough left to get batters out, she thought. There was sufficient speed on her fast one, and the curveball Babe Ruth had taught her seemed as good as ever.

It was also enough to impress the crowd of sportswriters. For most of them, the sight of a girl uncorking fastballs of any velocity made a good story. She knew she'd be all over the sports pages tomorrow and again on Thursday and Friday, after her first appearance in a game.

The photographers got everything they could possibly want. Colonel Fielding stepped up to the plate with a big black bat somebody had found and pretended to take swings against her. Ruby posed with Jake Conlon ("Could you give us a grin, Jake?" the shutterbugs asked, to no avail), with Allie and Amanda, even with the writers, all to emphasize how petite she was compared to the cigar-smoking men in sloppy suits who were going to write about her.

Ruby smiled upon request, demonstrated her grip, posed mid-windup like some strange statue dug out of the ground. She held out her arms again and again at whatever angle the photographers wanted, so that the newspapers' readers could gasp and point and discuss the quirk of nature that had provided her with her unusual talent.

At some point the girls got bored and headed home with Mrs. Connell. Ruby couldn't blame them. She found it all pretty tedious herself.

·　　·　　·

Around the time that the reporters began packing away their pads and pens, there was a sudden commotion over at the gate leading into the clubhouse. Ruby heard a confused gabble of voices, a shout, and her first thought was: It's Wilcox, coming back for me.

Then she knew it couldn't be, and shook her head at her moment of fear.

The photographers came streaming past her, more excited than they'd been at any point that day. She saw them clustering around two men who were just stepping onto the field. One was a portly, distinguished gentleman with a square face and a graying mustache. He was wearing a lightweight pinstriped suit and a dark red bow tie.

Beside him stood Babe Ruth, his plaid sports jacket slung over his shoulder, showing off a crisp white shirt, red-and-white-striped tie, red suspenders, and perfectly tailored trousers.

Ruby, breathless for a moment, took a quick glance at Colonel Fielding. The Colonel was leaning on his stick, smiling, looking like a cat that had just feasted on several canaries.

Seeing his expression, Ruby suddenly understood everything.

Surrounded by excited newspapermen, the Babe and his companion came walking out toward the mound, where Colonel Fielding stood waiting. As the three exchanged greetings, Ruby felt eyes on her. She turned her head quickly and caught the gaze of the cat-eyed man. He was standing amid the crowd out near second base, arms crossed, his face full of interest and amusement as he observed the tumult around him.

He met her gaze and grinned. With another rakish tip of his hat, he turned and walked with an easy, unhurried stride toward the centerfield exit.

"Ruby," Colonel Fielding said, "I'd like you to meet Colonel Jacob Ruppert, owner of the New York Yankees."

Smiling, his eyes twinkling, Ruppert shook her hand. "I've

heard a lot about you," he said, "and I hope to see you pitch someday soon."

He looked over at the Babe. "Mr. Ruth I gather you already know."

"I'd say so," the Babe said, grinning at her. "How you doin', kid?"

"All right." She tilted her head. "And you?"

"Never better."

"Hey!" someone called out. "Can we get some shots of you two together?"

But before they did, Colonel Fielding stepped forward and waved for attention. He took Ruppert's arm, and in a moment they stood side by side, two completely self-confident men, accustomed to the spotlight, used to having all eyes on them.

"On this historic day," Colonel Fielding said, "standing here, Colonel Ruppert and I want to announce an exhibition game to be played between the Brooklyn Typhoons and the New York Yankees at Yankee Stadium on Saturday, the twentieth of October, after the conclusion of the World Series—"

"Which will mark the Yankees' first World Championship," Ruppert interjected.

Colonel Fielding laughed. "With the assurance that, at some point in the course of the game, the Bambino will step to the plate to face Diamond Ruby Thomas, the Typhoons' new pitching sensation."

And a sensation it was, a swirl of shouts, pushing crowds, questions with no time for answers, popping flashbulbs, and in the middle of it all, Babe Ruth, in clover.

23

"*T*ania Negoda?" Colonel Fielding said when she finally had a word with him after practice ended on Monday. "From Coney Island?"

He looked doubtful. Ruby already knew that he preferred to think of everything himself. Unexpected requests displeased him.

She stood her ground. "I should have a companion," she said. "Remember?"

"Yes, I remember. A confidante." The Colonel leaned on his cane and peered at her. "Do you want one?"

Ruby nodded.

"I suppose I can understand why." He sighed. "And it does make sense to keep the women's organizations happy. You have, in fact, become quite the cause célèbre for them—perhaps they'll even come to our games."

A pause as he pondered. "But why this particular girl from Coney Island? We could supply one just as easily. Perhaps someone who already works for us here at Washington Park. I have one in mind, her name is Millicent, a switchboard operator, very sweet girl. Or perhaps—"

"I want Tania," Ruby said.

So Tania it was. She was already waiting when Ruby arrived at the ballpark hours before game time on Thursday. She looked just the same, her face worn, her smile revealing missing teeth, but her dark eyes full of life, even merriment.

She was leaning against the wall outside Ruby's tiny dressing room, carrying her usual bulky canvas bag slung over one shoulder. A cigarette dangled from the corner of her mouth, its coal glowing in the dark hallway as she shook her head at Ruby's approach.

"Really coming up in the world, aren't we?" she said.

The two of them embraced. "Yeah, well, wait till you see where they gave me to change," Ruby said, swinging the door open.

Tania surveyed the small room with paint peeling in the corners, a moth spinning around the globe on the ceiling, the clothes rack with Ruby's new uniform and a few empty hangers dangling from it, a splintery wooden table with a pitcher of water sitting on it, and two chairs.

She gave a low whistle. "What'd they get you for?" she asked.

Ruby looked at her.

"Bootlegging? Disturbing the peace? Assaulting an officer of the law? I think you maybe should appeal—anything would be better than this jail cell."

Ruby smiled. "Oh, Colonel Fielding said this is just for a while. He'll find me something . . . more suitable."

"Like an air shaft?" Tania sat down on one of the chairs and placed her bag on her knees. "Well, I guess you can't blame him. Doubt he ever expected to have a girl pitcher on his team."

Ruby shrugged. "I don't care. This is fine. It's not like I'm going to be living here. Not this time."

Tania gave her a sideways look. "Yeah, I heard you've moved in with that blind lady in some fancy neighborhood."

Ruby said only, "The girls are safe there."

Tania nodded as if to say, "Fair enough."

"I miss them, though," Ruby went on. "It's different, not having them with me all day."

"Yeah." Tania laughed. "It'll be quiet in here without them, that's for sure. Especially the little one."

Someone knocked on the door with an officious rap. The second knock, just an instant later, was softer, more tentative, as if seeking to take back the first.

Ruby said, "Come in." Tania stood beside her, arms crossed.

The door swung open to reveal Jake Conlon, looking simultaneously nervous and irritated. Ruby guessed that he was more used to slamming doors open than knocking on them.

His eyes shifted to Tania for a second. Then he shook his head and looked back at Ruby. "Out on the field in ten minutes," he said.

"I'll be ready," Ruby said.

He nodded, then paused. At his sides, his fingers twitched. He glanced down at them and up again, and then said, "Ruby."

"Yes?"

"I'll be bringing you into the game in the seventh."

"Okay," Ruby said.

"Colonel says that the crowd'll keep growing as people wait for you to come in, and nobody who's already there will leave."

He seemed to be waiting for a response to this, so she said, "Makes sense to me."

"I was thinking of you starting the inning, getting your feet wet that way."

Again he waited. Ruby felt a twinge of annoyance run along the muscles of her back.

"Just do what you think is best for us," she said. "For the team."

He blinked, surprised by her tone, and Ruby understood that he didn't think of her as part of "us." Amanda had been right. For now she was the Colonel's girl, a stunt, a trick to draw the crowds, like the mule that could kick a ball or the fans who were allowed to join the team for a day and play an inning in the field.

It was her job to convince him different. "I think I can help us win," she said. "Don't you think so? You've seen me throw."

He stared at her with that unnerving intensity she'd already come to know well. She held his gaze, though, and after a moment he nodded. "Maybe," he said. Then again, "Maybe so. You'll pitch the seventh inning."

Ruby said, "Thank you."

When he was gone, Tania gave a short laugh. "Real piece of work," she said. "A problem?"

"No, I don't think so."

Or, at worst, the least of her problems.

Two hours before game time, there were at least two thousand people in the stands, and many more on the way. Attendance had already exceeded what the team usually drew for a game at Washington Park, and the crowd hadn't come only to see the tightrope walker that Colonel Fielding, showman as always, had hired to walk from the stands behind home plate to the center-field fence.

Stepping out onto the field, Ruby heard a sound, an odd hum like bees disturbed in their hive, rising from the stands. She knew it was a buzz of enthusiasm and interest as the fans got their first look at Diamond Ruby in her Typhoons uniform.

It was a brilliant, sunny day, with little shreds of cloud scattered around the sky. Rain the night before had brought a fresh, cool breeze, and instead of the reek of the nearby canal, Ruby could smell the scent of newly cut grass.

Papa would have looked around, drawn in a big breath through his nose, and said, "It's a great day for a baseball game."

Most of her teammates were already on the field, clustered around the batting cage. Ruby saw them pointing up at the crowd, shaking their heads, laughing. Some stared at her, knowing she was the reason for the tumult.

But none, not a one, came over to speak to her.

"Aunt Ruby!"

The shout came from halfway between home plate and first base. It was Allie, of course, and now Ruby spotted her and Amanda sitting there in the second row, along with Helen, Paul, and Mrs. Connell.

Colonel Fielding, his eye on the best publicity at all times, had asked them to join him for Ruby's first appearance. He'd seen how photogenic little Allie was, how much human interest both girls contributed to Ruby's story, and when you added Helen, the blind butterfly, well, you couldn't pay for better human interest.

If he could have arranged it, he would have had them sitting there for every home game.

Ruby took a step toward them, but then saw Colonel Fielding coming across the grass to meet her. He was gray-faced with anxiety, and she found herself wondering how much he had invested in the team, how much he was depending on her success.

"Ruby, can I talk to you?" he said as he came up to her.

She looked around. There was nobody else within earshot. "Sure," she said. "What's going on?"

The Colonel nodded. He opened his mouth, closed it again. His eyes skittered to her face and away, as if he'd been studying body language from Jake Conlon. Finally he got the words out.

"There's been a threat," he said at last.

Ruby thought about this, and was surprised to find that she wasn't surprised. "What kind of threat?"

The Colonel's lips were actually quivering. Suddenly he looked very old, a hundred years removed from his time in the military.

"Against your life."

She'd already figured that out. "Who from?"

"I don't know," he said. "It was in a letter mailed to my office. Unsigned." His face was full of misery. "It merely said that women were not meant to play baseball, and that they—whoever they are—would make sure that you were not the first."

Ruby took a breath. She didn't feel afraid. No, what she felt was . . . quiet inside. Still. Unmoved.

"Have you told the police?" she asked.

The Colonel shook his head. "I just found out—"

"Well, don't," Ruby said.

"But—"

She took his arm. "Don't tell *anyone*."

She thought again of the lunatic young man who had attacked her in the Birdcage, of the house burning near Surf Avenue as firemen just watched, and of the Ku Klux Klan.

"Until we learn more, learn how serious it is," the Colonel said, "we can't risk letting you pitch."

"Oh yes, you can," Ruby said. "You must."

He opened his mouth but didn't say anything.

"I signed a contract with you," Ruby said. "Now I expect you to live up to it."

"But what if they—" His hands described some incomprehensible shape in the air. "Whoever they are, what if they attempt something?"

Ruby's eyes strayed over the Colonel's shoulder to where the girls and Mrs. Connell were watching them with curiosity. Allie had brought her mouth close to Helen's ear.

It was time to bring this conversation to a close.

"Listen," she said to the Colonel. "Don't you think Babe Ruth gets death threats?"

The Colonel didn't reply, just looked at her with his frightened eyes. For all Ruby knew, he'd sent men into battle, to their deaths, without half the worry he was showing now.

Of course, they'd been men, and she was just a girl.

"How about Ty Cobb?" she said. "Do you think he only gets friendly letters after he spikes someone?"

"That's different," the Colonel said.

"No, it's *not*."

He blinked at her tone.

Ruby stepped closer to him. "It's no different at all. He steps out onto the field every day knowing that almost every baseball fan in America hates him. Plenty of them would like to see him dead. But he steps out anyway, just like I'm going to do."

The Colonel started to speak, but Ruby didn't let him.

"I'm going to do the same thing Ty Cobb would do, or the Babe, or Walter Johnson, or any other ballplayer," she said. "I'm going to go out onto that field when my manager tells me to, and I'm going to *play*."

And with that, she turned and walked away from him.

24

a lone. That was the word.

Alone among eight thousand people.

Eight thousand. That was how many fans came to see the Brooklyn Typhoons play the Allentown Silkworms that Thursday afternoon. Row upon row filled with men in suits and bowler hats, women in dark skirts and pristine white blouses, their short hair nearly hidden under their cloche hats, children running up and down the aisles. The sun winked in and out of the clouds, and the breeze caught bits of paper and sent them whirling out across the field.

It was a multitude. And that didn't even count the hundred or so camped on the roof of the four-story brick apartment building just past the rightfield wall, or the dozens of others standing in the building's open windows, watching.

Or the couple dozen newspapermen and photographers from the local tabloids, along with *The Sporting News*, *Baseball Magazine*, *The Saturday Evening Post*, and others.

All here to watch her.

Was there also someone here in the stadium with a different goal?

On the field just before the game began, throwing a few easy tosses with the second-string catcher, Stu Hunter, Ruby couldn't actually believe that anyone had come to the game to kill her, merely to prevent her from "sullying" professional baseball. Most likely, whoever wrote the letter had believed that the threat itself would be enough to send her fleeing.

Wrong.

Ruby sat on the bench in the home dugout. Not one of her teammates would even acknowledge her existence, except for Andy Sutherland, the Typhoons' veteran starting catcher. When she caught his eye, Andy, who had unruly dark hair, shrugged and gave her a sympathetic look, but even he didn't sit close to her. There were five feet of splintery old bench between her and the next closest Typhoon.

Jake Conlon was different, a little. Twice in the early innings he plunked down beside her and asked if she was okay, if she was ready. Both times she said, Yeah, sure, and both times he nodded and said, Good, and then was back up again, sitting with the rest of his team, leaning against the railing, racing out to argue a call with the umpire, never still.

But also never telling his team to welcome her, or suggesting that she go sit with them.

Ruby watched the game. The Typhoons' pitcher, Mike something, was a thirty-five-year-old who relied on a variety of slow balls and changes of pace mixed with an occasional fadeaway and an even more occasional fastball. Ruby admired how he kept the batters off balance, out of rhythm, and thought that if he made it through the sixth inning, she'd have an easy time of it with the batters when she came in. Her fastball would look like a meteor to them after all Mike's slow stuff.

The Silkworms' pitcher was a cocky young speedballer who was more impressed with himself than he had any right to be. He'd stalk around the mound if anyone as much as hit a foul off him, and gripe loud enough for Ruby to hear if a pitch he liked was called a ball. If someone got a hit, he'd abandon his curveball, shake off his catcher's signs, and try to throw even harder against the next batter. This resulted in his pitches beginning to stray from the strike zone, and to come in straight down the center of the plate when they were accurate.

Jake Conlon watched this performance for an inning or so, and then gathered his team around him in the dugout and told them what to do. The Typhoon batters began to take a pitch or two and to try to make contact on the good pitches, even if just to foul them off, while waiting for a straight one to hit hard.

It was a good strategy, Ruby thought. As the red-faced Silkworm hurler raged at himself and the fates, the Typhoons broke through in the fourth inning, grouping two walks, a bunt single, a long fly ball to score a run, and a ringing double by Andy Sutherland that hit the BVD sign in right field on a bounce to score two more. The moment the ball left Andy's bat, the pitcher flung his mitt to the ground.

When the players who'd scored came back to the dugout, everyone gathered around to congratulate them. Ruby stood, too, but no one paid any attention to her.

The big crowd cheered the rally, and cheered again when Mike struck out two men with the bases loaded to end the sixth after the Silkworms had scored two runs. But the yells and applause were muted, distracted, and Ruby realized the challenge that Colonel Fielding faced. The fans simply hadn't given their hearts to this team yet. They rooted for it, but not passionately.

And anyway, the fans weren't here to see the Typhoons. They were here to see the girl.

Clearly, word had gotten out that Ruby would pitch the top of seventh inning, because as the Typhoons came to bat in the bottom of the sixth, the crowd began to buzz with anticipation. Ruby could see her teammates glancing at her, their expressions combining curiosity with doubt.

Jake Conlon squatted in front of her. "Go warm up. You're on next."

Ruby nodded, picked up her glove, and stood. The moment she stepped out of the dugout, the crowd noise swelled, an odd chattering sound as people pointed at her. She felt the pressure of thousands of eyes during the short walk to the pitchers' warm-up area in foul territory down the first-base line, but could distinguish only the voice of her younger niece, hollering her name so loudly that Ruby was sure Allie would have no voice left by the end of the game.

Then there was another sound, a woman's voice, more than one, a group of women, shouting her name, cheering her. Without thinking, Ruby looked up to find the source of the hullabaloo. The first person she saw was Josephine Collier, face red beneath her gray hair. Beside her, all around her, sat other women, a whole section of the stadium filled with pearls and diamonds and expensive hats and parasols to keep off the sun. As Ruby's eyes found them, four of them held up a pair of cloth banners. On one had been printed RUBY'S ROOTERS! and on the other DIAMOND RUBY: *Modern Girl!*

She had a fan club.

The Typhoons' other pitchers were arrayed along the bench in the warm-up area, sitting back, lazy in the hot sun, arms crossed, looking at her with expressionless faces as she walked to the practice mound. Stu, the backup catcher, was already standing beside the plate, wearing his mitt, his mask pushed to the top of his head. Hip-slung, relaxed, he watched her as well.

Ruby picked up the brown, worn baseball that lay beside the mound. She rubbed it up, then looked down at Stu and nodded.

He squatted behind the plate, and the ballpark went quiet.

It was the strangest thing. The Typhoons were up, with a man on first, yet it was obvious that the entire stadium was watching Ruby, not the action on the field. The sound of a Silkworm pitch hitting the catcher's mitt rang like a gunshot, the home-plate umpire shouted, "Strike three," the batter jawboned a little before heading back to the dugout, and *no one noticed*.

Ruby threw her first pitch, an easy one, just loosening up, and heard the crowd buzz as it popped into Stu's glove. She had to stifle a smile as the ball came back, imagining Allie saying to anyone who would listen, "You think that's something? Just wait!"

After about ten easy throws on this hot day, she nodded to Stu and he held on to the ball. They watched a Typhoon batter rap into a double play to end the inning. The score was still 3–2, Brooklyn. The Silkworms ran off the field and the Typhoons came on more slowly, picking up their gloves where they'd left them on the field.

Ruby jogged over to the real mound as the crowd noise grew into a low, anticipatory roar. She stood there, alone, as the fielders threw balls around behind her and Andy Sutherland finished putting on his catching gear. Then, holding a ball in his right hand and his glove in his left, he walked out toward her. She took a few steps to meet him.

This was the time when the entire infield usually clustered around a new pitcher, but no one else on the team joined them.

She could tell by the set of Andy's jaw that he recognized the slight as well, but all he said was, "You okay?"

"Okay?" she said. "This is the easy part."

He laughed. "Yeah, well, you throw half as good as you can,

you better get used to seeing crowds like this every time you pitch. They're stuck on you."

"Yeah?" She shrugged. "I'm thinking we should give these guys a lot of speed at the start. After what they've been seeing all game, it should mess up their timing, for a while at least."

He thought about that and nodded. "Yeah, let's go right at them."

Then he made a little move toward her before stopping suddenly. Ruby realized that he'd been intending to pat her on the rear, just as he would one of his other teammates.

Instead, he gave his head a shake, grinned, said, "Hands off the chassis," to himself, and headed back toward home plate.

After a few more warm-up pitches, Ruby felt wonderful. The sweat rolled down the sides of her face and beaded up under her uniform. Her arm and shoulder, given the chance to rest after her rescue from the Birdcage, felt loose and easy. Andy Sutherland's beat-up old mitt looked about four feet wide.

The first batter was a pinch hitter, a big ham-armed guy with a heavy beard and too much belly. Ruby knew he'd been sent up to blast one against her, to show the girl pitcher, the stunt, the freak, what a man could do.

She had to stifle a smile. Standing out here, yards from cover, in plain view of thousands of people, she didn't feel the least bit threatened, or overwhelmed, or even nervous. If someone *was* gunning for her, she couldn't do anything about it anyway.

Andy called for a fastball. Ruby reared back, her motion feeling so smooth it was as if her blood had been replaced by lubricating oil, and let go.

The ball slammed into Andy's glove. The umpire's arm shot up into the air. "Strike one!" he shouted, with more gusto than Ruby had heard from him all game.

The crowd roared. The batter, who'd flinched when the pitch

went by, stepped out of the batter's box and knocked some imaginary mud out of his spikes with his bat. The umpire told him to get back in, and he did, though he looked reluctant about it.

Ruby's second pitch was even harder, the hardest she'd thrown in weeks. This time there was an audible gasp from the crowd, eight thousand pairs of lungs all filling at the same moment. Ruby knew that, if she had any voice left, Allie would be shrieking, but she couldn't begin to hear her over the turmoil.

Andy tossed the ball back, got down in his crouch, and signaled for a change of pace. Ruby kept her face expressionless, but inside she was laughing. Andy's pitch calling was like a challenge to the Silkworms, designed to show how helpless they were against her.

She wound up, her arm flashing forward just as it did for a fastball. Only the ball floated in, perhaps twenty miles an hour slower than the previous pitch. The batter was swinging when it had barely left her hand, and then, trying to hold up, to check the swing, he lost his balance and went down onto his knees.

"Strike three!" bellowed the umpire. "And out!"

The crowd roared.

As the next batter came toward the plate, Andy walked halfway out to the mound. He made a quelling gesture with his hands as she went to meet him. "Looks like you're hitting on all sixes," he said, "but keep your head."

She stood there in front of him, hands relaxed at her sides. "Do I look like I'm losing it?"

He looked at her, then grinned. "Hey," he said. "It's one of the things they pay me for, keeping my pitchers on the straight and narrow. Don't blow my cover."

The next batter was another older player, with a creased face and eyes that bulged a little, as if they had too much white in them. He had the thick torso, strong biceps, and slender legs of a slugger, and a big, heavy-barreled bat that he swung easily while waiting for his turn. Ruby remembered that he'd already had two hits today, including a long double to center field.

"This guy, Tracy, he can hit," Andy said. "'Case you didn't notice. Got a couple hundred at-bats with the Athletics a few years ago."

Ruby shrugged. "I can beat him."

"Okay, but better have your best fastball."

Back behind the plate, he gave the signal. Ruby threw a good fastball, and Tracy swung violently and missed.

At the tail end of his swing he let go of the bat.

Ruby watched it fly toward her, spinning end over end like one of those whirly seeds that fell from the maple trees on East Twenty-first Street in summer. She stood very still as it came closer and closer, seeming to move in slow motion as it spun, dipped, hit the ground with a puff of dust, and took a big, unpredictable leap toward her, still spinning as it headed for her legs.

Ruby waited until it was almost upon her—hearing, as if from a distance, disordered cries from the crowd—and then leaped upward, as if she were attempting to fly. She heard a low whirring sound as the bat went past and under her, and then she landed lightly on her feet, turning like a cat to see it come to rest out near second base.

The crowd booed Tracy so loudly that Ruby felt the inside of her ears vibrate. The second baseman and the shortstop looked at the bat lying there, but made no move to pick it up. Jake Conlon came popping out of the dugout to complain to the home-plate umpire. After a moment, a kid, maybe the Silkworms' mascot, came running out of their dugout, picked up the bat, and brought it back toward the plate.

Ruby hadn't noticed Andy Sutherland come out to join her, but now she saw him there, his body rigid as a hunting dog pointing at its target.

"Leave it be," she said.

Scowling, he turned to look at her. "That was on purpose."

"Oh, you think so?" She smiled. "No harm done. Let's play."

After a moment, he nodded. But before he could go back to his position, he looked past Ruby and his eyes widened. They were being joined by the rest of the infield, clustering around her like she was any other pitcher, not the freak, not Diamond Ruby.

"Listen, Rue, that guy's been a rowdy for fifteen years," one of them said.

"And in the bottom of the bottle for just as long," said another.

A couple of them said, "You okay?"

Ruby said, "I'm fine."

"Throw the next one at his bean," someone suggested. "That'll sober him up."

When they were gone, Ruby said to Andy, "Thought we might go with a curve."

He considered the idea, then nodded. "Owled old bastard'll want to kill the next pitch. Curve should cross him up."

But Andy was wrong. When Ruby let go of the pitch, Tracy stuck his bat out and bunted the ball up the first-base line. Andy leaped up from his crouch in pursuit, but Ruby, scampering toward it, could see that it was her play. The ball was hugging the chalk baseline as it rolled. All she needed to do was pick it up and tag Tracy as he came past.

Hearing the pounding footsteps approaching, she got to the ball and snagged it in her bare left hand. Straightening, she turned, just in time to see Tracy raise his elbows and, without slowing down even a fraction, barrel into her. The next thing she knew she was flying through the air, the ball still clutched in her hand as she landed with a bone-shaking thump on her back in the grass.

Either the crowd went completely silent as she hit, or the impact stunned her sense of hearing along with everything else. Regardless, it was in a kind of humming silence that she scrambled to her feet, got her bearings, took six quick steps, and hurled herself at Tracy as he stood facing her, grinning, ready to fight.

She hit him like a battering ram, planting her head into his chest. The attack was so quick, so sudden, that he went over backward, all the air leaving his lungs with a whooping sound (she could hear *that*) as he slammed into the ground with her on top of him. Before she could inflict any more damage, though, someone grabbed her by the shoulders and hauled her up and off him.

Almost spitting with anger, she fought against whoever held her, twisting and writhing like a snake. Turning her head, she would have bitten her captor, if she hadn't seen that it was Jake Conlon. Even then it took great force of will for her to stop struggling.

Conlon looked a trifle alarmed at her expression, but his eyes were filled with amusement. "You've done your part, Diamond Girl," he said, not letting go. "Now let the guys help out."

She looked back to see about six of the Typhoons piled on top of Tracy, Andy Sutherland on the bottom of the pile. Both umpires were trying to pull the mob apart. Other Typhoons and Silkworms shouldered and shoved and glared at each other all over the infield, though no real punches were thrown.

A cacophonous mixture of boos and cheers cascaded from the grandstands.

Finally, the defiant Tracy was pulled from the pile and marched off to the locker room to the accompaniment of derisive howls from the crowd. The other players returned to their dugouts, and Jake Conlon judged it safe to release Ruby. As the Typhoons still on the field gathered around, he stepped back and took a look at her. There was still amusement in his moist, never-still eyes.

"Now you look like a ballplayer," he said, gazing at the rip in the knee of her uniform, the grass stains across the jersey, the scrape across her cheek. "You okay?"

Ruby could feel bruises rising on her breastbone, her right forearm, her left thigh. Her head still felt a bit muzzy, and a drop of blood from the scrape tickled her cheek as it tracked down toward her mouth.

"I'm fine," she said.

"We could bring in Charlie." Conlon gestured toward the relievers' bench. "You're only in for an inning today, anyway—"

"No!"

Everyone hid their grins at this deep-throated sound coming from the mouth of the girl.

"I need one more out," Ruby said. "Let me get it."

Conlon looked at Andy Sutherland, who had a fat lip. The catcher shrugged and said, "Listen to her."

"Okay." Conlon's eyes gleamed. "I don't, she might bite me."

"This next guy can't hit a curve," Andy told her when Conlon was back in the dugout and the other players at their positions.

Ruby looked at the batter approaching home plate. He was tall and slender, with long arms.

"No," she said. "No curveball, no fadeaway, no change of pace. Fast stuff."

"He murders fast stuff," Andy said.

"Not mine he won't," said Ruby.

It took three pitches. The first may have been the fastest ball she'd ever thrown. The batter was so stunned that he ducked back from the plate, the bat never leaving his shoulder.

The second was even faster, and his weak swing missed it by a foot.

The third was the fastest yet, slamming into Andy's mitt. The batter clearly decided that taking strike three would be less embarrassing than offering at it, because he made absolutely no effort to swing.

Andy joined her as she walked to the dugout. He was shaking his left hand.

"I'm gonna have to get myself a new mitt, the days you pitch," he said.

A group of the Typhoons was at the top of the dugout steps to congratulate her. After, Ruby turned to head to her spot on the bench, but someone called out, "Hey, Rue! Over here."

They'd cleared a space for her, right in the middle of the bench.

She hesitated for a moment, then went to join her teammates.

She took a long, hot, luxurious bath, dirt and blood floating off her bruised body in equal measure.

She ate a steak and two baked potatoes and a big slice of what Allie called Celebration Cake, actually a devil's-food-cake recipe she and Amanda had made out of their old Marion Harland cookbook, and drank three glasses of orange juice and one of milk.

She told them about the endless interviews she'd done after the game. Helen had laughed and said, "Oh, Ruby, after this, you are going to be more famous than you can even imagine."

Now, late at night, no one able to sleep, they were all sitting around the table, drinking milk and picking at the remnants of the cake. Ruby's family.

Amanda, as always more aware of Ruby's shifts in mood than anyone else, gave her an anxious glance and asked what was wrong.

Ruby said, "Nothing."

But the tone of her voice sharpened everyone's attention. After a moment, Helen said, "What is it you want, Ruby?"

This was exactly what she'd been wondering herself, but it took hearing the question spoken aloud to bring the answer.

"I want—" Her hands grasped at the air before her, grasped at nothing. "I want . . . *this*," she said. "*All* of this."

Helen nodded, unsurprised. But Allie and Amanda merely stared.

It was the first time in their lives they'd heard their aunt ask for anything for herself.

25

OPPONENTS MAY "RUE" THE DAY TYPHOONS SIGNED GIRL PHENOM
"Diamond" Ruby Thomas Pitches Inning, Strikes Out Two, Engages in Brawl
BY GEORGE LITTELL

First discovered by this reporter flinging scarlet baseballs at a wall amid the bearded ladies and wild men of the Coney Island carnival sideshows, Ruby Lee Thomas moved up in weight class when she was signed to pitch for Colonel Fielding's struggling Brooklyn Typhoons. What drew thousands of fanatics to old Washington Park yesterday afternoon was a simple question: Is "Diamond Ruby" a mere stunt, or a real baseball pitcher?

If yesterday's game is any indication, perhaps the better question should be: Which of our three big-league teams will sign her first?

A BASE TOO FAR
An Editorial

Longtime readers of the *New York American* editorial page will know that we have always been strong supporters of women's participation in organized athletics. Our recent series of features, "Sports: Accenting the Feminine" spotlighted the achievements of such stars as swimmer Ethelda Bleibtrey, golfing sensation Glenna Collett Vare, and tennis whiz Suzanne Lenglen.

But sometimes too much of a good thing is . . . simply too much. Such is the case with Ruby Thomas, the so-called Diamond Ruby of Coney Island sideshow fame. We can venture no opinion on Ruby's athletic ability with a baseball, not having attended Thursday's game at Washington Park, but we also cannot help but notice that chaos followed her onto the field.

Color us unsurprised. We do not condone the behavior of an Allentown roughneck known as Jim Tracy, but we understand well the emotions that tempted him off the straight and narrow. There are places where women—and especially 18-year-old girls—do not belong, places that should remain a gentleman's domain. The baseball diamond is one of them.

And as for the planned "grand confrontation" between "Diamond Ruby" and Babe Ruth in October, well, in our opinion it is a rank travesty that insults America's Pastime. We would expect no more from the man-child known as the Big Bam, but will not some saner heads prevail?

ANOTHER TRIUMPH FOR THE MODERN WOMAN

BY JOSEPHINE COLLIER

President, New York City Federation of Women's Clubs

Special to the New York Tribune

The women of New York City—nay, of the entire world—witnessed the next step in a revolution on Thursday, in the most unexpected of locations: a ramshackle old ballpark hard by the Gowanus Canal in Brooklyn.

What did they see? Merely a slightly built, long-limbed teenage girl named Ruby Thomas step out onto the pitcher's mound and face down a glowering lineup of male baseball stars in a professional game at Washington Park. And what did she do when she got there? She struck out two batters and showed the third she would not be bowled over . . . not on the baseball field, and not anywhere else, either.

If a woman can do this, what can't Women do?

NO DECREE FROM THE CZAR

When asked his opinion of the appearance of 18-year-old (female) pitcher Ruby Thomas in Thursday's game, Judge Kenesaw Mountain Landis, the commissioner of Major League Baseball, declined comment. His office did reveal, however, that the Czar is monitoring the situation closely.

"Enjoying your fame?" Babe Ruth asked. "Everything you expected so far?"

Ruby rolled her eyes at him. He laughed, and beside her Jack Dempsey smiled as well.

"How many times do they expect you to answer the same questions?" she asked. "The press, I mean."

"About a thousand," Jidge said.

"Every day," Dempsey added.

Riding in a yellow-and-chrome breezer, a Roamer, which may have belonged to the Babe, or may just have been borrowed for the occasion (and driven by a chauffeur of the same uncertain provenance), they were on their way to the Hebrew Orphan House, just as Ruby had promised they would all those weeks ago in the Birdcage.

Dempsey had recently moved to New York to prepare for his upcoming fight with Luis Firpo. He was training upstate in some place called White Sulfur Springs, but he did make publicity appearances in the city, and somehow Jidge had convinced him to come along on this visit to the orphanage.

Ruby had never met anyone more persuasive than Babe Ruth. If President Harding had been traveling in New York this day, she had no doubt that the Babe would have had him sitting beside them as well.

The Babe, occupying the front passenger seat, was twisted around to face them. "Heard about that hubbub on the field," he was saying. "You know, kid, that guy, Tracy, he was a sonuvabitch even back when he was with the Elephants."

Ruby was startled. "You knew him?"

"Knew him? I faced him when I pitched." Jidge grinned. "Knocked him on his ass at least one time I can recall. Made my day."

"I'll remember that the next time I pitch to him."

Dempsey was shaking his head. "He really ran right over you, on purpose?"

"Uh-huh. I've got the bruises to show for it."

And she did, big greenish welts along her rib cage, on her breasts, and on both of her forearms. She was wearing a long-sleeve cotton blouse, although the day was likely to be hot, so as not to frighten the orphans. Fortunately, the scrape on her face had mostly healed.

"I think he was hoping to break something, or maybe just scare me so I'd stop throwing the ball so hard."

Looking thoughtful, Dempsey scanned the street. Aside from tired workers coming home from nighttime shifts, it was mostly empty. A few people stopped to gaze at the outlandish car passing by, trying to figure out who was in it. Every once in a while someone would shout out the Babe's name, but he didn't seem to notice.

Dempsey's gaze returned to Ruby's face. "Next time somebody else with the same idea comes at you, and you don't have a baseball handy, just hit him on the nose," he told her. His fist jabbed the air, a blur, too fast for her to follow. "Doesn't have to be a big roundhouse, just a quick shot like this. You won't hurt your hand, the way you might if you hit him in the mouth or on the chin, and I guarantee he'll start to cry. His hands'll go up to protect his face, leaving the rest of him open. You can run or hit him again, your choice. Most people, they just can't handle being hit in the nose."

He reached up and touched his own flattened one, with its bumps and ridges. "'Course, when you've had yours broken as many times as me, you don't feel much of anything, you get hit there again."

"Wow, boxing lessons from the Manassas Mauler," the Babe said. "Watch he doesn't charge you for them, kid."

"They pay me enough to fight in the ring, Jidge," Dempsey said calmly. "A load more than you get for hitting a baseball."

Ruth was unperturbed. "I do just fine."

Dempsey looked back at Ruby. "You hear me?" he said. "A quick, sharp jab, the nose, no fuss."

Ruby thought about it, remembering, as she did so often, Mel Walters, his camera, his roving hands. "I can think of another place," she said carefully, "where men will cry if they get hit."

Both men looked at her. Then the Babe guffawed. But again Dempsey remained serious. "Yeah, that's a fact," he said. "Problem is, plenty of men will be expecting that, guarding against it. But not many will expect a straight shot to the honker, especially not from a girl."

He kept his eyes on Ruby's. "But whatever they leave open, if the chance is there, take it. Hit 'em in the nose, kick them in the balls, jam your thumb in their eyes. Do whatever it takes to win."

"Just like you do in the ring, right?" the Babe said.

"Whatever it takes," Dempsey said.

Ruby had expected to see a crowd of reporters and photographers waiting for them outside the front door of the Hebrew House, but no one was there but Deborah, the harried young woman who'd accompanied the orphans to the Birdcage.

The Babe noticed Ruby's expression and grinned. "I tell the press not to come, and they don't."

"I need to learn how to do that," Ruby said.

Deborah came to meet them as they stepped out of the car. "Mr. Ruth!" she said, grasping his hands. "Welcome. The boys and girls are *so* excited." Her tired eyes shone. "The staff, too."

Then she stepped back and looked at Ruby. "Miss Thomas. Thank you so much for coming."

"Please, call me Ruby."

"And I'm Jidge." The Babe gestured with one big hand. "Oh, and this is another pal of mine. Guess you can call him Jack."

Deborah stepped forward, her hand out, and only then heard the words. All the color flooded out of her face. "Jack *Dempsey*?" she gasped.

Shaking her hand quite gently, he nodded.

For about the first five minutes, the children all looked like they'd been struck by a thunderbolt. Then they forgot their paralytic shyness—and also, Ruby thought, the strict instructions they'd received to be respectful of their famous guests.

There were perhaps thirty of them, ranging from roughly five to fifteen. They were all dressed in what Ruby assumed was their Sunday best, dark shorts and white shirts for the boys, knee-length cotton skirts and half-sleeve white blouses for the girls. All the clothes were old but carefully mended and washed.

They'd clearly been required to scrub their hands and faces before their guests' arrival, though a few had spoiled the effect by snitching bits of icing from the big chocolate cake that someone (she guessed the Babe) had sent over, and which now sat, sweating in the warm, close air, on one of the old wooden tables lined up near the kitchen area. The evidence of their theft was apparent on their fingers and around their mouths.

Ruby watched the Babe bend over, put his hands on his knees, stare at the line of smallest children, and say, "Anyone want cake?"

Still the children didn't move. Finally one of the middle-size ones raised a hand and said, "But Miss Deborah says that cake isn't for breakfast."

The Babe gave a disbelieving snort and straightened. "Not for breakfast?" he boomed, patting the bulge of his stomach. "I eat chocolate cake for breakfast every day, and what harm does it do me?"

"None!" one of the braver kids shouted out.

"Do I still hit home runs?"

Now a few voices joined in a chorus of assent.

"Does chocolate cake taste as good at eight-thirty in the morning as it does after supper?"

Everyone seemed to agree loudly with that.

"So I don't think Miss Deborah would mind if we broke the rules just this once. Would you, Miss Deborah?"

Faced with the unstoppable force that was Babe Ruth, what

else could poor Deborah do but tell them to go ahead, to cheers led by none other than Jidge himself?

Chocolate cake opened doors, Ruby learned.

She also learned a few other things as they all dug in. First was that little children knew Babe Ruth was one of them. They couldn't keep away from him, and he delighted in every bit of their attention, laughing and talking even when the chocolate on their hands smeared his formerly white shirt.

Jack Dempsey, on the other hand, was most involved with the older boys. Ruby couldn't hear what he was saying, but she could see him sitting down at the far end of the table, his slice of cake untouched before him, speaking quietly but forcefully to a group of wide-eyed boys who drank in every word he was saying.

The older girls chose to sit with Ruby. At first they were all quiet and shy, but then one of them, a slight, diffident girl who looked about thirteen, asked, "How old are you?"

"Eighteen," Ruby said, "just recently."

They all blinked at that. "You look older," said one.

"And sound older, too," another added.

After that someone asked about her family, and Ruby told them about Allie and Amanda. As it became clear that she was the girls' main means of support, and that she herself had lost both parents in the great epidemic, they became wide-eyed and silent once again.

They understood right away, though, that her life hadn't differed that much from theirs, so they gradually loosened up and became more talkative. After her experiences with the press, Ruby was amused and relieved to find out that this audience was far more interested in other aspects of her life—the jobs she'd held, the food she liked to eat, the movie stars she thought were handsome—than in her ability to throw a baseball.

.　　.　　.

"Anybody ready to go to the park?" Babe Ruth asked.

There was a general roar of approval, and off they went, clomping down the stairs in neat lines, the Babe at the head. On the sidewalk, they drew barely a glance from the pedestrians out on this hot morning, and if a few people noticed a couple of familiar faces among the orphans, nobody came running up, shouting out Babe Ruth's name, or Jack Dempsey's.

They entered the park, walking past horse-drawn carriages and bicyclists to reach a field just east of the Lower Reservoir. Amanda and Allie were there to meet them, shepherded by Mrs. Connell. Helen had been struggling with a chest cold and was resting at home.

"Got a hug for me, kid?" Babe Ruth said to Allie. A moment later he was introducing both girls to the crowd of children clustered around.

"Look," Mrs. Connell said.

Several young men carrying boxes approached the field. Dempsey and the Babe went to meet them, and without delay the adults were handing out old baseball mitts, balls, bats, and even well-worn, well-padded boxing gloves to the excited children.

For the next hour or so, the Babe, assisted by Allie and two of the young men, taught the youngsters how to hit, Jack Dempsey instructed his avid teenage followers in pugilistic techniques, and Ruby showed her grave, smitten admirers how to hold a baseball, how not to throw "like a girl." When one managed to deliver the ball into a mitt with a satisfying smack, Amanda was always there to guess how fast the ball had traveled. No matter the number, the pitcher was always thrilled.

Miss Deborah and the other teachers sat in the shade, bestirring themselves only when one of their charges grew too rambunctious. This didn't happen often. The children were too riveted to wrangle.

All too soon it was time to go. The Babe and Dempsey were due at yet another press conference for yet another round of photographs. Then the Babe would head up to Yankee Stadium for the day's game, just as Ruby would go to her own, more modest, ballpark and Dempsey would board the train for White Sulfur Springs.

They said good-bye to the boys and girls, provoking many tears and a hearty and well organized three cheers in return.

When they had gone, Babe Ruth came walking up, Allie riding on his shoulders. He'd lit a cigar and looked entirely pleased with himself, though his face was red and his clothes were hopelessly stained and drenched in sweat. Jack Dempsey followed, as usual less expressive, but seeming relaxed as he tossed a boxing glove in the air and caught it.

"Good kids," he said.

The Babe nodded and took the cigar out of his mouth. "Sure. They always are."

"How often do you do things like this?" Mrs. Connell asked.

"Whenever he feels guilty about how much money they're paying him to hit a little white ball," Dempsey said.

"Better than hitting some poor old palooka in the head," Ruth replied. But he seemed preoccupied, looking at the girls and frowning. "Not enough room in my car," he said to Mrs. Connell. "I'll get you a cab."

She smiled at him. "Thanks, Jidge, but no need. We'll stay in the park for a while. The girls have hardly ever been here before."

"Exactly never," Allie said.

"We thought we might go boating."

The Babe grinned, relieved. "Swell." He bent over, and Allie jumped off to the ground. Her bare knees were covered in grass stains, there was a fresh scrape on her left arm, and she'd skinned her right elbow. She'd rarely looked happier.

She and Amanda both thanked the Babe and Dempsey very

politely, even curtsying (a skill Ruby had never mastered), and then Mrs. Connell led them south toward the lake. The Babe, frowning, looked over at one of the young men who'd brought the treasures for the kids, and without a word passing between them, the man walked off in the same direction.

"He'll make sure nothing happens to them," the Babe said. "Three females alone in this park, you just don't know."

Even though it's the 1920s, Ruby thought.

"So what do they have planned for you, the Colonel, and old Jake?" Jidge asked as they walked toward Fifth Avenue.

"They're starting me on Sunday," Ruby told him.

Dempsey grunted. "'Course they are. Bring in a lot more fans, they know you'll be in the game at the start."

The Babe nodded, then shot her a quick glance. "How much they paying you, kid?" he asked.

Ruby thought about it, then told him.

He and Dempsey made identical sounds of disgust. "Man's cheating you," Dempsey said.

Ruby shrugged.

"Ask for a raise, now, before your first start, and hold out if he won't give it to you. He'll bend soon enough—he knows the crowd will be lucky to reach a thou if you're not there. Hold out."

"I don't think so," Ruby said. "But thanks."

They walked in silence for a little while. Then the Babe said, "Okay, I get that. Someone gives you the chance to pitch in a real game, you take it. I'd've done the same thing, I was your age—I did do the same thing. But don't forget, kid, he'll be coining money every time you pitch, and even when you're not. You deserve a cut of that dough, but you won't get it if you don't make a fuss."

"And if my 'fuss' doesn't work, what then? I punch him in the nose?" She jabbed. "Like this?"

That got a laugh from both of them. "Not the worst idea, but I've got a better one," Dempsey said. "Let me do it."

"The Colonel would break into pieces." Ruby shook her head. "Forget it. He's a nice enough fellow, and I owe him something."

"But he owes you, too," Babe Ruth said.

26

*N*ick was waiting on the front steps of the Connells' brown-stone when the car pulled up.

Ruby was by now the only passenger, the Babe and Dempsey having departed at the Excelsior Hotel in Manhattan for their meeting with the press. Seeing her brother, she thought of telling the driver to keep going, but before she could decide, he'd pulled to a stop and Nick had spotted her.

He raised a tentative hand, as if expecting to be ignored, and she felt pity twist in her stomach. For a moment, she thought she glimpsed the old Nick, the smart, funny young man who would have done anything to protect her. The Nick that Evie had loved so deeply.

Then her eyes cleared, and she knew she was being foolish. That Nick was never coming back. At least Allie and Amanda weren't here to see this one. At least they didn't have to be re-minded of what he'd become.

The driver's eyes were on Nick as well. "You okay getting out here?" he asked, the first words she'd heard from him. "Want me to chuck that guy off your stoop?"

Ruby sighed. "No. It's fine."

"Mr. Ruth, he'd want me to take care of you."

"I'll handle this. But thanks."

She stepped out and waited for him to pull away from the curb, his eyes still on her in the mirror as he drove off. Then, steeling herself, she turned to face her brother.

She could see why the driver had been concerned. Nick looked worse than ever: gaunt, haggard, haphazardly shaven. She'd sent him a box of new clothing soon after moving here, but he seemed to be wearing clothes that were years old, and they hung on him. The collar and cuffs of his shirt and the knees of his trousers were frayed, and there were stains under his arms and down his front.

Most likely he'd never worn the new clothes, but had brought them back to the stores for cash.

Cash to buy what? Going by his ghost-pale face and bloodshot eyes, the answer to that question, at least, seemed obvious. Even from a few feet away, Ruby could smell him.

She regretted giving him her new address.

"Why are you here, Nick?" she asked.

His eyes shifted to her, and then away, up to the solid, shut front door. "Will you show me your house?" he asked. His voice was hoarse, as if he'd burned the inside of his throat.

Though not with tears, Ruby was sure.

"It's hot," he said. "The light hurts my eyes. Can we please go inside?"

Ruby crossed her arms and looked down at him. "No."

He blinked at the finality of the word. "Maybe we could go someplace to get something to eat?"

Ruby shook her head. "Whatever you have to tell me, you can say it right here."

For a moment, anger contorted his face. But just as quickly, it drained away. Ruby couldn't tell whether this was because he had it under control, or whether he no longer had the strength to sustain it.

In the end, all he did was reach into his pocket and pull out a creased envelope. "I was told to give this to you."

Ruby took it. Her name was written on the front in cursive in a thick, rough hand, but there was no other mark on it.

"Who is it from?" she asked.

Nick didn't reply.

With a shrug, she unsealed it and pulled out the single sheet within. The words inside were written with the same ink, but this time printed in block letters.

HALF JEW, HALF CATHOLIC

DEFORMED

YOU WILL NOT PLAY

IT WILL NOT STAND

WE WILL DEFEND PURE WOMANHOOD

ARYAN BROTHERHOOD

100% AMERICAN

NO IMMIGRANT SCUM

NO DIAMOND RUBY

And, at the bottom of the page, a flaming cross: the seal of the Ku Klux Klan.

Deformed. Ruby took a breath. There was an odd fluttering feeling in her stomach.

She looked up from the paper at her brother. "You're half Jew, half Catholic, too," she said. "Immigrant scum, just like me."

Nick stared at her. "What?"

"This letter you came all the way here to deliver," she said, struggling to keep her voice even, but failing, "comes from the

Klan. Warning me against playing baseball." She paused. "When you took this, when you agreed to give it to me, did you know what this letter said?"

"No. No, of course not."

Ruby had always thought that the more denials you heard, the more likely someone was lying. "Who gave it to you?" she asked.

"I don't know. Some guy. I didn't know him."

Another lie, most likely.

Ruby stepped closer. The smell of speakeasy gin coming out of his skin was mixed with the rank odor of fear.

"Nick," she said, "tell me: How much did he pay you for this little errand?"

He wouldn't hold her gaze, but eventually the truth came out. "Ten dollars."

"So you took ten bucks to bring me a threat on my life?"

This time he didn't even try to deny it. "I was so hungry," he said. "And . . . thirsty."

Ruby had to harden her heart. This shattered husk wasn't her brother. Her brother had died in 1918.

"You stay here," she said.

She walked past him up the stairs and let herself into the quiet house. The still air smelled of soup and some medicine that Helen had cooked up for her cold, but Helen herself appeared to have gone out.

Ruby went upstairs to her bedroom, knelt in front of the built-in cabinets that lined one wall, and slid open the false back of the left-most cabinet. From the roll of bills she kept there against a run on the bank (she'd inherited her father's cynical distrust of the people who held your money for "safekeeping"), she counted out one hundred dollars.

Then she went back downstairs and out into the blistering sun. Nick's back was to her, his chin in his hands, his thin bird-like shoulder blades pressing against his shirt.

"You can have this," she said, and when he lifted his head she showed him the cash.

He stared at it, then put out his hand.

She made no move. "You can have it if you tell me who you work for. The one with the jewelry and the shiny hair. Who is he?"

Before she was done with the sentence, though, he was shaking his head violently. "No," he said. "No, I can't. You don't want me to do that. You don't want to get near him, not that guy."

"You're right, I don't." She dangled the money closer to him. "But I don't seem to have any choice, do I? He showed up at Washington Park my first day there. He knows the connection between us, just like the Klan does. He knows Wilcox. Tell me his name."

Nick looked like he might faint. But finally, his eyes skittering around, he said, "Frankie."

"Frankie what?"

Nick didn't know, or wouldn't say.

"And where's Frankie from?"

"Someplace out west," Nick said. "That's all I heard. Really!"

It wasn't enough. Ruby gave him the money anyway, as she'd known she would, but not before she made some things clear.

"This is it," she said. "This is all. There's no more where it came from."

He nodded, though she could see calculation in his eyes.

"You stay like this, I don't want to hear from you again. I don't want the girls to see you. They've had a hard enough time already. You come back, and I'll have the bulls on you in five minutes."

He had nothing to say.

"But if you want to clean yourself up," Ruby said, "get word to me, and I'll help you."

She saw the mulish look on his face, and knew she was wasting her words. But she had to try. "You get off the juice, I'll help you get away from the guys you work for. But until then—stay away from me."

With that, she handed him the money, turned, and walked back up the stairs. He let her go without saying a word.

"You look terrific," Gordon said. "When I was busy, you became a young woman, not a girl."

She'd dialed the number on the card he'd given her, and he'd responded with pleasure, saying he was delighted to hear from her. He was glad to learn that Allie and Amanda were doing well, and especially happy to hear that Ruby had some information he might be interested in. Would she be free for a cup of coffee or something to eat? He didn't trust talking on the telephone. You never knew who was listening.

They met at a small cafeteria on the corner of Montague and Court streets. Gordon himself looked just the same, gray-haired, erect, cheerful, although now he was dressed in a better suit. He'd been following her exploits, of course, he told her. He regretted missing her first appearance (especially the "brouhaha"), and said he'd try to make it to her start on Sunday.

"I heard from some of the Coney Island regulars who were at the game and saw the brawl," he went on. "They said you stood up for yourself like a man." He laughed. "Of course, it's not the same for them, now that they're scattered around that big ballpark. They feel like you're not theirs anymore. You belong to the whole world now."

Ruby let all this pass without comment. "What's in the Birdcage these days?" she asked.

"Oh, some lady with tattoos that wiggle when she dances, I hear. Tedious stuff. The place is usually empty."

"How about the storage room?"

He looked at her, considering what to say, and finally settled on, "It's empty now. That's why I'm not forced to watch the tattooed lady."

"Any idea why they shifted it?"

"Happens all the time," he said. "Gives them a better chance of losing us, they keep switching their drop-off points. But I think in this case David Wilcox made it happen because he was afraid you'd tell some Prohi about it. He never figured out we were already there."

Again he hesitated before going on. "I think Wilcox's having a tough time of it. As long as Samuel Cooper was his boss, he did just fine. But in charge? He keeps canning people, or they quit. He's had to switch food suppliers twice already. Rumor has it his whole sideshow business might go belly-up or get taken over."

"Maybe I'll feel sorry for him tomorrow," Ruby said, "if I think of it."

There was a short silence. Then Gordon gave her a curious look. "It's a pleasure to see you, Ruby, especially looking so well. You've put on some weight, which you needed, and you seem . . . more settled than I've ever seen you. But I don't think you called me to reminisce, or to talk about David Wilcox, or just to see my old face again. So what's cooking?"

That's when she told him about her conversation with Nick, and the man named Frankie from "out west."

"He's the fancy guy I told you about before, the one with the oiled hair and the gold cuff links that I saw once in the Birdcage. Remember?" She took a breath. "And he was there for my first practice with the Typhoons, too, watching me. I wish you'd been there to see him."

Gordon gave her a long, considering look. "Listen, Ruby," he said. "Since the Dry Law passed, there's always someone showing up trying to get a piece of the pie. It's a big pie, you know?"

Ruby nodded.

"Where else is like here?" Gordon went on. "The long

coastline, miles of beaches with empty storefronts and hidden storage rooms close by, hundreds of boats coming in every day, fleets of trucks, train lines leading everywhere. You could smuggle in anything from alcohol to opium to a squadron of Sopwith Pups, and send it onward without anyone even half suspecting. It happens every day of the year, even Christmas. No wonder folks from 'out west' want a piece of it."

Ruby said, "Okay."

"The problem is that this man, this Frankie, hasn't yet showed a single sign of trying to get into the gin-smuggling racket. And until he does, there's no reason for me to know him, no reason to chase after him."

Ruby stayed quiet.

Gordon turned his hands up. "He threaten you in any way? Then I might be able to call someone in."

"No. He just . . . watched me. Like he's got a plan, and it includes me, but I don't know how."

Gordon frowned. "I'm sorry, Ruby."

Ruby kept her eyes on his for a long moment, then shrugged and got to her feet. It had been a long shot anyway.

He tilted his head. "Something else bothering you?"

For a long moment, she didn't move or reply. She'd come intending to show him the threatening letter she'd gotten from the Klan.

But instead, thinking of the policemen she'd seen flanking Wilcox at the ballpark, she just shook her head.

"No," she said. "That's it."

27

*O*n Saturday, one day before Ruby's first start for the Typhoons, Washington Park's little conference room was overflowing. Colonel Fielding surveyed the crowded room, filled with irritated reporters with wrinkled suits and sharp elbows, satisfaction on his face. "This keeps up," he said, "and I'll have to make some renovations, add some space."

Sitting beside him at a table crowded with microphones—shiny copper, metal springs, and twisted wires—emblazoned with the call letters of a dozen radio stations, Ruby took a deep breath. What did the press want from her? Everything. With a few exceptions, like Grumpy George, they had no respect, no compassion, no desire to treat her fairly. To them, she was the story, and the story was her. They wouldn't hesitate to embarrass her if they thought the audience wanted it.

So it was up to her to control them.

"How're you feeling, Ruby?" said the beat guy from the *Daily Eagle*. "Ready for tomorrow?"

"I'm fine." She pretended to look startled. "Wait—is something happening tomorrow? Why am I always the last to know?"

There was a ripple of laughter through the room. Good. Always let them know right away you're willing to play along, Dempsey had told her.

"You nervous about your first start?"

"Well, no—but these little dancers doing the tango in my stomach are."

More laughter.

Ruby leaned forward, placing her arms carefully on the table amid the nest of microphones. Cameras clicked and flashbulbs popped. "Of course I'm nervous. Who wouldn't be? There'll be thousands of people watching the game—"

The Colonel interrupted. "We think we may sell out," he said. "Eighteen thousand fans."

He sounded stunned even as he said the words, and the reporters shook their heads and exchanged glances. They were onto a good story, and they knew it.

"But I think I'll be able to shut out the noise—and my nerves—and pitch my game," Ruby said. She sat back in her chair a little and looked out at the mob. "And anyway, so what if I've got the heebie-jeebies? It'll never compare to the way I *used* to feel, when I'd wake up every morning wondering how I was going to find enough food to feed my family."

There was a brief pause while pens scratched against paper. She was giving them good material.

And being smart about it, too. Tell them about your past, the Babe and Dempsey had said. They'll find out anyway, and this way you'll be able to frame it yourself, instead of letting them do it.

That's what Jidge had done with his years at St. Mary's School in Baltimore, and Dempsey with his youth spent knocking down drunks in western saloons. The two men had controlled the story.

And that's what Ruby had to do now. She knew that the press had dug around. They were aware of her parents' deaths in the epidemic—and, as importantly, of the struggles that had followed.

"Is it true that you ate squirrel?" This from a woman Ruby hadn't seen before, from the *Ladies' Home Journal*.

"When I could find one," Ruby said. She felt her chin lift, but when she spoke again her voice was as calm and measured as ever. "I know it's a popular dish among some people down south, but the truth is we only turned to it because we had to. When I see a squirrel today, I always remember how scared I was that my girls might starve."

She took a breath.

Thinking, Okay, that's good, but don't give them too much.

"What do you know about the Beacon Bowlers?" Grumpy George asked. She smiled at him, partly in thanks for changing the subject and partly because his question reminded her of how Allie had laughed with pure unbridled glee when she'd heard the name.

"I don't know much," she admitted. "Andy Sutherland talked me through their lineup yesterday, but I've never actually seen them play. I do know that they've scored a lot of runs. They have several heavy hitters. I plan to learn more watching the game today."

Everyone nodded.

"Also," Ruby said, "I like their uniforms."

A lot of the writers grinned at that, a rare answer that sounded like it came from a girl. Beacon wore steel-gray uniforms that contrasted with light gray stockings—bowler-hat colors, Ruby supposed, though mostly they made her think how wearing such dark uniforms must feel on hot midsummer days.

"Do you think you can handle them?" someone asked. "Those heavy hitters?"

Ruby shrugged, then gave them all a sideways look. "I'll do the very best I can," she said primly. "But . . . did you see me pitch on Thursday? Do *you* think I can handle them?"

More grins and exchanged glances. She was writing their columns for them.

"Don't ever give with the false modesty," the Babe had said. "Remember, they're here to talk to you because they think you're different, unusual, special. So act that way."

"Miss Thomas?"

It was a young man she hadn't seen before, blond, with a sharp jaw and very pale blue eyes. "Please, call me Ruby," she said.

He didn't acknowledge that. "Russ Haynes, *Brooklyn Town Crier*," he said. "I've been told that you've stirred up the Ku Klux Klan, and that they're considering condemning you publicly, and perhaps even staging a march or demonstration against your presence on the team. Do you have a response?"

Ruby heard the Colonel gasp beside her, and saw a wave of movement, like a shiver, pass across the crowd of reporters. She took a moment to answer, her mind scrambling as she tried to find the right approach.

"No," she said finally, deciding not to mention the note she'd received. "But I can't say I'm surprised that the Klan might object to my pitching, because I'm a girl."

The scribbling was very loud.

"And because you're a Jew," Russ Haynes said.

Ruby looked into his ice-cold eyes. "Don't ever hide anything," the Babe had told her. "'Cause it won't stay hidden."

"Well, I don't practice the religion," Ruby said, "but, yes, Mama was Jewish, so by the rules I am, too."

She took a breath. "Of course, Papa was Catholic, so I guess I'm that, too. I understand that the Klan doesn't approve of Catholics, either." She looked around at the sportswriters. "They disapprove of so many things, I marvel that they approve of baseball itself."

"Yeah," Grumpy George said, loud enough for everyone to hear. "It's damned hard to play when you're wearing those robes and white hoods."

That got a few laughs and made Russ Haynes frown. But Ruby knew she couldn't be done yet, and beside her she could feel the Colonel shifting around, preparing to speak. The last thing she wanted was for him to put his two cents in now.

"But mostly what I am," she said, "is a pitcher. Someone who loves this great game, who's loved it since I was eight years old and my papa took me to the first-ever game at Ebbets Field, before it even opened for real, that exhibition game against the Yankees."

She saw many of the older reporters exchange glances, and knew that they'd been there, too.

"It was the most beautiful place I'd ever seen, and the most magnificent structure, and then Casey Stengel hit a foul ball to me."

Smiles, easier now, at the mention of ol' Casey's name.

"The most exciting day of my life," Ruby said. "But I know that tomorrow will top it."

Pens applied themselves to paper, and Ruby knew they were back on the story she wanted them to tell.

She allowed her gaze to drift over to Russ Haynes. There were red spots on his fair cheeks, and his pen was busy as well.

The Colonel leaned forward. "Regardless of what the Klan says or does, Ruby will pitch for us tomorrow. She's a member of the team, and, you know, we're not in Texas or Georgia. We make our own decisions about what's right or wrong in New York City— and especially here in Brooklyn."

And that's where they left it.

Ruby's teammates, sweaty and flushed from batting practice under the summer sun, clustered around her when she finally made it out onto the field. Jake Conlon walked over, too, looking curious.

"See you didn't drown in all that ink," he said.

"Not yet." She glanced into his face. "Listen, Jake, all of you, there's something I've got to tell you."

She filled them in on Russ Haynes's question, the Ku Klux Klan's threat, even her religious background. She saw several of the players' expressions change, turn thoughtful.

As she spoke, Jake Conlon's face grew stormy, but Ruby thought she wasn't his target.

When she finished by saying, "The Colonel thinks we should let me pitch anyway. And of course, I want to," he looked at her like she was crazy.

"'Let you pitch'?" he said, his hands jerking like he wanted to hit someone. "You're our starter tomorrow, got that? That group of rabble-rousers shows their faces—or their hoods—around here, and we'll give them a lesson they'll never forget."

There were nods all around.

Even though there was no chance that Ruby would pitch that afternoon, at least six thousand fans showed up at Washington Park. Of course, it was a hot, sunny Saturday in July, perfect baseball weather in a great baseball town. Plus, both the Robins and the Yankees were on the road, while the Giants were playing the St. Louis Cardinals, no powerhouse this season.

Still, on other summer Saturdays the team had drawn no more than three or four thousand. It was as if Ruby's arrival had introduced the Typhoons to Brooklyn. Curious about her, they were beginning to give the team a chance as well.

As the game got under way, Ruby saw that Andy Sutherland's report on the Bowlers had been accurate. Except for the leadoff hitter, a slightly built young man with wiry, close-cropped hair and olive features, none was a skilled or patient hitter. It was one big slugger after another in the Babe Ruth mold, but without the Babe's quick hands and explosive power.

Still, three of them got their forty-ounce bats around on the assortment of middling fastballs and slower ones thrown by the Typhoons' Henry Bonsall, and sent them in high, lazy arcs over the outfield walls. After the third one, and six runs in, Jake Conlon went racing out to the mound, took the ball from crestfallen Henry, and then jabbered in his ear while the relief pitcher came in and for several minutes in the dugout afterward as well.

"What do you think?" Andy asked, sitting beside Ruby when the Typhoons next came to bat.

What Ruby thought was that her stomach felt like it had eels wriggling around inside it. But she just shrugged and said, "Think I can get my fast one past them."

Andy bent over to strap on his shin guards. "Yeah, I agree. Just don't treat 'em like they're slower and stupider than they are. Bowlers are in first place, you know, and scoring about seven runs a game. Your fast one won't be enough. Pitch smart."

Ruby looked out on the field. "That shortstop they have batting first? He looks like he can hit, and run, too."

"Yeah, Cesar Dukes." Andy looked up, his catcher's mask in his hand. "That guy's really good. He should be leading off for the Robins, not the Bowlers."

"Then why isn't he?"

"He's too dark."

The inning ended, and Andy got to his feet. "Just like you're too female," he said, and headed onto the field.

The game was over, an 8–3 loss. As soon as it ended, Jake Conlon spent fifteen minutes laying into his team for their ineffectual efforts on the field. By the time he was done, even Ruby felt drained, and she hadn't been in the game.

"You all better come out tomorrow with your heads up, or some of you are going to start watching the games from the dugout," Jake concluded. "Or from the roof of that tenement across the street."

When he finally dismissed them, Ruby bathed and changed in her private washroom. Then, dressed in black slacks, a navy blouse, and flat shoes, she walked back to her dressing room and told Tania about the threat. She didn't know where else to turn.

"Yeah, like I would know anybody in the Klan?" Tania said. "Like they'd have anything to do with a Jew off the boat from the Ukraine?"

Ruby felt an unexpected stab of disappointment. "Guess not."

There was a soft knock on the door. It didn't sound like Jake Conlon's impatient rapping or the Colonel's polite double tap. Tania got to her feet and swung the door open. Then, almost as if she was disappointed, she turned to Ruby and said, "One of your ballplayers."

It was young Albert Gillespie, a right fielder by trade who usually rode the bench for the Typhoons. Very tall, skinny, and likely to blush at the least provocation, he stood in the doorway, uncomfortable in an ill-fitting suit, his freshly washed hair plastered across his forehead. His face was already bright red.

Ruby said, "Can I help you, Albert?"

He gulped again before getting the words out. "Some of the boys are going to get a hamburger at Gino's," he said, speaking quickly in his high tenor as if afraid that he might lose his train of thought. "We was wondering if you might like to come, Ruby." He took a breath and then gave Tania a panicked look. "You, too, of course, miss."

Tania gave him a sardonic look. "Of course."

"It sounds fun, Albert," Ruby said quickly in her sweetest, most feminine tone—quite a difficult task, given that her voice was deeper than his. "But I don't think it would be a good idea, not today." She smiled at him, provoking another furious blush. "I have to get home to my family, and I'd better make sure I have a good night's sleep tonight. It's a big day for me tomorrow."

She'd wondered if her refusal, however gracefully couched, might send him fleeing down the hall, but surprisingly he stood his ground. "Another time, then?" he said.

"I'd love to," Ruby said.

"Okay. Good. I'll ask you again."

She nodded. "That would be fine. Thank you, Albert."

"You're welcome." His eyes shifted around. "Bye." Finally he made his escape, shutting the door gently behind him. Hands over their mouths, Tania and Ruby listened to him retreat down the hall. Only when he was out of earshot did they exchange smiles.

"Oh, he's stuck on you!" Tania said.

Ruby thought about it for a second, then shrugged off the idea. "He's just a boy."

She saw Tania's smile fade, replaced by something that looked almost like pity. "Older than you are, Ruby."

"And much, much younger," Ruby said.

"You could, you know," Helen said.

It was late, close to midnight, and the house was quiet. Both girls were long asleep, and Mrs. Connell was up in her bedroom. Only when she and Helen were alone had Ruby spoken about the real events of the day, the appearance of the reporter Russ Haynes, the looming shadow cast by the Klan, Albert showing up at her door after the game.

"I could what?" Ruby asked.

"Go out. Let the boy buy you a soda or a hamburger."

"Albert? I don't think so."

"Not him necessarily. But some boy."

Ruby was silent.

Helen paused, then went on. "I can tell you from personal experience," she said, smiling, "that there's a lot to be said for it. Dating, I mean."

"Well, if you have someone like Paul," Ruby said. "But who else is nice like him?"

"Oh, there are others, I promise you." Ruby could hardly believe it, but Helen giggled. "Some of them might even be more of a darb than my Paul."

"Impossible."

"You deserve it, Ruby," Helen said, serious again. "You deserve to be happy, too, just as I am."

Ruby was startled to feel her breath catch. She found herself remembering that spring day at Ebbets Field in 1913, when she had sat in the sun with her family and felt pure, uncomplicated happiness.

Maybe it was true that she deserved to be happy now as well, but it was just as true that you didn't always get what you deserved.

28

*t*ania crumpled the newspaper into a ball and threw it across the room.

Ruby watched it bounce off the wall. "Nice arm," she said. "Maybe the Typhoons could use you."

"Bastards," Tania said in a venomous tone. She grabbed another newspaper from the pile on the table before her, snapped it open, and hid behind it.

With a sigh, Ruby walked over, picked the crumpled pages off the floor, and flattened them on the table. It was, as she'd guessed, the *Town Crier,* a rag she'd never seen before. It was printed on cheap paper, and in many places the ink was smeared as if it had been sold still wet, but unfortunately it was legible.

The headlines of Russ Haynes's article took up half the front page:

THE SHAME OF BASEBALL
Who is "Diamond Ruby" Thomas?
Daughter of Immigrants Disgraces America's Game
BY RUSSELL HAYNES

Born to a Jew from Russia and a Catholic from Ireland, merely two of the countless thousands of immigrants polluting America's shores early in this century (until God struck them down during the great 1918 plague against foreigners), Ruby Thomas was no more than a freak with arms like spaghetti strands until Colonel Edward Fielding betrayed the white race and

"Spaghetti strands?" Ruby said.

Tania, her face still tight with anger, lowered her newspaper. "If you insist on reading that out loud," she said with immense dignity, "then please do it someplace else."

Ruby shrugged. Her cheeks felt hot, but what was the use in getting angry? "I just need to see what it says about the Klan." She scanned ahead in the article, past the descriptions of what he labeled her deformity, her godlessness, baseball's place as America's pastime despite its unfortunate immigrant taint, and the proper role of women in modern society, before she finally found what she was looking for.

"'It is a disgrace to America that this foreigner-spawned, tenement-raised girl should be allowed to step onto the pitcher's mound in a professional baseball game,' proclaimed the Grand Cyclops of the Brooklyn Den, who must be identified only as 'Bill' due to the shameful persecution of the Klan in New York. 'Be sure that we are watching closely. If our warnings are not heeded—well, when the consequences fall upon their heads, the only ones to blame will be Colonel Fielding and Ruby Thomas herself.'"

The room was quiet. Then Tania said, "What does that mean?"

Ruby thought about it. "I believe it means that they won't do anything yet. For now, they're just waiting to see if their threats work."

"I hope you're right," Tania said.

Then she reached under the pile of newspapers, retrieved a thick envelope, and held it out. "There's also this."

Ruby took the envelope, shook out a piece of fine, thin stationery, and unfolded it to peer at the spidery handwriting under the logo of the Washington Senators.

"'Dear Ruby,'" she read, "'I have been following your progress with great interest. Congratulations on your success! Having seen you throw, I cannot say I am surprised. One small piece of advice on the day of your first-ever start, which you may feel free to take or discount: Do not feel like you have to throw every pitch at your hardest. Remember that the game is nine innings long, and that by conserving your energy when you can, you'll have a better chance to still be pitching in the later innings—and in the late innings of your career as well, as I am. Good luck and all my best wishes, Walter Johnson.'"

Ruby stared at the signature. She felt stunned.

"There's something else in there, too, right?" Tania asked.

There was. Ruby pulled it out, a sheaf of papers clipped together. She could tell at a glance that it was an old article from *Baseball Magazine,* one she'd never seen before. Written across the top of the first page was, "Thought you might be interested in this—W.J."

Ruby looked at the title: PITCHING SCIENCE IN ALL ITS ANGLES. Above the headline was a picture of Walter Johnson himself, shirtless, his right arm extended. "Walter Johnson, the Speediest Pitcher in the World and His Wonderfully Long Pitching Arm," read the caption.

And it *was* long. Very long. Almost as long, proportionately, as Ruby's.

"What's that?" Tania asked.

Ruby didn't answer. She glanced through the pages, half a dozen of them, maybe more, all about how Johnson's arm length was the secret to his pitching success. Pictures, too, revealing again and again how long his arms actually were.

"Not just me," Ruby said in a low voice. "Helen was right."

"What?" Tania was staring at her. "Right about what? Girl, you're acting sozzled."

Ruby merely shook her head. How could she explain? How could she describe what it felt like to realize she wasn't alone in the world?

She was saved by a knock on the door, which she recognized as Jake Conlon's impatient banging. He gave them about two seconds, then swung the door open.

Jake looked excited, his face already sheened with sweat, his eyes seeming about to leap from their sockets.

"You ready?" he asked. Then he gave a sudden, surprising grin, wolfish in the way it showed his teeth. "Of course you're ready. Let's go."

Had it only been a few days ago that a crowd of eight thousand had seemed huge to Ruby? Compared to this, that was an empty ballpark.

Looking out of the dugout just before the game, Ruby saw that every seat was filled, and half the aisles as well, and someone said people were still lined up at the front gate, hoping to get in. The roofs and windows of the apartments past the outfield wall were jam-packed as well, and people must have been perched on ladders and stepstools at the walls themselves, because Ruby could see heads poking up over the cigarette and candy ads.

Even Jake Conlon seemed a little taken aback by the size of the crowd. "Haven't seen this many fans since I was with the Browns," he said. "And not so often back then, either."

Then he focused and glared at his team. "Guess I'm going to find out whether you're men or little boys. My teams always used to play our best when the crowds were biggest. Want to show me you deserve the spotlight? Do the same."

Sitting comfortably on the bench in his gear, mask in hand, Andy Sutherland jerked a thumb at Ruby. "What about her?" he asked. "You want her to be a man, too?"

As Ruby knew Andy had hoped, the question brought some grins and a slight but noticeable lessening of tension. Even Jake briefly showed his teeth, but his eyes were thoughtful.

"Nah," he said, "Ruby'll do fine. She's already twice the man some of the rest of you are."

Ruby'll do fine.

Easy for him to say. He was sitting in the dugout, free from having to swing a bat or throw a single pitch. If he did come out, it would likely be to argue a call or bait the umpire—which would bring cheers—or to take a pitcher out of the game, in which case the boos would cascade down on the pitcher's head, not his.

The pitcher's head. Ruby's head.

Throwing her final warm-up tosses, Ruby managed to bounce one five feet in front of home plate. As Andy, having retrieved her errant toss, came walking up to the mound, she scanned the crowd for those she knew were, in fact, here to cheer her. In the press area behind home plate, she spotted Grumpy George. Down the first-base line, in their usual seats, sat Helen and Mrs. Connell and the girls, beside Colonel Fielding and his wife. Farther from the field, Josephine Collier and Ruby's Rooters were out in force, a hundred of them at least. Ruby saw that each was wearing something red to show their support.

"Waiting for someone to let the lions out?" Andy asked, standing beside her and looking up at the crowd as well.

"Didn't you read the *Town Crier*? I'm no Christian."

"Yeah, that's right." He shrugged. "Oh, I'm sure the Romans had no trouble throwing Jews into the ring, too."

Ruby smiled.

"Good," he said. "That's what I like to see. Because there's no lions, and I don't see any Klansmen, either. And the folks up there who *are* ready to turn their thumbs down, they don't matter."

"But—"

"They don't matter," he said again. "All that matters is your left arm and this—" He dropped the ball into her palm. "And this." He held up his glove. "Don't forget it."

"I won't," Ruby said.

Cesar Dukes was leading off for the Bowlers. Andy gave her the fastball sign, one finger, and then shifted his glove to the inside part of the plate.

"You move him off the plate, he'll get annoyed, and that means he'll swing at bad pitches," the catcher had told her. "But don't miss, or he'll pull it down the line for two bases, maybe three. Quick bat."

Ruby didn't miss. She put the pitch right where she wanted to. But Dukes crossed her up, bunting the ball, poking it up the first-base line before dropping the bat and streaking for the bag. As Ruby scrambled after it, she found herself remembering the last time this had happened, and the bone-jarring collision that had resulted.

But Cesar Dukes wasn't going to steamroll her. He was aiming to teach her a different lesson. By the time she got to the ball and picked it up, he was already near first base. Ruby didn't even bother to make a throw, but just stood there watching him cross the bag as the crowd thundered.

Dukes brushed his hands against his gray uniform pants as he turned and came back to the bag. He caught her eye and winked at her.

Ruby put her glove up in front of her face to hide a smile and immediately felt better, easier, more relaxed.

Who knew how nerves worked?

Andy was waiting for her when she returned to the mound. "Well, so much for your no-hit game," he said.

Ruby nodded. "I'm fine," she said. "Forget it. Let's get to work on the next guy. Curveballs and change-ups till we have him at two strikes, and then a fastball. I don't want him bunting the hotshot over."

Andy's mouth opened, then closed again. "Okay," he said. "Good plan."

Ruby struck out the next batter with a sharp curve over the inside corner, a change-up for a ball that had him backing away from the plate, a big slow curve that he bunted foul, and a fastball on the outside of the plate that he waved at weakly.

On the second pitch to the third hitter, Cesar Dukes stole second base. Ruby had thrown over to first a couple times, to keep him close to the bag, but she had no real pickoff move, nothing to put any fear into him. It was another thing she'd have to work on.

She sighed and went back to work. She was beginning to understand that the home-plate umpire, a squat man with a big chest and belly behind his protector, was no friend of hers. Three pitches in a row that she and Andy knew were strikes were called balls, the third of which looked to be right across the heart of the plate. The crowd jeered and catcalls came from the Typhoons' dugout, but the umpire appeared deaf to them.

Andy came out and said, "Guess he's got it in for you. Better make them hit the ball."

So Ruby let the hitter get wood on the next pitch, a sharp grounder that went straight through the legs of Carl Crutcher at shortstop and into left field. Cesar Dukes scored easily, and just like that, the Typhoons were losing and Ruby had given up her first-ever run.

She didn't show a thing, but inside she was seething, not at Carl Crutcher or the umpire, but at herself. It was *her* job to get these men out, not theirs. She looked at the cleanup hitter striding up to the plate, a beefy slugger, and decided that, umpire or no, she wasn't going to *allow* him to hit the ball. He had to earn that right.

And she knew that he wouldn't wait for a base on balls, either, even if the umpire was determined to give it to him. He'd want to hit the girl pitcher's fastball six miles into the heart of Brooklyn.

She shook Andy off when he called for a curveball, nodded when he switched to a fast one, and blazed it across the inner half of the plate for a swinging strike. The next one was even harder on the outside corner, and though the umpire would likely have called it a ball, the batter swung, succeeding only in dribbling it foul.

Two strikes. Andy, suddenly thinking along the same lines she was, called for a slow curveball, and Ruby threw it exactly as she wanted. It went up and then down like a roller coaster, and the batter missed it by a foot.

The crowd roared.

The next hitter was another hulking brute, but even before he got to the plate, he seemed nervous, unsure of himself, ready to fail. His big forty-ounce bat looked heavy in his hands.

It was exactly the frame of mind any pitcher would want a batter to be in. Three pitches and he was out, on a weak foul pop that Andy caught.

Ruby went jogging off the field to deafening cheers, stone-faced but relieved. Her teammates ran past her, congratulating her on her successful inning. Before she made it to the dugout, though, Carl Crutcher came up to her to apologize for his error. "We'll get that run back for you," he said, "and more."

"'Course you will," she said.

And they did, with two runs in the first inning and another in the second. The Bowlers' pitcher, a right-hander, threw hard, but his fastball sometimes ended up over the middle of the plate, making it easy to hit. Also, the Typhoons seemed much more focused and ready to play than they had been during the sloppy game a day earlier.

Ruby got her first at-bat in the second inning, with one out and no one on base. She'd worked hard on her hitting during her week with the Typhoons, but she knew no one would mistake her for Ty Cobb, or even for a pitcher who knew how to hit. Her long arms, the secret of her success as a hurler, made it hard for her to get the bat around fast enough to make good contact.

"Told you," Jake Conlon had said, watching her struggles. "You gotta be born with it."

Still, wanting to contribute, she got herself set and peered out at the pitcher. He went into his windup, which involved a high kick of his right leg, and whistled his first pitch directly at her rib cage. Next thing she knew, she was lying in a heap beside home plate. She had no idea how she'd avoided the ball.

The crowd was quiet, holding its breath, and she thought both teams, staring at her, waiting, might be, too. Everyone in the ballpark knew of her brawl with Jim Tracy, and now they were waiting to see how much of a hothead she might be.

The answer was: not much of one. As the crowd jeered at the pitcher, Ruby just got to her feet, shook the dirt out of her pants, picked up her bat, and got back into her batting stance. She wasn't angry at all. It was part of the game, a welcome-to-the-league calling card and nothing more. And it wouldn't be the last brushback she saw, either, not if she had any prolonged success.

Three more pitches and she was walking back to the dugout, swearing that she'd take batting practice for six hours a day, if Jake would let her, in order to become a respectable hitter.

She thought about what Walter Johnson had written to her, about pacing herself, not throwing too hard too early. She hadn't talked about it with Andy, but she could see he was guiding her in the same direction, calling for curveballs and change-ups when she might choose instead to throw as hard as she could.

Deep down, she thought she could throw two hundred pitches at ninety miles an hour in a day, if she had to. But if all she did was throw hard, harder, hardest, maybe her fastball would stop zooming upward or tailing away from the batter, perhaps her curve would flatten out.

Better to listen to Andy and the Big Train, and keep something back for when she needed it.

As it turned out, she didn't much need it. By the sixth inning she'd pitched, she'd given up three more hits (including a double to Cesar Dukes) but no more runs, and the Typhoons led, 3–1.

Then, in the bottom of the sixth, with two outs, the Typhoons' seventh and eighth hitters got on base. Ruby, who'd been swinging a bat on deck and wondering what she could do to bring the run home, heard Jake Conlon call her name.

She turned to look and saw that he was gesturing at her. "That's it for today, Ruby," he was saying. "Gillespie's gonna hit for you."

That's it for today.

That's *it*?

How could he take her out of the game?

This was the moment she truly realized that she was part of a team, and not always the most important part. Jake Conlon's only goal was to win, and he knew he had a better chance with Albert Gillespie batting than with Ruby Thomas.

As Albert ran past her toward the plate, and she walked

disconsolately back to the dugout, the sound of the crowd swelled. The fans—her fans—were cheering so loudly that the players on both teams glanced around nervously, as if wondering if the grandstands could take the punishment.

Ruby looked up and, just before stepping down into the dugout, raised a hand to acknowledge the crowd.

Then she accepted the congratulations of her teammates, pats on the back, touches on the arm, a murmured "Good job" and "We'll hang on and get you the win." Ballplayer-to-ballplayer talk. It was hard to believe that just a few days earlier she'd been sitting by herself on the end of the bench.

She sat down to watch just in time to see Albert loop a single in front of the right fielder to score another run. The succession of relief pitchers that Jake brought in managed to hold the Bowlers to just one more tally, Andy Sutherland drove in two with a double in the eighth, and as the last Bowler was put out in the top of the ninth Ruby realized that she had, in fact, just registered her first win in a professional baseball game.

Running out of the dugout to congratulate those on the field, she was the center of attention again, both from her teammates and from the fans. She wanted nothing more than to escape to her dressing room, to Tania. But Jake Conlon nudged her and said, "The boss wants to see us."

As they walked over to the stands where the Colonel, Allie, Amanda, and the Connells sat, all with varying expressions of pleasure, Jake said to her, "Remind me how old you are."

"Eighteen and a bit."

"And this is your first win."

She gave him a curious glance. "You know it is."

"That means you have time for about three hundred more." He shook his head. "Three hundred, *minimum*."

She smiled. "I'll settle for another in four days."

. . .

She was dressed and sitting in her little room, waiting to muster enough strength to go find her family—who'd rented a car for what they'd all sworn would be a triumphant ride home—when someone leaned in through the open door. She raised her head wearily to see that it was Cesar Dukes, freshly shaved, wearing a stylish suit, his glossy black hair brushed down over his forehead.

"We're getting on the bus in a minute," he said, "but I wanted to say congratulations. I liked watching you pitch . . . and hitting against you."

She looked at him. "Well, I didn't much like pitching against *you*."

That got a grin. "You'll have more chances."

As he turned to go, she said, without thinking, "You're good enough to be in the majors, you know. Good as plenty they got playing there already."

He looked back at her, surprised, and then slowly nodded. "Yes. I know. And I think with a little more time, you will be, too."

Ruby leaned back in her chair. She was so tired. "That day will never come."

"No," Cesar Dukes said, "not for either of us."

The ride back to Brooklyn Heights was quiet. An afternoon spent in the hot sun watching their aunt had taken the starch out of the girls. Allie actually fell asleep during the drive, her arm and cheek hot and rubbery against Ruby's side. The two Connell women up front talked quietly, smiling and relaxed, while Ruby drifted in a half daze, revisiting in her mind every pitch she'd made, every important moment in the game.

Mrs. Connell found a parking spot down the block from the house. Ruby shook Allie's shoulder, saying, "Wake up, girl. I'm too tired to carry you today, and anyway you're too big."

"Aren't I in bed?" Allie asked, her eyes still closed. Then she sighed and struggled out of the car after Amanda, Ruby following the two into the angled early evening light.

When they stepped through the front door, they could hear the telephone ringing. Helen walked quickly over to it and grabbed the handset, only to replace it with a shrug. "Too late," she said. "They'll call back if it's important."

But almost as soon as the handset was back in its cradle, the bell rang again. Helen laughed and picked it up as Ruby walked past her toward the kitchen, wanting only a cold drink.

She heard a cry of distress, a sound so raw that it seemed to claw Ruby's throat.

When she turned she saw that Helen was lying on the floor, the handset swinging from its cord above her head.

An instant later, Mrs. Connell was squatting beside her, grabbing the handset in one hand and speaking into it while touching her daughter's face with the other. She said a few words that Ruby couldn't make out, and then went completely still as she listened, her face washed of color and expression.

"Paul's been arrested," she said.

Helen put her arms over her head and wept. Amanda came over to stand by Ruby's side, and Allie stood there, eyes wide, fingers in her mouth.

"What for?" Ruby asked.

"They say he assaulted a woman." Mrs. Connell swayed where she stood. "How could such a thing happen?"

Ruby didn't speak.

But she knew.

29

"How long were you planning to make me wait?" Ruby asked Russell Haynes.

They were sitting in the *Town Crier*'s conference room, which was in truth just a small, barren nook in the tabloid's offices, its soot-stained windows looking out over Flatbush Avenue. The street four floors below was crowded with midday shoppers in the markets and clothing stores, and Ruby found herself wondering how someone like Haynes navigated this part of Brooklyn, or Brooklyn as a whole, filled as it was with recent immigrants. He must hate seeing it all, much less being immersed in it. He probably took a bath as soon as he got home every night.

As he had been at the press conference, Haynes was neatly dressed, his face carefully shaven—or perhaps, with his fair complexion and ash-blond hair, he couldn't grow a beard. His suit was well tailored, the cuffs of his white shirt clean and sharp. He looked, Ruby thought, entirely too presentable for the *Town Crier*, or for his coworkers, who seemed a noisy bunch and smelled of cigars and printer's ink.

Ruby guessed he'd ended up at this rag because no other paper would allow him to openly espouse his views, at least not in New York City.

His icy eyes scanned her face. "Make you wait?" he repeated. "You weren't sitting here even five minutes."

"You know what I'm talking about," she said.

He raised a silky eyebrow. "Oh, do I?"

Ruby had wondered, coming in, whether she'd be able to keep her temper. She was still wondering. How tempting it would be to fly across the table and knock the smug expression off his face.

But she didn't. She restrained herself. Attacking him might bring her a moment's solace, but it would do no good at all in her efforts to get Paul Fitzsimmons out of Kings County Jail.

"He's been there for three days now," she said. "How long before you decided I'd be soft enough, frantic enough, to do what you asked? Five days? A week?"

"Miss Thomas, I have no idea what you're talking about."

She took a deep breath and looked into his eyes. "Mr. Haynes," she said, "both you and I know that the Klan arranged my friend's arrest."

He smiled. "Oh, do we?"

"Yeah, we do. And I know you have contacts there, with the Grand Bicycle—or whatever he was called—you quoted in your first article about me."

"Grand Cyclops," he said, his expression turning sour.

"Right. 'Bill.' The man who's so proud of what he does that he hides behind a false name."

Ruby had decided that supplication, femininity, weakness, would do no good. She might not be able to intimidate him physically, but she wasn't going to beg either, or pretend to be afraid.

Haynes sipped his coffee. He hadn't offered her any. "Yes," he said. "So?"

"I want 'Bill'—or you—to tell me something."

A pale eyebrow lifted. "What?"

"What the Klan wants from me, in exchange for getting Paul out of jail."

Though she thought she already knew.

Paul had been walking down State Street, just a few blocks from the Connells' house, when he'd spotted a young woman being assaulted in an alley. He'd gone to help her and confronted the attacker, a heavyset man who'd eventually broken free and run.

The woman appeared very shaken, and her blouse had been torn. As Paul was asking if she was all right, two policemen entered the alley. They'd shown up so fast that Paul thought they must have been just around the corner.

He began to explain what had occurred and was dumbfounded ("undone" was the word he used) when the woman turned on him and scratched him across the face. Then, as he stood there in shock, she accused *him* of assaulting her, and despite all his protestations the policemen arrested him. Now he sat in jail, and seemed likely to stay there for a long time to come.

A setup from the start—and only one possible reason behind it.

"Here's what happened," Ruby said to Haynes. "The Klan threatened me, warned me not to pitch—and then, when I ignored them and went ahead, what did they do? Nothing. I couldn't figure why."

The reporter gave a little shrug. "So?"

"So then I figured it out. They had to change their plans.

They made a mistake by threatening me openly. They underestimated how much support I'd get, and how fast. Articles in every newspaper, editorials in the *Times* and the *Daily Eagle,* interviews in newsreels, *Baseball Magazine,* and *The New Yorker.*"

"Doesn't mean they're right and we're wrong," Haynes said, dropping the pretense that he was merely an observer and reporter.

Ruby shrugged. "I know that the Klan is just now trying to get a toehold here in the Northeast—"

Haynes looked a little offended. "We already have more than a toehold. We're gaining strength wherever the immigrant tide—"

"Yes, I know, I heard," Ruby interrupted, and watched pink spots rise to his cheeks. "But you still have to tread carefully here in New York City, don't you? It's not your natural home field. Everyone's an immigrant around here."

"Not everyone," Haynes said.

"And plenty of Jews and Catholics, too, aren't there? And women who don't follow your rules. You're not as popular as you expected to be, are you? The city government's done a pretty good job in busting up some Klan rings recently, rounding up kleagles and klonks and who knows what else you call yourselves."

Haynes flushed more deeply, but didn't speak.

She watched his face. "What to do? I can imagine the conversations. You'd already threatened me publicly, you had to back it up. But how? Yeah, a big demonstration out at the ballpark would get you in the news. But it wouldn't exactly help you spread the word—the flaming cross—around here. Even worse would be attacking me directly, like you threatened to do. I'm pretty popular, and everyone would know who'd done it."

She stretched her arms, saw him recoil just a bit, as if she had the flu, as if he might catch it from her.

"So you chose Paul. Didn't you worry that I might not care enough to try to save him?"

Russell Haynes's lips twitched. Looking at him, Ruby had the answer. "Oh," she said, "I get it. Paul isn't the point, is he? It doesn't matter whether I care about him. He's just your first shot, your way of showing what you can do, what you're capable of."

Haynes sipped his coffee and watched her.

"If I don't heed the warning, then you'll move on to someone I really care about, like Helen." She took a breath. "Or the girls."

Russell Haynes smiled. "Of course we will," he said. "If you force us to."

There it was. Now they were really talking.

"But we don't think it will be necessary. You have your . . . priorities."

"So what do you want me to do?" Ruby said.

Haynes tilted his head. "Oh, I think you already know. You'll disappear, quit the team, get out of baseball forever. Do that, and your blind friend's sweetheart will go home and nothing will happen to anyone you love. Don't, and all bets are off."

"I'm pitching tomorrow," Ruby said.

"No, you're not."

She held her tongue until her temper was under control. Then she said, "Smarter to let me pitch, don't you think? I disappear now, some reporter might start looking for a connection, and find it, and start digging. I quit next week, Paul's already forgotten."

This sounded only half convincing in her own ears, but after a few seconds Haynes nodded. "All right. Pitch tomorrow. Pitch your little heart out."

Ruby took a breath.

"But this is what you'll give us in return for getting one last chance." Haynes looked into her face, his eyes shining with malevolence. "When you quit, and the press asks you why, you'll tell them—"

He paused, thinking about it. Then he said, "You'll tell them that you've seen the light. That you've realized it's not proper for a girl to play a man's game."

"Everything okay?"

Andy Sutherland had caught a glimpse of her face, un-guarded.

"Everything's fine," Ruby said.

"You look like you want to kill someone." Andy shrugged. "Not that I'm griping. Just remember who the enemy is."

As if Ruby could forget.

Today was her second start, this one against the Bethlehem Steelmen, the worst team in the East-Coast League thus far. Ruby hadn't yet seen them play.

Not that it mattered much to her, whom she was pitching against and whether she'd studied them. Get the ball, throw the ball, get the ball back, throw it again. Clockwork girl. She knew she could overpower the Steelmen regardless.

Overpower them in her last appearance with the Typhoons.

"You've got that look on your face again," Andy said.

Ruby said, "Good."

After four innings she had seven strikeouts and had given up just one hit, a Texas Leaguer that fell in between the Typhoons' second baseman and right fielder. The Typhoons had scored six runs, the Steelmen were looking discouraged, and it was clear to everyone that the game was already as good as over.

But that didn't matter one iota to Ruby. On this gloomy day with its lowering clouds and occasional spatters of rain, she was throwing every pitch with absolute concentration.

She was a clockwork girl with a single purpose. She'd never thrown harder in her life, and if she was risking the future health of her left arm, she didn't care.

Throw the ball. Get it back and throw it again.

The enormous crowd began the game by cheering every pitch, roaring at every strikeout. Ruby barely noticed. She knew that an entire section of the stands was filled with Ruby's Rooters. The writers packed the press area, other familiar faces were scattered here and there, and for all she knew even Gordon had shown up. Nearly everyone she knew had come.

But not the most important people. Helen was at home, of course, waiting for visiting hours to see Paul. Mrs. Connell was with her. Amanda and Allie, with no one to bring them to the game, were trapped in the house.

Ruby struck out the side in the fifth inning on twelve pitches. By now the fans had grown quieter, greeting each explosive pitch, each strikeout, with a little gasp, beginning to realize that something was happening here that they'd never seen before.

"Did you see?" Andy asked when she sat down on the bench after the inning had ended, mopping her face with a damp towel. "They're scared of you. They're switching their bats—putting down the ones they usually use and taking lighter ones so they can get around faster."

"Oh?" Ruby hadn't noticed. "Doesn't matter," she said. "They could use toothpicks and they still won't catch up with my fastball. Not today."

Andy looked at her, and though he was smiling, there was something else in his expression as well. "I'm glad you're on my team," he said. "I wouldn't want to face you when you're in this mood."

Ruby looked over at Jake Conlon, standing as he often did with one foot on the first dugout step, looking out at the field. Without thinking about it, she got up and walked over to stand beside him, facing outward as well.

She could see his unfriendly sideways look. You didn't bother Jake during a game.

"I want to pitch nine innings today," she said.

His expression was stony. "Not your choice."

"How many pitches have I thrown?"

He didn't reply for a while, as another Typhoon got on base and the fans cheered. Then, grudgingly, he said, "Sixty, maybe."

"In five innings."

He gave her another look. "Not leaving much in the tank for later, are you?"

"Later when?" she asked. "Later tomorrow? Later next week? I have plenty left. You seeing anything different?"

Eventually he shook his head.

"So leave me in," Ruby said. "I get in trouble, pull me. But I won't. These guys can't hit me, not today. They know they can't. Let me finish the game."

The Steelmen's manager had gone out to the mound to talk to his hurler. Jake turned to look at Ruby. She met his gaze, let him look into her eyes.

"We'll see," he said at last, and turned away from her.

In the end, though, he did. He left her in. As the crowd hung on every pitch, she added two strikeouts in the sixth, gave up a walk in the seventh as the rain momentarily came down harder, making the ball slick, and then surrendered a run on a double down the line in the eighth, while adding two more strikeouts.

Then it was the ninth, 11–1 Typhoons. Despite the weather, not a fan seemed to have left. As Ruby walked out to the mound, she saw movement, a shifting around in the crowd, and she realized that the fans were all getting to their feet to watch her last inning.

After her warm-ups, Andy came out to the mound, as he so often did.

"Just don't break your arm," he said. "We'll need you in four days in Allentown."

Ruby said, "I'm fine."

The first batter tried to bunt his way on, but popped the

ball up foul. Andy caught it, and the hitter, who'd never even dropped his bat, trudged off the field to thunderous abuse from the crowd. They wanted nothing but strikeouts.

Ruby fanned the second batter on four pitches. The last, the strikeout pitch, was the first change of pace she'd thrown all day, and it had the hitter swinging when the ball had barely left her hand.

The Steelmen's final hope was a pinch hitter, a big, burly guy with a belly, carrying the kind of massive war club that the rest of the team had given up on innings earlier. Ruby watched him approach the plate and knew that the game was over. Three pitches later, she was right.

Nine innings pitched. One run and four hits given up. Sixteen strikeouts. Her second win.

Her last?

She ran in, barely noticing the congratulations of her teammates or the roaring of the crowd, heading instead to her dressing area and the shower. She stood under the steaming deluge, her mind a blank.

After she was dressed, Ruby headed over to the press room. The sportswriters laughed and jabbered, knowing they had a great story for the next editions. The Colonel talked in glowing tones, Jake Conlon ventured his more restrained opinions, the hitting stars and Andy Sutherland added their perspective, and Ruby didn't register a word.

When she was asked a direct question, she answered it. Luckily, the reporters seemed to chalk up her lack of emotion to weariness from her complete-game victory.

As soon as she could, she escaped and fled back to her dressing room. She locked the door and sat there, quiet, not moving, for at least an hour. Once, then again, someone knocked on her door and called her name, but she didn't respond, and eventually they went away.

· · ·

Finally she got to her feet and went out. The hallways were dark, and the only people she saw as she headed for the players' door were those hired to clean the big ballpark before the next game. They seemed surprised to see her, but no one asked what she was still doing there.

She saw the man as soon as she stepped out onto the nearly deserted avenue in the dim light of early evening. Dressed in a blue checked suit, his white straw hat tilted low over his eyes, he was leaning against a parked car, as if he'd been there for a long while and was prepared to stay forever. A cigarette dangled from the corner of his mouth, and several stamped-on butts littered the ground beside his shiny shoes.

Ruby recognized him immediately, his gaudy clothes, long, narrow face, and most of all his strange catlike eyes. Seeing her, he straightened. "Ruby Lee Thomas," he said, his voice a throaty, casual purr. "At last."

She kept on going. "Sorry, no time."

As she walked past, she heard him laugh.

"Even if I'm the answer to your prayers?" he asked.

30

*r*uby had heard enough. Had *had* enough.

She rounded on him. "First of all, I don't pray," she told him. "And second, even if I did, *you* wouldn't be the answer."

He grinned at her. He had very clean, straight teeth. "And how would you know that, Diamond Ruby?"

She didn't bother to reply, just turned and headed down the street toward the subway. He slipped into an easy stride beside her.

Hit 'em in the nose. Ruby got ready.

The man read her thoughts. He stepped in front of her, out of reach, and raised his hands in a placating gesture. "Listen," he said, "you probably think I'm a dapper, some drugstore cowboy just wanting to cash a check with you in the back of my struggle buggy."

He was wrong: that wasn't what she thought. Enough men had tried to cash checks with her since she'd become famous that she knew the signs. He was after something else. "So why are you chasing me?" she asked.

"Stop running and I'll tell you."

Ruby looked up into his canny eyes. "Some kind of business deal, right?"

He smiled, as if what she had said pleased him.

"Well, save your money," she said. "Today was my last time on the mound."

"So I've been told," he said.

Ruby stopped short and stared at him. "Told by who?"

He gave his head a little shake. "Listen," he said. "There's this restaurant a couple blocks from here, a quiet place. Let me buy you a cup of coffee or a pop and something to eat, whatever you like, and we can talk about your problem. I think I can help you out."

Still she hesitated. He grinned. "You just want to eat and go, that'll be fine, too. But you'd be missing out on your best chance."

She let a little more silence pass before she said, "Okay. We'll talk."

"That's my girl." He stuck out his hand. "The name's Chase."

After a moment, she shook it. His grip was firm and strong. "Ruby."

"Uh, yeah," he said, "I know."

They sat at a table in the corner of the armchair lunchroom down Fifth Street near Seventh Avenue, nearly empty now in the late afternoon. Ruby drank four glasses of water, they ordered coffee, and, on Chase's insistence, she also asked for a hamburger.

"You want anything else?" he asked. "All the work you did out there, I'd expect you to want to eat half a cow or something."

"You saw the game?"

"Yeah. Looked like you wanted to bounce the ball off every batter's head."

Ruby eyed him across the table. "You said you know why—why I'm walking away from the game. Was that the truth?"

He nodded. "Sure. You're scarpering because the Klan told you to. They said jump, and you jumped."

Ruby drew in a long breath. "What are you?" she asked. "One of them, stopping by to rub my face in it?"

"One of them?" Chase smiled, though there was a glint in his gray eyes that made her skin feel cold. "Nah, I'm not one of that gang. I'm not the problem. Told you, Ruby, I'm the solution."

He leaned across the table toward her. "Here's the deal. They're always scrambling for cash, those guys. And that goes double for the bulls who helped them set this up. All those rules they have, who can play baseball, who can't, those'll disappear if you make it worth their while."

"That's not what Russell Haynes said."

Again the eyes glinted. "Don't worry about Haynes. You work with us, and we'll be able to get you the dough you need to oil the lock on your friend's jail cell and keep the Klan off your back."

Ruby said, "You're not looking for me to advertise some shampoo or car, are you?"

Chase grinned.

"Or pose for pictures in lingerie." She swallowed a bitter taste. "Because I've already done that, and I'm not doing it again."

"No," Chase said, "that's not our business, either."

Ruby felt the same rushing in her veins as when she'd been about to lie to David Wilcox. She was at the edge of something. The crossroads.

"Then what is it you want me to do?" she asked.

Chase stared at her across the table, still assessing her through those odd, slanted eyes.

Then he nodded.

"Lose," he said.

Lose.

Like anyone with even the slightest knowledge of baseball, Ruby knew exactly what Chase was suggesting. She'd been fourteen when the powerful Chicago White Sox had fallen to the much weaker Cincinnati Reds in the 1919 World Series, and fifteen the next year when the truth came out. Those years, she'd been doing everything she could to keep herself and her family alive, but even so she'd heard about Joe Jackson and the other White Sox players throwing the Series, accepting paltry payment, most of them, in order to make gamblers rich.

And she remembered all too well the fact that the accused players were acquitted in court of doing anything wrong—but that hadn't mattered. Judge Landis, the commissioner of baseball, had banned them for life. "As long as I'm alive," he'd said, "these eight men, who have disgraced the game of baseball, will never play professionally again."

That's what losing on purpose meant.

She raised her eyes and saw that Chase understood her dilemma. There was sympathy in his expression, and patience, and behind those, a kind of hunger.

"But not yet," he said. "Not right away."

He read her confusion and gave a little nod. "After all, you're just getting started."

Ruby took a moment to sort it out. Then she said, slowly at first, "I'm still very new."

"Yup. Two starts and an inning in relief. Sixteen innings total. You're just a baby."

"People don't believe in me yet."

Chase said, "Let's just say they still have their doubts."

"But you don't?"

He slowly shook his head back and forth. "Not since I started watching you in Coney Island."

"In Coney Island." Ruby felt her stomach twist as something occurred to her. "Was it you? You who got me onto Colonel Fielding's team?"

Hoping desperately that the answer would be no, fearing that it would be yes.

"No." Chase turned his hands up. "He's a very straight old bird, the Colonel is. If we had approached him, he never would have gone near you. He would have given us the bum's rush."

Chase gestured toward his face, as if acknowledging that he might not look like the most trustworthy person in Brooklyn. "It had to be his idea, signing you, and it had to smell like a daisy. And it was, and it did."

Ruby felt an onrushing sense of relief, followed by a surge of anger she kept hidden.

And now you're asking me to betray him, she thought.

"But you don't want me to lose yet," Ruby said, "because . . ." She paused. "Because you're making more money off me winning than you would if I lost."

He smiled. She got the sense that he was impressed. A horse who could count, a dog who could sing, that's what she was to him.

"Exactly right," he said. "People still think you're a stunt, a trick, lucky to win. And remember, just a few, comparatively speaking, actually have seen you pitch. The rest only read the newspaper stories—and who trusts the press these days anyway?"

"So people have been betting against me," Ruby said.

"So people have been betting against you." There was a faint gleam in Chase's eyes. "We've done very well, taking those bets."

"But that's going to change."

"Yes, and faster than we'd like." But he didn't sound terribly put out. "If you'd kept pitching like you did last week, give up a run or two, people were *still* not going to believe. We'd have probably gotten another four starts, cashing in on you, before the money started swinging the other way."

He frowned. "But after today . . . well, the tabloids are going to be trumpeting that performance, no doubt about it. And everyone who was there will tell everybody they know what they saw. How many strikeouts did you say you had?"

"Sixteen."

"And you wish you could have fanned more, don't you?"

She met his gaze.

"Well, don't," he said. "Not yet."

She didn't say anything.

"I was thinking about this all afternoon, watching you." He looked down at his hands, and Ruby noticed how long and slender his fingers were. Unscarred, too. He'd never worked in a factory or a foundry.

"I mean, you strike out sixteen batters every game, the money's going to start running your way real soon. And when it starts, it's *really* gonna run. We'd make such a killing the first time you lost, we could almost fold up our tents and go home right then."

Home where? Ruby thought.

"But would that be smart?" he went on. "Would people get suspicious? Would our first paycheck also be our last?"

On the table beside his coffee cup, his slender hands moved as if he was reaching for something.

"So here's what you need to do," he said. "You need to keep winning, just like you're doing. But not like today. Not wanting to kill everyone, not for a while. Don't make yourself look so good that when we ask you to look bad, you get in trouble. Understand?"

After a moment, she nodded.

"And try not to lose before we want, okay?"

"I won't lose," Ruby said.

His slanted eyes gave a quick little blink. "Meaning you won't lose by mistake these next few starts, or you won't lose when we tell you to?"

Ruby let a few seconds pass. Then she said, "How much do I get?"

Some of the tension seemed to flow out of his body. "Five hundred dollars every time you lose, a hundred whenever you win."

Ruby couldn't help it. She gasped. It was so much more than she'd earn from the Colonel for the entire season.

Chase smiled. "You'll only have to lose every three or four starts. Maybe five times the rest of the year. You'll still end up with one of the best records in the league."

He waited for her to speak. When she didn't, he said, "And, because of the tough situation you're in, we'll advance you your first big payment, so you can take care of your friend."

Ruby thought about it. She thought about having that much money in her hands. She thought about talking to the cops who had arrested Paul, trying to find the Klan's "Bill," having to ask Russell Haynes for help. Having to beg.

"No," she said.

The skin on Chase's taut cheekbones tightened. But before he could speak, Ruby continued.

"How strong are you?" she said.

"Strong?"

"How fast is your fastball? Here, I mean. In New York."

Realizing as she said it that she'd known from the start he was from out of town. It was a matter of vowels, she thought, the way he pronounced them. It wasn't an immigrant's accent—he'd been born in this country. Just not around here.

"Fast enough," he said.

She shrugged at that. "Yeah? And why should I believe you? How do I know that you're not just feeding me a line? What have you done to prove that you're worth losing games for?"

Another blink at this barrage, but then the corners of his mouth twitched upward. "Want something from me, do you?"

"Yes." She paused. "I want you to show me something other than smooth talk. I want you to use your own money, your own oil, to get Paul out and to keep Haynes and the Klan away from me—for good."

Chase drew a deep breath in through his nose. "And then you'll do your part?" he asked.

Ruby's stomach rumbled. She reached down and picked up the hamburger. The roll was a little stale, but she took a big bite of it. Chewed and swallowed before she looked back at him.

"Then I'll think about it," she said.

"Think about it?" He grinned. "Okay. It's a big step, I know that."

He leaned toward her. "But while you're doing all this thinking, you should keep something in mind."

Ruby waited.

Chase got to his feet and tossed a couple of bucks down on the table.

"Whatever I do for you," he said, "I can undo just as fast."

31

*P*aul was released from jail three days later.

According to the official story, the woman in the alley had disappeared, leaving only a note admitting that she'd lied about the whole thing. Without her and her accusation, there was no case, and Paul had to be set free.

Ruby wondered how much it had cost to get the woman out of town.

Or maybe money hadn't been involved at all.

She'd told no one about her meeting with Chase, or the deal they'd made. Amanda had seen that something was troubling her, and so had Tania, but Ruby had shrugged off their concern. It was mostly a matter of keeping her face studiously blank and answering any direct questions with vague, off-the-point replies.

At the ballpark all the talk had been about Ruby's spectacular performance during her last start. If she appeared remote and reserved with the press, well, the reporters really didn't expect much more from a teenage girl facing her first brush with real fame.

And her teammates, who were unsure how to treat her at the best of times, mostly gave her a wide berth when they saw the mood she was in.

After all, they thought, you never knew with girls. Better just to stay away.

Ruby got the news of Paul's release in a message from Amanda at the ballpark after a game. By the time she got home, he was already there, encamped in the last remaining spare bedroom because he was in no condition to return to his own apartment. The doctor had come and gone, but the house smelled like a sick-room, an odor Ruby remembered all too well.

Mrs. Connell had taken the girls out for ice cream. Helen was sitting beside Paul as if it would take a steam shovel to evict her, yet when he saw Ruby he pushed himself up on his pillows and asked in a breathy voice to speak with her privately for a moment. Helen looked surprised, but without complaint got to her feet, embraced Ruby—just a quick touch—and went out, closing the door behind her.

Ruby sat on the chair beside the bed. Paul looked as if he'd lost fifteen pounds since she'd seen him last, the loose skin hanging in folds on his cheeks and under his chin. There was an ugly purplish bruise across his forehead and raw patches, painted with iodine, showed on the knuckles of his right hand.

He followed the direction of her gaze. "I had to fight," he said, and laughed, his lungs rattling. "I'm a terrible fighter. I should have gotten your friend Dempsey to stand in for me."

"What did the doctor say?" Ruby asked.

"I'll be fine."

She wasn't sure she believed him, but didn't push the point.

He fixed his eyes on her. She saw the whites were yellow and shot with red. "Ruby," he said, "I know I'm out because of you."

She shook her head, but he reached out and grabbed her right hand with his left, uninjured one. "Don't deny it." He coughed, his face crumpling, then gathered himself. "One of the cops told me. 'Thank that girl, the pitcher—'"

"Forget it," Ruby said.

"I know the truth when I hear it." He coughed again. "You got me out, Ruby."

She wrapped both of her cold hands around his warm one. "Have you told Helen?" she said. "Have you told anyone that I had a part in this?"

He quailed a little at her expression. "No, not yet."

"Don't," Ruby said.

The phone rang after dinner. Amanda answered it and listened. Then, her face full of questions, she held the handset out to Ruby.

"It's a man," she said.

Ruby took it, knowing who it would be before she heard the purring voice say, "So, how's my fastball?"

She said nothing, and heard Chase laugh. "Time to start believing in me, Diamond Ruby, because I always do what I say." He paused and then repeated, "Always."

She turned away from the curious gaze of her nieces and said in a low voice, "Okay. What next?"

"I'm on the corner of Clinton and Atlantic. Got something to show you."

He hung up. Ruby stood still for a moment, as blank as a statue, before replacing the handset on its cradle. Behind her, she heard Amanda ask, "Who was that?"

Ruby turned to look at her, finding it hard to meet those serious dark eyes. "Just a friend," she said. "I have to go see him for a minute."

"I'll come with you," Amanda said.

"No." Ruby tried to arrange her expression into a reassuring shape. "It's fine," she said. "I'll be back soon."

Neither of the girls looked reassured.

•   •   •

Ruby could see Chase leaning against a streetlamp on the corner, his white boater glimmering in the milky light. There was another man with him, shoulders hunched, head down. Not until she got close did Ruby recognize that it was Russell Haynes.

"See? Ask and ye shall receive," Chase said as she came up to them.

Ruby looked at Haynes, but the reporter didn't raise his head.

"I didn't ask for him," she said.

Chase smiled. "Still, thought you might like to hear the last word from the bluenose himself."

He reached out and gave Haynes a little poke. "Talk, Rusty."

Haynes finally looked at Ruby. His eyes shone in the streetlight, and in his face Ruby could see exhaustion and terror.

Chase poked him harder. *"Talk."*

"The word is out to leave you alone," Haynes said. His voice was high, wavering, a far cry from the icy tone he'd used in his office. "Both at the *Town Crier* and . . . other places."

"For how long?" Ruby asked.

"Forever."

Chase's hands moved faster than Ruby could follow, and suddenly there was a knife in his right one, its shiny flat blade at Haynes's throat. The reporter gasped and closed his eyes.

"Let's just make sure we're clear what forever means," Chase said, his voice harder than Ruby had heard before. "Is the Klan ever going to get in the way of my money again?"

Haynes shook his head, a tiny movement back and forth.

"Didn't think so." Chase gave him a shove. "Now get out of here."

Haynes turned and took a stumbling step away, then another. But just as he regained his balance, Chase leaped forward, his hands again a blur. The knife blade caught the light for an instant, a quick gleam like the blink of a distant beacon.

Then Chase was standing back, his arms crossed, watching. The knife had vanished.

For a second, perhaps two, Haynes stood still, his arms hanging limply at his sides. Ruby heard a sound like water trickling, then spattering, and saw black spots begin to speckle the sidewalk.

Making a guttural sound deep in his throat, Haynes fell to his knees. At the same moment, Ruby heard the sound of an engine starting up. A car she hadn't noticed before, parked perhaps fifty feet from where they'd been standing, pulled away from the curb, lights out, and approached, coming to a halt right in front of Haynes.

The reporter fell face-first onto the pavement and rolled onto his side. His black blood spread out along the sidewalk's cracks like tiny rivers.

Two men emerged from the car. They were wearing dark suits, and their faces were hidden in the shadows under hats whose brims had been pulled low over their foreheads. One was carrying a thick blanket.

Haynes barely moved, merely letting let out a low groan that was little more than a sigh as the two men rolled him up in the blanket. A moment later they'd hoisted their bundle and tossed it into the back of the car. Without a word or a glance, they climbed back into the front seat.

The car pulled away. Ruby watched it go, saw its taillights come on as it neared the corner, saw it make a slow, smooth turn and move out of sight.

She looked down at the spatters and rivulets, then raised her eyes to Chase. He gave a shrug. "Couldn't trust the guy," he said. "He was a true believer."

Ruby didn't say anything. Chase looked into her face. "You okay?" he asked, sounding genuinely concerned.

Ruby nodded. She felt numb, but she wasn't going to admit it. "I'm fine."

"Good." He moved a step toward her. She wondered where the knife was. Had he wiped the blade before he put it back? Or was it still dripping? Was it staining his clothes?

Ruby shook her head. She had to concentrate. "What now?" she asked.

Chase said, "You do what I told you. Win your next start, but don't show off. Let them get a hit or two, okay? A couple runs, if you've got the room."

Ruby said, "All right."

"And every day, whether you're pitching or not, an hour after the game ends, walk by the lunchroom where we talked last time. If I'm there, it means I have something to tell you. If not, just keep doing what you're doing until you hear from me. Got that?"

Ruby nodded. Then she said, "My next start's on the road, though. In Beacon. What do I do then?"

"Just pitch." He made a shrugging motion with his hands. "We need you up there, we'll find you. If not, be out here at ten the night you get back in town."

"You planning to kill anyone else that night?"

He grinned. "Not unless I have to."

She turned away from him. But when she'd only gone a few steps, he called her name.

She looked back and saw he was holding something in his right hand. He tossed it to her.

It was a small paper sack. Ruby looked inside and saw that it contained two candy bars of a kind she'd never seen before. She pulled one out and held it up to the light. It was called the 18th Amendment Bar and featured a colorful drawing of bottle of rum on the wrapper.

"For your daughters," Chase said.

"They're not my daughters."

Chase's teeth gleamed in the streetlight. "Care about them as much as if they were, though, don't you?" he said.

· · ·

"What's wrong?" Andy Sutherland asked.

Ruby tried to hide her alarm. She'd only thrown a few warm-up tosses, and here he was, standing in front of her, mask off, face filled with concern.

"Nothing," she said.

"Is it the mound?"

That would make a handy excuse. Highland Stadium, where the Beacon Bowlers played, was a beat-up old yard that seated maybe ten thousand on decrepit old benches and seats. The infield dirt was covered with pebbles—some were more like boulders—the outfield grass was brown, and the mound was steep and lumpy.

"I don't know," she said, kicking at a pebble. "Maybe."

"Then what else?"

Someone's telling me how to pitch. Ordering me to lose on purpose. That's what else. That's what's wrong. And I can't tell anyone about it. Not you, not Helen, not Tania, nobody.

But she just said, "Andy—"

"Yeah?"

"I'm going to listen to Jake today. I'm not going to bear down all game. I'll save something for the end."

He blinked, then gave her a grin. "Never thought I'd hear *those* words coming out of Diamond Ruby's mouth," he said.

Ruby had never thought she'd have to speak them.

As it turned out, Ruby didn't stick around long enough to make it worth saving her strength for the end. She pitched seven innings, giving up three runs on six hits while striking out eight, and the Typhoons won the game, 7–4.

It would have been a creditable enough performance, even one to be proud of, for anyone but her. But the crowd, which filled every seat in the old ballpark, had come expecting more, hoping for fastballs so speedy you couldn't see them and curves that made the batters' knees buckle. They filed silently out through the exits, and it wasn't easy to tell whether it was because their team had lost or because Ruby hadn't given them the show they wanted.

The press was disappointed as well. They hadn't gotten much of a story: better for them if she'd either repeated her dominating performance of her previous start or lost in equally spectacular fashion. GIRL PITCHER WINS BORING GAME! wasn't going to sell many newspapers.

Even Ruby's teammates seemed a bit let down. When Jake pulled her from the game, they reassured her that everyone had days like this, that they were sure she'd be back in form the next time, and anyway, a Typhoon victory was all that really mattered.

No one suspected anything. On the whole, she'd gotten off easy.

Except from herself.

It had rained in Brooklyn while she was up in Beacon, leaving the streets uncharacteristically clean. There was no trace of Russell Haynes's blood on the sidewalk below the streetlamp.

Ruby had heard some reporters talking about Haynes's disappearance. But no one seemed to care about it very much—people disappeared all the time, and anyway, who could miss a guy like that?

Chase was waiting for her when she arrived on the corner on Thursday at ten o'clock, as he'd commanded. "Did the girls like their candy bars?" was the first thing he asked.

Ruby nodded. In truth, neither had been able to tolerate the ersatz rum flavor, though Allie had loved being able to add to her candy-wrapper collection.

"You did a good job the other day," he went on. "Very convincing. You showed people you were human, just like I told you to. But not enough to make anyone suspicious."

Ruby stayed silent.

"So, next start you lose," Chase said.

The dizziness struck Ruby unawares, as if a sudden, powerful gust of wind had whistled up, threatening to lift her off the ground. She put her hand out against the streetlamp.

"You need to sit down?" Chase asked.

"I'm fine," she said.

He crossed his arms. "Having second thoughts?"

"I'll keep my end of the deal," Ruby said. "I told you I would, and I will. Now, where's my first payment?"

Saying the words because she knew they were what he expected from her. But not feeling them. Feeling nothing at all.

Numb to her soul.

"Your first payment went to the New York City Police Department and the Ku Klux Klan." Chase grinned. "And to my cleanup crew. But I tell you what. An hour after the game ends, after you lose, meet me at the lunchroom. We'll talk about how you did, and I might have a bonus for you."

He stepped closer to her on the quiet street corner. She looked down at his hands, but they were empty.

"Just don't let your pride get the best of you," he said.

Ruby was quiet.

"Because in my world, you're the one with no fastball."

32

*t*wenty-four cheerful, trusting young faces, and each one was like an accusation.

The early-morning event at Washington Park had been arranged by Josephine Collier and other leaders of New York's women's organizations, with the eager support of Colonel Fielding. After a series of art and writing competitions in Brooklyn's classrooms, these two dozen girls, aged seven to fifteen, had been selected to meet Ruby and have a pitching lesson.

Hearing about it in advance, Ruby had wondered—why art and writing? Why not an athletics competition? Wouldn't it have made more sense to choose girls who already knew how to throw a ball? Wouldn't they have been the ones who could learn the most from her?

But Tania had laughed at that. "They want girls who do the best they can at what they love to do, even if it's drawing," she'd explained. "They're not scouts looking for the next Diamond Ruby."

Ruby had looked down at her arms, crossed in her lap. "Put it that way, then thank goodness," she'd said. "One of me is enough."

At the time, she'd spoken lightly, and had been greatly looking forward to the day. She enjoyed being with kids, helping them learn. It was the one thing she missed from the Birdcage.

Only now that the day had come, she dreaded every moment.

They were so happy for her, these girls, so excited, resembling a team in their dark pants and white blouses, all wearing the red neckerchiefs that had come to represent Ruby's Rooters. Red-bordered name tags were pinned to their blouses. Faces flushed, eyes sparkling, they stood in orderly formation, holding their winning paintings, drawings, sculptures, stories, or poems.

One by one, as cameras clicked and clattered and the Colonel beamed and Josephine Collier kept strict order, they showed Ruby their work. There stood Diamond Ruby on the mound in ink or watercolor or oil paint, resolute, staring in toward the plate or in midmotion. There she was, in wire and clay, her arms and legs like a spider's. There she was, sketched in words, brave and true, overcoming tragedy and the blindness of today's backward men to achieve great things.

Here she was, standing among them, a fraud.

She did the best she could, smiling, thanking all the girls, shaking hands, accepting the occasional hug from a girl willing to endure Josephine Collier's rebuke. No one seemed to notice that her smiles were forced, that her husky voice lacked its usual vigor, that during the rare moments when everyone's attention was drawn elsewhere, she took deep breaths, as if to stave off drowning in fresh air.

No one noticed but Amanda and Allie, her intrepid and worried helpers. They whispered to each other and then redoubled their own efforts to entertain the girls, to make up with their own energy their aunt's lack of it.

Ruby had trouble even meeting Andy Sutherland's gaze. Andy was here to catch Ruby's demonstration pitches and to provide a big, reassuring target for the girls' efforts to fling a baseball sixty feet, six inches and have it end up where they hoped it would. Five minutes after he was introduced to them, all the older girls had already fallen in love with his strong chin and big smile, and even his knotted catcher's hands.

Ruby felt sick. She didn't deserve Andy, either. He would never throw a game. He would figure out a way to get out from under.

Then—

"You're so strong," the girl standing beside her on the mound said.

Ruby looked at her. *Emma*, her name tag said. Emma, a skinny, waiflike girl, perhaps ten, with lank ash-blond hair and smudges like bruises under her pale blue eyes. Her pitching lesson had resulted in only two throws so far, with time spent catching her breath after each one.

She looked like she'd had consumption, but at least she'd survived. And her painting of Ruby awash in light had been one of the most beautiful of all.

"I wish I could be as strong as you are," Emma said.

Ruby knew the young girl was talking about physical strength, nothing else. But still, to her amazement, she felt a lump form in her throat. *Strong?* What good did it do to be strong?

"I look at you," Emma said, "and I know for sure you can do anything."

Ruby felt like putting her hands over her ears. She felt like running away. How could she listen to this?

But she couldn't run. She couldn't stop hearing.

"Sometimes it's hard," she said.

Emma looked up at her. "My mama always says, if a happy life was easy, everybody would have one."

Someone was calling out from near home plate. While they'd been talking, the other girls had taken their places again. With a last quick smile, Emma hurried over to join them. Ruby, feeling dizzy, the ground unsteady beneath her feet, stayed where she was as Josephine Collier stepped forward to give a speech.

Her voice carrying like a trumpet across the infield, Miss Collier spoke about women, about the new generation, about what today's young girls might expect in the 1930s and beyond. But mostly she spoke about Ruby, going on about strength and dignity and opportunity, and how sometimes you could find inspiration in the strangest places.

It was too much.

And when something was too much, what did you do?

As Miss Collier went on and on, Ruby felt the numbness that had afflicted her begin to dissipate. She'd been walking around as if asleep these last few days, and now she was waking up again.

What did you do? You *acted*.

"Something's different," Tania said. She was standing at the ironing board, hands uncharacteristically still, looking at Ruby with an inquiring expression.

Ruby, buttoning her shirt, half turned away, said nothing.

"*You're* different."

Ruby paused. "Am I?"

"Sure. You been walking around like someone put rocks in your stomach. Now . . . well, now you're not."

At last Ruby turned to face her friend. "Tania, do you like me?" she asked.

Tania laughed. "Recently, not so much," she said. "Before that, well enough, I guess."

"Enough to help me?"

Tania looked startled. Then she laughed again. "What a question," she said. "Listen, I wouldn't *have* to like you to want to help. Case you didn't notice, you're my meal ticket. You make money, I do, too. You get yourself in trouble, where am I?"

Ruby thought about that.

"Liking you's an extra, a bonus." Tania shrugged. "And you've been good enough company, least till recently."

"Thank you," Ruby said.

"Sure. So, what's your problem? What do you want me to do?"

"Nothing yet," Ruby said.

"No?"

"Just be ready."

"Me?" Tania turned her hands up. "Me, all I ever am is ready."

Ruby's nightmare day was postponed for twenty-four hours due to a larger nightmare: the death of President Harding.

Not that Harding's passing on a warm and sticky Thursday had much of an effect on Ruby. She'd known he was ill, because it was all over the newspapers: something about a long, exhausting whistle-stop tour to places like Alaska and Oregon, followed by a bout with an unidentified illness in San Francisco. After days of reports on his health, the newspapers had claimed that he was finally recovering. That was quickly followed by the announcement of his death.

His passing was due, it was said, to a kind of explosion in his brain brought on by the demands of his job. Ruby had seen enough photographs of the late president, though, to guess that overeating might have contributed, too.

She honestly couldn't have cared less. What did the president have to do with her and her life? But the rest of America seemed possessed by grief, at least according to Friday's newspapers, which ran great black-bordered headlines proclaiming Harding a true friend of the common man, a great patriot who was responsible for the comfortable, happy times the American people lived in today.

It was all very distracting, but the only direct effect it had on Ruby was that Judge Landis, baseball's commissioner, ordered all games from the major leagues on down to be postponed on the nationwide day of mourning. The former president's body, visible to onlookers on its bier aboard a special train car named the *Superb,* was making its way east from California. Even those who did not live along its route were expected to ponder the vagaries of life, and how quickly it could be taken away.

Ruby didn't need a funeral procession to tell her *that.*

After the team gathered, Colonel Fielding made a small, quiet speech about President Harding and sent them home. Jake Conlon, looking quite put out, held his tongue. Many of the players seemed to have no idea where they should go.

Even though the schedule had changed, Ruby decided to walk past the armchair lunchroom. Chase was there, sitting in the same corner as before. Her stomach lurching, she went in.

The restaurant was half full with lunch goers. Those who were speaking at all were doing so in low voices, which made Chase's cheerful, "Well, there you are, Diamond Girl!" sound as raucous as a siren in comparison.

Everyone in the restaurant glared at him. He stared around, unabashed, and then said to Ruby, "What's their beef?"

Ruby slipped into the chair across the table from him. "They're staying quiet out of respect," she said, keeping her voice low as well.

"Respect? For who?" Chase's voice rang like a bell, and Ruby saw that he was doing it on purpose. "For President Harding? *That* crook?"

The waiter, a doddery old man, came over. "Please, sir—"

Chase shot him a scornful look, but lowered his voice just a trifle. "I'd have respected old Warren a little more if he'd been any good at his job—which was getting as much money out of the Treasury for his friends as he could. The man was a fraud, and a fool, too."

The waiter walked away in the middle of this speech, and Chase switched his attention to Ruby. He was acting as if the dead president had insulted him personally.

"Anyone who ever played an angle knew about Harding as soon as they laid eyes on him," Chase said. "He was an embarrassment, not even good at cheating. He was the pigeon you took at cards. Luckiest thing he ever did was check out when he did. Just watch, a year from now everyone will see—"

"Honestly, I don't care," Ruby said before she could stop herself.

Chase interrupted his speech and gave Ruby a sudden, piercing inspection. She realized too late that she'd made a mistake. The one man she wanted unaware of her newly discovered resolve was sitting across from her, and here she was, not five minutes in his company, raising his suspicions.

Only thing to do now was to go with it. "The world is full of crooks, and we all have problems," she said. "My problem is earning that money you've been promising me, but which I haven't seen yet."

He gazed at her with a cat's insufferable inscrutability. Then he gave a slow grin, which didn't quite seem to include his eyes, and switched to a much quieter voice. "Now, that's the Ruby I expected to meet right off the bat—the one always looking for the best chance. The one who seemed to have gone missing for a while."

"She's right here," Ruby said. "She got lost, but now that you sprang Paul, she's back."

He gave a slow nod. "Well, you'll see the money tomorrow, after the game is played."

Ruby said, "Okay."

"Glad I've got your permission." Chase got up, tossing a bill on the table to pay for the coffee. "You know how to handle this tomorrow. Don't shake the fans' faith in you."

In other words, lose, but make it seem like a fluke. So people will bet on you just as heavily the next time you lose . . . and the time after that.

Ruby looked up at him. "I know what I have to do," she said.

Chase frowned. His eyes darkened as he stared down at her. "Ruby," he said, and there was a world of threat in his voice.

Ruby's heart thudded. She could almost see the knife in his hand, almost feel the bite of the blade cutting into her flesh.

But she didn't look away from his eyes. "I *understand*, Chase."

After another moment, he nodded and went on his way.

Only after he was out of sight did she put her head in her hands and wait for her heart to calm.

That evening Ruby made two phone calls and went to bed early. But sleep was a long time coming. She lay on top of the sheets for hours, staring at the ceiling, thinking things over.

You can do anything.

But not alone.

33

*r*uby prayed for rain on game day, but Saturday dawned bright
and sunny, the summer heat cut by a wind from the north-
west. A perfect day for baseball.

The Typhoons were playing the Monroe Cheesekooks, visiting from somewhere on the other side of the Hudson River up
past Beacon. When Ruby had first heard the name from Jake
Conlon, she had stared at him in disbelief. He'd scowled and
wriggled his shoulders, as if trying to ease a stiff neck, and said,
"The bosses said the league'll get more attention if the teams have
names you remember."

"You mean, instead of boring ones like the 'Yankees' and
'Giants'?" she'd asked.

Conlon had glared at her. "Typhoons, Silkworms, Cheesekooks. Can't believe we even put our uniforms on in the morning."

Still, the Cheesekooks had ability. During a two-game series
up in Monroe the previous week, Ruby had watched them carefully and had seen that they were well coached. They played strong

defense, bunted a lot, stole bases, and slapped the ball the other way instead of cranking up to hit home runs.

Ruby had to admit that Chase was smart. After her rage-filled, dominating performance two starts ago, and her winning (though less impressive) most recent effort, the betting money would still be flooding in her direction for this start. But the Cheesekooks were good, legitimately good, so a loss to them wouldn't raise any alarm bells among bettors. They'd just shrug their shoulders and pay off their debts—no one won every time, not even on supposed "sure things." And though they might hold off betting on her the next time, they'd be back soon enough when she started winning again.

It was a perfect setup. Ruby might even have admired it, if it hadn't required her to do something that made her feel sick to her stomach.

Alone in the corner of the dugout in the hours before the game began, she and Andy went over the Cheesekooks' batters, one by one. Andy kept glancing at her face as they talked, and finally he said, "Ruby, you're sitting there looking like somebody died, and I can tell you're not listening to what I'm saying."

Ruby said, "Sorry."

"Jeez." Andy glared at her. "I don't care if you're sorry or not. I just want to know what's going on."

She'd known this moment was coming. She'd long since made her decision. Still, it was almost impossible for her to speak. She felt sweat break out on her arms and the back of her neck.

"For God's sake," Andy said, alarmed, "what's wrong?"

So she opened her mouth, closed it again, and then some-how, her voice even hoarser than usual, got the words out. "I have to lose this game," she said.

She was unable to look at him as she explained. Feeling more like a little girl than she had in years, she wondered, Will he hate me now? Will he get up and walk away? Will he . . . tell?

There was silence when she was done. Finally she raised her eyes and saw that the muscles in his face had set and his lips were pressed tightly together.

"I'm sorry," she said again.

He gave a jerk of the shoulders like he was flicking off a fly. "Who's doing this to you?" he asked. "What's his name? Where can I find him?"

Ruby said, "Andy—I can't tell you. Not yet."

"So don't do it." He leaned toward her. "Ruby, just don't."

"I've got no choice," she said.

Seeing Chase's shining knife blade as vivid as a shooting star in her mind.

Andy sat back a little. "Tell the bulls."

"Tell them what? It's not down on paper, you know. The threats have been . . . careful. And anyway—you'd trust the cops?" she asked. "'Cause I don't."

He grimaced at that. "So you do what? Lose whenever he tells you?"

"That's what he thinks. But I can't. I can't." The words almost seemed to burn her mouth. "Just today, that's all. Then I'll have time to—"

She shook her head. "Andy, you could beg off the game. Say you have an aching head or belly gripes or something. Let Stu catch instead."

Andy thought about it and slowly shook his head. "Nah. I'll play. You have to do this, I have to share it with you."

He leaned over and spat onto the dirt floor of the dugout. "But only this once, you say?"

"Only this once," Ruby said.

His eyes brightened a little. "And you've got a plan?"

"Yeah," Ruby said. "I've got a plan."

The beginnings of one, at least.

·   ·   ·

The game was as bad as Ruby could have imagined. Worse. Her insides felt clawed to pieces, shredded, with every hit she "surrendered," every walk the Cheesekooks "earned" off her.

What was worst of all is how hard she had to work to lose, but lose in the right way. Chase had warned her against getting knocked around in the first couple of innings, but at the same time to look like she was struggling. But how was she supposed to do that? How was she supposed to pitch just well enough not to win?

She gave up two runs before the first inning was even over, a soft hit, a stolen base, a ball down the line, just fair. It was the first time she'd ever pointed her pitches in the wrong direction. She felt like she was betraying herself.

Andy came out to the mound, where Ruby was standing with her head down. It was what he would have done in a normal game, to ask her what was wrong.

Instead he said, "How you holding up?"

"Oh, everything's fine," she said, her voice bitter.

"Keep yourself together, Ruby." His voice was sharp. "And pitch better. Jake thinks you've got a sore wing, and he's going to yank you if you don't get back in control."

See? Ruby felt like saying. It's impossible. You can't pitch a baseball game like this. You can't guarantee a loss that won't make people suspicious.

She got out of the first inning without any more damage, and made it through the second unscathed as well, though she struck out only the opposing pitcher. The hometown fans, who had begun the game cheering wildly for her every pitch, began to realize that they weren't seeing the Diamond Ruby they'd expected. They murmured at each ball hit sharply, even if it was into a Typhoon glove. And when, after the Typhoons had tied the game in the third, Ruby gave up two more runs in the fifth—on the first home run she'd ever allowed—she heard, for the first time, groans and other sounds of disappointment from the stands.

The claw gouged at her insides. She was profoundly glad that she'd asked the Connells and the girls not to come. She'd blamed it on superstition, but in truth she just couldn't stand the idea of them watching her lose.

She was gone from the game after six, having surrendered another run in her final inning. The subdued crowd cheered her anyway, thanking her for her past efforts, forgiving her.

Which only made it worse.

As they had in her last, albeit winning, start, her teammates consoled her with quick, encouraging words: *We'll get 'em tomorrow. You know this means you'll throw a no-hitter next time.*

But she barely heard them, didn't want to listen, preferring to sit in pure, blind misery alone on the end of the bench as the rest of the game unfolded.

While she still sat there, as the quiet fans filed out and the rest of her team headed for the locker room, Jake Conlon squatted down and looked her straight in the eyes. "I'm giving you a couple of extra days before your next start," he said.

She was shaking her head before he was done. "I'm fine," she said. "I just didn't have it today."

"Not by what I'm seeing. I think you're hiding something from me."

She reached out toward him. "Jake, please," she said, "Please let me take my next start. I'll be fine. I'll show you I still have it. But how can I show you if I'm not on the mound?"

It was the closest she'd ever come to begging.

He hesitated, biting the corner of his lip with uncharacteristic indecision. Then his expression softened a bit. "Tell you what," he said. "Don't touch a ball for two days. Then you'll do some light throwing, with me and Andy watching. You look good, we'll let you go ahead. We see anything that bothers us, you're going on the shelf till I say you're ready."

He frowned. "You're still just a kid. Don't want to break you."

It was the best she was going to get. Ruby wrapped her arms around her belly. "Okay," she said. "Jake—thanks."

He nodded and straightened. As soon as he'd walked away, she got to her feet and almost ran down the corridor toward her washroom.

She barely made it in time. Then she was crouching over the cold white bowl, vomiting explosively, endlessly, until there was nothing left in her stomach, and not stopping even then. She retched until her throat burned and her stomach felt like it had been scoured with lye.

Finally, her head spinning, she got back to her feet, made it to the sink, and rinsed out her mouth. But she didn't think the bad taste would ever go away.

She washed her face and looked at herself in the mirror, pale and thin with black circles around her bloodshot eyes. She felt like she'd broken something inside herself the moment she'd agreed to lose the game, and was receiving her rightful punishment now.

Never again.

Chase sat back in his chair. "Conlon thinks you're hurt, huh?"

Ruby nodded.

"But you convinced him otherwise?"

"I tried to." She took a breath. "Thought you'd want me back out on the mound quick as possible."

"Yeah, true. Still—"

Interrupting himself, he looked down at the tabletop, drumming his fingers against the stained wood. While he worked things out, Ruby took the time to glance around the armchair lunchroom. As always, there was no one at any of the tables within easy earshot. It occurred to her that maybe Chase was paying off the manager to keep those tables empty while he held court with Ruby.

Paying him off, or using some other form of persuasion.

At tables farther away, two elderly, white-haired women sipped tea, a young couple whispered to each other like they were planning something, and a cheerful man with sandy hair enjoyed a sandwich.

Finally Chase said, "Good. You'll get back on the mound, as you said. But meanwhile, the word will get out." He smiled. "*Somehow* the word will get out that maybe you're hiding an injury. That'll send the money running in our direction. All you'll have to do is pitch like yourself again, and we'll clean up."

He reached inside his jacket and withdrew a thick white envelope. "Congratulations, Diamond Ruby," he said, pushing it across the table toward her. "You're handling this like you were born to the business."

She didn't say anything.

He laughed at her expression. "Take it. Buy yourself something nice. You'll feel better."

After a moment, she picked up the envelope and slipped it into her bag.

Chase was still smiling. "Next time out, go ahead and win. Just don't throw the ball like you were aiming it at my head every pitch," he said. "Take it easy. We don't want you ruining your arm for real."

Across the room, the elderly ladies were leaving. A few minutes later, the sandy-haired young man followed. Only the young couple seemed to have nowhere else to go. Outside, Ruby could see the low-angled early-evening sunlight turning the sidewalks and car bumpers a glowing orange-yellow. Suddenly she was very tired.

"You okay?"

She turned her head to look at him. "I threw up after the game. A *lot*."

Chase seemed interested in this. "You always do that? Up-chuck?"

"No. Just this time."

He grinned.

"Next time," he said, "will be easier."

34

*t*he doorbell rang at nine the next morning, just as Ruby had requested. Anticipating it, she'd asked Helen and Mrs. Connell to take the girls out for an early breakfast, and Paul—just beginning to venture outside again—had gone along, too. Ruby wanted to be alone for at least the beginning of this meeting.

She swung open the heavy oak front door to find her visitor waiting patiently on the top step. Looking at him, she felt momentarily like a street-corner magician pulling a scarf out of her sleeve or making a nickel appear from some child's ear.

The young man standing at the door, a black leather portfolio case under one arm, was dressed in a suit that looked like it could use a good cleaning and pressing. Beneath a mop of unruly, sandy hair, his expressive, fine-boned face and piercing blue eyes were alive with interest and speculation.

Looking at him, Ruby drew in a slow breath. Even though she knew he must be in his late twenties now, he looked as if he'd barely aged a day since the last time they'd been face to face. That had been the day they buried Mama and Papa. The day Ruby and Nick and Evie and this man, Jim McKay, had dug for hours, desperate to get the two coffins underground amid the abandoned ones stacked all around them.

Jim had helped back then because he'd been Ted's friend, a fellow artist. Ruby had remembered the two of them laboring over broadsides as the Great War neared its end, just before the epidemic struck. She'd discovered he was now an editorial cartoonist for the *Examiner,* creator of devilish, funny sketches lampooning the mayor and other local politicians. In turn, he'd known Ruby as soon as she identified herself over the telephone, and now he was peering at her and smiling.

"Sure, I recognized you right away," he said, shaking her hand with a gentle clasp. "Would've even if your picture wasn't in the paper every day or two."

She gestured him into the living room. "Would you like some coffee?"

He shook his head and sat on the sofa, laying the portfolio case on his lap and undoing the straps.

"I was glad to see you there," Ruby said. "I didn't know if you'd show up."

"And miss the fun?" Jim opened the case and pulled out a handful of sheets of rice paper. "I felt like Mata Hari."

But Ruby was barely listening. She was staring at his hands.

Her instructions over the telephone had been simple: Show up at the armchair restaurant after the game, sit unobtrusively but within sight of Chase, memorize his face without being noticed, and then go home and draw his portrait. Oh, and feel free to eat a sandwich on her nickel.

But Ruby had expected a single drawing as the result, not a pile of them.

She sat down beside Jim and looked at Chase's face staring up at her. His slanted eyes were filled with amusement, his lips turned upward in one of his casual, meaningless smiles. It was a brilliant likeness.

"Don't much like the manner of that man," Jim said.

"Me either."

With delicate hands, he paged through the sheets. The next four drawings were nearly identical to the first, as like to each other as if he'd photographed the original and then made several prints from it.

"How long did it take you to draw these?" Ruby asked.

"Not so long." He shrugged. "I work fast. And I don't need much sleep."

"Thank you. They're great," she said. "Exactly what I was hoping for."

Jim grinned and flapped a hand to dismiss her thanks. Then he stared at her through disconcertingly blue eyes. "What about that other guy we talked about?"

Ruby hesitated. "You've already done so much . . ."

Ignoring her, he stood. "Let's move to the table."

They did, and once he was seated, Jim reached into his case and pulled out a small pile of unmarked sheets, three pencils of different weights, and a gum eraser. Taking one of the pencils, he said, "Please begin."

Slowly at first, and then with increasing confidence, Ruby described Frankie, the man with the brilliantined hair. Jim's pencil moved across the page, capturing the details from her words: not only the thick, shiny hair, but the soft dimples on the cheeks, the close-set eyes, the cruel droop to the full lips, the fleshiness along the jawline that would someday soon become jowls.

Occasionally he'd wield the eraser, but by the time they were done he had captured the look, the spirit, of the man Ruby had seen. "That's it," she said. "That's him."

Jim regarded his work. "Another prize specimen."

"Yeah."

He slanted his gaze at her. "This one and the other, they're acquainted?"

Ruby nodded.

"Well, from the looks of it, they deserve each other." He smiled at her. "Ruby, if you could leave me alone for a few minutes? And I will take some coffee now, if you don't mind."

By the time she returned with the tray, he was just finishing the third copy of the original drawing. As he reached for the cup, though, they heard the front door swing open and the tumult that always announced Amanda's and, especially, Allie's arrival.

They came in, glowing from the summer sun, followed by the grown-ups. Ruby introduced them all to Jim, the girls instantly becoming quiet and shy, at least for a moment.

Ruby said, "Mr. McKay has been kind enough to help me."

Whatever shyness remained in Allie was entirely banished when she spotted the drawings on the table. "What are these?" she asked, plunking herself down beside Jim.

"Just some people," Ruby said. "Don't touch."

Amanda was staring at them. "Which one is the man you go out to meet at night?"

There was no point in lying. Ruby pointed.

"I wish you didn't have to," Amanda said.

"Me, too."

Mrs. Connell had been staring down at the drawings. Now she gave Ruby a shrewd look. "What are you planning to do with these?"

Ruby shook her head and didn't say what she was thinking.

Whatever it takes to win.

As he was packing up his pencils, Jim suddenly stopped. "This man, Chase," he said. "Where's he hail from?"

Ruby said, "I don't know."

"Not from around here, though."

Ruby stopped and looked at him. "How can you tell?"

Jim rubbed his chin. "I'm not sure. I couldn't hear his voice clearly from across the restaurant, but there was something about the tone—and the way he moved—that told me he was from out of town." He grimaced. "Couldn't tell you where, though."

"Chicago," Allie said.

Everyone stared at her. Ruby saw her hand creep toward her mouth, but she held up under their gazes.

"Wait here," she instructed.

She turned and ran up the stairs. As her sister's footsteps thumped across the wood floor above, Amanda suddenly gave a decisive nod, as if she'd figured something out.

When Allie came pelting back down the stairs, she was bearing her prized scrapbook. She placed it on the table in front of them and began turning the pages. Ruby caught a glimpse of the candy wrappers pasted carefully within, as colorful and exotic as the flags of distant countries. Konabars and Mounds and Cherry Balls and Baby Ruths, all these treats that hadn't existed when Ruby was Allie's age, that she'd grown past without ever tasting.

"Someone once approached me to design a candy-bar wrapper, but nothing ever came of it," Jim said.

Allie flipped one last page. "Look," she said, pointing.

It was the wrapper for the 18th Amendment Bar, with its cartoon jug of rum.

"I threw mine away," Amanda said. "It tasted awful."

Allie gave an irritable twitch of the shoulders. "That man," she said, gesturing at the stack of drawings. "The one you meet. He's the one who gave you the candy for us, isn't he?"

Ruby nodded.

"Well, it's from Chicago. Look."

Ruby bent close to the wrapper to read the small print. "Marvel Company, Chicago, Illinois."

"See?" Allie's voice was triumphant. "I *can* read!"

"Think, too," Ruby said.

"Chicago, huh?" Tania said.

Ruby nodded.

"Yeah, I saw him." Tania was gazing at the drawings. "Seen both of them."

She shrugged. "But just the same times you did, lurking around at the Birdcage and also the day you got famous here. Wondered about it because, you know, why were they there? They weren't throwing the ball at the Cage, they weren't writing anything down like reporters here at the ballpark."

She looked down at the drawings again. "I just figured them as creeps. They more than that?"

"Well, this is the guy deciding when I win and when I lose."

As Ruby filled in the details, Tania's mouth tightened. "Oh, yeah? Knew I didn't like him. And the other?"

"His game is rumrunning, I think. Could be he supplies the cash, too. I don't know." Ruby turned her palms up. "I don't know enough about either of them."

"And that's where I come in," Tania said.

"If you want."

Tania didn't even dignify that with a response. She took a copy of each drawing, folded them in half, and put them inside her cloth bag.

"Please," Ruby said to her, "be careful. Don't take any risks."

Tania laughed out loud. "Living's a risk, sweetie," she said.

"I played in Chicago for six years," Andy Sutherland said. "I told you that once, right? For the Logan Squares of the City League." He grinned. "I pitched *and* caught, though never at the same time. Had a pretty good fastball back then, too, though not as good as some I could mention."

Ruby said, "You still know people from back there?"

They were sitting in her dressing room, the two of them, with Tania, the mother hen, standing off to the side, arms crossed, listening.

"I'm from Champaign originally," Andy replied. "Still got family in that area, and plenty of old friends. So, sure."

Ruby took two of the drawings and slid them across the table to him. He looked down, frowning, and said, "These two Chicago guys?"

"I think so."

"Huh." He rolled his eyes. "I was in France during the war. Met a guy who asked me, 'You're from America? Do you know Harry?'"

Ruby sighed. "I get that it's a long shot. But these two are trying to make a mark for themselves in New York. Seems to me that they must've had some pull out there, let them believe they could do the same here. *Someone's* got to know them."

Andy looked back down at the drawings. Then he poked a thick finger at the one of Chase. "This guy I might have seen once or twice before."

"He's around the ballpark a lot."

"He the one got his hooks into you?"

Ruby nodded.

"What if I just go out there and knock his ass back and forth across the street a few times?"

She smiled at the idea, though Andy seemed perfectly serious. "Like to try it myself," she said, "but it wouldn't do any good."

"Why not?"

"Because someone else would show up right behind him."

Thinking about it, Andy puffed out his cheeks.

"No, when I get him—them—off my back, it's going to be for good," Ruby said. "I've got to make sure I never see Chase—"

"What did you say his name was?"

"Chase."

Andy sat back in his chair. "Very funny."

Ruby said, "I don't understand."

"Ever hear of Hal Chase?"

The name sounded familiar, but Ruby couldn't come up with why.

"Old Prince Hal, just the crookedest player you've ever seen." He whistled through his teeth. "Great player, was Hal, smoothest at first base I ever saw, when he wanted to be. He played with the Highlanders here in New York for a couple years, with the Giants, a bunch of other teams, too. And wherever he went, he'd try to convince some of his teammates to start throwing games for the gamblers. Sometimes he'd succeed. Everybody knew about it."

Ruby said, "So?"

"So the word was that his fingerprints were all over the 1919 World Series. He made something like ten thou betting against the Black Sox. Hear he's still at it someplace out west, some out-law team with Chick Gandil and some of the other bastards from the Sox."

Ruby looked down at the drawing. "But this isn't him."

"No—too bad. That would be easier." Andy flexed his fingers, as though his hands were hurting him. "This guy, *your* Chase, whoever he is, he's, like, playing with you. Why else would he take that name?"

For fun, Ruby thought. For the same reason he'd given the girls 18th Amendment candy bars. For the same reason he grinned every time he looked at her.

Because he could.

Because he thought he was untouchable.

Andy picked up the two drawings. All the humor had drained out of his expression.

"I'll find out who these jokers are," he said.

.   .   .

"Come out and see me," Chase said, his amusement coming clearly over the telephone line.

It was late. Ruby was exhausted. She didn't feel like jumping just because he told her to.

"You can say what you need to say over the phone," she said.

There was a brief pause. Then she heard him laugh. "Well, okay," he said. "How about this: Your brother's in jail."

Ruby almost said, "I have no brother." She almost said, "Remind me why I'm supposed to care?"

She almost just hung up.

But then she took a breath and realized that she had to follow her own advice. It wasn't time yet. She had to play this all very carefully.

Chase was leaning against the lamppost, relaxed in the yellow light as he watched her approach. "Nice of you to show up," he said when she was close enough to hear.

Ruby stopped five feet away from him and didn't say anything.

Frowning, he looked her up and down. "So, I'm waiting," he said finally.

"Waiting for what?"

"For you to beg me to get your brother out of jail, just like you did for that guy your friend is sweet on."

Ruby looked into his face. She had no trouble keeping her own a blank.

"You've got me read all wrong," she said. "I couldn't care less what happens to Nick."

Chase blinked, and his mouth opened a little. It was the first time she'd surprised him.

"My brother walked out of my life, out of his daughters' lives, a long time ago," she went on. "He made that decision, not me, not them, and now he's got to live with it."

Chase said, "But—"

Ruby didn't let him continue. "Whatever happens to him in there, that's his decision, too. So don't bother to tell me about it. I don't need to know."

After a moment, Chase said, "Okay."

Ruby took a step closer to him. "I'm tired. You're going to want me to win next time, right? You'll want me hitting on all sixes. Right? Well, then, I've got to get some sleep. So is there anything else?"

After another pause, he shook his head.

"Then I'll see you after the game," she said, and walked away from him.

"How could you do that?" Helen asked. She shuddered, her shoulders shaking. "Just abandon him? Paul told me how—how awful it is in there."

"Helen," Ruby said, and there was something in her voice that made her friend stop short.

"Helen," Ruby said again, more gently, "Chase was never going to get Nick out for me. He was just dangling the idea so I'd jump at it, and then he could slap me down."

Helen's hands knotted in her lap. "Are you sure?"

"Yeah. I'm sure. Right now, the biggest favor I can do for Nick is to act like he doesn't matter. That way, Chase won't use him as a hammer to beat me with."

Helen was silent for a long time. Then she said, "Ruby, how do you know all this?"

Ruby didn't answer.

But she was thinking: Helen, how do you *not*?

35

"What's this thing like in a storm?" Ruby asked.

Jack Dempsey smiled and bounced a little on his heels. "The movement helps you stay light on your feet. Anyway, after you've been hit a few times up here—" He pointed at his head. "You feel like you're on the high seas anyway. This evens it out a little."

They were standing in a crowd of people on the deck of the *President Harding,* a big, low-slung militia training ship docked in the Hudson River. At least that's what Ruby had been told it was, though to her it seemed more like a skyscraper laid on its side.

Ruby had never been on a boat before. She shifted her feet, trying to adjust to even the tiny movements of the great steel hulk on the water, her stomach lurching with every unexpected shift.

They'd come here, to this ship smelling of rust and paint and the sea, for the press's sake, of course. The *Harding* was an old boat with a new moniker, hastily renamed after the death of the president a few weeks earlier. Ruby could see where the old letters had been obscured with fresh steel-gray paint. The new name had been painted in white that was already yellowing.

No one had even mentioned the dead president in days. People in New York had quickly put aside their silent grief over his death and were back paying attention to things that really mattered to them, like restaurants and shows and the Yankees' and Giants' spectacular seasons and Diamond Ruby's ongoing success with the Typhoons.

And, above all, New Yorkers were focused on the upcoming heavyweight championship boxing match between Jack Dempsey and Luis Firpo, the Argentine "Wild Bull of the Pampas," at the Polo Grounds. Ruby had never paid the slightest attention to boxing, but even if she hadn't gotten to know Jack Dempsey, she would have been aware of this fight. It was the talk of the town.

All Dempsey had to do was sneeze, and there would be an article about it. All Firpo had to do was grunt, and columns were filled with speculations about what the glowering Argentine meant. And the more breathlessly the tabloids covered the impending battle, the more the public seemed to want to read about it.

The event staged today on the *President Harding* was just one of a series that had interrupted Dempsey's training up in White Sulfur Springs. "The last thing I need is a break for *this*," he grumbled to Ruby as they stood on deck waiting for the event to begin, for the press to ask the same questions they always asked. Already they were surrounded by reporters hoping to get a quote before anyone else did.

"You look like you could fight tomorrow," she said. And it was true: Dempsey seemed as quick and powerful as some jungle creature. She glanced at his fists, and wondered what it would feel like to be struck by one.

"Huh," he said, but seemed a bit mollified. Then he gave a sudden smile. "Tell you what's bugging me," he said. "I trained on this boat before a fight I had back in 1920."

"Bill Brennan," someone said. "In Madison Square Garden."

Dempsey nodded. "Wintertime. I remember it was damn cold." He gave Ruby an apologetic glance, as if worried she'd never heard the swearword before. "Got myself into perfect shape—and then they postponed the fight for three weeks. By the time it finally came around, I was as stale as an old piece of bread. Brennan came too damn close—" He gave Ruby another glance, and she rolled her eyes at him. "Too darn close to beating me. And you should've heard the boos from the crowd at the Garden! Thought they might lynch me."

Scowling, he looked around. "Lousy memories."

"This time it'll be different," Ruby said.

"Yeah?" He grimaced. "Against Firpo, it'd better be. That man can throw a punch."

His gaze lifted and he looked over toward Riverside Drive. "Speak of the devil."

There was a buzz from the assembled crowd as a taxicab pulled up at the foot of the pier. Dempsey gave a quick nod and said to no one in particular, "I'll see you all down below."

Ruby gave him a questioning look. "Man deserves his moment in the sun," he explained, and then was gone through a white-painted door at the top of a flight of stairs.

Publicity.

Along with everyone else, Ruby watched the muscular figure emerge from the backseat of the cab. Luis Firpo was taller than Dempsey, much more massive, with a barrel chest and thick legs. He was clad in a fine dark suit jacket, a white shirt that shone crisply even at a distance, a dark red tie, perfectly creased trousers, and shiny black shoes. He looked, Ruby thought, less "the Wild Bull of the Pampas" than the "Best Dressed Dandy on Manhattan Island."

He was handsome, too, with a broad, olive-toned, serious face, close-cropped, wavy black hair, and deep-set dark eyes.

He walked up the gangplank, accompanied by his sour-faced manager and a couple of other hangers-on. His eyes shifted past the reporters and photographers as if they didn't exist and settled on Ruby. A moment later, he was standing beside her, looking her up and down. "You are Miss Thomas?" he said, his voice deep, his accent one she'd never heard before.

She nodded.

Reaching into his pocket, Firpo extracted a new, white baseball and held it out to her. It looked like a golf ball in his huge palm. Ruby had the odd, irrelevant thought that he would make a great catcher, and then wondered if they even had baseball in Argentina.

"Throw this, if you like," he said.

Ruby heard a murmur from the onlookers, and the familiar sound of camera shutters clicking. She thought about it, and then nodded. Publicity.

"Sure," she said, taking the ball.

She walked over to the railing, the crowd following her, and then waited for Firpo to join her there. There was little boat traffic on the greasy river, and the air was so thick she could barely make out the opposite shore.

She threw. The ball streaked away from them, a white dot growing smaller and smaller until it vanished into the fog. Luis Firpo watched it, his face thoughtful, then turned toward Ruby and gave a small bow.

"Thank you," he said, and for the first time he smiled. Ruby saw that he had good teeth, straight and white, and wondered how you kept your teeth when you were a boxer.

Then his manager, who'd been standing by impatiently, murmured something into his ear. Firpo nodded, bowed once again to Ruby, and turned away. A moment later he and the whole crowd were heading toward the back of the ship and then descending the same staircase that Dempsey had used a few minutes earlier.

When Ruby followed, she saw that the downstairs—or whatever it was called—was a gymnasium. It smelled of perspiration and fresh paint and something Ruby couldn't identify. Fish?

A wooden-floored boxing ring had been built in the center of the floor, surrounded by steel walls beneath flaking pipes snaking along the low ceiling. The slight sliding movement of the ship was less noticeable down here.

Dempsey had changed into high-waisted white boxing shorts, and was standing shirtless beside a heavy training bag suspended from the ceiling in the center of the ring. Ruby had never thought he'd seemed all that big and powerful, but now she could tell that his strength came from the remarkably taut, long muscles along his back and arms, and the coiled power of his chest muscles as well. Just as the length of Ruby's arms gave her pitches their speed, Dempsey's muscles must provide his punches with their explosive force.

He waited for Firpo to join him, and then they shook hands and posed for photographs, the flashbulbs blinding in the enclosed space. An incongruous match, with Firpo still in his fine suit and Dempsey in his shorts, they answered some questions that Ruby, standing at the back of the crowd, couldn't hear.

Then Firpo disappeared through a door into a room beyond the ring, and Dempsey began to hit the heavy bag.

Ruby could see that his heart wasn't in it, at least not at first—it was all just another show for the newspapers—but still she was astounded by his quickness and the strength and power of his blows. Then he grew more serious, bobbing and ducking as if he were fighting a stronger opponent, and soon the heavy bag was jumping. Each impact echoed off the metal walls.

Ruby was sincerely grateful that her chosen profession did not require getting hit by fists.

Eventually Firpo returned, clad now in black shorts. He was more massive than Dempsey, especially in the chest, but also softer. He didn't look like he'd been training as hard, at least not yet. There were still four weeks to go till the fight.

But when he started hitting the bag, Ruby saw exactly why he was a threat to win. He didn't have any of Dempsey's speed and agility, but his huge fists looked like sledgehammers as they landed. If one of those blows caught Dempsey on the jaw, he would go down.

Dempsey, standing to the side, his face expressionless but his eyes intent, was probably thinking the same thing.

When the two men were done, the crowd began to disperse. Ruby was just heading up the stairs to the deck when she felt a tap on the shoulder. It was Dempsey.

"What did you think?" he asked her.

She took a moment before answering. "I think he's dangerous," she said finally. "Don't let yourself get stale as a piece of bread, not with this one."

"No chance of that." He paused. "Want to see it?"

"The fight?"

"Yeah."

She thought about it, then said, "If you promise you'll win."

Dempsey smiled. "I'll get you two tickets, ringside," he said. "You can bring that friend of yours and Jidge's."

"Helen?"

He nodded and turned away. Then stopped and looked over his shoulder at her.

"Oh, by the way," he said.

"Yes?"

"I'll win."

When Ruby got home late that afternoon, David Wilcox was waiting for her.

She couldn't believe it. It had already been a long day—the press event on the *President Harding* followed by an off-day workout at Washington Park—and the last person she wanted to see was her old boss.

He was slouched back against the sofa cushions, his feet up on the coffee table, a glass of orange juice balanced on his round belly. He looked like he lived there. He looked like he owned the place.

Helen sat opposite him. Her hands were clasped in her lap and her expression was furious.

The girls were nowhere to be seen. Ruby guessed they were hiding upstairs in their bedroom.

She felt her hands curl into fists. "I don't have anything to say to you," she said.

Wilcox grinned at her. His face was mottled, his nose mis-shapen. His little eyes were shot with red. He smelled like gin. Ruby knew, without having to look, that he had a flask somewhere on his body, and that the orange juice he was drinking had been doctored.

"Sure you do," he said.

He looked over at Helen. "You, blind girl, get out. We need to talk, Ruby and me."

Knowing it was a mistake, but unable to stop herself, Ruby took two large steps and slapped him on the face.

The sound of the blow echoed around the quiet room. Her palm stung and a red mark blossomed on Wilcox's right cheek. Juice sloshed over the rim of the glass and stained his shirt. He stared up at her, stunned, breathing heavily, his face coloring so that the imprint of her palm was no longer visible.

"Don't talk to my friend like that," she told him. "This is her house."

Wilcox looked like he wanted nothing more than to get his hands around her throat. But first he had to struggle into a sitting position and put the half-empty glass down on the coffee table, and by the time he'd accomplished this, he'd gotten a grip on his rage. Whatever he'd come for—and Ruby had her suspicions—it wasn't to kill her.

Helen had gotten to her feet. "I'm calling the police."

Wilcox looked at her, then back at Ruby, and waited.

Ruby took a deep breath. The image of Wilcox carted off by the police was an enticing one.

But then she sighed. "Don't bother. I can listen to what he has to say." She paused. "Would you leave us alone for a minute?"

"Are you sure?" Helen said.

"I'll be fine."

Helen jittered on her feet. Finally, though, she said, "I'll be in the next room if you need me."

Ruby waited until she and Wilcox were alone, then dropped into the chair Helen had vacated. "I'm not coming back," she said. "Ever."

Wilcox looked up from where he was mopping at his shirt with a white handkerchief. "Sure you are," he said. "As soon as you and Babe Ruth put on your great exhibition." He smiled, all confidence again. "Just imagine the crowds when Diamond Ruby, the star, returns to the place that introduced her to the world."

Ruby could imagine. She could imagine working fourteen hours a day. Throwing three hundred pitches through the mesh against the steel plate on the wall. Coming home with her arm hanging like a dead thing, until finally it fell off entirely.

"No chance," she said. "I've got a real job now. I don't need your money."

He leaned in a little toward her. "We never know," he said. "exactly what it is we'll need."

Then Ruby got it. He understood something she didn't.

"Listen," she said. "No matter what my future holds, I'm never going inside the Birdcage again, not as long as you have anything to do with it."

Wilcox pulled himself to his feet. She stood, too, so he wouldn't be able to loom over her.

But he was already turning toward the door. "You'll start the week after you face the Babe this fall," he said. "With the right ballyhoo, and your name, we'll get people to come out to Coney Island even in the off-season. Then we can ramp up again in the spring."

"When I'm going to be pitching for the Typhoons," Ruby said.

"Oh, yes?" he said, still smiling. "You think?"

"We'll leave tomorrow," Ruby said.

Sitting on the sofa, Paul gave her a long, probing look. Helen and Mrs. Connell's expressions betrayed a simpler shock.

The girls were upstairs, asleep. Ruby hadn't told them yet.

"What are you talking about?" Helen said. "Leave why?"

But before she could answer, Paul said, "I know why. To protect us."

Ruby looked at him. He kept his eyes on hers as he continued. "Everything's changed since that guy, that Wilcox, came by today. That's what Ruby thinks."

He paused, but no one interrupted.

"She's already been killing herself because of what happened to me," he went on. "She blames herself, and it's eating away at her. Don't you see it? I do." He managed a grin. "I see it, and she knows I do, even though she keeps as far away from me as she can."

Ruby didn't say anything. Didn't know what to say.

"Then you—then I got out," he said to Ruby, "and you allowed yourself to think you'd still be safe here."

After a long moment, Ruby nodded. "Until today."

"Yes, until today, when Wilcox stopped by." Paul's face was full of sympathy. "But now you can't ignore it—the danger you think we're all in because of you."

"Not think," Ruby said. "Know."

"And your solution is to move out." Paul settled back against the cushions, his voice scratchy. "To protect us by leaving."

Ruby looked down at the floor, then raised her eyes. "Helen," she said, "he's right. Wilcox and those men in Jim's drawings—they have no interest in you, except as a way to get to me. I walk away from here and they'll leave you alone."

Before she was halfway through this little speech, she saw Helen start to shake her head. But Ruby didn't let her friend interrupt. "I can't do it anymore," she said. "I just can't. I can't be everywhere. I can't protect everyone." She took in a breath that shuddered in her throat. "I can take the girls with me, do my best for them, but the rest of you—they'll hurt you again. It's what they do. They'll hurt you to make me do what they want."

"Ruby—" Helen said.

"So the only choice I have is to leave. I'll find a place tomorrow—"

"Ruby, *shut up*!"

She'd never heard Helen sound so angry. She shut up.

Helen said, "You're not going anywhere, so stop wasting your breath. And if you act all pigheaded and insist on leaving, well, you're *certainly* not taking the girls."

She came over and put a hand on Ruby's arm. "Honey, it's time for you to calm down and let us help you," she said, her face filled with a mix of affection and exasperation. There might even have been a trace of amusement there, too.

"Yes, help *you*," she went on. "Ease your burden. What's so hard to understand about that? It's what people do for each other, isn't it? It's what friends do, and family."

"Even if—" Ruby began.

"Yes, even if it puts them in danger. Listen," Helen said, "I'm sure you're working on a plan to deal with those men?"

"Yes."

"And would it be easier to put it into action alone?" Her voice was calm now. "Or here, with us helping, with a home to live in?"

Ruby didn't say anything.

Helen nodded and dropped her hands to her sides. "Then we have nothing further to talk about. You're not going anywhere. The subject is closed."

Ruby looked at her, at Mrs. Connell, at Paul. None showed any sign of doubt, of worry, of anger at her.

"All right," Paul said at last. "Since I can't volunteer to challenge these cads to a duel, what are we going to do?"

Still Ruby hesitated.

"Sweetie," Helen said quietly, "sometimes you just have to rely on other people."

So Ruby told them what she was thinking.

36

"It's that time again," Chase said.

Ruby looked at him, leaning back against the lamppost, his slanted eyes gleaming in the smoky light, and didn't reply.

"People've begun to think your winning streak's going to go on all year," he said, pausing as a young couple, a sailor and his girl, walked hand in hand past them down toward the river. Watching them, Ruby found herself wondering what it would feel like to be with a man you liked enough, trusted enough, to let him hold your hand.

It had been a long day. Her brain felt slow, filled with sludge, but she couldn't afford to let Chase outthink her.

She looked up at him, and saw that he was regarding her with curiosity. "I start the day after tomorrow," she said. "Wednesday."

"I know."

"You could have told me tomorrow, at the restaurant."

Chase's lips twitched. "Thought you might need a day to get used to the idea," he said. "You weren't so enthusiastic the first time, I remember right." He gave a little shrug. "The details I'll give you tomorrow."

Inside, Ruby's stomach was twisting itself into knots, but she was determined not to reveal it. The last thing she needed was for Chase to guess her thoughts. Too often he seemed able to look inside her, no matter how hard she tried to conceal her expressions from him.

Even now, he shot her a look. "If you're planning something . . ."

Her temper flared at once. "Don't," she said. "Just don't. I know everything you're about to say. I know my girls aren't safe. I know my friends can be hurt. I know all the things you can do to me. We've been through this before. I'm getting tired of hearing it—it's as stale as old bread."

She stopped for a moment, Jack Dempsey's phrase giving her an idea, then hurried on. "You should come up with a new line."

He grinned, but there was an odd shine in his eyes she didn't like. With a sudden movement, he leaned in close to her. She smelled something sweet on his breath.

"How about this line?" he said, putting his hands on her shoulders. It was the first time he'd touched her since the handshake the day they'd met. "Helen and her mother and that sick boyfriend, and your little Allie and Amanda—they're all just meat to me."

He gave her a little shake, and she could feel his fingers digging into her shoulders like steel spikes, like the tines of two forks. "Less than meat," he said. "I'd kill them if it meant an extra ten bucks in my pocket."

Then, without another word, he let go and walked away from her.

"You okay?"

Ruby raised her eyes to look at Andy Sutherland. In its own

way, his concern was as bad as Chase's menace. She had no time for either, no time to be distracted.

"I didn't get much sleep last night," she said finally.

In truth, she hadn't gotten any. She'd lain in bed all night, thinking, and almost before she knew it, the sky was lightening through her curtains and she could hear the sleepy voices of the girls in the bedroom next to hers.

"Well, you better catch up tonight." Andy tilted his head. "Big start for you tomorrow."

The Typhoons were only a game out of first place, and they'd be playing the East-Coast League's front-runners, the Allentown Silkworms. It would be the first time Ruby had faced the Silkworms since her initial appearance, when she'd gotten into the brawl with Jim Tracy.

"We'll be there to protect you if that goon makes a move," Andy said.

Ruby didn't say a word, just looked into his face. After a moment, she saw him grimace. "Oh, it's that way, is it?"

Ruby suppressed a shudder, hearing Chase's voice in her head. *They're all just meat to me. Less than meat.*

"No," she said. "I won't do it again."

"Well." Andy shook his head, as if uncertain about something. "I don't know, but maybe this will help—"

Ruby said, "What? Tell me."

"You going to stick around after the game today?"

"Always do," she said. He knew she did. "Why?"

"I met somebody, she wants to talk to you."

Ruby felt her heart give a leap. "She knows something?"

"Maybe." Andy's face clouded. "I don't know. She wouldn't say a word to me. Said she had to talk to you directly. She's going to want to be paid—I told her you'd be able to fork over twenty bucks, if she gave you what you needed."

"Sure." The back of Ruby's neck felt cold, though she didn't know exactly why. Maybe it was the expression on Andy's face. "What?" she said. "What aren't you telling me?"

After a moment, he shrugged. "Nothing. It's just—" He grimaced. "She's had a tough time of it, is all. Tougher than most. And she's scared. She might not even show up."

But the woman did. She was already there, in fact, when Ruby went back to her dressing room after the game. Ruby hadn't anticipated that, and regretted banging the door open when she saw her visitor start and cringe away.

Tania was standing over by her ironing board. When Ruby's eyes met hers, she frowned and gave a tiny shrug. Curious, Ruby turned her attention to the visitor, who was dressed in a stained, faded skirt and ragged blouse. Then she had to be very careful to keep her expression a blank.

The woman's face was layered with scar tissue, along the cheeks, surrounding both eyes, across her puffy lips. Her nose had been flattened like a boxer's, and her left eye, but only her left, shone with tears. She sat there at the little table in the center of the room, an untasted bottle of Coca-Cola in front of her, her eyes slanting toward the door, as if she were considering making a run for it.

Ruby sat down opposite her and said, "I'm Ruby Thomas. Thanks for coming to see me."

The woman took a while answering. Finally, though, she sighed and said, in a surprisingly high, breathy voice, "You'll pay me?"

"Of course," Ruby said. She reached into her bag and withdrew twenty dollars, then added another ten, and placed them on the table.

Some of the tension seemed to leave her guest's body, but still she hesitated. Ruby gave her time, and eventually the woman said, "Do you have those pictures? The ones that the man showed me?"

Ruby nodded. Tania handed her a copy of each drawing, and Ruby laid them down carefully side by side. The woman looked at them, saying nothing, but after a moment Ruby saw her start to cry. The tears welled up, more of them from her left eye than her right, and ran down her face. After a few moments, she used a fragment of white linen to mop at them.

Then, with careful movements, she reached out a fine-boned hand, so much more delicate than her ravaged face, and turned the drawing of Chase over. She asked for a pencil, and Tania handed her one.

In a voice that was breathier than ever, she said, "His name is Rourke. Jimmy Rourke." She lifted her gaze. "At least, that's how I knew him back home. In Chicago. He lived on the South Side, not far from Wrigley Field."

She wrote the name carefully in crude block letters on the back of the drawing, and then an address as well. "This is where he lived when I knew him."

"Did he ever call himself Chase?" Ruby asked.

The woman shrugged. "He tried on different names," she said, "like hats. He always had his reasons. But he always went back to Rourke."

Something was troubling Ruby. "How did Andy find you?"

"One of his teammates back home talked to someone who knew I'd moved here. She called me, and I got in touch."

Ruby said, "That was lucky."

The woman shrugged. "Not so much. A lot of people knew Rourke back there—he always had his hand in this and that—and a lot of them knew me because of him." She breathed in through her flattened nose. "Never realized how easy I was to find *here*, though."

"Was it Rourke," Ruby asked, "who did that to you?"

The woman gave her a disbelieving look. "Jimmy? No. He uses a knife."

She pushed the facedown drawing away to reveal the glowering image of the man with the shiny hair. Then she raised her eyes. Under its scars, her face was pale.

"No," she said. "It was him who made me like this. *He's* the one who likes using his fists."

The words hung in the air for a moment. Then the woman went on. "His name is Frank Colgate."

Frankie.

"His real name is Francis Coletti, but he likes Frank Colgate better," the woman went on. "Thinks it makes him sound more American."

She wrote both names on the back of the sheet.

"This Coletti," Ruby asked. "He's a bootlegger?"

The woman shrugged. "Other things, too, but yeah, sure."

"And Rourke?"

"Gambling. Fixing." Another shrug. "You know all this, right?"

Ruby nodded. "Who's the boss? Who gives the orders? One of these two, or someone else?"

"Neither. They each have their own thing. Sometimes they work together, is all."

Ruby took a deep breath. Good. That was good.

The woman reached across the table and took the cash. Then she got to her feet.

"If I think of anything else," Ruby said, "how can I reach you?"

"You can't." The woman stood. "I'm taking this and going straight to Penn Station. And if you think I'm telling you where I'm headed, you're spifflicated."

Ruby stood as well. "Well . . . thank you," she said.

The woman fixed her with a sharp gaze. Even her left eye was dry now. "Want some advice?" she said. "Leave them alone."

"I can't," Ruby said.

"Then one way or another, they'll kill you."

Ruby didn't reply.

"And before they do, you'll look worse than me."

Ruby was ten minutes late to the armchair restaurant. She'd walked in wondering if her tardiness would anger Chase, cause him to repeat his threats of the previous evening, but one glance told her he was onto something else. Something that excited him very much.

Chase. Jimmy Rourke.

Ruby felt a deep, illicit thrill. She knew his name. She knew things about him he wasn't aware of.

She had power over him.

"Was thinking you might not show," he said as she sat down. But there was no menace in the words. Instead there was a tone she hadn't heard before, a deeper purr.

"I'm too smart for that," she said. "I know who I answer to."

Jimmy Rourke.

She couldn't do this. She had to think of him as Chase. Otherwise she might let his real name slip, and that would be a disaster.

"Glad to hear it," Chase said.

Still he seemed almost absent, working through something in his mind. The excitement showed on his face, which for the first time since she'd met him revealed something other than amusement or menace. In fact, he seemed exhilarated, his normally pale cheeks flushed, his mouth turning up at the corners.

"Okay," he said, leaning forward and wrapping his hands around his coffee cup. "There's been a change of plans."

Ruby felt her stomach swerve. "You want me to come up with a sore wing."

"No." Chase looked surprised at the very idea. "I want you to win."

Ruby said, "What?"

His grin grew wider. "I want you to win every time you pitch from here on in."

Ruby couldn't speak. She felt her jaw loosen, her mouth drop open, and for long moments all she could do was stare at him.

Looking back at her across the table, he laughed, and the joy created by whatever had happened since they'd last met bubbled in his throat. "This place isn't so clean, you know," he said. "You'll catch flies looking like that. Flies or worse."

He was making a joke that wasn't at her expense. It was almost enough to make her jaw drop even farther. But instead she closed her mouth, let her mind start working even as her spirit soared, and said, "Why the change?"

He didn't answer, just laughed.

"How does it help you for me to win?" she said. "I don't get it. Every gambler on earth will be putting their money on me by the time the season ends."

Chase tapped his chin. "Hmm, you're right," he said. Then he clapped his hands together, a sharp sound. "You've convinced me. I've changed my mind back. You should lose."

Her look of alarm set him to laughing again. "No," he said, making a reassuring gesture. "Please, pitch your little heart out. Strike out all twenty-seven batters in a game, if you can. Make those men look like little sprouts."

She sat back, picked up her coffee cup, held it so she could feel the warm steam caress her chin. "Chase, what's going on?"

He tilted his head and gave her a catlike sideways look. "Do you really need to know?" he asked. "Isn't it enough that you're allowed to win?"

No, Ruby thought.

"I guess so," she said.

"Anyway," Chase said, "you'll find out soon enough."

I want to know *now*, Ruby thought.

· · ·

At home later that evening, she described everything she'd learned that day, and everything she'd failed to learn. Helen's hand went to her mouth when she heard that Ruby had discovered the real names of the two men in Jim McKay's drawings. Ruby thought her friend was finally beginning to understand how high the stakes had become, how much they all had to lose.

"You know the girls and I could still move out," she said.

Helen made an impatient gesture. "Stop being tedious." She paused. "What now? Are you going to tell the police, or that Prohi friend of yours?"

Ruby had been thinking about that all day. "Not yet. It's not time."

She went on to describe Chase's barely restrained joy, his setting her free to pitch as well as she could. Helen got the point right away. "He'll be expecting some gigantic payback, won't he?" she asked.

"Yes," Ruby said, "he will."

"What, though?"

Yes, that was the question.

Allie and Amanda still left a lamp on in the corner at night. Standing in the doorway, Ruby couldn't remember the last time she'd spied on them while they slept. She'd been too busy, too distracted, too tired.

Too focused on trying to take care of them to tend to them.

Allie, as always, slept in a tangle of bedclothes, her nightdress twisted around her, one plump bare leg hanging off the edge of the mattress. Ruby saw that her fingers were in her mouth.

Amanda, also typically, was sleeping neatly on her back, the sheets pulled up to her chest, her long arms bent at the elbows, one hand on the pillow on each side of her head. She looked as if she'd fallen asleep right at a moment of surprise, but her long, narrow face was as grave in repose as when she was awake.

Ruby walked silently to Allie's bed, grabbed her dangling leg, hoisted it back onto the mattress, then yanked the sheets up around her. Once she was solidly asleep, you could barely wake Allie with a brass band, and all she did now was murmur around her fingers and then suck them harder.

When Ruby straightened and turned, she saw that though Amanda hadn't moved, her eyes were open and fixed on Ruby's face.

"I dreamed," she said, her voice still clogged with sleep. "I dreamed you left us."

Then she lifted her arms and held them out, a more needful gesture than Ruby had seen from her in an age.

Without a word, Ruby walked over and sat on the edge of the bed. She saw Amanda come up toward her, felt the slender arms wrap around her, absorbed the warmth of sleep emanating through the thin nightgown.

After a few moments, she peeled Amanda's arms away and settled her back down onto the bed. Then she lifted the sheets and climbed in beside her. Looked a few inches across the pillow into her niece's closing eyes.

"I will *never* leave you," she said.

Amanda smiled as she slipped back into sleep.

"I know you won't," she said.

37

*e*very time he came to the plate to hit, right before he settled into his stance, Jim Tracy took a big wad of chewing gum out of his mouth and stuck it on his cap for safekeeping.

Ruby had noticed this the last time the Typhoons played the Silkworms. It had made her laugh. Big and hulking, with those bulging eyes, Tracy looked like the kind of palooka who'd fill his jaw with some kind of chewing tobacco, Mammoth Cave or Red Man or something, then spit the juice everywhere and end up making the area around home plate resemble the Gowanus Canal.

But no, it was chewing gum, a wet shining mound that gleamed right at the spot where the gray brim met the navy-blue cloth.

And it was at the chewing gum that Ruby aimed her first pitch to Tracy.

Remember me? the pitch said.

It was still the top of the first inning, a hot, airless day with the old ballpark packed to the rafters as always when Ruby was pitching. If anything, the crowd was even bigger than usual: Ruby wasn't the only one wondering what would happen the next time she faced the Silkworms and Jim Tracy.

Remember me? She sure remembered him.

The pitch flew toward the spot where the chewing gum had recently been, but the gum, the cap, and Tracy himself were now groveling in the dirt at home plate as Andy Sutherland reached up and snagged the pitch.

The crowd howled its approval, mixed with disappointment that she'd failed to hit him.

But Ruby had never intended to bean Tracy. Hit someone in the head and you risked killing them, and Ruby didn't want to kill anyone.

At least she didn't want to kill Tracy.

That's why she'd thrown it where she had. The batter's instinct was always to duck down and back from an errant pitch, or one thrown at him on purpose. If you wanted to hit someone in the head, you threw behind his neck. Without being able to stop himself, he'd move right into its path. Aim at his cap, however, and pure instinct would cause him to dodge out of danger.

She'd taken something off the pitch anyhow, just in case Tracy froze up there.

But he hadn't. He'd moved with more speed than she'd thought possible, and was now struggling to his feet, tangled up with his big bat, shouting and cursing as the crowd's noise shook the stands. Ruby saw Andy drop the ball and his glove and get between her and Tracy, but she still got herself ready for another brouhaha.

She was expecting one. It was part of the price of doing business. You did what was necessary to claim your territory. After the way Tracy had treated her the last time, she'd needed to let him know who was in charge.

He seemed to get the message, because he made no effort to

go around Andy and get at her. Curses seemed to be enough for him.

The umpire got it, too. He walked the ball out to her, and before he was halfway, she could see he was grinning. McGinty, his name was, and if she remembered right he'd played ball himself way back when, with a rowdy team in St. Louis.

"Seen you pitch before," he said when he reached the mound. He held the ball in his big, callused right hand, in no hurry to give it to her.

"Didn't you work one of my other games?" she asked.

"Yeah, but not your best one. Not the one you pitched like your pants was on fire."

He took a step closer to her. "But I saw enough. You can put the ball pretty damn near where you want to, every pitch."

She waited, not denying it.

"So I also know that you meant to drop that guy in the dirt," he said, "and why."

"And you're telling me don't do it again."

The ump nodded. "Quick learner, are you?"

"Quick enough."

"You get a pass because the guy's a goon and because he tried to hurt you last time. But I see another beanball, and I'll have to run you. Rules of the league. Got it?"

Ruby nodded.

"Got it?"

"Yes, *sir*," she said.

He grinned again and finally dropped the ball into her waiting palm. "Just so long as we understand each other."

The language of baseball. Ruby loved it.

Her next pitch to Jim Tracy was on the outside corner of the plate. But because he was stepping away from it almost as soon as it left her hand, he couldn't have hit it with a tent pole. He was an experienced hitter, though, and managed to dig in for the third one. He even got his bat on the ball, which he hit on a fly to center field for an out.

He stared at Ruby as he returned to the visitors' dugout. She merely looked back at him, calm, expressionless, waiting for the ball to get back to her from the outfield. No need to humiliate him. They both knew where they stood.

After that, the game seemed to fly along. Ruby didn't strike out all twenty-seven batters—she didn't seem to possess her best fastball—but she struck out her share, and managed to keep the rest off balance with her curve and change of pace. After six innings, the Silkworms had only three hits, a little pop fly that fell in short right field, a grounder that made its way past Ruby and up the middle, and a sharp double down the leftfield line.

But the score was still 0–0, because the Silkworms' pitcher, a guy named Ryan who was their ace, was almost as good as Ruby on this day. He was a lefty, too, but with a completely different approach. He threw submarine style, his pitching hand nearly brushing the ground as he completed his quick, hunched windup and released the ball. The resulting pitch seemed to rise if it was a fastball, or rise and then dip if it was a curve. Every pitch either ran in toward or away from the batter. Nothing was ever straight, and the Typhoons spent most of their at-bats taking weak swings at pitches they didn't see clearly, or worse, standing there with their bats on their shoulders as Umpire McGinty bellowed "Strike three!"

It was all very demoralizing. Ruby struck out on three pitches her first two times up, mesmerized by Ryan's pitching delivery and absolutely unable to pick up the flight of the ball until it was almost past her.

The Typhoons had precisely zero hits going into the bottom of the seventh. Andy Sutherland was sitting beside Ruby on the end of the bench, and as Scott Mathis, leading off, swung and missed, Andy suddenly sat up straight.

"Goddamn," he said.

Ruby glanced at him. "What?"

"Hush." He was leaning forward again. Another pitch, another swing and miss. "There it is," he murmured, and now he was beginning to grin.

"What?" Ruby said.

"Watch his glove, that pitcher. Watch what he does when he's about to throw that little fadeaway of his. The one we've been missing all day."

Ruby watched. Ryan stood, waiting for the sign from the catcher, glove up in front of his chest, left hand inside it holding the ball out of sight. The next pitch was a curve for a ball, but on the one after that she saw it: a telltale waggle of the mitt as he shifted his grip for the fadeaway.

"He's tipping the pitch," Ruby said.

Andy nodded. His eyes were gleaming.

The equation was simple: if batters knew what pitch was coming, they could prepare for it. No pitcher could survive long after surrendering the power of surprise.

"You going to tell everyone?" she asked.

Andy shook his head. "They see me talking, the guys in the other dugout, they're going to know I'm onto something." He gave a wolfish smile. "Anyway, I want him for myself."

When Carl Crutcher worked out a walk with two outs, Andy got his chance. Patiently, he took a fastball for a strike and a curve for a ball. Then Ruby saw Ryan's glove waggle. Andy moved up a half step in the batter's box, the pitch came in, a fadeaway, the bat flashed across the plate, and the ball soared upward in an enormous trajectory and disappeared over the leftfield wall.

"Easy as pie," Andy said, when all the congratulating and

backslapping were done. "Though I never understood why pie was supposed to be easy."

When Ruby went out to the mound to start the eighth, Andy came with her, gesturing to the infield to join them. What looked like a discussion of defensive and pitching strategy, though, actually gave the catcher a chance to spread the word about Ryan's fatal flaw. "Let the others know," he said.

In the bottom of the inning, the Typhoons scored three more runs, driving Ryan from the game and making sure the outcome was no longer in doubt.

Ruby gave up a run in the top of the ninth, but that was all, and just a handful of pitches later it was over. Easy as pie.

Before heading to the dressing room, she walked to the stands, where her family was sitting.

"My aunt Ruby is really wet," Allie said to Helen.

"Allie!" her sister said in her most reproving tone.

Helen laughed. "It's the 1920s," she said, "and girls are allowed to sweat."

"How do you feel?" Mrs. Connell asked Ruby.

"Great."

And it was true. Despite everything, at that moment it was true.

Colonel Fielding was standing outside her dressing room. She hadn't seen much of him recently, and had heard he'd been preoccupied with his other businesses. He normally didn't approach her until she'd had time to shower and change after a game. Yet here he was, leaning heavily on his walking stick, clearly waiting for her.

Though he managed a smile, he seemed distracted, even upset. He looked older somehow, and his wiry hair, usually so well groomed, seemed unkempt.

"Excellent game, Ruby," he said. "You really showed that hooligan."

"Thank you," Ruby said.

She waited while he looked down the hall, at his hands on the stick, in her direction but not quite at her face. He wouldn't meet her eyes.

Finally he got to the point. "Er, Ruby," he said, "Judge Landis wants to see us, you and me, in the morning."

It was the last thing she'd expected to hear. "Who?"

"Kenesaw Mountain Landis." He blinked. "The commissioner of baseball."

Ruby knew who he was. "Why does he want to see me?"

But even as she asked, she knew. Her mind, so occupied a moment before with the satisfying events of the game, finally shifted focus. There was only one reason why Judge Landis would want to see her, and it wasn't to invite her out to dinner, or to suggest she try out for the Yankees.

"He's never approved of me, has he?" she asked, remembering the "no comments" in the press that spoke volumes, now that she looked back on them.

The Colonel, his face haggard, shook his head.

"He sees me as a distraction, a sideshow, a *freak*." Ruby couldn't believe she hadn't thought about it before. Of course he did.

Of course she was.

"What's he going to do?" she asked. "What have you heard?"

But the Colonel merely shook his head again, took a deep breath, and tried his best to regain his paternal manner. "Let's just wait and see what he says, why don't we? Why put words in his mouth? Perhaps we can reason with him."

But his attempts at being reassuring were a failure, to himself as much as to her. He looked miserable, like he was about to cry. Watching him, Ruby felt a hole open up in her heart.

It was too much. It was all too much. How many people, how many men, was she expected to contend with at one time? She'd spent all these days planning her counterattack on Chase and on Frankie Colgate, figuring out how to get them off her back while she kept pitching for the Typhoons. And now here came that old curmudgeon, that Mr. Grundy, Judge Landis, and she knew exactly what he was going to say.

Why wouldn't he just leave her alone? What harm was she doing by feeding her family while throwing a baseball every four days?

But just like that, ten seconds after these thoughts began, Ruby banished them. She might be only eighteen, but she'd already lived too long to allow herself to succumb to self-pity. It didn't get you anywhere. It merely slowed your mind.

There was always a strategy, a solution. You just had to learn all the facts, and then you could put them to use.

And she'd start learning them tomorrow.

No, today.

"What time is our meeting?" she asked.

The Colonel blinked at her, as if he'd been so absorbed in his own thoughts that he'd forgotten she was there. He rallied himself again and said, "Nine A.M. I'll send a car to bring you to the commissioner's office. It's on Park Avenue."

"Thank you," Ruby said.

He stared at her, and it was as if the small politeness had finally loosened his tongue. "Things were going so well," he said despairingly. "The crowds, not only here—sellouts every time you pitch, ten thousand seats sold even when it's not your turn—but all over the league, they've been beyond what we ever dreamed. We were planning a postseason tour, between the two top teams—"

Ruby was amazed to see that his eyes were shining with tears. "And we would have been one of them," he went on. "It was obvious, with you and the way everyone else has been playing. It's like you inspire them, Ruby, you and the crowds. They believe in themselves now, and in this league. We were just days from closing down when I contacted you, and now—"

She put her hand on his arm to stop the flood of words, a gesture of intimacy she would never previously have dared with him. He looked down at her hand, then up into her eyes again, and his face seemed even more stricken.

"Colonel," she said gently, "don't give up."

He said, "But—"

"Trust me," she said. "I'll come up with something."

Now she just had to figure out what.

38

*e*verything about the old man came in shades of gray.

His wiry hair flowed like a stiff, unruly wave from the ragged part on the right side of his scalp. His bushy eyebrows resembled aggressive caterpillars perched above his piercing eyes, themselves a pale, icy shade that Ruby had never seen before. Even his sharply angled face, every line a mark of strict rectitude, seemed gray in the unforgiving light of the floor lamp beside his wooden desk.

Judge Kenesaw Mountain Landis, the Czar, the first and thus far only commissioner of baseball, had dressed for this meeting in a charcoal tweed suit, its jacket straight over stiff upright shoulders, all seven buttons of its vest fastened. Beneath it was the only bit of color Ruby could see on him: his high-necked white shirt. Was white a color?

Ruby and Colonel Fielding had met just a few minutes earlier in the small waiting room overseen by a silent, stern-faced secretary. The Colonel was shredding the corners of the newspaper he'd brought with him. Little pieces of wadded-up newsprint lay on the floor around his shoes, drawing ever-more-severe glares from the watchwoman.

Looking at Colonel Fielding's bloodless face, she'd felt a pang of sympathy, maybe even pity. Though she doubted he'd ever been starving, ever worried about where his next meal might come from, she'd understood how much he was dreading their meeting with the Czar. And she'd wondered, as she had before, how far he was in debt, how much he depended on the financial success of the Typhoons.

The Judge had remained behind his desk as the silent secretary led them inside the dimly lit office, with its bare furnishings and framed certificates and diplomas on the dark, paneled walls. The room smelled of wealth and cigar smoke, and reeked of privilege and decisions being made in private.

Ruby felt very calm.

As they approached, the Judge stood. Ruby was surprised at how short he was, no more than five foot seven. Her own height, give or take an inch. And he couldn't have weighed more than one-thirty. If he'd played baseball as a young man, she found herself thinking, he must have been a light-hitting infielder, a leadoff man, slapping at the ball and working out walks.

"Thank you for coming to see me," he said in a gruff voice. Leaning over the desk, he shook Colonel Fielding's hand and then, after a moment's hesitation, Ruby's.

Ruby looked into his face, shadowed by the sideways lamplight, and read annoyance, even exasperation, in his expression. Friend, I feel exactly the same way, she thought.

As soon as they were seated again, the Judge started speaking. "No sport in America's great history has occupied a more central place in our nation's imagination than baseball," he began, then glanced at Ruby as if making sure she was paying attention.

She said nothing, allowed no emotion to cross her face.

Beside her the Colonel nodded and murmured, "Yes, very true."

"Are you aware that after the War Between the States," the Judge went on, still looking at Ruby, "baseball was one of the most important forces reuniting our shattered country?"

He waited for her to respond, so after a moment she shook her head.

"It's true," he said. "Northern boys taught the rules to southerners who'd been taken prisoner, and the southern boys brought the game back home once the war was over."

Ruby said, "Oh."

"Yes, and soon both sides, the former enemies, were uniting over this great game."

Ruby couldn't control her tongue any longer. "What does any of this have to do with me?"

"It was the boys, the soldiers, who played," the Judge said, speaking each word distinctly, as if she were slow-witted, "and the girls who *watched*. They all understood what you don't: baseball is far too strenuous a pursuit for women."

Ruby laughed, a loud, sudden sound in the quiet room. She couldn't help it. Her mind went back to the frigid days she'd spent hunting squirrels, packing boxes until her hands looked like gnarled claws, coughing till her throat bled from the fumes she'd been breathing all day in airless factories with painted-shut windows.

She thought of Tania, whose hardscrabble life showed in every scar on her face and hands. Of that poor battered woman who had bravely come forward to identify the man who had hit her. Of brave Evie. Of all the women who died in the tenements and were never given proper burial, all those who drowned in the vast treacherous tides of New York City.

And this old man had the nerve to tell her that *baseball* was too strenuous?

"You can't be serious," she said. "Most women would fall on their knees and pray to trade their labors for mine." She glanced at Colonel Fielding, who'd apparently been struck dumb by her outburst. "They'd thank God to be blessed with the opportunities I've been given."

But the Judge appeared only to have heard her first sentence. He glowered at her, the lines on his face looking like caverns. "In fact, Miss Thomas, I am entirely serious," he said in a frigid tone.

Ruby stood and held her hands out. "Look at me," she said. "I'm fine. Healthy as a soul could ask to be."

The Judge's shoulders stiffened. "You don't understand my point."

Ruby took a deep breath. "Judge Landis, sir, I haven't done anything wrong," she said. "I haven't hurt anybody. My teammates accept me. The fans—" Another breath. "The fans enjoy coming out to watch me."

She glanced at Colonel Fielding, but he seemed to be in a daze. Why didn't he argue? Why didn't he defend her?

The Judge said, "None of those is the point either."

"Then what?" Ruby turned her palms up. "Why do I even— matter to you?"

The Judge sat back in his chair. His gray lips were turned down at the corners.

"Why do you matter? I'll tell you," he said. "Women's organizations with banners. That's why you matter. Girls creating teams at school—I've heard of dozens. Movie cameras and reporters and who knows what else turning away from their proper subjects to focus instead on the new sensation, the female with the fastball."

He looked at her as he might a bug, a flea. "By your very presence, you make a mockery of the game," he said.

"Babe Ruth doesn't think so," Ruby said.

She realized her mistake at once. Malevolence flowered in

the Judge's expression. "Oh," he said in a scathing tone, "so now we're taking lessons in deportment from *Babe Ruth*?"

Ruby had no response to that. After a moment, she turned to Colonel Fielding, whose head was slumped over his walking stick. "Can he do this?" she asked. "Can he ban me?"

Colonel Fielding looked up and gave a weary nod. "Of course he can."

"But—" She took a moment to gather her thoughts. "But the East-Coast League is independent, isn't it? Why should the commissioner of major-league baseball have the right to ban me from a league that he's not commissioner of?"

Out of the corner of her eye, she saw the Judge's lips twitch in a small smile, the first she'd seen from him.

But it was the Colonel who replied. His face showed an odd mix of emotions, pity, and exhaustion and perhaps even a trace of exasperation at her ignorance. "Ruby," he said, "Judge Landis may be commissioner only of the major leagues, but every owner and player at every level does what he says."

"Why?"

Judge Landis took over. "Because no ballplayer grows up dreaming of playing in Allentown or Beacon, or even Washington Park, Miss Thomas. Because they all strive to make it to the big leagues—or, if they've had a taste of it already, of making it back, even for a year, a week, a day. It's all they think about."

Colonel Fielding nodded. His old hands lay heavy on the walking stick.

"And if I determine that you cannot play, anyone who defies the edict—who plays beside or against you—will never set foot in the majors, no matter how much he otherwise deserves to."

His gaze held Ruby's. "For example, it's been nearly three years since I banned Joe Jackson from the game. Can you imagine how many fans a team that signed him would draw?"

For a moment, Colonel Fielding's eyes swam with the

prospect of packed ballparks. "He'd be a guaranteed ticket wherever he went, from the smallest town to the biggest city in this country," he said. "But I could never sign him—no team owner could. And not because we're all too moral, too principled, to do so."

This time the Judge's smile was more genuine. "Hardly," he said.

"It's because we know that any team that took Jackson would have a black mark on it forever—and so would all his new teammates. They'd walk off the team rather than risk their futures. So no one will sign him."

The Judge sat up straight, a small ramrod of a man. "And when you are banned from the game, Miss Thomas, the same will hold true for you. You'll carry the black mark, and the doors of every ballpark will be shut to you."

All three of them let the words, the final sentence, hang in the air. Then Ruby said, "When will it start? Right away?"

Frowning, Landis took his time answering her question. "I've been debating that with myself," he said finally. "Going back and forth. And I must admit that was my first instinct. Out of sight, out of mind." His voice regained a note of asperity. "The sooner this repellent sideshow is brought to an end the better, as far as I'm concerned."

Then he shook his head, and the look he sent Colonel Fielding's way contained a surprising amount of sympathy. He might not give a hoot about the ballplayers or Ruby, but he did care about the magnates.

"But I don't wish to lay such a burden on you, Ted," he said. "So I will permit her"—Ruby noticed that he would not even use her name—"to finish the season."

"And the exhibition game with Babe Ruth?" she asked.

The Judge gave her a grim look from under his bushy eyebrows, and Ruby knew that he wanted nothing more than for her to hold her tongue. Perhaps he thought that speaking was too strenuous a task for women as well.

But eventually he sighed and said, "It would be unfair both to you, Ted, and to Colonel Ruppert to cancel a game—a confrontation—that has aroused such public interest. So I will allow it to proceed." His eyes flickered in Ruby's direction. "I also think it might be . . . beneficial . . . for you to face your comeuppance at Ruth's hands."

Ruby kept her mouth shut.

"And the postseason series between us and the Silkworms?" Colonel Fielding asked.

The Judge shook his head. "The series can go on, of course, but without the girl. Enough is enough. I'll make my announcement right after the exhibition at Yankee Stadium. And my ruling will be effective immediately."

Colonel Fielding opened his mouth to protest, but the Judge cut him off. "This decision," he said, "is final."

Then he bent over his desk, reached for a stack of papers, and pulled them close to him. "Good day, Ted," he said.

After a moment, Colonel Fielding got to his feet. His hands were shaking on the head of his stick, and Ruby found her heart going out to him again. But then her pity changed to anger, and she turned back toward Judge Landis. Stepping up to his desk, she said, "I'll make you change your mind."

He raised his head and looked into her face. In his eyes she thought she saw a glint of amusement.

"Oh no," he said. "I really don't believe you will."

"He's banning me," she said to Chase.

"I know."

"After the exhibition against the Yankees."

"Yes, Ruby, I know."

She'd begun speaking while still standing beside the table.

Now she sat down, but found she could barely keep still. She'd been like this, jumpy and unpredictable, all day. Her mind was working hard to find a way to prevent the Judge from destroying her career, but coming up empty.

In the car on the way to the ballpark, the Colonel had requested—begged was actually a more accurate word—her to keep the banishment a secret. It would be a calamity if the word got out, he said. Just imagine the firestorm in the press, and there were financial considerations as well, considerations she couldn't possibly understand.

Well, that might have been true, or it might not. But such things didn't concern her. If she kept silent, and she would, it would be for her own good, not Colonel Fielding's. He hadn't done anything today to deserve her loyalty.

Looking at Chase's grin, she said, "How long have you known?"

But before the words were out of her mouth, she knew the answer. "You found out before yesterday's game," she said. "Before my start."

He tilted his head.

Ruby was thinking fast. "And you were happy."

"Still am."

"So the question is, what's in it for you?"

Chase laughed. "Yes, that's the question, isn't it?"

"And the answer is—" She paused. "Well, I guess you just might enjoy seeing me suffer."

"Hey." He was offended. "I like you, Ruby."

"Yeah? The way you'd like a piece of meat?"

He shook his head but didn't reply, and Ruby saw that it could be true: he could simultaneously be fond of her and kill her without a second thought, if the situation demanded it.

"Forget it," she said. "It's not important. What's important is that I know you're going to get something, some profit, out of Landis's decision."

Chase raised his eyebrows.

"Or . . . not." She drummed her hands on the table. "It's something—something else."

He said nothing.

"Chase, what are you going to make me do?" Ruby asked.

He gave her a slow, happy smile. "All in good time," he said, "clever girl."

39

*a*fterward, the newspapers claimed that 125,000 people had turned out for the Dempsey-Firpo fight. As far as Ruby was concerned, though, it could have been a million, or a billion, at the Polo Grounds that night.

Dempsey had come through with the tickets he'd promised, and Helen had agreed to go, though not without some trepidation at having to face the crowds. "I won't let go of you," Ruby had told her.

They left the house early, hours before the fight was scheduled to begin. But not early enough. Traffic was nearly at a standstill, even in Brooklyn. Sightseeing buses Ruby hadn't glimpsed since her days in Coney Island had been dragooned into use to carry fight goers across the Brooklyn Bridge and up to the ballpark. The streets echoed with hurrying footsteps, as if some people planned to walk the whole way to watch two men pummel each other.

Belowground was no better. Already the subway stations were

overrun, and people were packed into each train car like pickles in a jar. The smell of sweat and cigarettes and alcohol filled the dark, dirty platforms.

When finally a train came that was slightly less packed than the others, they pushed their way aboard, Helen holding tightly onto Ruby's arm.

Emerging from the 157th Street station, they found the streets around the ballpark in turmoil. The crowd surged everywhere, some people clutching their tickets, others empty-handed, looking for ways to break through the lines and enter the ballpark unobserved.

Stone-faced policemen on horseback, clubs held high, tried to keep order amid the flood. Their horses were skittish, all white rolling eyes and sweaty flanks, picking their way on clattery hooves across the cobblestones and through the milling crowds to form a ragged barricade between the unruly crowd and the park, the Polo Grounds.

A sudden breeze, carrying with it a breath of autumn, whirled scraps of paper and brown, dry leaves and even, briefly, a woman's white hat into the air. The gust also brought the sound of a thousand voices, a low, discontented, constant grumble occasionally erupting into shouts of anger and frustration. Here and there people fainted, men and women alike, disappearing from view before being hoisted to safety. Pushed and shoved, some in the crowd panicked, shouting that they would pay five dollars, or even ten, for transport away.

Somehow Ruby and Helen worked their way to within sight of the entrance. Then, without warning, as if it had been pre-arranged, several hundred men broke free of the crowd and stormed the gate. Before they reached it, though, they encountered the police line, mounted cops and others on foot, all with clubs raised. Horses reared, voices rang out, bodies fell to the pavement. More policemen, and still more, appeared as if out of nowhere to bolster the line, and fists and clubs alike flew freely.

"Is it a riot?" Helen asked.

But even as she spoke, it was over. Watching the defeated rebels fall back, nursing their wounds, Ruby said, "I'd say more of a lively encounter."

But her mind was on other things. She was looking at the cops, hundreds of them, brought in from precincts across the five boroughs to keep order in this one small corner of Manhattan, and she was thinking.

Who's watching the rest of the city?

Inside the ballpark it was nearly as crowded, though considerably less tumultuous. Night had fallen as they made their way inside. The grandstands, looming up like old castle walls above them, were plunged in darkness, and the packed crowd's white blouses and shirts and hats gleamed like ghosts, brighter when you didn't look directly at them.

Glancing up at the full stands, Ruby laughed at herself. Had she once thought that a crowd of a few hundred was impressive? Had she really been awestruck to stand before two thousand fans?

Putting her arm around Helen's shoulders and edging across the field toward their seats, Ruby felt tiny, insignificant, a speck that could be brushed away without anyone even noticing.

She heard the sound of blows and some halfhearted cheering, a muffled roar deadened by the thick evening air, the exhalations of a hundred thousand throats. There was already a preliminary bout taking place in the ring, which had been placed in the center of the infield. It was lit by arc lights as bright and harsh as little man-made suns.

Finding their seats just three rows from the ring, Ruby guided Helen onto the rough-hewn wooden bench, then sat down beside her. Next to them was an elderly couple, the man resplendent in a long dark coat, the woman drenched in pearls and scent. Both looked bored and impatient.

In the white light, Helen's face was alive with excitement, and there was merriment in her dark eyes.

"Have we survived?" she asked.

"Barely," Ruby said.

With a sudden motion, Helen put both arms around her and hugged her, hard. "I can't believe I'm here."

Ruby said, "I feel exactly the same way."

Helen let go and sat back, turning her head this way and that as if surveying the scene. "Oh, damn," she said in a tone of frustration, "I wish I could *see*."

It was the first time Ruby had ever heard this sentiment from her. "I'll describe it as best I can," she said. Then, "I wish I had half the way with words that Allie does."

Helen smiled, self-possessed again. "You'll do fine."

Ruby tried. For the next half hour she described every sight she could—the busy writers, the ghostly look of the looming crowd, the fancy dress of the ringside attendees, even a shooting star that streaked across the sky above the field, drawing gasps from the crowd. But then Helen, ravenous for information, detail, *color,* asked Ruby to name the members of society who'd made it to ringside.

"Are the Rockefellers here?" she asked, her animated face filled with interest. "Horace Whitney? I heard Florenz Ziegfeld was planning to attend. Do you see him? What about W. K. Vanderbilt? The newspaper said he was bringing ten friends."

Ruby looked at the aristocratic men and their bejeweled wives, the fat cigars clenched in well-manicured hands, the cigarettes held in long polished holders, smoke curling upward like ghostly worms, and was at a total loss. "I have no idea," she said. "I don't know what they look like."

Then she had a thought. "Would you like me to ask them?"

Helen looked horrified. "No!"

Ruby said, "Really, it would be no trouble." She raised her voice. "Excuse me, ma'am? Are you society?"

"Ruby!" Helen, face flushed, gave her a shove. "Stop teasing me."

At ringside and perhaps ten feet over, Ruby spied Grumpy George, already bent over his typewriter. Grantland Rice was there, too, and Dan Daniel, and Jack Lawrence, and others she recognized from her own press conferences, her own odd brush with fame. They seemed to be paying no attention to the vast crowd, the swells perched on the makeshift ringside benches, the spotlit stage above them, the band playing military marches somewhere out of sight, and the cold breath of autumn swirling down from above.

Helen touched her arm. "Wait, is that Jidge I hear?"

Ruby looked around and saw that it was indeed the Babe, down at the far end of the ringside benches, exchanging greetings with a skinny old guy who looked to Ruby like an ex-ballplayer. Dressed in a superb silk suit, Ruth turned away and walked through the crowd to his seat as if expecting everyone to move out of his way, and of course they did.

Ruby couldn't help noticing that Jidge's seat was in the eighth row, farther back than theirs.

"Did he see you?" Helen asked.

Ruby said no.

Helen grinned. "Too busy basking in the glow of his adoring public?"

Ruby saw the Babe sit down unceremoniously, his ample form forcing a glowering matron several inches farther down the bench than the woman wanted to go.

"That's one way to put it, I guess," she said.

. . .

The last preliminary bout ended, followed by a pause that seemed to last for hours. Finally there came a stirring from beside the ring, and men started to clamber up between the ropes. Some officials were followed by photographers, other men Ruby couldn't identify, and then Dempsey himself arrived with his handlers and manager.

A mix of boos and cheers cascaded down from the grandstands.

"Why are they booing?" Helen asked.

"Lots of reasons, I guess," Ruby said. "He doesn't fight often enough, he doesn't win fast enough, he wins too often."

He does whatever it takes to win.

Helen sighed. "No one is less forgiving than the public. I used to get booed if my dives didn't seem death-defying enough."

In the ring, Dempsey and his handlers ignored the catcalls. The boxer strode around inside the ropes, as if marking the edges of his territory.

"What's he wearing?" Helen asked.

"White shorts," Ruby said, "and a white hooded jacket. He's got it kind of half on, half draped around his shoulders."

"How does he look?"

"Strong. Confident."

Helen gave a little shiver. "Can you imagine being on the receiving end of one of his punches?"

Thinking about the times she'd been hit, Ruby said no. Those blows had been bad enough, but nothing compared to what Jack Dempsey could unleash.

There was another stir in the crowd, some boos, some cheers. "Now Firpo is coming in," Ruby said. "He's wearing a long robe, white and black checks—no, I think it's yellow, not white. Hard to tell in the lights." She took a breath. "He's *big,* much bigger than Dempsey. I'd forgotten."

There was another delay while photographers and newsreel cameramen filmed the boxers together and apart, officials made announcements—a loud garble in Ruby's ears—the press hammered at their typewriters, and the last ringside seats were filled.

The fight began.

And then, just a few minutes later, after all the weeks of anticipation, all the newspaper headlines, all the newsreels and radio broadcasts and street-corner conversations, it was over.

About four minutes of counted time, that was all, that's what the clock and the newspapers said. But so much happened in those four minutes that Ruby went quite breathless trying to describe it to Helen, shouting into her ear above the constant ocean's roar of the vast crowd. For days afterward her throat ached.

The bell rang, and Dempsey demonstrated from the start that he was in a hurry to get to the end. He strode across the ring and started punching, powerful blows aimed at Firpo's thick chest, which looked to Ruby as solid as a tree trunk. But then, in a blink, things changed. As Dempsey reared back to strike again, Firpo got his left fist in first, an odd, awkward blow that somehow connected with Dempsey's right cheekbone.

The roaring crowd leaped to see, Ruby pulling Helen up with her. "Dempsey's down!" she shouted, but even as she did he was back on his feet. She was close enough to see that there was a dazed look on his face as he half swarmed, half stumbled toward Firpo, raining fierce but mostly inaccurate blows on his ducking opponent.

Ruby's attention was distracted for a moment by a rending, tearing sound that rose even above the bellowing of the crowd. She turned to see one long bench, then another, then dozens, begin to splinter and collapse as frantic fans jumped up on them to attain a better view. Several rows back, the Babe went down, knocked over by a stumbling man who looked like a boxer himself. Rising, Ruth shoved the man, and for a moment it seemed like a fight would break out between them.

But then the crowd's roar grew in intensity, impossible as that might have seemed a moment before. Helen cried out, "What's happened?" and Ruby turned back to the ring to see Dempsey send Firpo to his hands and knees with a thunderous blow.

Firpo got back up, but now Dempsey was all over him, clenching and gripping and hitting him in the ribs. Again and again the Argentine went down, rose, was knocked down, got back to his feet, and was punched to the mat once more. Ruby, already hoarse—hoarser than usual—shouting into Helen's ear, saw Dempsey standing over Firpo, hitting him again before he even had the chance to regain his feet. The crowd howled.

How many knockdowns? Six? Seven? And even as Ruby silently begged Firpo to give up, to acknowledge defeat, the Argentine got back up, even managed to land a few punches while taking fearsome punishment in return. Would he only stop fighting when he died?

Amazingly, he found a new reserve of energy. Suddenly he was striding forward, unleashing a series of brutally powerful looping blows with his right hand, his arm swinging like a scythe. First one got through Dempsey's defenses and connected, then a second, and then a third. Finally, there was a one more, almost a shove, and Dempsey came toppling through the ropes and plunged into the press row, just fifteen feet from where Ruby and Helen stood. As the crowd gasped, a great undersea sound, and people screamed and shouted nearby, Ruby saw Dempsey's hip bang against the board the reporters were using as a desk, saw Grumpy George and the others grab their typewriters and duck out of the way, saw many hands lift the dazed champion up into the ring.

Can they do that? Ruby wondered. But the referee, standing

by the ropes watching, allowed it to happen. Dempsey crawled through the ropes, got back onto his feet, and took several more punches between clinches before the bell rang, mercifully, to end the round.

He made it to his corner and slumped onto a stool, his handlers desperately waving smelling salts under his nose. "I think he might lose," Ruby told Helen.

But she was wrong. She'd underestimated the champion. The bell rang to start the second round, and Dempsey seemed to have regained his strength and awareness. He rushed the bigger man, ducking beneath his wild swings, hitting him with blows to the body and face, knocking him down, then almost wrestling him to the canvas. Somehow, yet again, Firpo got to his feet, but by now his movements were vague and unfocused, and when Dempsey broke out of a clinch and landed two punches, a left and then a right to the head, the Argentine went down one last time. He rolled onto his back and lay there, then managed to get back onto his stomach—and even onto his hands and knees—but it was too late. The referee had counted him out.

"It's over," Ruby said into Helen's ear through the howls of the crowd. "Now Jack is helping him—he's picking him up, getting him back on his feet."

"I hope they're both all right," Helen said.

Ruby linked her arm through her friend's, but already her mind was far away from the spectacle they'd just witnessed. That's what sports did, she was thinking. Boxing matches, baseball games, horse races: they all took you away from your world, your problems, for a few hours.

And sometimes, if you were lucky, they also helped you figure out what to do next.

40

*i*t was seven o'clock in the evening, three days after the championship fight. Ruby was pretending to look over the *Herald*'s sports pages, but she barely saw the newsprint. In truth, she was thinking about her next start, in two days. Her last start of the season.

Her last start ever, if her plans didn't start coming together soon.

The Typhoons had won thirteen of their last seventeen games and now, with just two to go, had an insurmountable three-game lead over Jim Tracy, his chewing gum, and the rest of the Allentown Silkworms. In just two days, the Typhoons would be proclaimed champions of the East-Coast League.

But what did the championship mean? Very close to nothing. It only mattered, Colonel Fielding said, if it was followed by the postseason series between the two teams. And *that* would only matter if Ruby was still on the team.

The Colonel, more haggard by the day and clearly unable to

enjoy his team's strong season and robust crowds, had never wavered from the opinion that the entire series would be canceled for lack of interest if Ruby didn't play. "You make the whole team seem . . . *different*. And that's all that matters these days."

Well, Ruby had thought, I certainly am different. There was no arguing with that.

"We'll figure something out," she'd told the Colonel. "Don't give up hope."

He'd managed to produce a wan smile. "'Hope' and 'Judge Kenesaw Mountain Landis' don't belong in the same sentence," he'd said.

Deep in thought, Ruby didn't hear the telephone's polite jingle. It was Amanda who got up from the living-room sofa to answer it, then turned and said, "It's for you, Aunt Ruby."

Ruby not even noticing the odd look on her niece's face.

She took the handset from Amanda and said, "This is Ruby."

"Next time," said the slow, deep voice on the other end. "Next time I call, you better stop scratching your nose and get to the phone quicker."

And just like that, Ruby's attention was on the task at hand. The hair on the back of her neck and along her arms prickled, and the image of a sullen, full-lipped face rose unbidden to her mind.

This would be what Frankie Colgate sounded like.

"You know who I am?" the voice asked.

"Yeah." She shooed Amanda, pale and wide-eyed, away. "And why should I give a fig what you want?"

There was a moment's silence after this—*angry* silence—and then the voice spoke again, slower yet and full of menace. "Listen, you chimpanzee," he said, "*this* is why."

There was a clatter on the other end of the line, the sound of muffled voices, some words Ruby couldn't make out, and then some she could.

"Ruby, don't do what they tell you," said a voice.

Tania's voice.

But there was something wrong with it.

Ruby heard a thud, a cry, the sound of a scuffle. She stood, not breathing, keeping her face expressionless as her eyes darted over to check on Allie, half asleep on the sofa, on Helen and her mother, working on a crossword puzzle together at the table, on Amanda, pretending to read her book while sending worried glances Ruby's way.

Ruby thought of the woman Andy had found, who'd risked so much to share Colgate's name with them at the ballpark. The woman whose every inch of exposed skin had been turned to scar tissue.

The man got back on the line. "Twenty-seven West Thirty-first," he said. "Just off Mermaid."

"I know where it is," Ruby said.

"Good. Be here in an hour or—" Again he moved away from the phone, and again there was the sound of a fist against flesh. Ruby felt like shouting, like somehow reaching through the handset and getting her fingers around his throat, but all she could do was wait for him to return to the line.

When he did, he didn't bother to wait to see if she was still listening. He just said, sounding a bit breathless, "Get moving."

Drops of sweat rolled down Ruby's neck, sticking her blouse to her back. "Leave her alone, or I'll call the bulls on you."

The man laughed, a sluggish *huh-huh* sound.

"Don't bother. They're already here," he said, and hung up.

She asked the taxi driver to stop two blocks down Surf Avenue from her destination. As she stepped from the cab and straightened, the familiarity of it struck her like a blow—the smells of frying food and horse dung, the tang of salt from the nearby ocean, the lights of the Ferris wheels and roller coasters, the sounds of

carousel music and the murmur of the crowds over on the Boardwalk. She felt as if she had never left, never escaped.

She gave the cabbie five dollars, a bounty, and told him to
wait for her. "Shouldn't be long," she said.

He grinned at her from behind the wheel, and said, "I won't
go anywhere, doll."

Ruby turned and looked down the block toward the row of
small wood-frame houses on Thirty-first Street. She walked
through the crowd as if it was filled with ghosts, her eyes and
thoughts only on the squat house that was her destination.

Before she even crossed Mermaid Avenue, she saw the cop
standing in front of it. For an instant, a kind of wild hope filled
her, and she imagined that Gordon and the Prohis had swept
in, captured Frankie Colgate and Jimmy Rourke and the rest of
them, rescued Tania, and solved all of Ruby's problems at the
same time.

But just as quickly she knew that such hopes were absurd. If
she had been able to laugh, she would have laughed at herself. No
one, no Prohi or bull, was going to help her, not unless there was
something in it for them. No one did anything except out of self-
interest in New York City.

The cop, a young man with a fair, unblemished face, watched
her without expression as she crossed the street and walked toward
him and number 27. Ruby could tell he was expecting her.

When she reached him he gave a nod and pointed with his
chin at the stone steps leading up to the wooden front door.
Though the gas lamp that normally would have illuminated the
stoop was unlit, Ruby could see by the rim of pale light on one
side that the door was ajar.

"They're waiting for you," the cop said.

Ruby imagined they were. She walked along the cracked flag-
stones and up the slate-topped concrete stairs, pushed the door
wide, and stepped through it.

She stood for a moment in the front hall. Old white paint was peeling off the walls in strips, rectangular lighter patches showing where paintings or photographs once had hung. The dead air smelled of spoiled food and rotting wood.

And of fresh blood. Ruby knew that smell.

Straight down the hall was another door, also ajar, brighter lights beyond, and low voices coming from within.

She walked silently down the hall, shoved open the door, and stepped inside.

Just as they did on the baseball diamond, her eyes and her brain worked fast together. She saw Tania sitting on a wooden chair in the center of the small room, her ankles tied to its legs, her arms behind her back. Her face was a mass of welts and bruises, and blood ran freely from her nose down onto her blouse, which was already stained scarlet. She stared at Ruby, and Ruby saw that blood was dripping from the corners of her eyes as well.

Four men also occupied the room. One was Chase. Two were cops in uniform, older, heavier, than the one who guarded the front entrance. More dangerous. When Ruby came in, they'd both tensed. But a quick shake of the head from Chase had caused them to relax a fraction.

Chase was dressed in a fine suit as usual, his white hat held in his left hand. As always, his eyes gave away the intelligence and ruthlessness within. Now, though, there was something in those eyes Ruby hadn't seen before. She thought it might be worry.

Grim-faced, he nodded at her. She nodded back, then turned to look at the fourth man, the one who stood just behind Tania's left shoulder.

Frankie Colgate looked very much as he had at the Birdcage and on the field at Washington Park on Ruby's opening day. The same petulant, well-tended face and piggish eyes half obscured by the flesh of his cheeks, the same mass of shiny hair, the same expensive suit.

Only now he'd stripped off the jacket, revealing a billowy, and obviously expensive, white shirt. Red against white, streaks and spatters of blood marked his sleeves from the gold-linked cuffs up to the elbows.

Ruby glanced at his hands. They looked hard, harder than the rest of him. Big and callused under the dried blood, under the layers of cloth bandage he'd wrapped them in to protect the bones inside from the impact of his blows.

Ruby raised her eyes and met his gaze. "Let her go," she said.

In the corner, Chase grimaced and shot her a warning look. But Ruby was a long way from caring how Chase wanted her to proceed.

"Let her go," she repeated, "and I'll answer your questions. Don't, and I'm just going to walk out of here, and you can do whatever you like to her."

Colgate stared. He made a strange chewing motion with his jaw and took a step in her direction.

The cops just watched, as if faintly interested in what was going to happen next. But an instant later Chase was standing in front of Colgate, talking urgently into his ear in what Ruby guessed was Italian.

After a moment, Ruby saw some of the tension leave the big man's posture. "Okay," he said. "Okay." He made a dismissive gesture with his hand, and Chase, after a moment's hesitation, retreated to his corner.

Colgate didn't come any closer, but was still chewing on something when he fixed his eyes on Ruby and said, "I don't believe you." His voice was deep and thick, as it had sounded over the phone.

He pointed down at Tania, whose eyes were closed. "I think you wouldn't leave her."

Ruby didn't say anything.

"So she's going to stay with me, and I'm going to ask you a few questions, and you're going to give me the real answers." He shot her a flat look through those half-hidden eyes. "And then maybe, if I like what I hear, I'll let her go. Maybe."

Ruby said, "What do you want to know?"

A tiny, victorious smile twitched the corners of Colgate's mouth. Ruby kept her true emotions hidden, showing only what she wanted him to see.

"I want to know why this one—" He pointed at Tania, whose eyes flickered fearfully in the direction of his hand. "Why this one was walking around Brooklyn with a picture of me."

"I gave it to her," Ruby said.

Colgate blinked, and his gaze strayed toward Chase. Ruby thought that they'd guessed this, but hadn't known it for sure.

Which meant that Tania hadn't told them. Ruby's friend, her minder, her confidante, had made her job much easier.

Colgate said, "Gave it to her why?"

"Because I wanted to know who you are." She jerked a thumb in Chase's direction. "And him, too. So I could figure out a way to get you two off my back."

"Yeah?" Colgate's jaw clenched. "And what did you learn?"

"Nothing," Ruby said. "She gave me nothing."

Her most important lie, and her riskiest.

"See?" Tania's voice was hoarse, wet. "Like I said."

Colgate raised a wrapped red fist, then restrained himself. "Yeah, and you been lying."

"Maybe she has," Ruby said. "But if she knows anything about you, she never spilled it. I never heard a word. Far as I knew, she came up empty."

"I *told* you." Ruby could hear a trace of the old asperity in Tania's cracked voice. "I was going to ask her for double the money." Amazingly, she managed to grin through her bruised and puffy lips. "But nobody would talk. They're all too afraid of you."

Again, Ruby saw the little smile tease Colgate's mouth. He was just a child, she thought, a brutal child.

She didn't look at Chase.

"For what it's worth, Tania," she said, "I would have paid double, just to learn about these hoods."

Tania smirked. "Maybe I would've asked triple."

"Shut up." Colgate looked at Ruby. "As for you, you're gonna stop snooping and save your money."

"Sure." Ruby shrugged. "Don't know who else to ask, anyway."

But inside she was celebrating. They hadn't learned about Andy Sutherland and his friends in Chicago. No one had told them about the beaten woman who'd come to see her. They didn't know half of what they thought they did.

Colgate made a flicking gesture with his hand. "Okay. Fine. Now get out of here."

Ruby crossed her arms over her chest. "Only if she comes with me."

"Even though she was tryin' to cheat you?"

"Even though," Ruby said.

For the first time, Colgate truly smiled at her, a half-moon curve of red lips. "No," he said. "You go. She stays here."

Tania closed her eyes.

Now, finally, Ruby looked at Chase. He gave her a little shrug that meant, "Sorry, this part has nothing to do with me."

Already Colgate was turning away, tightening the wrap across his palm.

Ruby reached into the waistband of her pants and with her right hand pulled out from a makeshift sheath the knife she'd brought with her. The razor-sharp, evilly curved fish-gutting knife that was part of a set Helen and her mother had brought back from a trip to Germany, sitting unused in the block until Ruby had borrowed it.

Colgate turned his head and blanched. He knew how vulnerable he was. He knew that with just two quick steps Ruby could be on top of him. Fish weren't all this blade could gut.

But Ruby didn't move, and within another moment both cops had pulled out their guns. Ruby could see down the barrel of one.

"Wait!"

Chase came leaping out of the corner, seeming to turn in the air and landing on his feet between her and the cops. "For God's sake, don't shoot!"

Ruby had to give him credit for bravery.

By now Colgate was facing her. His cheeks had turned from a bloodless white to a flushed, feverish red, and both of his fists were clenched at his sides. "You were going to kill me," he said.

Ruby said, "If I'd wanted to, you'd be dead already."

The words echoed around the room, and everyone stared at her, even Tania.

"And then, a second later, I'd be dead, too," she said to Colgate. "You must be fried to the hat to think I'd make *that* trade."

She lifted the knife slowly and placed the blade against the biceps muscle of her left arm. Despite her care, the edge bit into her skin, and a thin line of blood began to seep out on either side.

"I'm not going to use it on you," she explained. "I'm going to use it on *me*."

The room was completely silent. Ruby could hear the rattle of Colgate's breathing, the bubbling, blood-filled sound coming from Tania's lungs, and the tense exhalations of the two cops. Chase, however, looking over his shoulder at her, did not seem to be breathing at all.

And it was Chase whom Ruby addressed. "I have no idea what you're planning for when I face the Babe next month," she said. "But whatever it is, I bet it depends on my throwing a ball."

She looked down at the knife and back up at him. "Get someone to untie Tania, and let her walk out the door with me, or I'll push the blade in and cut this muscle. That would put me out of action for a while, don't you think?"

No one said a word. Ruby looked over at the cops, then up at Colgate, finally back at Chase. "And after I'm done, you can do what you want with me," she told him. "Honestly, I don't care. If I can't pitch, I won't have anything to live for."

She saw Chase's eyes glint, and saw that he alone here knew the truth: as long as her nieces existed, she had everything to live for. The question was, would he tell Frankie?

"So what's it going to be?" she asked. "Do you untie her, or do I cut?"

For a long moment, no one spoke or moved. Then Chase's lips slanted into a grin. "Put your guns away," he said to the cops. "She's no threat."

He turned to Colgate. "You bluffed, you lost," he said, squatting down beside Tania and producing a small, light-bladed knife of his own.

Colgate's wrapped fists clenched. "That was no bluff."

"Yeah," Chase said, "it was." His expression hardened. "And now you're going to let these two walk out of here, and find some other girl to . . . enjoy yourself with."

Colgate looked furious, but said nothing as Chase cut Tania's bonds. A moment later she was on her feet, shaky, in obvious pain but not bowing to it. Droplets of her blood speckled the floor, reminding Ruby of Russell Haynes.

She waited till Tania was standing beside her and then said, "One more thing."

Chase, hands empty again, raised an eyebrow.

"No one follows us. No one finds out where she's going. She's done with this now. Out of it."

Before she'd even finished her little speech, Chase was nodding. "Okay. She's out of it," he said. "Now it's just us, Ruby, you and me."

He paused. "I'll go out with you, make sure our guy lets you pass." He looked amused at her expression. "And then I'll come back in."

Ruby's hands were sweaty, and her arm stung where the blade had bit. But she kept it against her skin and said to Tania, "You go first." Together, they walked down the little hall, Ruby putting her body between her friend and Chase. She heard the door to the little room slam shut behind her, then heard the sound of a thud that she hoped was the impact of Colgate's fist against a solid wall.

"Go inside a minute," Chase told the surprised young policeman at the front door. "They're leaving."

After a moment, the cop obeyed. When he was inside, Chase said, "Okay?"

"Okay."

"By the way—nice work with that knife."

Ruby didn't reply.

He grinned down at her from the top of the stairs. "I'll be in touch."

She sighed. "Aren't you always?"

They walked as quickly as Tania could manage onto Mermaid Avenue, which was still crowded. It felt like hours since Ruby had been here, though she realized it had only been a few minutes. It wasn't even late yet.

Some people glanced at Tania's bloody face, and then away, but no one said anything. Nor did Tania or Ruby speak. Ruby kept the knife in her right hand, though hidden against her shirt, and continually looked over her shoulder and around. But it seemed that Chase had been as good as his word.

Amazingly enough, the taxi was still there. The cabbie swore when he saw Tania and said, "Do you want me to bring her to the hospital?"

Tania said, "No—"

"Just take her wherever she wants to go," Ruby said, and handed him a ten-dollar bill. Then, to Tania, "But don't tell me where! I shouldn't know."

Ruby put an arm around her to help her climb into the backseat. But Tania resisted long enough to say, "Ruby—"

"Save your strength." Ruby got her seated against the cracked seat. "And get yourself to a doctor."

She stepped back and watched the cab pull away. Then she spun on her heel, watching for followers. She saw nothing but horse carts and parked cars and the floods of people heading the opposite way, toward the glories and delights of the Coney Island dreamlands.

Ruby wriggled her shoulders, slipped the knife back into her waistband, and headed for the subway.

41

She didn't sleep well. Her arm, tended with iodine and sticking plaster, stung all night, and her thoughts wouldn't stop whirling. After kicking at the damp sheets for hours, she gave up when dawn finally arrived and went down to breakfast.

Allie and Amanda were still asleep, of course. Nor had Helen or Mrs. Connell yet emerged. Only Paul was sitting at the table, already dressed, looking at the *New York Times* and drinking coffee.

Ruby was surprised to see him. "Why are you awake already?"

"Well, good morning to you, too." He shrugged. "I don't know. Think I've spent so much time lying down these past weeks that I've lost my taste for it."

Picking up the coffeepot, he poured her a cup. "You look tired, Ruby. Eat something—there's oatmeal on the stove."

"I'm not hungry." She reached for the cup. "And anyway, who has time to eat?"

They heard the doorbell chime. Ruby said, "See?"

Paul looked at his pocketwatch. "Who on earth could be calling here so early?"

"I'll find out."

It was the scissor grinder. Ruby had often seen him around the neighborhood, an ancient man with a face like a shriveled walnut and an air of immense dignity, walking slowly under the heavy load of the wooden stand and stone wheel he carried in a harness strapped to his back. Up one side of the street and down the other he'd trudge, swinging a brass handbell to alert all the women inside the fine brownstone buildings that he'd come to sharpen their scissors and knives.

But scissor grinders didn't make house calls, so Ruby stood in the doorway and merely looked at the old man who had struggled up the stone steps, his stand already set up on the sidewalk below. His sharp blue eyes regarded her with interest.

"Have any knives that need sharpening?" he asked. His voice was high and nasal, and didn't sound like he used it all that often. "Any scissors or shears?"

"No." Ruby felt disconcerted. "Maybe next time."

"Yes, next time," he said. Then he made a gesture toward his stand, and for a moment, Ruby was afraid he was going to topple over and tumble down the stairs. "Would it be too great an inconvenience if I were to conduct my business here, on your property?"

Ruby smiled at him. "I don't think we own the sidewalk," she said. "And anyway, it's fine."

"Well, then, thank you kindly." He turned to go, but as he did, his shoe caught on a crack in the stoop and he stumbled. For a moment, he stood there, teetering, but before he could fall Ruby grabbed his arm and held on tight as he regained his balance.

"Well, thank you *very* kindly," he said to her.

"Let me help you," Ruby said. Together, they slowly made

their way down the steps, Ruby holding onto his arm. She was surprised how strong and wiry it felt under his shabby clothes.

At the bottom he bowed to her, then turned to attend to the small group of women who had gathered to avail themselves of his services.

It wasn't till Ruby was back inside that she discovered the scrap of paper he'd somehow tucked into her sleeve.

The scrap had an address on it, that was all, written in an unsteady hand with smudged black ink. An address on Fifty-sixth Street, "near Fourteenth Ave."

That was in Borough Park, Ruby knew.

But who'd sent it? It felt like a trap.

Ruby stood indecisively in the front hall, looking down at the paper, half tempted to crumple it up and throw it away.

Then she saw the brownish thumbprint at the bottom of the scrap, realized who'd sent it to her, and knew exactly what she was going to do about it.

"The bloodstain was a dead giveaway," she said.

Tania grinned. "Knew you'd figure it out."

They were sitting in the living room of a small fourth-floor apartment, not a fancy place but a far sight better than the one on Mermaid Avenue they'd both been in just the night before.

Tania's guards here weren't bent cops, but the silver-haired couple whose apartment it was and their four enormous, muscular, stern-faced sons. No one, not Frankie Colgate, not even Chase, could get at Tania unless they permitted it.

Tania had introduced them as longtime friends of hers, bearing Russian names that Ruby didn't catch. The older couple had smiled, shaken her hand, given her a glass of tea with a sugar lump to suck it through (the way Mama had always drunk it), placed a plate of pastries on the table, and left them alone.

"I also liked how you used a man who sharpens knives for a living. That was a nice touch."

Tania looked positively smug. "I thought so."

Ruby inspected her friend. "You don't look as bad as I expected."

"Thanks a lot."

It was true. All of the blood had been washed off, and Tania had used some of her potions to bring down the worst of the swelling around her eyes and in her lips. What was left was the rainbow of colors, reds and purples and yellows, that bruises took on as they waxed and waned. It was a palette with which Ruby was all too familiar.

"I've had worse," Tania said. Then her face grew serious. "I *would* have had worse if you hadn't showed up." She shook her head, remembering. "How did you think of that trick?"

Ruby shrugged. "It worked, that's all I care about."

"That man is a monster." Tania's mouth turned down at the corners. "Wouldn't feel right to me to clear out without helping you take care of him. And I got some ideas how."

"Good," Ruby said.

Tania sat forward. "Rumrunning is Frankie's business. You know that, right?"

Ruby nodded.

"Well, I heard that the day of your game against Babe Ruth, Frankie's arranged this big shipment—something like a hundred thousand gallons—to get brought onto the beaches down Seagate way."

Ruby remembered her stray thought the night of the Dempsey-Firpo fight. "And most of the city's cops will be keeping the peace around Yankee Stadium."

"And plenty of what's left is on Frankie's payroll, not just the three we saw yesterday." Tania frowned. "But he's not taking any chances. Just before the big shipment's coming in, I heard he's going to leak about another haul, a little one, east of Manhattan Beach. The Prohis will all run over there, and nobody will be around to bother him at Seagate."

Ruby thought about it. "Bet one of his crooked cops will be the one to get the tip about the Manhattan Beach shipment, too."

"Bet you're right."

Ruby was impressed. Sometimes you had to acknowledge a good plan when you heard it.

"Probably all Chase's idea," she said.

Tania shrugged. "Who cares? It's what's going to happen. I heard this yesterday, but before I could get in touch with you, Colgate's goons scooped me up."

"And you didn't tell him anything about what you knew, even when he hit you."

"'Course not." Tania shook her head. "You know this just like I do, Ruby," she said. "Guys like that, they don't stop beating on you when you give 'em what they ask for. They just hit harder and want more."

Ruby drained her tea and crunched up the sugar cube. Then she stood. "Are you going to stay here? Seems like you've got all the protection you need."

But Tania shook her head. "Uh-uh. Had enough, you know? I got an aunt in Los Angeles, and I think I'll head there. Plenty of jobs for a seamstress out Hollywood way, I've heard."

She gave Ruby a quick look through sparkling eyes. Colgate hadn't been able to bruise those. "Wouldn't say no to some help paying the train fare, though."

Ruby reached into her bag. She'd known this was coming.

"Cheap at twice the price," she said.

Tania laughed. "That's for sure."

"Are you clean?" Ruby asked Gordon. "On the up-and-up?"

He looked stunned. "What? Of course I am."

"I'll take you at your word," Ruby said. "So here's another question: Do you actually *do* anything?"

"*What?*"

They were sitting opposite each other in Steiner's Delicatessen on Avenue M, in Ruby's old neighborhood. Three booths down from where Colonel Fielding had offered her a job and changed her life.

Ruby had insisted on meeting here. The last thing she needed was for someone to be staking out the Connells' house and follow her to Gordon's office. Even so, she'd taken three separate subway trains in a roundabout route, keeping a close eye all around to make sure she wasn't being trailed.

Now she sat back, her arms crossed, and stared at the man whose lined face she knew so well from her days in the Birdcage. She saw that his habitually cheerful expression had darkened under the assault of her questions.

He said, a little plaintively, "I haven't told you as much as I could have, Ruby, because I wanted to protect you."

Ruby snorted, a loud sound that drew glances from the crowded tables around them. "Protect me!" she said. "What's happened since you started protecting me? Let's see. First my best friend's fiancé was arrested, and then my brother was. And he's still in. Right?"

Gordon nodded. He looked as if he was sucking on a sourball.

"Another friend was beaten and would've been killed if I hadn't been able to get her out." She glanced down at the long scab on her left biceps. "Where were you when that happened?"

All this question got was a shake of the head. He had no idea what she was talking about.

"I have one man who's trying to run my life, and another who wants to do the same thing to me with his fists he did to my friend, and a bunch of crooked cops who'd as soon shoot me as cash a check with me." She put her hands flat on the cool table-top. "Some protector *you* are!"

For long moments he just gazed at her. He looked sorrowful and old. Then he took a deep breath, nodded, and said, "Ruby, I'm clean. My whole team is clean. We know all about the corrupt officers in this police department, but we're not like them."

Ruby waited.

"And we do a good job, though we're not perfect." His eyes held hers. "To be frank, I think Prohibition is a big waste of time and money. But until the Dry Law gets overturned, I'm a rum snooper. I work at it as hard as I can. And I get results."

Ruby didn't say anything.

"But you need to know if you can trust me." He leaned forward. "You can. And I promise you that if you have information I can use, I'll go after it with everything I have."

Ruby stayed silent and looked into his face. After a few moments, she saw him give a little nod. "You want something from me in return," he said.

She waited.

"What?"

Ruby leaned forward. "First, you promise you'll get Nick sprung."

Gordon said, "Well—"

"That's first," Ruby said. "I want more, but it starts there. You promise to get him sprung, and to send him someplace to dry out. Even with Prohibition, there's got to be sanitariums or hospitals that help people who can't stop drinking."

"Of course there are."

"Well, find one for Nick, and arrange to get him into it. On your dime."

There was a glimmer in Gordon's expression. "And next?"

She took a breath. "The thing I'm about to tell you, it's set to happen on a certain day. If you rush in before that day, you'll ruin everything." She looked into his eyes. *"Everything."*

He paused before speaking. "Ruby, I can promise that I'll get Nick out of jail and into someplace that can help him. That's easy. But the second thing—waiting—I can't swear to. Not until I know the details."

She began to protest, but he held up a hand. "Think about it. What if people will die needlessly if I wait? My job, my responsibilities, would demand that I act, and any promise I made to you—well, I'd have to break it."

Ruby felt numb. She saw Gordon's expression soften. "But I'll do what I can to hold off. I promise you that much."

He gave her an odd, gentle smile and said, "I *am* on your side, Ruby."

Still she didn't speak for a long while. But then she came to a decision. With her heart pounding in her chest, she told him about Frankie Colgate and his plans for October 20, the day that the Yankees and the Typhoons—and Babe Ruth and Ruby Thomas—would meet on the field of Yankee Stadium.

Gordon sat in silence, a trace of color rising to his cheeks as he listened. When she was done with the story, giving him every detail she knew, he sat back in his seat, his expression turning inward as he went over it all.

Then he said, "You're certain of all of this?"

"Certain as I can be." Her chin lifted as she thought of Tania, keeping the information to herself under the assault of Colgate's fists. "I trust my source."

Gordon nodded. "You were right. This is a big deal, Ruby."

"I know."

"This Colgate fellow, he's been laying low so far. We haven't gotten a whiff that he's been planning something like this. I guess it's going to be his introduction to Brooklyn."

Ruby waited. After a few more moments Gordon nodded again, as if reaching a decision of his own. "Like I said, I'll arrange to get Nick someplace that can help him—right after October twentieth. We don't want Colgate wondering why your brother's suddenly getting special treatment."

He paused. "And I also won't beat the pistol and sweep Colgate up before the twentieth."

As he spoke, Ruby felt something unclench inside her. "Thank you," she said.

Gordon grimaced. "Honestly, waiting's in our own best interests, too. This way we'll sweep up all the garbage at one time: the people bringing the liquor in, Colgate and his men, maybe even the restaurants and gin joints waiting for the shipment."

He smiled. "But . . . you're welcome anyway, Ruby."

She got to her feet and looked down at him, a peaceable, rumpled man enjoying the last sips of his coffee. Surprising herself, she said, "Gordon, do you have any children?"

His smile widened. "Yep," he said. "Three grown daughters."

Of course he did.

"Why do you think I put up with you?" he said.

42

She was sitting in her silent dressing room before the Silkworms game, missing Tania, when there came a knock on the door. She called out, "Come in."

After a moment, the door swung open, and in walked Jim Tracy.

Ruby straightened in her chair, but she could see that he didn't mean to make trouble. His head a little bent, his Silkworms cap held in both hands, he looked . . . humble.

And old. Ruby had never gotten a clear look at his face before, but now she noticed the lines and sun wrinkles and scars on it from a lifetime of hard work and tough baseball. His hair was drawing back at the temples, and there were speckles of gray in it. His long jaw worked at a mound of chewing gum.

"Bothering you?" he asked.

Ruby gave him an askance look. "Not yet."

He shook his head, opened his mouth, closed it, decided to plunge ahead. "Guess I was wrong about you, Ruby," he said.

It wasn't what she'd expected. "Yeah?"

"Yeah." He looked down at his cap, crumpled between his thick hands. "Shouldn't have thrown my bat at you, that first time."

"You're right, you shouldn't have." Ruby paused. "How about steamrolling me near first base?"

He looked at her. "Dunno," he said. "I'd do that to anybody."

Ruby laughed, and after a moment he grinned.

"Listen," he said. "You're okay. You just go out and play, nothing fancy. You don't make yourself better than anybody or expect to be treated different." He looked around her room. "Well, this is different, but not like it's fancy."

"No," Ruby agreed.

"Anyway, just wanted to say that you're a good player, and I don't have any problem with you being out there on the mound." He paused. "Except for the fact that you throw too damn hard."

Ruby said, "Thanks."

He nodded and turned to go, then looked back. "Hate days like this," he said. "Colder than a witch's tit out there—excuse my language. Makes my bones ache, it does. Maybe it'll be nicer when we have that series after the season ends."

He paused, then grinned again. "I like those exhibition games, especially the bonuses. Me, I might not have to sell shoes this winter, and I know you're a big reason why."

She nodded, then got to her feet and held out her hand. He shook it with his callused, knuckly one, and with that they established their truce.

When he was gone, she sighed and sat back down.

You're a big reason why.

And the only reason why not.

Ruby sat there, stiff in her chair, and thought about Judge Kenesaw Mountain Landis.

·   ·   ·

It wasn't much of a game, as it turned out. And Ruby didn't even get a win out of it, or a loss. No bats were thrown in her direction, though she did give up a hit to Jim Tracy, a single off her curveball. She was gone for a pinch hitter in the eighth inning with the score tied 2–2, and the Silkworms ended up winning, 4–2, on a couple of errors and a little ten-bounce single up the middle in the ninth.

It was a trifling and meaningless contest that didn't matter a whit to anyone on either team. Except Ruby. It meant everything to Ruby, who knew what none of her teammates did, that she might just have made her last appearance with the Typhoons.

She went back to her room after the game, showered, and dressed in her regular clothes. She was holding the scuffed-up ball with which she'd thrown her last pitch, rolling it around in her hands, examining it, her mind a blank, when the Colonel came in. He'd sat through the entire game with some business friends, and the frigid wind had chapped his cheeks and left his eyes watery and red.

"An inglorious conclusion to a wonderful season," he said, sitting down heavily in the other chair.

Ruby was still looking at the ball. There were a few nicks on it from her fingernails, smudges from the grip she used for her curveball, and a grass stain left by the sharp grounder to third base that had ended the eighth. The last out she'd induced before leaving the game.

She looked up. "Have you talked to Judge Landis?"

"Yes, of course I have." He sighed. "A deputation of us, six of the eight owners, went to plead our case. We told the Judge that our league would likely fail if you were banned. We showed him figures from our accounting books. But he was adamant. He kept speaking of 'the integrity of the game,' as if it were some law written in stone and carried down from a mountaintop. Your expulsion from organized baseball will stand."

Ruby was suddenly on her feet, spinning around and firing the baseball at the wall. Throwing as hard as she could, putting every ounce of her anger and frustration into it.

The ball hit the plaster wall and went right through it, flying straight out into the hall. Ruby could hear it bouncing off the walls out there, and an exclamation of alarm from someone it had narrowly missed.

The two of them stared at the round hole in the wall, at the scraps of plaster that hung from it. Flakes of paint drifted down from the ceiling.

Then Ruby turned to Colonel Fielding. "That man," she said, and her voice was hoarse. "That man is *not* going to stop me from pitching."

The Colonel stared at her. "That man," he said, "always gets what he wants."

Ruby drew in a deep breath, then another.

"Not this time," she said.

"You have a plan," she said to Chase. "I'm involved. So tell me what it is."

He leaned back in his chair and inspected her face. Then he shrugged. "Not yet."

Ruby slammed her hands down on the table, making his coffee slop over the brim of its cup and drawing the startled, covert glances of the few other diners in the armchair restaurant this cold afternoon.

Lovers' quarrel, they were probably thinking.

"I'm tired of this," Ruby said, her voice a venomous whisper. "I'm tired of *you*. Tell me what you're planning, *now,* or I swear I'm walking away. And then what will you do? Slice me up? Well, go ahead. I've had enough."

He opened his mouth to speak, but she didn't let him. Now that she'd started, she thought she might never stop.

"And don't bother to threaten my family, either," she said. "Enough of that, too. I won't hear it. It won't work. No matter what you want, no matter what you're planning, I have to be on the mound against the Babe, don't I? Don't I?"

She didn't wait for an answer. "Yeah, I do. Don't bother telling me any different, But I can promise you one thing: You hurt anyone in my family, any of my friends, anyone I care about in the slightest, anyone I've ever *met,* and you won't see me on October twentieth. On the mound or anywhere else. It's so important, *you* go out and pitch the baseball to the Babe, because I sure as hell won't be there."

She leaned toward him over the table. "Chase, I have nothing to lose."

"Sure you do."

She bit down on her words and stared at him. "Yeah, like what?"

"Like your career."

Ruby snorted. "I have no career. Not after today."

But Chase was grinning at her. He always seemed to like her best when she was acting like a bearcat. He must have thought it was cute.

"Sure you do," he said again. "Fact is, it's just beginning."

Ruby said, *"Then tell me how."*

Chase's eyes scanned the room, settled on the distant diners, judged their threat. Then he nodded. "Okay," he said. "I guess it's time."

Ruby closed her eyes for a moment. Infuriatingly, her voice almost cracked when she said, "So what do you want me to do?"

"Hit Babe Ruth with a pitch," Chase said.

Ruby stared at him. "What?"

"That's all," Chase said. "Bean him. First pitch, if you have to. Or waste one. Just don't let him belt one out of the ballpark before you hit him."

Ruby didn't know what to say.

"But it can't be just a brushback," Chase went on. "And you can't just graze him in the rear with a slow curve or some other slop. It's got to be a fastball, and it's got to hit him straight on. He's got to go down on the ground, and stay there for a while."

Chase's eyes brightened, the cat imagining a mouse. "Think you could actually bean him? Hit him in the head and do some damage? That would be even better."

Ruby just looked at him, and after a moment he shrugged. "Yeah, well, I guess that's asking too much. No one can hit someone exactly where they want to, not even Diamond Ruby. But I know you can plunk him somewhere that'll hurt. On the hand or the knee or the chin. Just make sure you drop him in the dirt."

Ruby said, "Why?"

He smiled. "Let's just say that I want every eye, every camera, focused on the field for about thirty seconds that day."

Ruby thought about it, her eyes on the tabletop in front of her. She let her finger trace a long scratch in the wood.

Then, filled with an odd, cold certainty, she looked up. "Judge Landis is going to be at the game, isn't he?"

"Yes." Chase's eyes were those of cat sitting on a radiator on a winter's day. "Yes, he is."

"What are you going to do to him?"

Chase extended his arms in a lazy, comfortable stretch and yawned. "Let's just say we're going to throw a scare into him."

"Why?"

Chase blinked. The closer they got to the heart of the discussion, the crux, the sleepier—and more dangerous—he seemed to become.

Then he appeared to reach another decision. "Ruby, I bet you already know the answer to that one," he said. "I mean, I've never hidden what I do from you. It's why we understand each other, you and me, isn't it?"

His smile anticipated an outburst from her. But she merely said, "You take money from pushovers."

He nodded. "Well, sometimes we give money to them, too. But yeah, mostly we take."

Ruby was thinking hard. "And a lot of your money has always come from baseball."

"It's America's pastime," he agreed.

"But Judge Landis, since he became commissioner, he's gotten in your way. He's made it harder for you to cash in on baseball."

"Much harder." For once, Chase's true emotions showed in the steely expression in those gray eyes. "It's crazy. This guy tosses players out, bans them for life, who haven't done a thing wrong except maybe hear from somebody that somebody else was throwing a game. Ever since they named him commissioner, he's got all our players running scared. No one wants to be the next guy he bans without even a fair trial."

It was funny in a way to hear Chase complaining about the lack of justice, but Ruby didn't laugh. "So what are you going to do to Landis, while everybody's watching Babe Ruth rolling around at home plate?"

Chase didn't answer. Ruby looked into his eyes and said, "You're going to kill him, aren't you?"

"Nah." Chase discarded the suggestion with a flick of one hand. "Too dangerous, and besides, not necessary. Like I said, we're going to scare him. Give him a message."

"What message?"

"That he might be the Czar of baseball, but not of the rest of the world." Chase's face was grim. "Not of the *real* world."

"And what happens when he gets that message?"

"Oh, he'll step down from the job." Chase gave her one of

his slantwise looks. "He'll step down, retire, poor old guy, and we can go back to doing our business like we used to."

"How can you be so sure?"

"Because he'll know that we won't be giving him a second warning. So he'll have a choice—do what we ask or spend the rest of his life looking over his shoulder." Stone-faced, Chase paused. "His *short* life."

Ruby let the silence stretch out for a while. Then she said, "What does this all have to do with me?"

"That's the good part. Only a few people know that Landis is planning to kick you out—you, me, your owner. After Saturday, believe me, he'll have too much on his mind to bother with any of that. More . . . immediate concerns. Banning you? All it'll ever be is a rumor that didn't come true."

Ruby said, "And what about the next commissioner? He'll be able to do it as easy as Landis could."

Another flick of the hand. "The next commissioner? Who says there's even going to be one? There never was one before Landis. We make our point clear enough, who else is going to want the job?"

He gazed at her. "And anyway, excuse me, Ruby, but who the hell are you? A freak-armed pitcher on some ragtag team in a ballpark that's about a week away from falling down, part of a new league that's barely able to pay its way. The only reason you're in Landis's gunsights at all is because he's a power-hungry old buzzard who thinks he controls every game ever played, whether it's in the big leagues or some empty lot in Flatbush."

Chase jerked his shoulders. "Say there *is* a new commissioner, say someone's dumb enough to take the job. You think he'll care one iota about Ruby Thomas or the Typhoons? He'll be too busy worrying about his own health."

He sat back and looked at her. "Coming clear yet?"

Ruby nodded. "And all I have to do," she said, "is put the Babe in the dirt?"

"That's all. But for real. Think you can do it?"

"Sure."

But suddenly he didn't seem reassured. His mouth turned down at the corners and his eyes bored in on her. "It's not going to bother you to hit your old pal?"

Ruby returned his gaze. "If it meant saving my career," she said, "I'd do it to my best friend."

"No best friends necessary." Chase relaxed. "You don't have to bean the blind girl, just the Babe. Hit him and leave the rest to us, and we'll all end up happy."

He got to his feet and began to turn away. Then he stopped and looked down at her. "You need to know something else."

She waited.

"If someone does come after your family," he said, "it won't be me."

"Who, then?" she asked.

"Come on, Ruby, you're a bright girl." Chase looked a little put out. "Just give it a minute's thought."

"What you read is true—I don't remember a thing. I had to watch the newsreel to see how I won."

Jack Dempsey's soft voice was crackly and distorted by the long-distance telephone lines, but still recognizable.

"The first time I went down, that first punch Firpo hit me with, it almost put me out. I never got hit so hard in my life. And that fall out of the ring didn't help any."

During the pause that followed, Ruby could hear the ghostly echoes of what sounded like a hundred other voices on the line. Then Dempsey went on. "No excuse for my hitting him when he was still getting up, though. I was in a fog."

Ruby had left a message for him at the Hollywood Hotel, but

hadn't really expected him to return her call. When he had, her heart had leaped.

"What's it like out there?" she asked. It was still amazing to her that she could be talking to someone thousands of miles away, their voices traveling down wires all that distance.

"Hot," he said. "Sunny. It's a desert. And boring. They take an hour to make me up just so I'll look like myself on the screen. I feel like a clown by the time they're done. I think they should build a camera that shows what we actually look like, and skip the clown part."

Ruby thought of her own experiences in front of the newsreel cameras. "Yeah, I know what you mean," she said.

Then her heart thumped again in her chest. It was time to get to the point. Uncharacteristically, her voice wavered when she said, "Mr. Dempsey—"

"Jack."

"Jack—are you planning to come back to see me and Babe Ruth in that exhibition game next week?"

She heard him laugh. "Wouldn't miss it. Already got my railroad ticket."

Ruby felt relief flood through her. But she was only halfway home. Less than halfway.

"Jack," she said again. "Listen—"

43

*b*abe Ruth gobbled down another steamer clam. To Ruby, the big muscular thing in its cracked yellow-gray shell looked disgusting, but the Babe, sweating happily in his suit, his cigar dropping ash on the white tablecloth, was polishing off a whole bucketful of them. In the history of eating, she guessed, no one had ever enjoyed steamers more than the Babe.

Someone whose name he couldn't remember had recommended this wooden shack built on stilts over the lapping waters of Sheepshead Bay, and that was enough to send the Babe to a back corner of Brooklyn. Ruby was beginning to feel that she was spending half her life in restaurants, usually with powerful men who thought they knew everything.

In a way, it was inspiring to watch someone who relished food so much. But Ruby couldn't do more than pick at the sandwich she'd ordered, because every time she looked at the Babe, she imagined him lying on the ground, his hands covering his face, blood leaking out between his fingers. All because she had hit him in the head with a pitch.

She'd read an article once by a reporter who'd been at the Polo Grounds the day the Yankees' submarining right-hander Carl Mays had struck Cleveland Indians shortstop Ray Chapman in the head with a pitch. The pitch that killed him.

Mays threw hard, but not as hard as Ruby. Yet the writer had said the sound of the ball striking Chapman's skull was so loud that everyone watching thought at first it had hit his bat. The ball rebounded out toward the mound, and Mays even picked it up and threw it to first. Only then did everyone notice Chapman lying crumpled on the ground, one of his eyes hanging out of its socket. He died hours later in the hospital.

Ruby felt her stomach wrench, and only shook her head when Ruth, concerned that hunger was making her unwell, offered her a clam from his enormous pile.

The Babe had set up this lunch with his business manager, a distinguished-looking man whose name Ruby didn't catch, and poor haggard Colonel Fielding, neither of whom seemed to have much more appetite than Ruby did. The purpose was to discuss the upcoming great confrontation, the one that the tabloids were already calling "Big Bam vs. Great Gams."

The confrontation was suddenly only twelve days away. "Be better to meet even closer, I know," the Babe said, going at his melted butter with a hunk of bread, "but I got something to do first."

That something, as Ruby well knew, was the World Series, the Yankees' third consecutive tilt with John McGraw's New York Giants. The Yanks had simply crushed the opposition in the American League, while the Giants had captured the senior circuit by a narrower margin.

"Going to be different this year, or the same old?" Ruby asked.

Colonel Fielding, who'd barely said a word since the meal had begun, looked stricken, but the Babe grinned at the needle. The Yankees had lost two consecutive World Series to the Giants, and had, in fact, dropped seven Series games in a row. The previous season had begun with the Babe being suspended for weeks by Judge Landis for barnstorming. It had ended with a disastrous World Series that—except for one game halted while tied—the Giants swept. The Babe, who'd had an indifferent season, had had an even worse time of it in the Series, getting just two hits in the five games.

"Oh, it's going to be different this year," the Babe said. "You can bet on that."

Ruby thought of betting, and of Chase, and felt cold inside.

Babe's business manager winced, and Ruby imagined him and Colonel Fielding commiserating with each other later on the unpredictability of star ballplayers. But if anyone could make a rash promise stick, it was Babe Ruth. All he'd done this season was hit over .390, with forty-one home runs and some unbelievable number of doubles, triples, walks, and runs driven in. It might have been his best year yet.

The Babe was reaching into a pocket and pulling out a sheaf of tickets. "Game one," he said, pushing them across the table toward her. "For everybody."

"Thanks." Ruby took the tickets. "You going to swat one for Allie?"

The Babe laughed. "Won't guarantee a home run. Just winning the Series."

Wiping his mouth with a napkin, he leaned over the table, the stack of clamshells teetering precariously. "Okay," he said, "time to make a plan."

Ruby said, "A plan?"

The Babe nodded. "Yeah. This has got to be fun, for us and the crowd, too."

"Oh, I promise you it's going to be fun, Jidge," Colonel Fielding said.

Ruth shot him a look that shut him up, then turned back to Ruby. "Tell you what, kid," he said slowly, working it out. "Why don't you bounce the first one, make me jump rope over it."

He guffawed at the expression on her face. "Don't like that idea, do you?"

"No," Ruby said, "I don't."

"Think it'll make everyone feel like you're a joke, just a stunt, right? Or scared, maybe. Scared to throw the ball over the plate."

Ruby shrugged. But it was exactly what she thought.

"Well, hold your horses and listen." The Babe was still grinning. "You bounce that one, and I'll make a big deal about it. Like I thought you threw at me on purpose, you know? I'll shake my fist and send some curses your way—"

He glanced at the two old men and gave another laugh. "Oh, nothing that'll singe the poor girl's ears," he said.

Then he winked at Ruby. "They don't trust me."

Ruby rolled her eyes. "All right," she said. "I'll bounce it."

"Good."

"And on the second pitch, you'll swing and miss. I'll give you a big curve, and you'll miss it by three feet."

"What?" The Babe thought about that. He didn't look as happy as he had a moment earlier. "Three feet?"

"Yeah, you know, blow people's hats off, spin around, lose your bat. *Miss the ball.* The fans will love it."

Ruth was beginning to grin. "Yeah," he said. "Yeah! That's good."

It must be nice, Ruby thought, to have such self-confidence that you had no fear of making a fool of yourself in front of sixty thousand fans.

"It's foolproof," the Babe said, by now completely won over.

"I'll swing and miss. Then I'll throw my bat on the ground and stomp around and point at you, like I can't believe what just happened. Like, 'How could this kid, this *girl*, get one past the great Bambino?'"

"They'll be hollering, all right," Colonel Fielding said. Even he looked a little happier, the old showman brightening at the prospect of a great flimflam.

"The question is," Ruby said, "what happens on pitch number three?"

The Babe had an answer ready. "On the third pitch," he said, "no script. No shenanigans, no playing to the crowd. Just you against me."

"I throw the ball," Ruby said.

"And I hit it," said the Babe.

Ruby said, "If you can."

The Babe sat back and looked at her, cheeks crinkling under his pale hunter's eyes, and she found herself smiling back at that familiar moon face. The language of baseball went beyond words. In the end, all that mattered was skill and competition and the pure joy of being out there on the field, doing something you were good at. You couldn't truly understand it unless it was inside you.

"I love this," she said. "Don't you?"

The Babe's grin was full of affection. "Nothing like it, kid."

And at that moment, after all those hours, all those long days and sleepless nights filled with worrying, Ruby put the finishing touches on her plan.

As they got into Colonel Fielding's car, the Colonel said, "You want to be dropped off at your place?"

"You mean Helen's?" Ruby shook her head. "No, could you take me to Manhattan?" She thought for a moment. "Madison Avenue in Midtown will do fine."

He looked surprised, but merely said, "You've got an appointment?"

Ruby sat back against the cool leather seat. "Just someone I need to talk to," she said, and that was all.

The next time she saw the Babe he wasn't dressed in a fancy suit, stuffing his face and clowning around. Clad in the Yankees' white uniform with black pinstripes, he was deadly serious as he took the field in game one of the World Series. He seemed quite grim-faced with tension, as did most of his Yankee teammates and their tiny manager, Miller Huggins.

"What does Huggins look like?" Helen asked. She'd never been much of a baseball fan before she lost her sight, and didn't have many of the game's faces in her memory.

"Like a depressed leprechaun," Paul told her.

They were sitting just three rows in on the first-base side, Ruby and her clan, amid an enormous crowd that paled only in comparison to the one at the Polo Grounds for the championship fight. It felt strange to Ruby to be on this side of the railing during a baseball game. She'd seen them sitting together so often, Helen and Mrs. Connell and the girls, watching her play, but she'd nearly forgotten what it felt like to be merely a spectator.

Down on the field, the two baseball clowns, Nick Altrock and Al Schacht, were replaying the Dempsey-Firpo fight in slow motion. There went Dempsey through the ropes and onto his back. Fans in the nearby stands laughed, but most didn't respond to the antics.

Allie, watching the routine with a critical eye, said, "Is that what it was like? The fight?"

"No." Ruby glanced at the two men below. There was something distasteful about their act, about turning that great, life-threatening, thunderous battle into a joke. "No. It was fast and loud and . . . big," she told her niece. "Big . . . like this game feels."

Allie spread her arms and gave a smile that dimpled her cheeks. "Me," she said, "I *like* big."

Helen draped an arm over Allie's shoulders. "Me, too, honey."

Colonel Fielding sat across the way, gazing sorrowfully at the crowd and pondering his dismal future. A host of former ballplayers, managers, and magnates filled many of the best seats: Johnny Evers looking as crabby as ever and out of place in a wrinkled suit; Connie Mack resembling a distinguished scarecrow; Christy Mathewson, the old Giants' hurler, whose health problems had left him looking fearfully worn out.

And there, flanked by glowering Ban Johnson and John Heydler, presidents of the American and National leagues, sat Judge Landis, sterner than ever, just fifteen feet or so away. Ruby knew he'd spotted her, knew just as well that he would never acknowledge her presence.

Beside her, Amanda, her elegant face somber, said, "Who's that, Aunt Ruby?"

"The commissioner of baseball," Ruby said.

"Why are you looking at him that way?"

Ruby just shook her head.

Was that who Ruby thought it was?

Yes. There, peeking out from the Yankee dugout, was Carl Mays, the man who'd killed Ray Chapman with a pitch three years earlier.

Ruby had forgotten Mays was still on the Yankees. But she did know that his career hadn't come to an end after his pitch left Chapman dying on the ground. In fact, if Ruby remembered right, he'd even won twenty games in a season a time or two since then.

Ruby looked at his dour expression. How often did he think about that day, that moment, that pitch? Had he meant to hit Chapman? Or had the ball just slipped? He always swore it was a mistake, but wouldn't anybody lie if they'd killed someone?

Wouldn't Ruby lie, if she ended Babe Ruth's career ten days hence? Wouldn't she say that it was all a dreadful mistake? Of course she would.

And maybe eventually she'd even come to believe it.

Beside her, Amanda looked up into Ruby's face, slipped an arm through hers, and leaned against her shoulder.

Babe Ruth had been smart not to promise Allie a home run, because he didn't hit one this day. In fact, the first two times he came to the plate, he didn't even get a hit. To Ruby's eyes, he looked nervous out there—even the Babe!—and the crowd was definitely on edge, too. It was as if they thought that his magnificent season had been a mirage, and that he could revert to the player who'd struggled so in last year's World Series.

The Yankees jumped out to a 3–0 lead, but they couldn't hold it, and by the seventh inning the Giants had moved ahead, 4–3. His third time to the plate, the Babe slammed a triple down the leftfield line, and the Yankee fans in the stadium crowd erupted in relieved cheers. These sounds of happiness were cut off a moment later, however, when he tried to score on a short fly and was tagged out at home.

Ruby had trouble concentrating on the game. She had too much to think about. Perhaps worse, she kept traveling back ten years to her former life, the life that she usually preferred to forget.

Casey Stengel sent her there. He was playing center field for the Giants, and Ruby could see from his lined, cheerful face that the passing years had turned him from a brash youngster into a veteran. But he was still recognizably the same man who'd hit a foul ball to her during the first game ever at Ebbets Field, back when Ruby was not quite eight.

The years hadn't made Casey any less of a pest, either. In the second inning he hit a long fly ball to right field but was put out. In the fourth he walked. In the seventh he singled. He seemed to be everywhere, hustling down the base paths with his funny, awkward gait, grinning when he got where he was headed, jawing with the Yankee fielders, drawing a laugh even from stoical Wally Pipp over at first base.

Then, in the top of the ninth, two outs, the score tied 4–4, Casey came up one last time and hit a long drive to left center. The crack of the bat momentarily silenced the huge crowd, and then the scattered Giants' partisans began howling as the ball bounded free to the outfield wall.

Ruby was watching Casey. He was running as fast as she'd ever seen him go, making good time even though, with his bandy legs and long face, he reminded her of a broken-down horse being forced to race in the Kentucky Derby. To make things worse, somewhere around second base the sole of one of his shoes began to come loose, half tripping him as he staggered around third and headed home. It was a comical sight at such a crucial moment of the game, but somehow he pulled off an elegant slide to score the go-ahead run.

When the Yankees went down meekly in the bottom of the ninth, the Giants had taken the first contest. It was the eighth straight Series game that the Yankees had dropped to their crosstown rivals. The crowd was subdued. This wasn't how things were supposed to go.

Helen shook her head and frowned. "I wonder if Jidge will ever win a World Series with the Yankees," she said.

"Sure he will," Allie said. "He'll win this one."

"Oh, yeah?" Helen reached out and ran her fingers through Allie's blond ringlets. "And how can you be so sure?"

"Because he promised."

"Oh." Helen stifled a laugh. "Then that's all right, then."

But Allie wasn't done. "And people like Babe Ruth and Aunt Ruby," she said, "they always keep their promises."

Ruby knew it the moment they walked in the door.

He'd been there.

No one else seemed to notice, not even Amanda. Not even Helen, though Ruby saw her wrinkle her nose, then give her head a shake, as if dismissing her suspicions.

But Ruby had more than suspicions. She had certainty.

While they'd been at Yankee Stadium, David Wilcox had been inside their house.

It was the smell that tipped her off, Wilcox's characteristic odor. That mix of his cigar smoke and alcohol and that awful cologne he wore. No one else smelled like that.

And he'd been inside. For all she knew, he was still here.

While Mrs. Connell went to make dinner and the rest of the family gathered in the living room, Ruby walked upstairs to check. All along the way, she smelled him. She knew he'd come up here, taking his time as he explored Helen's room, Mrs. Connell's, Paul's. All empty now. Wilcox's odor in each one.

Next Ruby went into the girls' room. She looked down at their beds, Allie's messy and unmade as usual, Amanda's sheets neatly tucked in, shipshape. Except for the dent on top of the covers, the impression of a large, heavy body that had lain there.

Ruby leaned over and put her palm against the covers. Were they still warm? She couldn't tell. The room itself was warm as well.

With a violent move, she pulled the bedclothes from Amanda's mattress, and then Allie's, and carried them in a bundle to the hamper. She would have liked to have burned them, but a good washing would have to suffice. She remade the beds with fresh sheets.

Done, she continued her circuit, checking the bathrooms, and even the closets. Nothing.

The question was: Had he expected to find them home, or had he known they'd be at the game, and had shown up because he knew he'd be undisturbed?

Lastly, she took a deep, unsteady breath and went into her own bedroom. It, too, was empty, but there was a small, folded piece of white paper sitting on the pillow.

Ruby picked it up, her stomach twisting at the idea of touching something he'd so recently held, and unfolded it. Saw only a couple of pen marks on it, just a single date written in a scratchy hand.

Oct 27.

Ruby knew what that meant. It was the date he expected her back at the Birdcage, the date that he would once again take ownership of her.

And if she continued to refuse?

Well, look what he'd done. He'd come in here, just to show he could. Every step, every move, had been an implied threat.

Imagine what I'll do if you defy me.

It was Paul who looked into her face when she returned and saw something there. She was eternally grateful that he didn't say anything, only cast her a worried look when no one else was watching, then nodded in understanding when she raised her hands in a quick, quelling gesture.

Much later, after everyone else had gone to bed, he came back down to the living room. He looked tired but . . . serene. Ruby thought again that she'd spent too long underestimating him.

"You've thought of something I can do to help," he said.

She nodded.

"Finally." He smiled at her. "Good. What?"

"On the day that I pitch against Babe Ruth, stay home." She took a breath. "I mean all of you, Helen, Mrs. Connell, the girls."

Paul blinked. "All of us?" he said. "Why?"

Ruby had decided not to tell him, not to tell anyone, about Wilcox's visit. Was it the right choice? She had no idea. She was so far past knowing what the right choice was that she couldn't even guess at it anymore. All she knew was that she had a plan, and she was going to carry it through.

"Why?" he asked again.

"Because I think it might be dangerous for you all to be there."

This was the truth, though not the entire truth.

"Ruby," he said, "tell me what's going to happen."

She merely shook her head. "Just keep them here, and stay close to them." She held his gaze. "But let's let them think they're going till the day of the game, all right? It will save us a week of arguing."

Paul saw the logic in that.

"And when the time comes, I'll take the blame. But they can't go. You have to keep them here."

After a moment, he nodded. "Okay. I'll do that."

"Thank you," Ruby said.

"Just answer me one question."

"If I can."

He was looking into her eyes. "Ruby," he said. "Are we going to be . . . bait?"

Ruby thought of the vast ocean of New York City, filled with icy currents and hidden undertows and circling predators, and of the millions swimming in it, just trying to stay at the surface, just trying to breathe.

"We're all bait," she said.

44

So they'd come to it at last.

Two hours before game time, and the Yankee Stadium stands were already full. From what Ruby had heard, fans had been camping outside the stadium for two days in hopes of getting their hands on general-admission tickets in the upper grandstands. The seats closer to the field? They were long gone, snapped up within a day or two of going on sale. This was the place to be on a warm, windy October 20, sitting in the House That Ruth Built, getting ready to watch the Big Bam face off against Diamond Ruby, the Belle of the Ball.

Every seat was taken, it seemed to Ruby, except for six right by the railing a little way up the first-base line. Two rows of three, the painted wood a stark contrast to the overflowing stands all around.

Ruby had never been much for promotion, but she could admire it when it was done well. And in her opinion, the days leading up to the big game had been a model of effective publicity, both in the press and via word of mouth. Every day she'd endured another interview, another appearance at a department store, another thousand flashbulbs popped and hundreds of feet of film exposed. She'd posed more times than she could count with Babe Ruth, with Miller Huggins (whom she towered over), with Yankee players familiar from the Birdcage and others she'd never seen before, with Jake Conlon and Andy Sutherland and poor distraught Colonel Fielding. The result was that by the last few days people in New York City were talking about little else than the upcoming game.

The Yankees had done their part by capturing the World Series. It took them six games, but they did it, with the Babe hitting three home runs and the team overcoming another game-winning round-tripper by Casey Stengel to, in the words of Grantland Rice, finally "reach the shining haven where the gold dust for the winter's end lies ankle-deep in the streets."

(Midway through the Series, Ruby heard that Stengel had griped about missing out on some gold dust himself. "If we win, do *I* get paid to hit against a girl?" he'd asked. "Why does the Babe get all the breaks?")

The Yankees' first championship, in their new ballpark's first year, did nothing but make fans even more excited about the forthcoming exhibition. No one wanted to let go of such a marvelous baseball season in New York City, so the opportunity to return to Yankee Stadium just a few days after the last World Series game was heaven-sent.

Certainly the sporting press didn't want the season to end. It would be a long, cold winter to fill with stories of salary wrangles and threatened holdouts, with only the occasional manager's firing or big trade to enliven the dead months until spring training began. Sure, there would be other things to write about: football, basketball, hunting, even a horse race with some big-name entries over at Belmont Park later this same day, but of course none of them could compare to baseball in terms of provoking interest and enthusiasm.

The vast crowd had arrived in peaceful, orderly fashion. Ruby could spot the uniforms of New York City policemen here and there, but they didn't seem to have much to do. There were no fights, no signs of overindulgence in bootleg liquor, not even any loud debates between those who rooted for the Babe and those who might prefer Diamond Ruby.

The fans had kept up a constant cheerful murmur ever since arriving, and had gotten the chance to intersperse this with happy shouting as they watched the Babe and his teammates blast batting-practice pitches all over—and out of—the stadium. Ruby had never seen such an easy-to-please crowd; they even laughed and cheered delightedly when Joe Dugan, the Yankees' third baseman, let a grounder roll between his legs during fielding practice.

She knew that their attention would focus once the game started. Many of the fans would be expecting the Babe to hit one a mile against her. She hoped that some—and not just Josephine Collier and Ruby's Rooters, who she assumed must be somewhere in the crowd—would be rooting for her to strike out the Bambino. But except for those who were betting on the results, most of the fans were just here for the spectacle, to see the little left-handed female hurler pitch to Babe Ruth. They wanted a good show, of course, but how it turned out didn't much matter.

In their place, Ruby might have felt the same way. She would have looked upon today as a lark, much as the Babe—clowning around in the home dugout, whaling at the ball during batting practice—clearly did. But of course she couldn't. Too much was at stake, too much could go wrong, too much was expected of her that she couldn't bear even to consider. The general air of festivity might as well have been taking place in another city, on another planet.

All but a few of the Typhoons seemed to share her tension, though for more innocent reasons. They were awestruck just to be inside Yankee Stadium, consumed by a sense of inferiority that didn't seem to help their swings when it was their turn for batting practice. Most of them looked like children up at the plate, though a couple of the veterans, especially Andy Sutherland and the two others who'd had major-league experience, took the whole thing in stride.

"Notice anything special about the field?" Andy asked in the dugout.

Ruby looked out, and then back at him. "What?"

"No weeds."

"True."

"But the mound still gets chewed up. The dirt's a little soft. So don't forget to smooth it out before you pitch."

"I won't."

He grinned at her. "Why do I bother? You never forget a thing."

"It's my job," Ruby said.

For now.

She found Jake Conlon, looking harassed as he stood by the railing, answering yet more questions from the sportswriters. He seemed happy to see her, as it gave him the excuse to walk away from the press.

"Okay," he said as soon as they were out of earshot. "First thing is, I don't want you throwing where anybody can see you till I give the word."

Ruby shot him a curious look, but didn't say anything.

"And the second thing is, you're not starting."

Now she stared at him, her mouth open.

His sour face lightened a bit at her expression. "Hold your horses," he said, raising a hand. "The Babe is going to be batting third, like usual, so he's guaranteed to be up in the bottom of the first. I'm going to start old Solly Phipps. He'll pitch to Witt and Dugan, and then when it's Babe's turn I'll bring you in."

Ruby was shaking her head halfway through this explanation. "No," she said. "I want to start. It's my game."

"Oh, is it?" Conlon's expression hardened. "No, Ruby, it's not. It's not your game—it's Colonel Fielding's and Jake Ruppert's. You may be the draw, or one of the draws, but don't forget you're only here 'cause of your arm. And if the Colonel decides you're not going to come in until the Babe's at the dish—to make everybody lean forward in their seats, and to make sure you don't do something like throw your wing out pitching to Whitey Witt— well, you better believe that maybe he knows better than you do, girl. Not to mention, you'll do what any other player under contract would do, which is what I tell you. Got that?"

Ruby got it.

"Good." And with that, Conlon stomped away.

Ruby sighed. As she walked toward the dugout, she sensed a ripple in the crowd, and looked up to see a knot of police officers converging at one of the grandstand entrances. After a moment's consultation, most of them disappeared down the ramp and out of sight.

Frowning, Ruby went back to the press area. She ignored the whispers and pointing fingers of fans who, she guessed, had never seen her before, and said "be right back" to the children who were holding out objects for her to sign.

Amid the assembled press, some tapping on their typewriters, others merely tossing around lazy quips and soaking up the autumn sunshine, Ruby spotted Grumpy George. When she waved at him, he got to his feet and came down to see her.

"You guys look too comfortable," she said.

He laughed. "That's because we're not worried some heavyweight fighter's going to fall on our heads."

"Listen," Ruby said, jerking a thumb at where two or three

cops still stood close together, talking. "What's that about? Where'd the rest of them go?"

George shrugged. "Turns out there's a Klan demonstration going on—"

He made a quelling gesture with his hands. "No, don't worry, not here. Some poor colored shopkeeper in Fordham acted uppity, probably didn't bow before some white guy, and the 'invisible empire' is flexing its muscle." He frowned. "Whatever muscle it's got left. Anyway, things are quiet enough here that the department is redeploying a bunch over there to keep things under control."

Ruby had the vivid image of Chase holding his knife at Russell Haynes's throat, showing her in the most convincing possible fashion that he had the New York City Klan under his thumb. She had no doubt that the Fordham demonstration was no coincidence. It had been designed to empty Yankee Stadium of anything more than a skeleton police presence.

Good.

She turned to go. George said, "Ruby, I heard something—"

But before he could ask his question, a question she knew was coming but didn't intend to answer, she had responded to the beseeching voices of her young fans and was signing autographs too far away for him to keep trying. She had nothing more to say to him.

Across the way, she could see Babe Ruth, Miller Huggins close beside him, leaning against the railing in close consultation with his business manager, Colonel Ruppert, Colonel Fielding, and a variety of other men in suits and neckties. Ruby was glad not to be in his place. The world of business, of money, seemed to rule everyone's life, but it didn't interest her at all. As long as she had enough to keep her family safe and fed, that was all that mattered. What was the point of having more?

Ruth spotted her and grinned. "You ready?" he called out, drawing all nearby eyes to her.

Play along. "Ready to whiff you," she said.

There was laughter through the crowd, and the Babe guffawed. "In your dreams, little girl," he said.

Then she saw the expression on his face change. Looking over her shoulder, she understood why. Walking with all the stiff-legged dignity he possessed, Judge Kenesaw Mountain Landis, the commissioner of baseball, the Czar, came down the aisle toward his front-row seat just to the right of home plate. Dressed in gray as always, he nodded and exchanged words with acquaintances as he passed, but never did he betray a smile or hint of warmth.

Trailing behind him, looking everywhere but at the old man, came a couple of beefy young guys in ill-fitting suits. Bodyguards.

Shaking her head, Ruby looked back at the Babe. He was still glowering. She recalled how much he detested Landis, believing that his suspension and other penalties a year ago were unfair humiliations visited on him by a jealous competitor for public attention, not by a fair, impartial arbiter. Time, a magnificent season, and a World Series championship did not seem to have lessened the Babe's disdain.

But she could see Colonel Ruppert talking earnestly into Ruth's ear, and after a moment the Babe gave a reluctant nod. Accompanied by the two Colonels, he walked over, his moon face still curved into a pout, and muttered, "Time to make nice with the windbag."

Ruby went with them, photographers following like a flock of trained pigeons. For the next ten minutes, they all posed for photographs, and Ruby couldn't tell who looked more disgusted by the necessity of it, the Babe or the Judge.

Then they were done. The umpires were on the field, the Yankee players were headed out to their positions, and Waite Hoyt, the Yankees' hard-throwing right-hander, was warming up on the mound.

"About time," the Babe said.

"Past time," Ruby agreed. She hesitated, then said, "Jidge?"

"Yeah?"

"Listen." She looked up at him. "Whatever happens, let's stick to the plan."

He shrugged. "Sure, kid."

"No, listen. Even if there are—distractions, don't let them get in the way. Just stand in the batter's box and let's keep going, okay?"

He gave her a curious look, but merely nodded. "Okay, Ruby," he said. "That's what we'll do."

It was the first time she'd ever heard him use her name.

The Typhoons went down in the top of the first, felled like cornstalks by Waite Hoyt's arsenal of scythelike fastballs and tricky curves. Watching him from the dugout, Ruby understood how much she still had to learn about pitching. Right now she had speed and a halfway decent curveball, but the speed wouldn't always be there, and she could do with some baseball learning to go along with it.

Assuming . . .

"You know what his nickname is?" Andy Sutherland said from beside her on the bench. "Hoyt, I mean?"

Ruby looked at him.

"'The Merry Mortician.' He's a nice guy, and I hear he works as a funeral director in the off-season. Somewhere in Brooklyn, I think."

Ruby wondered if he'd been the man to prepare her parents' and brother's bodies after they'd died. But before such thoughts could take hold, Hoyt had finished dispatching the Typhoons, and it was time for Andy to head out onto the field and Ruby, with Jake Conlon's blessing, to go to the bullpen to warm up.

"Good luck," she said.

Andy grinned behind his mask. "I told Solly that if he put anyone on before you, he had to buy us both a steak dinner."

"I'll hold him to that," Ruby said.

She heard the fans closest to the bullpen gasp when she unleashed her first warm-up toss to Stu Hunter. But she'd heard such gasps before, every time she pitched, and paid them little heed. People would either get used to her, to her freak skill, or they wouldn't. She no longer cared.

What mattered was that her arm felt good, loose, easy in the shoulder. Her pitches had life and movement, her curveball was breaking more sharply than usual and her fast ones had a "tail," shooting upward at the last instant.

With stuff like she had today, she might just be able to fan the Babe.

She heard a yell from the stands, quickly cut off. Whitey Witt had slapped a line drive, but Carl Crutcher, the Typhoons' shortstop, had plucked it out of the air. One out.

"You ready?" Stu Hunter called.

Ruby nodded.

His mask pushed up to the top of his head, Stu walked the ball back to her, and together they watched Solly, working with extreme care and deliberation, fool Joe Dugan with a big, slow curve and get him to pop the ball up to second base. Almost before the ball was caught, Jake Conlon was out of the dugout and heading toward the mound.

Stu said, "Exit the old warhorse, enter the main event."

Ruby didn't reply. Her stomach was fluttering in a peculiar way.

As the buzz of the crowd turned into a roar, Jake Conlon tapped his left arm with his right hand, summoning her into the game.

·   ·   ·

"Strike out that big buffoon," Jake said, looking at the Babe swinging three big bats near the on-deck circle.

Andy Sutherland laughed. "Just think of the advice you'd be getting," he said to Ruby, "if your manager *hadn't* spent the past thirty years in the game!"

Jake scowled, but Ruby thought she saw a glint in his eyes. Could it be that he was enjoying all the hoopla as well?

"You remember that Jidge and I have set this at-bat up, at least the first couple of pitches, right?" she asked.

"Yeah, I remember." Now Jake's scowl was heartfelt. He didn't like anybody messing with the sanctity of the game.

But Andy just grinned. "Yeah, I hear you'll have me groveling around in the dirt like some damn puppy."

The home-plate umpire came strolling out to the mound. Ruby had been told ahead of time who it would be, but she still felt her heart quicken at the sight of pale-eyed, jowly Bill Klem. She knew that he was the Babe Ruth of umpires, or maybe the Judge Landis, dictating balls and strikes for nearly twenty years with an unshakably strict, no-nonsense demeanor. "It ain't nothin' till I call it," was his credo.

"Gentlemen," he said now, then inclined his head toward Ruby. "And lady. Is this a coffee klatch or a baseball game?"

Jake Conlon held his tongue, gave Ruby a pat on the back, and trotted toward the dugout. Andy waited till Klem was returning to the plate, then whispered to Ruby, "Whatever you do, don't call him 'Catfish.' He'll toss you right out of the game, no matter what the fans want."

Ruby said, "Got it."

When Andy was back in place behind the plate, she took her final warm-up tosses. Nothing too strenuous—she didn't need it. Her arm felt as good as it ever had, and the enormous buzzing crowd didn't bother her at all. Once she was on the mound, she might as well have been throwing at a tree trunk.

Rubbing the ball between her palms, she let her gaze drift to the stands. Her eyes rested for a moment on Judge Landis, who was leaning forward, elbows on the rail, head propped on his hands. His face was expressionless, but his eyes never left her.

A few seats away from the Judge, one to the right and one to the left, sat the two young men who'd accompanied him. Both were watching Ruby as well, but she couldn't make out their expressions at this distance.

She recognized no one else in that section.

She turned her head and saw that the six seats up the first-base line were still empty. Her stomach fluttered again, but she quickly pushed that and every other thought from her mind.

Her only job now was to throw the ball.

45

"*P*lay ball!" cried Bill Klem in his most stentorian tone. It seemed that he, too, had become caught up in the spectacle, in the excitement of the moment.

The crowd noise grew in intensity as Babe Ruth walked slowly up to the plate. He was carrying the heaviest bat he used, a long, thick-barreled war club that must have weighed fifty ounces. "The bigger the bat, the farther the ball travels," Ruby had heard him say, and he clearly intended to hit one of her pitches completely out of the park.

The Babe gave his bludgeon a couple of fierce swings, then settled into his coiled batting stance. Andy crouched behind him, "Catfish" Klem behind *him,* and for a moment they all were as still as a painting. The crowd, so loud a moment before, hushed in anticipation.

Then Jidge winked at Ruby, and the spell was broken.

She went into her windup and let go. The ball bounced a foot inside and two feet in front of home plate. As if it had a mind of its own, it skipped past Andy Sutherland (who did, in fact, grovel in the dirt trying to block it) and rolled all the way to the backstop.

The Babe, surprisingly light on his feet, dropped his bat and danced out of the way of the errant pitch. Then, as the crowd noise grew, he put his hands on his hips and stared out at her, as if considering whether she'd intentionally thrown at him, as if deciding whether he might want to charge out to the mound and challenge her.

The fans howled. Most were here for the show, the spectacle, the Babe. If the girl pitcher made a fool of the big slugger, that was fine with them. If she made a fool of herself, all the better. For some of them, Judge Landis certainly included, it would merely confirm their suspicions that a girl had no right to stand on the mound at Yankee Stadium.

Ruby had prepared herself for this moment, but still she had to stifle a surge of something that felt a lot like anger. She'd never bounced a pitch before in her life. No, that wasn't true, sure she had, once or twice, on rainy days, or frigid ones, when the ball felt like a chunk of ice. But it was warm and sunny today.

Andy retrieved the ball. Bill Klem held out his hand, inspected it, then tossed it back out to Ruby. She rubbed it again, as if trying to get a better grip on it, then peered in for the sign.

Curve.

She got set, holding the ball hidden in her glove at chest level as she always did. But something tickled at the edge of her mind, and she let her gaze slip once again to the box where Judge Landis sat.

And this time she saw him, the man with the silent, slippery grace and the catlike eyes that never seemed to miss a thing. Chase, dressed for once like everyone else in a dark coat and pants, his homburg pulled low over his forehead. He was standing in the aisle atop the stairs that led to the box seats and looking out at the field, at Ruby.

She thought he might have been smiling.

No point in waiting. Her role was out here, alone on the mound. She returned her attention to the game, took a deep breath, and let ease and relaxation flow through her muscles again.

She threw the pitch, a swooping curveball. The Babe missed it by at least two feet, spinning so hard after his wild swing that it looked like he was trying to drill himself into the ground.

The fans, equal-opportunity enthusiasts, rose to their feet and roared their delight. The Babe regained his balance, staring out at Ruby in a fine simulation of shocked disbelief, and then hurled his bat to the ground with such violence that it raised a cloud of dust when it hit. Stomping around the plate like a grizzly bear, he swore and waved his arms around, while Andy, Bill Klem, the players on the field, and the whole enormous bellowing crowd ate it up.

Ruby thought the great stadium's grandstands might come down around her ears.

She cut a glance toward Judge Landis. Frowning, his face all sharp disapproving lines, he was standing at the railing, staring out at her. In the crush of fans who'd pushed forward for a better view, several other onlookers had gotten between him and his bodyguards—neither of whom seemed to notice at all that Chase was, in his eel-like fashion, moving through the crowd and down the steps. There were no cops in sight.

Even when Chase ducked and glided and emerged standing right beside the Judge, no one paid him any heed at all. Ruby had a sudden revelation, that he'd gotten to the bodyguards, that they'd been paid off, that the police had been paid off, that everyone in the entire stadium was either blissfully unaware or was in cahoots with him.

She also knew for sure what she'd suspected all along: no way was Chase merely trying to throw a scare into Landis. Of course that wasn't it. That had never been his intention.

Looking for it, Ruby glimpsed a gleam of steel, the knife held half concealed at Chase's side.

But no one else spotted it, of course. All eyes were riveted on her, awaiting the next pitch.

Smiling out at her, Chase waited, too. He was nothing if not patient.

Ruby looked back at home plate, at the Babe. When he caught her eye he grinned. "Remember, kid," he called out. "Remember what we talked about."

Ruby nodded.

No script.

Just you against me.

It was time.

The most famous man in America standing at home plate, coiled in his stance.

The crowd vibrating with anticipation, with tension.

The cold-eyed old Czar on his feet like everyone else, perfectly still in his gray coat and hat.

The cat-eyed man beside him, teeth shining white, knife held easily in his palm.

The long-armed pitcher, the monkey girl, on the mound, standing in the vortex of a storm only she knew existed.

The long, waiting moment that preceded the pitch.

Ruby rocked back, raised her hands above her head, broke them apart, began the forward motion that would usually culminate in a fastball whistling across the plate. Only this time, in the middle of her motion, her foot caught in a divot in the mound, the chopped-up dirt she had neglected to repair, and she stumbled, taking a staggering step toward the third-base line instead.

Her arm whipped forward. Even as she went down flat on her face, she released the ball. Lying there, unmoving, the wind knocked out of her lungs, she heard a dull solid *thump*. There was a moment's pause, as if the entire crowd was holding its breath, and then the silence was broken by a woman's high-pitched scream. This was followed by confused shouts, a rising, shocked murmur from ten thousand throats and, above this, urgent calls for a doctor.

Ruby got slowly to her feet. Catching her breath, she took her time looking over. She didn't really need to. She knew what she had done.

But she had a role to play, so after she did look, she found herself running toward the stands. Surrounded by fans pointing, covering their mouths or their children's eyes, fanning themselves, Judge Landis stood rooted in his spot, his face ashen, looking like he might faint.

But alive. Unharmed.

At his feet lay Chase, on his back, head propped against a concrete step. His eyes were open, and an enormous purple egg had already sprouted from his left temple where the ball had struck him.

Ruby scrambled over the railing and dropped to her knees beside the stricken man. Her face was full of shock and concern as she put her mouth close to his ear.

"Rourke," she murmured. "Jimmy Rourke."

His dazed eyes flickered in her direction. He was hearing her. Understanding for the first time whom he was up against.

"You asked me a question a few days ago," she went on. "Here's my answer: I can hit anything I choose to."

He blinked, and his mouth moved, but no sound came out. His body lay so still and heavy against the cold concrete that Ruby wondered if she'd paralyzed him.

"And I *always* have a choice," she said.

Then she straightened, just as two policemen and a man carrying a doctor's bag pushed their way through the crowd. "Careful," Ruby said to them. "He has a knife."

That certainly caught everyone's attention. The sawbones backed away, along with the fans closest to the scene, and the cops handled Chase a lot less delicately than they would have otherwise. Especially when they got a look at the gleaming, deadly blade that had fallen beneath him when he went down.

Ruby straightened and turned to face Landis. He looked ancient, frail, and exhausted, hanging on the railing and staring down at his barely avoided future.

"See?" Ruby said. "Told you."

He raised his eyes to look at her. They were vague, unfocused, almost as if he was the one who'd been struck by the ball. But after a moment, they sharpened. He was listening.

"We have a deal," Ruby said.

He said nothing.

"We have a deal," Ruby said again. "Right?"

She'd gone to see the Judge after leaving the Babe's clam feast. Taking the wood-paneled elevator up to his office suite, she'd walked right past the silent, shocked secretary and straight into his sanctum.

His eyes had widened at her brazen approach, and he'd tried, but failed, to freeze her with his gaze. "Miss Thomas," he'd said, "we have nothing further to talk about."

"Sure we do," she'd replied. Then she'd perched on the edge of the desk, ignoring the look of disgust that crossed his face, and told him exactly what was going to happen.

At first he'd barely seemed to comprehend what she was saying, but as she went on she'd seen his attention focus, and concern, then alarm, enter his expression. When she'd finished, he'd said, "Then I simply won't go."

"Don't be a fool," she'd said immediately, having known this would be his initial response. "Chase could get to you anywhere—and anyplace else I won't be there to warn you. You want to be afraid every minute of the rest of your life? And say he does succeed, you want men like him taking over the game? You want more scandals like they had in 1919?"

She'd seen him thinking about that, his face pale, the lines and grooves more pronounced than ever. Finally he'd looked up and said, "What do you want in return?"

"You know what I want."

Even then, he'd shaken his head. Pigheaded to the last.

Somehow she'd kept her temper, though not her tongue. "Pay attention, Judge," she'd said. "If there's one thing I've learned, it's how to talk to sportswriters. And they love to listen to me. As good as write their stories for them, I do. Yet you'd still ban me the day after I saved your life? Believe you me, they'd have a field day with that one."

She'd leaned closer to them. "And don't doubt it: I'll talk to them, all of them, George Littell and Jack Lawrence and Grantland Rice and Damon Runyon—the whole caboodle. They like me already. They need me. So have fun explaining to them why you followed up such a good turn with such a bad one. And then imagine what it'd do to your reputation."

The Judge had tried to hide it, but she could tell he was horrified. He was a man for whom reputation was all.

"Look," she'd said, "I've got no interest in going to the major leagues. Even if the Yankees were to ask me, I'd say no. I just want things to stay as they are. I want to be able to feed my family. I want to keep pitching for the Typhoons."

He still hadn't said anything.

"And one more thing. Colonel Fielding gets to have his postseason series with the Silkworms. And I get to pitch in it."

Judge Landis had raised his eyes. Ruby thought it might have been the first time he'd actually seen her face, not just her body, not just her arms.

But still he had not spoken.

. . .

And now he was doing it again. Looking into her face.

Ten seconds passed, fifteen. The doctor was busy around the fallen man, and more policemen were on their way down the aisles. Ruby wondered how many of them had been in Chase's pocket, but she knew that none would dare admit it, not now, not here, not anymore. The balance of power had shifted, and for good.

The game had been halted until an ambulance arrived to take Chase away. Ruby had all the time in the world to wait for the Judge's response.

Finally, she saw some brightness, some spark, go out of the old man's eyes.

He nodded. "We have a deal."

That was all she was going to get from him, Ruby knew. No graciousness, no thanks, no warmth. Just a nod and a single grudging sentence.

But it was enough. It was the whole world.

Two men in white jackets came bustling down the aisle carrying a stretcher, cops clearing the way for them through the crowd. By now Chase had begun to stir, his legs moving, his slender fingers twitching. She hadn't paralyzed him.

The ambulance attendants bundled him onto the stretcher, also being less gentle than they would have been otherwise. An efficient police detective in street clothes, who'd taken over command of the situation upon arriving, told Ruby he'd want to talk with her after the game. She sighed and said of course, but when he began to turn away she put a hand on his arm to stop him.

"Could you tell me," she said, "was there a Prohi raid down in Coney Island today?"

The detective looked startled. "How'd you hear about that?"

"I know Gordon Gerrard."

Not much of an explanation, but in the tumult it was enough. "There were two," he said. "One was big, a big haul. Boats, suppliers, distributors, speakeasies, the whole deal. A clean sweep, and no casualties."

Ruby thought of Tania, of bloodstained hands wrapped in bandages. "Did they catch the man in charge? The big boss?"

"Yeah, red-handed, some guy from Chicago," the detective said.

Then he grinned at Ruby. "Well, maybe there *was* one casualty," he said. "They gave that schmo a real Brooklyn welcome."

Poor Colonel Fielding was sitting in his front-row seat, his shoulders slumped, clearly wondering what else could go wrong. Spotting him, Ruby took pity and walked over to his box.

"Cheer up," she said.

He stared at her. "Why?"

"Because Judge Landis just changed his mind."

She left him there looking like he'd just been struck by a bolt from heaven.

While she'd been busy, the six empty seats up the first-base line had filled. Feeling lighter at heart than she had in years, she walked over to them.

Her mood darkened a little when she saw the fresh shiner on Paul's right eye. But he raised a hand and, smiling, said, "Don't worry. I'm fine." He touched the bruise gingerly. "In fact, this is a war wound I'll wear proudly for as long as it lasts."

Allie half vaulted over the railing into Ruby's arms, a bundle of energy and warmth as always. "That terrible man came to visit," she hollered, loudly enough to make Ruby wince.

"Mr. Wilcox, she means." Amanda frowned. "He threatened us, Aunt Ruby."

"Repeatedly." Helen looked strained, but not overly so. "One thing after another that he promised to do if you didn't go back to his sideshow. It was quite tedious, actually."

"He asked if I remembered what he'd done to me before." Amanda shook her head. "As if I'd forget!"

So brave. They were all so brave. Ruby felt abashed. She didn't deserve them.

"After a while, I'd had enough and told him to leave." Again Paul touched his bruise. "That's when he clocked me."

Mrs. Connell gave a grim smile. "I was just about to brain him with that brass Art Deco ashtray we keep on the mantel."

"And I bit him on the leg," Allie said.

"And they would have handled him just fine," said the big man filling the sixth seat. "But that's when I came in and told them to let me take care of it."

They all looked at Jack Dempsey. He'd been busy signing autographs while they spoke, but apparently he'd also been listening to their conversation. Ruby saw an expression on Amanda's face that made her smile to herself. It seemed that her serious niece had a new hero.

"Did he know who you were?" Ruby asked.

Dempsey nodded. "Oh, sure."

"And what did he do?"

"He tried to slug me."

Ruby gasped. "No!"

"He did," Amanda said, to nods all around.

Ruby's eyes were wide. "And what happened then?"

"Mr. Dempsey hit him one time," Allie said, "and he fell down."

Dempsey gave them all a slow, satisfied smile. "Not my best punch, but good enough, I guess."

"I guess!" Amanda said.

Mrs. Connell laughed. "About ten minutes later, when Wilcox got up, we gave him some water, and ice to put on his chin. And then we sent him away."

"But before we did," Jack Dempsey said, "I told him that if he even *thought* about bothering any of you, I'd come looking for him. And the next time I wouldn't pull my punches, or go to a neutral corner when he went down."

They were all quiet for a moment, picturing that scene. Then Helen said, "Ruby, I really don't think you'll ever have to worry about him again."

Amanda gave a decisive nod. "With us all watching out for you? Of course not."

"Feel like playing some baseball?" Bill Klem asked her.

Ruby felt her face color. Everyone else was ready, her teammates out at their positions, the Babe leaning on his bat beside home plate, the crowd, still subdued by what they'd seen. Only she was holding up the game.

She nodded.

"Think you can get the ball over the plate this time?"

He was being kind, she knew. He thought she was upset by what she'd done. He had no way of knowing that she was exultant. Everything had worked as she'd planned. Everything. She was free and clear.

"I know I can," she said.

The Babe met her halfway to the mound. "What was *that* all about?" he asked.

"Tell you later."

He gave her a sudden, shrewd look. "You meant to throw that ball into the stands. You hit that man on purpose."

"Later."

He turned away, then looked over his shoulder at her. "Hey," he said. "I heard that old windbag Landis is going to toss you out after the game."

Ruby shook her head. "You heard wrong."

"Really?"

"Yup. I'm not going anywhere."

"Huh." The Babe gave a shrug, then grinned. "Well, good. Because, kid, you can pitch."

She smiled back at him. "And you can hit, Jidge."

He laughed and headed to home plate. Got right into his stance, no fooling now, all business.

Andy Sutherland signaled fastball, and Ruby threw one, hard and over the inside corner of the plate.

Somehow the Babe got his big bat around on it. There was a crack like the sky breaking in half, and the last anyone saw of the ball it was still rising as it disappeared over the rightfield fence and departed the ballpark.

The crowd erupted in deafening cheers as the Babe, laughing and bowing and waving his linked hands above his head like a victorious fighter after a championship match, slowly rounded the bases.

And Ruby? Ruby merely stood on the mound, face expressionless, glove up, waiting for Bill Klem to throw her a new ball.

But inside she was laughing as well.

Sometimes, she knew, you had to give the fans what they'd come to see.

AUTHOR'S NOTE

Jackie Mitchell, a teenage girl I never met, inspired me to write *Diamond Ruby*. How? By throwing a baseball hard enough to strike out two of the greatest sluggers ever to play the game.

In the spring of 1931, Jackie was signed by the Chattanooga (Tennessee) Lookouts, until then an all-male team in an all-male minor league. She soon attracted the attention of the mighty New York Yankees, led by Babe Ruth and Lou Gehrig. On their way to New York from spring training in Florida, the Yankees stopped in Chattanooga to play an exhibition game against the Lookouts—and to get a look at the girl phenom.

Jackie didn't start the game, but she came in as soon as the Babe strode to the plate. Four pitches later, he was stomping back to the bench. Gehrig was an even easier out, going down on just three pitches.

This amazing feat should have marked the beginning of Jackie Mitchell's ascent, but instead it was the end. Just a few days later, Judge Kenesaw Mountain Landis, baseball's commissioner, banned her—and all women—from baseball, major and minor league, on the grounds that the sport was "too strenuous" for them. (In truth, the possibility that a woman might succeed at America's Pastime was too strenuous for *him*.)

Jackie hung on for a few more years as a kind of sideshow with a barnstorming team, but she never got the chance to face Ruth or Gehrig, or any other stars, again. What she or another female pitcher might have achieved has been left to the imagination . . . and to fiction.

I created Diamond Ruby Thomas and many of the book's other characters, but the world they inhabit really did exist. In 1918, the arrival, explosive spread, and devastating consequences of the Spanish influenza in New York happened as I describe, as did the tragic Malbone Street train wreck and the ordnance explosions that destroyed several towns in New Jersey and threatened to topple New York City's skyscrapers.

The year 1923, when the bulk of the novel takes place, was truly an eventful one. Safe and Sane Fourth actually took place, as it did every year. (I wish they would bring it back.) Yankee Stadium and the Coney Island Boardwalk opened that spring, President Warren Harding died in office during the summer, Jack Dempsey fought Luis Firpo in front of an estimated 125,000 spectators in the fall, and then the Yankees won their first-ever World Series championship. Wouldn't it have been great if Diamond Ruby had wrapped up that vivid, exciting stretch by facing the Babe himself at the House That Ruth Built in late October?

ACKNOWLEDGMENTS

I am grateful to many for the arrival of this, my first novel. Above all, my wife, Sharon AvRutick, worked tirelessly to help get the manuscript in shape and put up with me during the writing of it, a pair of signal achievements.

My children, Shana and Jacob, provided day-by-day lessons in the behavior of smart, funny young people, helping me make Ruby, Amanda, and Allie believable. My intrepid niece, Morgan AvRutick, was also a major inspiration for Ruby and the girls.

I can't express sufficient gratitude to my writing mentors, who encouraged me to try fiction and in several cases gave me the chance to publish: S.J. Rozan, Ben Cheever, Laura Lippman, Reed Farrel Coleman, and James W. Hall, terrific writers all, were especially generous with their time and advice.

I also owe a debt to the high-school writing students I've worked with over the past twenty years. Noemi, Eleanor, Cameron, Emily, Matt, Nicole, Susie, and the others have provided me with an unmatched window into teenage life and many pleasure-filled hours of reading. Two extraordinarily talented actresses, Felicia Day and Carlie Nettles, also helped me both on this novel and on my next, which follows Ruby and the girls to Hollywood.

Major props to my brothers Jonathan (who read my original "Diamond Ruby" short story and said, "You know, this would make a good book") and Richard Wallace. My parents-in-law, Alice and Julian AvRutick, have been cheering me on since Jimmy Carter was in office, and David and Kay AvRutick, Shannon Spencer, and Meri Wallace have been supportive and encouraging as well. Among my friends, Michael Silverstein, Keith Bass, Karen Sullivan, and Shar Bass have long watched my wandering career with great interest; special thanks to Keith for one particularly valuable introduction.

I wish my parents, Stanley and Eleanor, were here to share in this adventure. They would have gotten great pleasure from it . . . especially the fact that most of the book takes place in their beloved hometown.

Every writer should be fortunate enough to have an agent as fierce and supportive as Deborah Schneider. Deborah made sure that Ruby ended up with Trish Todd, editor in chief of Touchstone Books, whose empathetic, insightful work improved the novel enormously. At Touchstone, I'm also very fortunate to be working with Stacey Creamer, Mark Gompertz (see you at the film center!), Marcia Burch, Lisa Healy, Megan Clancy, and the rest of the team.

I hope you'll visit my website at www.josephwallace.com, which will link you to my Facebook page, blog, YouTube channel, (www.youtube.com/user/DiamondRubyBook), and other sites where you'll discover much more about Ruby and her world. You'll find video trailers, interviews with me, a tour of the Brooklyn locations featured in the novel, and real-life footage of Babe Ruth, Jack Dempsey, and others. There's also a place where you can share your own memories of old-time New York City and its marvelous history. I look forward to hearing from you!

TOUCHSTONE READING GROUP GUIDE

Diamond Ruby

FOR DISCUSSION

1. "No matter how bad things are, they can always get worse" (page 172). Ruby learns this lesson early on, as one unfortunate event happens after another. Was there a singular event that you see as the pinnacle of Ruby's suffering? Did the suffering alone lead Ruby to success? Was there a point in the story where it seemed nothing could get worse? Was there a point where everything was okay?

2. How do Ruby's nieces, Amanda and Allie, factor into the story? Do you view them as minor characters or as necessary for the integrity of the story? How much or how little do you think Amanda and Allie aided Ruby's ability to survive? Do you believe the girls were the reason Ruby decided to pursue a career in baseball?

3. Why does Helen invite Ruby and the girls to live with her? She says it's because Ruby let Helen "touch [her] beautiful arms" (page 213). Do you agree? What is the author implying about inner beauty versus outer beauty? About sight versus blindness? Does Ruby's perception of herself change because of how Helen "sees" her?

4. How does the Brooklyn setting help shape the story? Consider class, race, gender, citizenship, and ethnicity.

5. Decisions about right and wrong appear frequently in the novel. Ruby elects not to share the threatening letter from the KKK with Gordon; she also decides not to tell anyone about her deal with Chase. Think of a few other examples when Ruby must decide

between right and wrong. Do you agree with Ruby's choices? Do you see any as clearly right or clearly wrong?

6. Do you see Chase as an inherently evil, selfish character? Often he helps Ruby out of difficult situations, though just as often he is the reason for Ruby's problems in the first place. What are Chase's motives? Do you think he has genuine concern for Ruby's well-being or not?

7. On page 184, Helen invites Ruby and the girls to the "Safe and Sane Fourth" celebration. Do you see this invitation as a turning point in the novel? Is it a symbol of Ruby's and the girls' return to safety? To what extent?

8. When Ruby signs with the Typhoons, she causes an enormous uproar in New York City media. The newspapers believe it is a women's rights issue. Does Ruby? What is her overarching reason for joining the Typhoons? How does she understand her role on the team?

9. A central theme emerges on page 393 when Ruby muses: "That's what sports did . . . they all took you away from your world, your problems, for a few hours." Describe the role of sports in the novel. Is baseball Ruby's only escape from reality? What role does sports play in Helen's, Jack's and Babe Ruth's realities?

10. Do you find any symbolism in the name "Diamond Ruby"? Do the words *diamond* and *ruby* seem incongruous, especially as a means to describe Ruby? Does Ruby live up to the sparkle and beauty her nickname implied?

11. *Diamond Ruby* is set amid significant historical and cultural events. Describe the events you felt are most important to the development of the novel. Does a particular event stand out? Were Ruby to live today, how would her life be different? How much does the spirit of the time influence the outcome of the story?

12. Is Nick a sympathetic character? Examine his shift from a strong, successful journalist to an alcoholic rumrunner. Do you forgive Nick for his actions? Do you think Ruby forgave Nick?

13. Judge Kenesaw Mountain Landis declared that "no sport in America's great history has occupied a more central place in our nation's imagination than baseball" (page 377). He goes on to say that

"baseball is far too strenuous a pursuit for women" (page 378). If baseball is an important part of our collective imagination as Americans, does Ruby embody the American Dream? By defying Judge Landis, does Ruby become a symbol of freedom?

14. Ruby, Helen, Amanda, and Tania are some of the strongest and most heroic characters in the novel. Who do you see as the most heroic and why? Does the fact that the author is male change your perspective on the book?

15. Predict what will happen to Ruby after the novel ends. Do you think she will continue to play baseball without interference? What do you predict for Amanda and Allie? For Helen and Paul? For Nick?

A CONVERSATION WITH JOE WALLACE

This is your first novel, though you have written several nonfiction books. How did you decide to write Ruby's story? Did any of your previous books influence you?

My previous nonfiction books were a big influence on *Diamond Ruby*. Whether I was writing about baseball or science and natural history, I've always been fascinated about how women, against great odds, have fought their way into fields traditionally considered to be "men only." These are real-life stories filled with drama, heartbreak, and (occasionally) triumph, and well worth telling.

Having learned about Jackie Mitchell (the actual girl who struck out Babe Ruth and was then banned from baseball) while researching one of my books, I decided I wanted to write a similar story the way it *should* have happened. That's the good thing about fiction—if you want to change the ending, you can.

Describe the journey you took while writing this book. Is writing fiction a different experience from writing nonfiction? Do you prefer one to the other?

Writing fiction is the most exciting, fulfilling, frustrating, and terrifying process I've ever been through. I can usually tell when my nonfiction books are going well, but during the first draft of *Ruby* I was always wondering if I was simply deluding myself. I was so relieved when my first readers liked it!

I enjoy telling fascinating true stories in my nonfiction books. But I fell in love with writing fiction while working on *Diamond Ruby*—which is why I'm writing a new novel right now. I think I'm hooked.

Describe the research you had to do in order to correctly represent historical characters such as Babe Ruth and Jack Dempsey. Were there any interesting stories you came across about your characters that did not make it into the novel?

It's impossible to read about New York in the 1920s *without* hearing a whole lot about Babe Ruth. He was larger than life even when he was alive—loud and charming and friendly and difficult all at once. He was up for anything: boxing, playing football, riding in rodeos, posing with kids, as long as it seemed like fun and would keep him in the public eye. He also collected friends, even though he rarely remembered their names. And children adored him. I really do believe that if Ruby, Allie, and Amanda had existed back then, the Babe would have "adopted" them as he did so many others.

Jack Dempsey was an interesting person, much quieter than Ruth and with a much more complicated relationship with the public. His public persona appears to have been more like I made Ruby's: not flashy, but determined to win at all costs. Many sportswriters at the time wondered if boxing fans would ever warm up to him. They did eventually embrace him, but not until he lost the championship a few years later.

What made you decide to set this novel in Brooklyn, New York? What effect do you believe the setting has on the book overall? Did you consider any other cities for the setting of *Diamond Ruby*?

I never doubted that *Diamond Ruby* would be set in Brooklyn. It's where I grew up, so I know it well: its sights, smells, even the color of the light there. More importantly, Brooklyn and New York City as a whole were among the most fascinating places on earth to live in the early 1920s. They were perilous and intoxicating at the same time, places filled with danger and opportunity. Between the opening of the Coney Island

Boardwalk and Yankee Stadium, the rise of women's rights, the flowering of the Ku Klux Klan, Prohibition rumrunning, and the kind of active tabloid press that would have loved her—well, where else would Ruby live?

We know Ruby's character is inspired by Jackie Mitchell from Chattanooga, Tennessee, the girl who struck out Babe Ruth and was consequently banned from baseball along with her entire gender. Why did you decide to write a story based on Jackie's experiences?

I was so frustrated at the way history cheated Jackie Mitchell when Judge Landis banned her! A photo I found haunted me: This slightly built teenage girl smiling as she posed with Ruth and Lou Gehrig, two of the most famous celebrities of all time, never knowing that her career was about to end. The more I thought about it, the more I decided I wanted to write a novel on a similar theme.

Diamond Ruby isn't about Jackie Mitchell, though. I purposely made Ruby a fictional character whose life shares little with Jackie's. My goal was to write a story about a girl who used her talent, smarts, and determination to overcome the people who want to control or destroy her.

Describe the process you went through while creating Ruby's character. What was it like to write from a female perspective? Was there any additional research involved in capturing Ruby's voice?

Before starting *Diamond Ruby*, I had written several short stories from the perspective of young women. I'm not sure why, but I'm very comfortable with that point of view. I haven't received any complaints (from women or men) that the stories don't ring true or that I shouldn't have tried, so I guess I'll keep at it!

As far as Ruby is concerned, her voice reflects that of many of the women I admired most from that era. In doing my research, I read dozens of journals, autobiographies, magazine articles, and other contemporary writings by women, finding that almost universally the writers were smart, self-aware, and determined to make a difference. I wanted Ruby to share their determination in pursuing her single goal: survival for her nieces and herself.

The novel is set during a turbulent time in American history and touches on many significant historical and cultural events. How did you decide which events to include in the novel? As a historian, do you consider this time period a turning point in American history?

Both in the early sections of the novel (set in the 1910s) and in 1923, when most of it takes place, I had to leave out many fascinating historical events or else the book would have been 800 pages long! (For example, while working at Coney Island, Ruby would likely have met Cary Grant, who was working there, too. Grant was a character in early drafts, but didn't make the final cut, alas.)

I retained some historical details (such as the great influenza epidemic) because they had such an enormous impact on anyone who lived through those times. Others, such as the Dempsey-Firpo fight and a World Series game at the new Yankee Stadium, were simply terrific fun to write and, I hope, to read.

I wish I considered the 1920s a turning point in American history! Instead, I think it was a brief golden age for women's rights; I found article after article celebrating the idea that women and men were finally equal and proclaiming that this would never change. No one guessed how much things would backslide just a few years later or that women's rights wouldn't get back to where they'd been until the 1960s.

Besides Jackie Mitchell, who else inspired Ruby's character? Would you consider Ruby more fiction than not? How much or how little is Ruby like her real-life counterpart?

Ruby is definitely fictional. I took only a powerful left arm and a confrontation with Babe Ruth from Jackie Mitchell and invented the rest of the story.

On the other hand, I'm surrounded by people who inspired Ruby, Amanda, and Allie. Much of my own teenage daughter's personality is reflected in my characters, and I've also learned a lot from my niece, from the high-school students I work with as a writing mentor, and from many other young women I've met along the way. I'm glad I got to thank many of them in the acknowledgments.

Who is your favorite character in the story and why?

Well, I'm crazy about Ruby, of course. I love how she never stops working toward her goals. She has no pretensions, no inflated sense of self-worth, no outsize ego. She simply loves her nieces and will do whatever it takes to keep them safe. The people who threaten her don't understand how far love and determination can take you.

I'm also very fond of Ruby's closest friend, Helen. I based Helen on Helen Carr, a real-life diver who went blind following a tragic accident, but who didn't let her terrible misfortune stop her from living a full life. I found only a couple of stories about the real Helen, but she inspired me.

And I have to confess to a sneaking affection for Chase, the main villain in the story. I like his style and I know that the highlights of his days were the times he got to cross swords with Ruby. (Well, at least until the very end!)

Who are your influences as a writer and historian? What are you reading now? What is next for you?

I love reading histories that bring long-lost times and places to life. Among many, many other authors, Doris Kearns Goodwin, of course, is superb at this, and before her I especially admired Barbara Tuchman. I also find Studs Terkel's oral histories (*Working*, *The Good War*, etc.) invaluable, because they capture the true voices of regular people. On the baseball front, Lawrence Ritter's masterpiece *The Glory of Their Times* (also an oral history) and Bill James's *Historical Baseball Abstract* top the list.

In fiction, I read very widely, and I'm especially drawn to mysteries and thrillers. (For example, although Dick Francis's heroes are always male, in their quiet, underestimated way, they share a lot with Ruby.) I just finished Lee Child's latest Jack Reacher novel, *Gone Tomorrow*. It's a portrait of a very different New York City than the one I wrote about, though equally perilous!

Right now I'm working on a follow-up to *Diamond Ruby*. It takes place in 1926, about three years after the first, because I want to explore the way the years have changed Ruby, Amanda, and Allie. This novel is set in Hollywood, a perfect place for Ruby to bear witness to—and confront—the excitement and dangers of the Roaring Twenties.